A Crown of Bitter Orange

A Crown of Bitter Orange

by LAURA FLORAND

Chapter 1

Well, look at that. Prince Charming. Malòrie should have known she'd stumble over him the instant she set foot back in his kingdom. The man was the bane of her existence even when she was halfway around the world.

She put her hands on her hips and looked down at him, so peacefully dozing out in the open that he hadn't even stirred at the sound of her feet in the great white pebbles by the river.

Tristan Rosier asleep looked exactly how Malorie had always imagined. Gorgeous. Insouciant. Not vulnerable in the least, except to being over-kissed by the sun. A wicked little smile curving his mouth as if that sun was a woman and he was quite used to this kind of treatment.

Shirtless and completely ripped, the definition of his muscles visible even relaxed in sleep. He'd probably just come down from that beautiful limestone cliff face rising on the other side of the gorge and his muscles were still pumped from it. One hand held a half-eaten apple, the other a small white paperback—Giono's *Hussard sur le toit*—and they had both slumped to his torso when he dozed off. In full sun.

She sighed. It would serve Tristan right to have his nose peeling for a week, but then forty years from now, if he got skin cancer, it would be all her fault, and the last thing a Monsard needed was more lives on her conscience.

Plus, knowing Tristan, a peeling nose would probably improve his ability to flirt with hot actresses, not weaken it—he always managed flips like that. And his ability to flirt with hot actresses was already freaking annoying.

1

Fine. She dipped her hands in the milky green river, high from the recently melted snow in the peaks, limestone giving it that beautiful color. She carried the water back across the round white pebbles, tightened herself and double-checked her buttons to make sure her clothes weren't going to melt off as soon as he winked at her, and then tossed the icy water over his bare torso.

Muscles flicked like a cat's—powerful, lean, surging awake—and he opened his eyes, blinking sleepily at her as if she was all shadow in too much light. "Malorie Monsard," he said, with a sensual, lazy pleasure, as if he'd just woken up on a Sunday morning and was quite happy to see that she was the woman draped in his bathrobe bringing him coffee in the hopes he would ask her to stay.

She had to dive fast into irony to protect herself, as she always did with him.

"You make a good Sleeping Beauty, Tristan." She used the masculine *beau au bois dormant*. "Or should I say Snow White?" A nod to the half-eaten apple resting against his washboard abs.

Tristan sat up, blinking, his eyes clearing. "Malorie Monsard." His voice flattened. He shifted to sit on the rock against which his head had been resting, cushioned by his backpack. "Trust you to replace the kiss in the story with ice water on a man's skin."

Yeah. Tristan had been as friendly to her as to any other female on the planet when they were in high school, but when they met again in New York, it had not gone well. For him.

Supple, expressive eyebrows that could lilt up subtly in amusement, invite a woman in with laughter, tease her wickedly, did what they always did when she was around. They drew together. "Malorie," he said for the third time, looking around them at the limestone cliffs and the rushing spring river as if finally processing it. "What the hell are you doing here?"

"I used to live here, you know," she said dryly.

A flicker in his eyes as his mouth popped open for the automatic response, and he caught it, pressing his lips together. *Ha.* He'd been such a geek in his younger days, despite his inability to actually care about school, and even in high school a little of that geekiness had clung to him. He'd shaken it off quickly once he started focusing on girls, though. Or made it seem like the ultimate in sexy hotness, rather.

These days, it gave her a warm, fuzzy feeling somehow to think of sexy, world-is-my-oyster Tristan as a kid, watching *Return of the Jedi* with his cousins with the same excitement that everyone else in the world felt.

She gave herself a mental kick in exasperation. Every time Tristan blinked those brown eyes it gave women warm, fuzzy feelings. The last thing she needed was to join the packs of females eating out of the palm of his hand.

"The last I saw you, you were in New York." Tristan shook himself, like a cat at the touch of water. Yes, of course, memory of interactions with her *would* be like water on a cat to him. "What, are you stalking me? Trying to figure out more comprehensive ways to ruin my life?"

"I know you're used to being the focus of most women's attention, but there must be something wrong with me, Tristan. I've been hiking for ten days now, and haven't thought of you at all."

Well, mostly not at all. Maybe thought of his face, when she came into her own again, made Monsard a name to be proud of, right there on the old perfume street by Rosier SA. Thought of, maybe, the way he might look at her when she walked into one of those ghastly parties of the Grasse fragrance elite, only this time, she wasn't an ignored member of a ruined old family with her dress from a cheap department store, she was one of the elite herself, and wore her clothes with all the confidence she'd gained in ten years far away from Grasse's crushing weight of social class and history.

Instead, in the vision, she was sexy and glamorous and outclassed all those models he dated and...okay, in ten days of hiking, the mind could wander a bit far off the trail.

"Besides...ruined your life? Seriously, Tristan? You look as if you're having a pretty good life to me." He was so damn *entitled*. Just never even realized how lusciously wonderful his life was, all its power and strength and confidence showered down on him by the gods who seemed to want to turn every single cobblestone in Grasse gold before a Rosier foot had to step on it.

He gave her a burning, dark look. "I gave you the most beautiful perfume created in a decade, and you smashed it into bits on the floor."

Fugace. *Here we go again.* "You listed absurdly expensive components and no average consumer could tell the difference between them and the substitutes that cost a tenth—sometimes a *hundredth*—of the price. Abbaye likes to make money off its perfumes. We've been through this, Tristan."

He gave her a bitter look.

"Now, in your head, you gave the perfume to me directly and I threw it on the floor? I was head of accounting. I was doing my job, Tristan."

"Do you think accountancy is one of those careers that draws a high percentage of sociopaths?"

"I think perfumery draws a high percentage of narcissists."

"A narcissist?" Tristan's head jerked back. "*Me?*"

Yeah, probably not. He sure as hell was charismatic, though. And adept at getting his own way.

Thus his incredulous frustration with her.

The only woman in his entire life to have ever thwarted his desires.

"You didn't answer my question," Tristan said. "Why are you hiking up here? Nostalgia? You never come back home."

"I come see my grandmother every Christmas," Malorie said, offended. How heartless did he think she was? "And whatever other family is around."

Past tense, she remembered on a wave of sadness. No more making the thirteen desserts with her grandmother for Christmas.

"You do?" Tristan said blankly.

What did he think she was, just a calculator in a pencil skirt? Probably.

"But your grandmother is—now she's—" He broke off. Studied her, his face growing serious, and with it, gentler. "I'm sorry. Is that why you're here? To...think about her?"

Not a single Rosier had been at the funeral. Which was normal, of course. It wouldn't have been appropriate for any of them to come. But...well, that showed what it showed.

"This is how I left." She gestured to the hills. Hiking out of Grasse with friends to celebrate passing her *bac*. Except that after a week, her friends had come back as planned, and Malorie...she'd kept going. She'd liked it too much out there where the wind blew all that dusty dirty past of her family away and she could just be her. The world stretched out below her and all around her, beautiful, dramatic, adventurous, hers for the taking.

She'd hiked her way north, and eventually made friends at a *gîte* with a family of four and ended up in Paris as their *au pair* for the summer. Started school there in an *alternance* program, where she worked part time for a company and got her degree in finance and management, and was desperately poor, as students were, and scraped by, and *flourished*.

And now what she needed to decide was whether this would be perhaps her last visit to Grasse—whether she would sell everything her grandmother had left and

5

continue to bloom where she had not been planted, or whether she would come back here and save her roots.

"I remember," Tristan said with an inexplicable grimness. "It was in fashion there for a while. People leaving me."

She gave him a confused look. She remembered his older cousins, of course. Half the girls in school had had crushes on either Raoul or Lucien (the other half preferring Damien, Matthieu, or, already even at fourteen, Tristan; Tristan's percentage of those crushes had grown bigger every year, too). And when Raoul had gone off to Africa and Lucien had disappeared into the Foreign Legion—just *given up his name and vanished*—it had sent a shockwave through the entire school. Hell, through the whole *pays grassois*.

Obviously, to Tristan, who had always quite visibly loved his cousins, their disappearance must have been a brutal blow. He'd been quiet that year. Very quiet, in comparison to the way he'd developed in future years.

But what relevance *her* leaving should have to Tristan, she had no idea.

"You were never tempted?" she asked. He'd spent quite a bit of time in New York and Paris, she knew, but never really established long-term residence.

"I travel. I love to travel. But I like to come back, too," he said with a hint of accusation. As if she'd personally attacked him by not liking to come back.

"Well." She gave him a faint, challenging smile. "Here I am. Back."

That athletic body that always seemed so supple and so on the brink of movement, as if he could fling himself up a rock just to stretch out his kinks when he got restless, stiffened subtly. "Back?" Brown eyes swept over her face. "You mean...*back*? To stay?"

"I'm thinking about it." She'd arranged for a three-month leave from Abbaye to try to get affairs in order here. Now she just had to make up her mind how she wanted to do that.

6

Tristan's eyebrows knit. "Who would you work for?"

They both knew that economic options around Grasse were still limited. The best jobs were in the fragrance industry, but around here, most of those were tied up in a Gordian knot of family. Meaning *he'd* had every opportunity he wanted here, but she'd had none at all.

La Maison de Monsard hadn't seemed an opportunity back then. Now...well. Her grandmother had "put La Maison de Monsard to sleep" fifteen months ago, letting it go legally dormant, and in retrospect...maybe that should have been a sign. Malorie had thought it normal a seventy-nine-year-old woman would want to retire from that thankless job, but maybe her grandmother had also been feeling her health fail. She'd equally divided her shares in her will among her granddaughters, twenty percent each, but she'd assigned to Malorie, the only one with business training, the responsibility as legal representative. Now Malorie had to decide whether to bring the dormant company back to life or dissolve it, before the two year time-limit on inactive companies ran out. "I'm thinking over my options," she said.

Tristan clapped his hand to his forehead. "*Bordel*, please don't tell me Damien offered you a job. Surely he wouldn't do that. Even to me."

She stiffened. "Rosier SA should be so lucky."

Tristan's breath left him in a collapse of relief.

Okay, you know what...? "What do you guys have to pay your finance people to put up with you?"

"Most of our accountants put up with me just fine," Tristan retorted.

Only if they were thinking with their hormones. "You flirt with them, don't you?" She could see it now. Handsome, utterly charming Tristan Rosier strolling into someone's office, winking at her, giving her some flowers, telling her what a godsend she was...and never having anyone sit on his extravagances at all.

7

Hell, she didn't even have to imagine it. He'd tried it with her. And not reacted *at all* well when it didn't work.

"No," Tristan retorted. "I treat them like human beings. Not everyone is a sociopath."

"Able to think rationally and control emotional responses?" Malorie raised her eyebrows.

He bared his teeth. "No heart, no conscience, no consideration for the pain you wreck on others."

"Other than the amusement and sense of power it affords me, of course," she said blandly.

His eyes narrowed. "I knew it."

"It's Sociopathy 101. I got top marks in gloating."

He glared at her. Their conversations always seemed to revert to the mean, didn't they?

"Well. I just stopped to save you from skin cancer," she said, rising. Actually, she had meant to picnic in the shade of the trees by the water. But she'd find another spot. "You might want to put a shirt on. There's nobody around here to faint over your physique anyway."

A dark glance. He stood and pulled a fresh T-shirt out of his backpack, one of those flimsy athletic shirts that rolled up into the size of a fist. Another one lay stretched out over a rock, drying—from the sweat from a recent climb, or the river, or a combination of both. "Not the fainting kind, Malorie?"

"Over *you?*" Malorie said incredulously. What, did he have to have fawning attention from *everybody?* Even a woman he hated and with whom he'd sat in class as a skinny fourteen-year-old geek, no muscle mass yet but all height and great cheekbones and gorgeous brown eyes that had a way of looking at a girl, when the teacher made them work on some group project together, that just...

Tristan had stilled. His eyes locked with hers, and on those lips that had long ago stopped smiling for her, there was a little curl of pure anger, like a panther baring its teeth.

Her last words re-played in her head. *Over you?* Maybe that had come out a little rude. But for God's sake, it was Tristan. Outside an assault on his perfumes, any other stick or stone the world could throw at him just turned to water against the quintessential duck.

"Not your type, Malorie?" he said, with an edge.

"Tristan." She shrugged helplessly. *You're any woman's type.* Didn't he have enough proof of that? "Is it true what they say about narcissists? That you have this black hole inside you that kind of sucks up all the praise and attention you can get, so that you truly feel as if you never have enough?"

His lips pressed into a thin line. The last time she'd seen him that furious, she'd just won the battle to change the formula on his Fugace juice. Unlike his cousin Damien, Tristan was terrible at coldness. But with her, and only with her, his ability for pure rage came out.

"I *wouldn't know*, Malorie," he said icily. "And the fact that there were so many fucking narcissists in your family doesn't mean you'll find them everywhere else you look."

She recoiled, shutting down entirely. God, she hated the Rosiers. Not even all the way back in Grasse yet, just set foot inside the region's extended territory, and already her family history was being thrown in her face. Yeah, her father had been a narcissist, desperate to fill some hole in himself with other people's attention, even if he gained it through affairs and gambling and eventually drugs. Her grandfather had probably been a narcissist—he sure as hell hadn't been a good guy, to leave a sixteen-year-old pregnant and disappear. And her handsome, charming great-grandfather had sold out human lives to feather his own nest.

Yeah. She got it. Letting a charming man into your life was like snuggling all your fragile baby dreams down in a nest of vipers for warmth.

"Next time, Snow White, I'll let you choke on your damn apple." She pivoted, a harsh sound in the big pale

9

pebbles of the bank, and strode toward the trail. "Or get a sunburn and die of skin cancer." Whatever.

"You're supposed to kiss not douse with ice water!" Tristan yelled after her. "You should try it sometime, Malorie. You might get better results."

Chapter 2

It was two days more hiking before she reached the end of the trail. Two days of Tristan twining himself around her head like an elusive whiff of one of his perfumes.

He'd always done that to her. Whenever she didn't want to think about difficult things, it was so much easier to think about Tristan.

Not that he wasn't difficult. But he was exasperating in such a charming way. So good-looking that he got away with murder. That dark hair of his, those great cheekbones, the supple, sensual mouth, the warm brown eyes, the easy muscled looseness of the way he moved...it all worked to make the prickles of anger something more sparkly. Like the bubbles in Perrier.

You could not stay mad at Tristan. You just could not do it. She'd tried, because, first of all, he'd wanted her to shaft her own career for him. Way better to stay pissed off about that than give in. But also, she'd always known that coolness and distance were far preferable to falling into the trap of believing in him.

He acted as if she could. Not that it was an *act* exactly. Tristan was just so used to being considered Prince Charming that he probably took it for granted that fairy tales existed and he was the hero.

She snorted faintly and brushed a spiderweb off her face. Which he might be, if you were Cinderella. But somehow those stories always glossed over how many other women were at that ball—the ones who didn't matter, who weren't chosen. As every single Monsard woman could attest, counting on a handsome charmer to give you a secure life was a lousy career plan.

And hamstringing your own career because he asked so passionately and persuasively? Yeah, right.

Cinderella could keep him. Malorie preferred to wear the kind of shoes in which she could go far. Climb over obstacles. Forge her own path.

An Über driver picked her up at the trailhead, and she gazed out the window at old familiar countryside—oaks and herbs and *maquis* and limestone cliffs—as he took her to her grandmother's old place near Vallauris. About fifteen minutes south of Grasse, still solidly in the *pays grassois*, the Grasse region that had once been full of flowers and liked to pretend it still was.

Her smile twisted. She had to hand it to the Rosiers. At least they were doing their part, to keep this region full of flowers. They hadn't sold off that land of theirs to the highest bidder and retired rich. Even Tristan, who from all appearances would have made a natural playboy, was actually one of the top perfumers of his generation, a creative genius who brought in millions a year for his family company and, through them, for the region. He worked. He made it look easy, but that was probably the way those gymnasts at the Olympics made it look easy. Prince Charming, to be that damn charming and accomplished at fighting his way through thorny hedges and dragons, dancing, and waking women with a kiss, probably had had to work his entire life at it.

She figured it was a status thing for the Rosiers. If they sold out, well, what were they, other than handsome men with a moderate fortune and no purpose? They would be rootless, pointless. Charming, minus the Prince. But if they kept the land, kept making Rosier SA a powerful player in the region and the industry, they were still the *Rosiers*. Grasse royalty.

Like her family used to be. Once upon a time.

Her mouth turned down, and the driver pulled up in front of a hedge-lined wall. Shouldering her backpack one last time, her feet and calves aching from the two weeks of hiking, she waved him off and turned to face...what?

Her past? Her happily ever after? La Maison de Monsard had been dormant for over a year, and long before that, it had stopped earning more than a modest supplement to her grandmother's retirement income. But the Monsard storefront in Grasse, plus all the beautiful collector's items in storage there, would bring in a tidy sum if Malorie used her power to dissolve the company. Some of that would go to shareholders outside the family—ten percent to a distant cousin who had agreed to serve as board member out of reluctant family obligation post-war and who was now in a nursing home, ten percent to be divided among the heirs of the third board member if the legal battle between those heirs ever reached a conclusion. Another twenty percent floated out there, and she would have to track down the owners, or at least the holding companies that protected their identity. But sixty percent would still provide herself and her sisters with a not insignificant lump sum.

And then there was this place. The private land that had been in the family since the end of the nineteenth century.

The orange blossoms from this land no longer earned enough to cover its taxes. But it had a gorgeous view to the coast, and over the years of decline in the Monsard company, the land itself had increased in value. Sell it all, give the government its cut, and she and her sisters would each end up with close to a million.

At the cost, of course, of yanking out the last roots any of them had. It wasn't so different from the Rosier choice, really—except the Rosiers had pulled together as a family and made it work. Hers had failed and dispersed.

She stopped at the ivy-covered gate.

Leaves had piled around the old bronze robin. Malorie pushed them away and rubbed the robin's shiny head, then picked it up to take the key, there where her grandmother had always left it for them. Malorie and her sisters had flown home when their grandmother's health failed, of course, although it had already been too late for her to say much to them. But after her death, they had all had to go back to work, and the key had been left one last time. The leaves had piled up. While Malorie was trying to negotiate a more extended leave from her work, no distant cousin in the area had come to care for the place, because unlike the Rosiers no one in her family did know how to care for each other anymore.

And the orange garden and my shares in La Maison de Monsard I give to my granddaughters, in case they might care.

Her throat ached, and she sniffed hard once and straightened. She had to push the ivy away to find the old square of iron and fit the key into the lock. It opened with that same heavy clunk that it always had when her grandmother was wielding the key and Malorie was beside her, her school backpack weighing on her shoulders. Maybe her father had found it so easy to justify his absences in their lives, the way he disintegrated and left nothing to hold them up, because her grandmother, in her quiet and even humble way, was so strong. So there.

She'd stayed here for them, keeping this place, even when all her granddaughters were leaving her as if everything she'd tended and tried to maintain had no value to them at all.

Malorie's eyes stung so badly. She pushed the door open, ducking under the ivy, and stopped still inside, taking a deep breath.

The old orchard of bitter orange trees stood a couple of miles from the sea, but all the land here sloped steeply from the Alps to the Mediterranean, and standing here at the top terrace of this great, walled garden, she could see straight out to the water and the island of Corsica blurry in the distance.

A breeze wafted in off the Mediterranean, catching the sweet, warm scent of orange blossom as it passed through the trees. Small white blossoms clustered among glossy green leaves. It was mid-April, and the trees were just starting to bloom.

She had to push through tall grass and scraggly brush to reach the smooth trunk of the nearest tree.

14

One of the last stands of bitter orange in France, and no one had taken care of it. Another sign, like the showroom across from the museum, of how far her once-great family had fallen.

Her grandmother had taken care of them, all their childhood, and then they had set out on their own, teenagers determined to become something other than a shameful last name. They hadn't thought that she was growing older and they were leaving her all alone.

"And the fact that there were so many fucking narcissists in your family doesn't mean you'll find them everywhere else you look."

She wondered how you unlearned selfishness, when it was such a fundamental survival instinct in her family. She wondered how you became someone like her grandmother, willing to be the roots three granddaughters had needed, no matter how lonely it left her.

Loneliness. That was another thing Malorie knew all about. If you had to forge your way alone, then you were...well. Alone.

She rubbed the back of her neck, fighting grief and guilt and the memories it woke of that deeper, underlying shame that her family always carried with it.

The past stayed alive here. New York was a brash, brisk city, too many buildings, too many people, too much concrete and steel. It wasn't always easy to live in New York, but there no one cared where you came from. Not only didn't they know, but it would never occur to them to even wonder.

Here where you came from...was where you were.

She stood there, her backpack weighing on her shoulders, dusty and tired, the youngest daughter returned from a long quest to find her fortune and now wondering what good the fastest horse or a firebird did when there was no one to show them to.

Slowly, she slipped her backpack off and set it in the tall grass. She picked an orange blossom and took a deep

15

breath of the fresh-honey scent of it and tucked it into the coil of hair at the top of her head. The grass was too tall and itchy under the orange trees, full of weeds, but she sank down into it anyway and curled against a trunk, wrapping her arm around it.

The orchard was entirely empty of human life.

No one was left here now. Only Malorie.

She didn't realize she was crying, until the tear slipped down her cheek and plopped on the back of her hand. She scrubbed her face automatically. She'd made her own decisions, and this profound grief that shook her now that her grandmother was gone seemed...so much too late.

Her grandmother would have *loved* to have one of her granddaughters stay. Stay and prove that everything her grandmother had lived for, fought for, had value to them, had meaning.

It did, Mémère. I just—I couldn't get any traction here. You of all people know how closed this place is. You're born to the right family or you can just forget about entering the perfume industry here. It would have been like churning my wheels in mud for ten years. I had to get out of this rut.

Now *I can do something.*

Now that her grandmother was no longer alive to see it, and her sisters and mother didn't care.

She wrapped in on herself against the loneliness, releasing the tree to hug herself, as she'd had to do when loneliness struck in her Brooklyn apartment.

And as always, Tristan slipped in. That guy *never* let her be alone. He'd been picking on her since they were only a few years old and her teachers always made her sit next to him to try to get him to behave. He'd been such a pain when they were little. Not mean, but always jumping out of his seat and trying to get her to play with him instead of paying attention. It was only as she got older that the way she'd thought about him had changed.

Well, he'd still been a pain, and he'd still wanted all her attention and everyone else's, but as he got older, all that energy and charm and restlessness in him had packed itself into a body that grew increasingly hot as he grew taller and taller and filled out and started to shave and just grew so...*male*.

But he kept that fundamental sweetness he'd had even as a boy who hated to sit still. Every single time she was homesick or upset in Paris and New York, he was there. So solidly freaking *there* it was ridiculous for someone who was a figment of her imagination.

You know that's not who he really would be in a relationship, right? He just can't focus on a woman that long.

But in her imagination he did. Amused, laughing, inviting her to quit focusing on her work and play with him. Friendly, supportive, encouraging. A wink, a smile, a touch of her cheek, a stroke of her hair. Exasperating, maddening, distracting her from darker thoughts with her desire to strangle him.

She was such an idiot that he had even been there that night after their worst fight over his stupid Fugace, telling her he didn't mean it, a warm figment of a presence she could curl up against.

She'd always been good at fantasizing about Tristan. When they were little kids she'd fantasized about beating him over the head with her stuffed animals, and when they were teenagers, well...

That hot, sexy body. The wicked, amused invitation in his eyes. His warmth and fundamental decency. What was there not to fantasize about?

She didn't have to *let him know* that she was one of the scores of women who fantasized about him, of course. But he had made her feel better, less lonely— helped her get through, persist, succeed—more times than she could count. To be honest, when she was by herself she didn't even bother to fight it anymore. The fantasies of Tristan were her refuge.

In a way, just the fact that he existed had helped her survive. Grow stronger. Deep in her heart, in secret, she owed him something for that.

Chapter 3

"Wait." Matt paused with the *cochonnet,* the little yellow jack, in one hand, and an unholy grin spread across his face. Big, rough, and growly, Matt was the middle cousin in age but the only child of their grandfather Jean-Jacques Rosier's oldest son, and thus the family patriarch in training. He had a heart like a marshmallow but an exterior as rough as his farmer's hands, and he also took his responsibility for interfering in his cousins' lives far too seriously. But then, so did Damien and Raoul, if you asked Tristan. "Malorie Monsard is back?"

Tristan had no insecurities.

He'd made peace with his failures in school as a child. He'd proven exactly how much he could do when he was freed from a desk and allowed to be him.

He'd survived being the youngest of these cousins. He'd even flipped it so that he was the one who was always amused at their emotional eccentricities, not the one being teased into crises of rage and tears like he'd been at four and five.

He'd become one of the top perfumers of his generation, and despite all the pressures from family and society to become someone else, he'd done it entirely his way. He hadn't had a choice, in fact. Try as he might, he had never been able to fit into any other mold than his own.

He was good with that. He was entirely—*entirely*—secure in who he was.

But trust his cousins to still, unerringly, find his one damn weak spot.

He took a sip of his Ricard. "Are you going to throw that jack any time soon?"

19

"Who's Malorie Monsard?" Matt's fiancée Layla asked, and at the other end of the court, their grandfather looked around at the last name.

Above them, the great branches of an old plane tree shaded their game, leaves spring fresh. In the late Saturday afternoon, the April air was gently warm not hot. Around them were the original old stone building of the *mas*, the outbuildings that had once housed farm animals, and, at a little remove, the extraction plant and a couple more buildings associated with it. Past that stretched the roses, leafing out but not yet in bloom, and steep slopes framed the valley. The Rosier valley. Not Tristan's—his house lay high on the slopes, the fields themselves destined for Matt—but home. The apricot and almond trees planted around the house were in bloom, the *amandiers* releasing that incredible sweet scent from their fragile white flowers. And under that, the scents of stone and green, the softer, humid scents of spring that would soon dry in the summer, baked under the sun. The tingle-sharp scent of his apéritif, the faint hint of dirt stirred up by their feet in the gravel as they threw.

"Only Tristan's worst enemy," Damien said, gray-green eyes glinting in amusement. He exchanged a glance with Raoul. *Merde.* That never ended well for the youngest cousin, when the oldest ones started exchanging glances with that grin on their faces.

Plus, Damien's wedding was only three weeks away and Matt, like an insane man, had agreed to having his and Layla's right at the tail end of the rose harvest a month later, so they both were probably just dying to relieve their stress levels on someone. Damien had originally tried to have a quiet, quick wedding last fall, but Tante Colette, his mother, and pretty much everyone connected to the family from here to Québec had all sat on that one *hard*. There were people who had been waiting thirty-five years for the next Rosier wedding. It would have been impossible for the first wedding in a generation—or any of their weddings—to invite fewer than five hundred people. The hurt and disappointment would have been terrible. Since Tante Colette was the person insisting on this and Damien could hardly articulate to her in response his profound fears that she might die before the ceremony, he had lost that battle.

And Tante Colette was going to live to be one hundred twenty-three. Tristan was positive of it. She'd see *his* children get married. If he ever found the right person to have them with.

"Malorie is not my worst enemy," he said.

"She eats him for breakfast." Matt held up a hand and made enthusiastic munching motions with it, grinning.

Tristan tried to keep his cool, the number one most essential thing to do for surviving being the youngest of this crowd, but his eyes narrowed just a little. "She *hardly* eats me for breakfast."

Just ripped his heart out and gnawed on it absently for a snack was more like what she did, but he'd be damned if he'd let his cousins know that. Unless they'd already guessed, in which case he was screwed.

"Makes him pay attention to bottom line and shit," Raoul volunteered, his arm across Allegra's shoulders, rubbing the curve of one shoulder idly as he sipped from a small glass of their grandfather's walnut wine. "It's horrible."

The oldest of the cousins—but *not* the son of the oldest son—Raoul had had a difficult relationship with Matt and an even more difficult one with their grandfather, and he'd run off to Africa at nineteen and eventually taken charge of their overseas operations. He'd come home Christmas before last to stay, his sienna hair streaked prematurely with charcoal gray, the only cousin besides the absent Lucien who didn't have black hair.

Of course Lucien didn't...that is, he wasn't...never mind.

"Tristan has an enemy?" Allegra said blankly. Slim and vivacious, an Italian-American who had originally come here while doing research for her dissertation, never-met-a-stranger Allegra had taken one look at Raoul when he came home for Christmas and just snatched him up, and he'd fallen head over heels for her.

It was kind of alarming how hard Tristan's older cousins had fallen when they'd fallen, in fact. Up until then, Tristan had been under the conviction that it was possible to fall in love and stay relatively sane.

"Tristan can pay attention to bottom line?" Damien said blankly. "Even for a girl?"

"You do know that my computer program automatically shows me the cost of every single ingredient I plug into a formula as well as the total production cost at all times, right?" Tristan pointed out.

"Oh, is that still working on your computer?" Damien said. "I couldn't tell."

Tristan narrowed his eyes at him.

"And the best part of it is that Tristan used to have the worst crush on her in high school," Matt said.

Tristan controlled his urge to snarl. He'd spent his entire life practicing unflappable amusement as a way to deal with four older cousins. The last thing he wanted to confirm was a weak spot.

"Ah, the girls in high school," he sighed dramatically. "Which one was Malorie now? The one who favored those little pink skirts?"

That had actually been one of Matt's high school girlfriends, and Matt stiffened in alarm, glaring at him at the threat that Tristan might bring up some of his old ridiculous relationships in front of Layla. Tristan smiled at him sweetly.

"The one you followed around like a puppy," Damien said, unfazed; even in high school, Damien had not acted ridiculous. His ball arced precisely and thumped to a stop a few centimeters from the *cochonnet*. The Rosier cousins had competitiveness down to a fine art. Damien added to his fiancée Jess, "He used to bump into her just so he could pick up her books when he knocked them to the floor. Smooth. Very smooth."

Jess, a sweet-tempered perfumer who had produced one of the most ghastly bestselling perfumes of the decade, laughed, staring at Tristan in amazed delight.

It was possible he shouldn't have showed such open amusement when Matt and Damien were bumbling around in their own relationships. But he could hardly have just watched them act like such idiots and not point it out. He'd been being helpful.

The guys would sink in the morass of their own emotions otherwise. What was he supposed to do for an encore, watch kittens drown without helping?

"Wait." Layla held up a hand. Her extravagant corkscrew curls were held back in a wide headband today, but they still escaped out all around the edges of it. "*Tristan* had an unrequited crush? Tristan? Whom girls fall all over just because he winks at them?"

"In contrast to these guys, any man looks good," Tristan explained modestly.

"*Desperately* unrequited," Damien said.

Matt snickered. "And then when he met up with her again in New York, she just—grrm." That gobbling motion with his hand again, as if Tristan was some helpless warm-blooded mammal to a cold-hearted T-rex.

Tristan picked up his own ball and knocked Damien's a full stride away, his own settling in to nestle cheek to jowl with the jack. "What she *did* was swap out your own jasmine in Fugace for cheaper stuff from Egypt. Among other crimes she was too damn pigheaded to understand she was committing."

Matt looked indignant. Finally. "What, she thought that stuff from Egypt was just as good?" he demanded, outraged.

"More likely she just wanted to do as much damage to the Rosiers as she could," their grandfather said coolly, coming up on them. "She's a Monsard, after all."

23

Tristan slid a glance at his grandfather. Despite the compression of age, the old man was still nearly as tall as his tall grandsons, able to hold their eyes with those faded blue ones, able to demand great things of them with the absolute confidence that they would achieve them.

Pépé made Tristan feel grounded, the same way a cliff face made him feel grounded—like he could climb to the top of the world, but with his fingers gripping granite all the way. He was a very great man. Tristan had always counted himself one of the lucky ones, to be born his grandson.

But there was a darkness in his past that Tristan had never known. He had killed people. He had seen friends killed. Three of them thanks to Pierre Monsard, who had betrayed them to the Germans. And sometimes he judged people through that darkness, a lens that had changed his perception of the world forever.

Or maybe it was the extraordinary acts of heroism and courage he'd witnessed and performed that had changed his perspective. Which was harder? To be judged by a man who believed that humans were capable of great evil or to be judged by one who believed that humans were capable of exceptional feats of greatness?

"I don't think Malorie's busy fighting her great-grandfather's battles, Pépé," Tristan said carefully. "She's busy fighting her own."

All on her own.

His eyebrows knit. Because there was something he'd never understood about Malorie, not since that day he'd learned that she'd hiked all the way to Paris by herself and set up a life there. When she was fighting, who had her back?

And if no one did, why had she never taken him up on his tacit offer to let that person be him? Didn't she trust him to be good at it?

Chapter 4

The fountain was dry.

Once this fountain had run with orange blossom in April, rose-scented water in May, jasmine in August, all the scents of the seasons of flowers around Grasse. That was what Malorie's grandmother said, dreamy-bright fairy-tale memories of her childhood before the war.

Now it had fallen silent, sticks cluttering the basins. Mary Magdalene, patron saint of perfumers, did not weep anymore, and no scented water ran through the carved marble of her hair nor spilled from the urn she tilted. Early Christian iconography had made of Mary Magdalene the closest the Church had to a sacred erotic figure, and the Art Nouveau sculptor of this fountain had delighted in that sensuality, until it was almost impossible to stand near the fountain and not reach out to touch its curving lines.

City officials had already contacted Malorie and her sisters, urging them to maintain it, so fine an example of Art Nouveau work that tourists went out of their way to see it. Malorie looked from the fountain's courtyard space to the museum and beyond it to the city's fountain of iron flowers at the main roundabout by the great terrace space of the esplanade.

La Maison de Monsard really had been built in the prime location in the city. It was the ideal place for a grand, elegant perfume house with a proud, ancient name. It always had been.

She looked up at the MONSARD graven in elegant capitals above the doors, the beautiful lines of the Art Nouveau façade, lines that, like the fountain, spoke of another time, when buildings themselves could be erotic, full of curves and flowers and balconies, like an invitation into Eden. She could sell the place, of course. Her grandmother had been approached by one of the major international perfume houses, which had fancied the idea of having such a symbolic showcase here in Grasse.

Hell, the Rosiers would probably take it. They liked owning everything in Grasse. *Tristan* would probably take it. He'd love having his own personal perfume playpen, where he could make whatever the hell crossed his fancy and no accountant would force him to make it financially viable. But they'd cover up that Monsard name with their own. Call it Parfums Rosier or something.

The grand set of double doors was not as flagrant in its design as another by the same architect in Paris, but there was something profoundly sensual about the flowing lines of iron and wood and glass, and the artist had engaged openly and playfully with that sensuality. Carved among the wealth of stone vines that framed the doors, Adam on one side was giving an astonished look to what was happening under his fig leaf while a completely naked Eve at the other corner beckoned, amused, curvaceous, inviting.

The open celebration of the sensual was perfect for a perfume house. Sensuality captured, distilled, spread forth again, via perfume.

Malorie pushed open the double doors. To either side were beautiful, huge windows that should have been displaying bottles like precious jewels. Bones of an older building still stood here, but the façade, the windows, and the interior had all undergone a major remodel just before the First World War, when La Maison de Monsard was at its most glorious height, one of the most powerful names in the Grasse region and one of the most influential in the entire perfume industry.

Her grandmother had photos of the beautiful Art Nouveau interior, but then in the 1950s, there had been a desperate second remodel, a greater paroxysm of a mania that had swept much of the country, an attempt to hide the past with everything new. And then Monsard had sold soaps and lavender sachets and perfume tours to tourists for a while and tried to pretend that still let them call themselves perfumers, until they discovered her father was siphoning off assets to support his *I'm-still-from-a-rich-family* pretense in Monaco and everyone in her family just lost heart. Her siblings never even looked at the perfume industry for a career.

After their father died in the fast car he'd sold part of their heritage to afford, and after the girls left and their mother could finally wash her hands of the whole mess a Monsard had made of her life and go teach on a remote island in French Polynesia, their grandmother, Chloé Monsard, had retired, shutting the place down.

Malorie ran a finger along the dust of a long display counter, looking around at the space. To think this had once been the most glamorous place in the city. Rich women from all around the world waltzed through here in their flapper dresses and cloche hats and tried on perfumes or, sometimes, retired into a second room for their special, hours-long, multi-session creation of a bespoke perfume.

The Monsards had worked with the Rosiers back then. Only the best went into Monsard perfumes, and the best meant roses and jasmine from the Rosier fields. The Monsards couldn't trace their history quite as obviously to the Renaissance, having risen to power in the second half of the nineteenth century when the Grasse perfume industry really took off. Both families mixed in multiple aspects of the industry, but the Monsards had focused more on the glamor, the perfumes, the shops, while the Rosiers had anchored themselves into the land. The things that grew.

La Maison de Monsard had opened a great store on the Champs-Elysées in the twenties, too, with a beautiful Art Déco look that Malorie had seen in photos, but it had long since been sold. Always a privately held company, just under half the shares had been sold too cheaply in attempts to earn money in the second half of the twentieth century. But the majority had come to Malorie and her two sisters in their grandmother's will.

Now the question was…sell it? Shake the dust of Grasse from their feet forever and go their separate ways? How long would the Monsards hold together without this anchor, how long would visiting each other in odd parts of the world at Christmas be enough, before they lost that sense of family that held the Rosiers together through all the storms that had hit them?

Malorie had been forging her way alone since she was nineteen. She'd felt the solitude. When she'd run into Tristan that first time in New York, she'd wanted to throw herself at him and sink herself into the sense of home that he carried with him wherever he went. *He* belonged. To a place, to a family.

But despite that loneliness, she'd never realized how much her grandmother had been the port for her brave little ship out there—the sense that she did have a place she could go home to. That she wasn't just adrift on a great big sea. She was more like…oh, an explorer. With a place to come back to, when she had the holds of her ship full of spices to sell and make her family's fortune.

She had never even realized how important that port of anchor was until she lost it.

Now she was anchorless. If she sold this place, the name Monsard officially meant nothing more, ever again, than a way for government officials to distinguish her from every other Malorie out there.

"It used to be a beautiful place, didn't it?" a voice said from behind her.

Tristan. She knew the deep, warm timbre, with a little edge to it that was only there for her, without even having to turn around. But she did turn and look at that long, pseudo-lazy masculine shape lounging in the doorway, silhouetted by the near-noon sun. She pretty much always did look at Tristan when she got the chance. The same way she looked at éclairs in the bakery window when she was hungry or watched beautiful sunsets—who could look away?

"Oh, for God's sake, you again?" she said. New York might be a bit safer for her emotions than Grasse. In the

Big Apple, a casual stroll down the street wasn't all that separated her from Tristan. "Don't you ever work?"

A little glint of annoyance in his eyes as he strolled forward into the middle of the great show space. "I get that a lot."

The thing was, she knew perfectly well that Tristan had not gotten to be one of the top perfumers of his generation by shirking his work. Not even with the Rosier name behind him. But he made it look as if he was playing all the time. Never had she seen a man just reach out and embrace life with so much pleasure. He *loved* the world.

"How was the rest of your hike? No trouble?" Those brown eyes did a surprisingly comprehensive scan of her body, head to toe, as if trying to penetrate right through to the sore muscles in her calves. *A flashing vision of Tristan's strong, rock-climber fingers sinking into her calves, massaging the soreness...*

Hey. Those fantasies are only for when he's not around, you idiot. "Well, I did keep an eye out whenever I went through any gorges, in case you were lurking up there ready to dislodge a boulder."

His eyebrows went up a little. His smile faded. "For someone who has known me all my life, you never chose to know me very well, did you?"

"We weren't exactly friends in high school, Tristan."

He cut her an odd, dark glance she couldn't quite interpret. Sometimes it kind of bothered her that Tristan didn't smile at her like he did at every other woman. He used to. In grade school, he'd been an utter pain in his need for her attention—or for anything else to keep his energy occupied. And in high school, he'd always been utterly charming to her. Not that they were friends, but it was a small high school, and they ended up in a lot of the same classes.

So of course they crossed paths. *She'd* felt more awkward around him, in high school, all her hormones waking up and noticing he was turning into a really hot

29

guy even as her own body transformed itself in ways she wasn't sure she liked and which made her not even sure who she was anymore. But he clearly hadn't felt the same self-consciousness.

It seemed as if he was always having to squeeze himself down beside her for the last spot on a bench, apologizing for crowding her. Or apologizing when he bumped into her, which he did a lot—a little clumsy for his height, still, perhaps, and for the crowded hallways, and anyway he was almost always surrounded by friends and not paying attention. Kneeling to pick up her books as he smiled into her eyes and made jokes about learning to watch where he was going. Reaching over her shoulder in the library to get a book he needed for some assignment. Teasing her in a friendly way when a teacher assigned them to the same group and sometimes, during that group work, just meeting her eyes with that gift he had for making a girl feel as if she was the most fascinating girl in the world and he'd love to know all about her.

The one time they had ended up on a project that had required the two of them to meet after school had been the worst. Antoine, the almost ruthlessly driven classmate with whom she competed for *premier* or first in class, was also a friend of Tristan's—who wasn't?—and supposed to be one of their partners, but bizarrely, he never showed. The only time in their entire school career when she had ever known Antoine Vallier to blow off schoolwork. So it had just been her and Tristan.

And Tristan would talk to her and smile at her and try to get her to talk to him, all that easy charm of his, and she always felt only one careless breath away from just falling so hard for him she'd never recover. She'd just be another one of the many, many girls at school who must have already found out how pleasurable it was to fall over backwards for Tristan and let him get everything he wanted.

"And we definitely weren't friends in New York," she said.

He said nothing for a moment, and then: "I was happy to see *you*." Flat and a little crisp. "At first."

Yeah, but Tristan was always happy to see everybody. Yes, he'd clearly been thrilled to run into her on the sidewalk as they were both heading into the same perfume launch party. And he'd been equally delighted to see all the beautiful models and actresses who had surrounded him before she even managed to check her coat and rejoin him. In fact, the sight of them had stopped her, and she never had rejoined him, never yielded to that homesick urge to cling to his arm as if *he* was home. He hadn't had an arm left free to cling to.

That moment—the surprised joy in seeing him and then turning around to find him thronged with women far more beautiful than she could ever hope to be—had been a brutal little reminder that Tristan's delight in most women could lead her down a very painful path. He could become someone so special to her that he drew her eyes no matter where she was, and she, on the other hand, wouldn't even be visible in the crowd around him.

Making him mad, now, *that* was a feat. She might be the only woman who had ever managed it. It gave her some secret, perverse sense of accomplishment. At least she stood out.

But sometimes she missed Tristan's smiles. Sometimes she missed those times when they worked on that history project and his friend Antoine never bothered to show up.

It had been a ghastly, horrible project to have to work on with a Rosier, too. It had to have been pure cruelty on the teacher's part that had put a Monsard with a Rosier for a project on the Occupation.

Or maybe everyone in the area didn't remember what her great-grandfather had done as much as she thought? "I thought we were natural enemies," she said, watching Tristan.

He snorted as he turned slowly in the middle of the room, looking at the high ceiling and the beautiful arches. "You're the one who decided to become an

31

accountant." She was fairly sure his lips could not curl more on her choice of profession if she'd chosen to kill endangered species and hang their body parts on her wall. "You can't blame me."

Sometimes, the temptation to hit Tristan over the head with one of his own perfume bottles was hard to resist. "I was talking about the Monsards and the Rosiers."

Tristan looked completely blank.

Must be nice to be so obliviously secure in who you were.

"Are you talking about seventy years ago?" Tristan asked warily. "Isn't that a little before our time?"

"You're still living on your grandfather's Resistance glory days, aren't you?" The way Tristan had swelled with pride whenever his grandfather was asked to speak to their school. Malorie had had a slight preference for his grandmother and his Tante Colette's talks—nice to see a woman's heroism remembered and honored, too—but mostly she had stared at her hands on her desk for those events and wished to God she hadn't been too stubborn to stay home sick.

"My grandfather is his own special challenge," Tristan said, with a softening of his mouth and a glint of laughter in his eyes that was exactly what was so irresistible about him. The open, amused affection which he bore for even the most difficult of the people he loved. "But I'm proud of him, yes."

"Yes." Pride and a heritage of honor, versus a heritage of shame and dishonor. He couldn't possibly get it, and she had nothing left to say.

Tristan's eyebrows knit, his face growing graver than she was used to seeing it. He looked back toward the great open doors of the building. Past the courtyard stretched a street she knew like the back of her own hand. The tall, close buildings painted in ochre and yellow, with their shutters in dusky blues and greens. The tiny lavender pillows being sold to tourists, who never seemed to realize that in April lavender could not possibly be fresh and local. The little café tables out in front of shops, to take advantage of the delicious spring.

And the museum of perfume and fragrance, which the Monsards had not been invited to help fund and to whose collections they had not been invited to contribute. Their story from the nineteenth century was there, of course. It ended abruptly in the section on the 1940s with, "Upon the family's disgrace at the end of World War II, the Monsards lost their influence in the regional industry and..."

Nearly every single year their class had taken a field trip to that museum. She swore sometimes Tristan stood next to her *on purpose* in that exhibit, his shoulder brushing hers as she stared at that sentence and he clasped his hands behind his back and gazed at the black and white photos of his grandparents and great-grandparents with roses spread in a layer around them on the floor, the way they used to have to air the blooms before they opened their own processing facility.

No overt reference in that particular museum to heroism, Resistance, collaboration. That was for the Musée de la Résistance. Another favorite school expedition.

"That has nothing to do with *us*," he said, slowly, like someone who knew as he said it that he wasn't telling the truth. "It's in the past."

Now he was just being a hypocrite. "So are we."

Entirely surrounded by medieval and Renaissance buildings. Even the modern monuments were in honor of the glory days of perfume and fragrance, attempts to keep that glory alive so that Grasse's economy didn't collapse. In the second half of the twentieth century continuing through to this day, the Rosiers had been a notable force in keeping Grasse central to the perfume industry, resisting that powerful pull of all things toward Paris and New York.

The Monsards had not been a powerful force in Malorie's lifetime. After her great-grandfather's *dégradation nationale*, which had prevented him from serving as the head of La Maison de Monsard, and the disgrace through him of the whole family, their economic and social power had collapsed and no one had ever rebuilt it.

Until now?

"Is that why you've never liked me?" Tristan said, his eyebrows knit but a little ah-ha light in his eyes like Pasteur after he finally got the rabies vaccine to work. "That old history?"

It was perfectly hilarious for someone who proudly traced his ancestry back to the Middle Ages to refer to something that had occurred within living memory as "old history". Or it would be hilarious, if his oblivion wasn't so infuriating.

"I don't dislike you, Tristan." It would be like disliking a hot, half-naked guy who had just climbed up into a tree to rescue a piteous kitten and was cuddling it against his bare muscled chest. It just wasn't possible. No woman could dislike Tristan.

However, she could take a long, hard look at the effect charming men had had on the lives of the women in her family and everyone else and stay the hell away from his emotional clutches.

He gave her a dark look. He didn't even have to say *Fugace*. She'd seen that dark look enough to know what word was in his mind.

"See, Tristan? This is what I mean about you being entitled. Whenever a woman treats you in a perfectly normal way—doing her job and making sure your perfumes don't cost more than a trip to the moon, instead of falling all over you—you take it as personal dislike."

"The perfumes aren't the only—" He snapped his mouth closed over the words. Those warm brown eyes were ablaze.

Score another point for Malorie. The only woman in the world who could make Tristan, the ever-amused and unprovokable, lose his temper.

An ability that made her skin skitter with energy and yet...she also wanted to sigh. Sometimes she wished she, too, like every other woman he knew, had just given herself up for Tristan's smiles. Then she would still get them.

Tristan gave a movement of his shoulders like a duck flicking water off its feathers, shaking his temper away, and cocked his head to study her. A gleam came into his eyes that she couldn't quite interpret but that made her skin prickle again. "So you don't dislike me, Malorie?"

"I'm human, Tristan."

His eyebrows shot up. "You are?" His surprise sounded so genuine that her own temper flicked her.

"Last I checked."

"Maybe you should let *me* check. I'm not sure your methods are accurate."

She narrowed her eyes at him. "What do you want to do, stab me to see if I bleed?"

Tristan put his hand to his forehead. "Do you *ever* think of non-violent solutions? Ice water, stabbing. What did we talk about last time?" He lowered his hand, and that gleam in his eyes grew, wicked Tristan fully waking. "I don't mean to be rude about your parents, Malorie, but I'm honestly not sure they raised you right."

Yeah. He might be right about that.

"At least *I* know what to do with a sleeping princess. Or one frozen in crystal, in your case." Those wicked brown eyes came to rest on her lips. And he drew his own lips just slightly in, as if he was tasting them.

"And here I always thought the guy should have given that girl sleeping in crystal a good shake to free the apple, instead of kissing her like some pervert," Malorie said sardonically.

"You would," Tristan retorted.

"I hear the Heimlich maneuver works."

"Oh, *bon sang.*" Tristan rolled his eyes skyward.

"Why don't you just check my pulse?" she said dryly, holding out her upturned wrist.

"You take all the fun out of things, Malorie." But his fingers closed around her wrist, his hand cupping hers, and instantly she knew she had made a mistake. The rub of his callused index and middle finger as he sought her pulse. The warmth that enveloped her hand and ran up the inside of her wrist as if it was racing for her heart.

Melting that little case of ice she tried so hard to keep cool around it to keep it safe.

Tristan's fingers rubbed gently, a shiver of callus and warmth, and his black lashes lifted suddenly. Their eyes met, his focused on her as if he was suddenly about to see right through her.

Malorie twisted her wrist free before that race of heat could reach her cheeks and turned away, smoothing her jeans. She wished she was wearing one of those crisp pencil skirts she usually wore around him, in her office, in control. Her nape prickled with a sense that he was watching it. *Don't blush. Don't blush.*

"Was there something you wanted, Tristan?"

An odd, low laugh from him, not so much a laugh as a pained puff of breath.

"Besides to see me melt at your feet," Malorie threw over her shoulder acerbically, brazenly stomping on that idea.

Tristan folded his arms. Temper tightened the corners of his eyes. It was hellishly unfair how hot Tristan looked when his temper pressed him. She didn't find male temper attractive, generally, but Tristan's charged her up every time. As if all the strength and energy he kept hidden under his carefree persona slipped out and focused on her.

Hot, sexy, and very, very tempted to do something physical to her.

"Trust me," Tristan said astringently. "I've long since given up any hope of *that*."

Seriously? He'd had hope of it at some point? That she'd just fall at his feet like all the other girls? She gave him a dirty look.

Tristan took a long, hard breath and tapped his fingers once against his arm. He pivoted, striding around the big room a moment, until his arms loosened back to his sides and his stride relaxed to a stroll. It took him about three paces. Damn, but Tristan had control of his temper. He flicked things off him as if they were *nothing*.

And she was a terrible person, because it made her want to carry one of his perfumes with her so that she could hold it over a cliff in a threatening way to keep his emotions heated up with her.

He turned back, perfectly relaxed now, his manner inviting her to relax, too. He toed the worn carpeting. "Is there still the original parquet flooring under here, do you know?"

Malorie nodded. There was something provoking about how easily he could calm down, when she was still feeling aroused. (To anger. Aroused to anger. Right.) But there was something very easing about it, too. She might not trust Tristan with her heart, and definitely not with her finances, but her physical safety around him was absolute. His strength might be greater than hers, but his control was more than equal to that strength.

"*Merde*, I'd love to rip this damn carpet up and refinish it," he said.

Malorie's eyebrows went up. "That would be a lot of work."

"The belief that I don't like to work is a misconception," Tristan said idly. "Based, I suspect, on the fact that I also like to play." He looked around some more. "Are the original display cases entirely gone? What happened, were they sold?"

"They're in storage downstairs, believe it or not." These gorgeous, long displays, made with flowering curves of metal and iridescent glass. "Along with the Guimard chandelier."

"*Merde*," Tristan whispered, arching his head back to gaze at the ceiling as if in a vision. "You still have that?"

"We have Guimard and Lalique pieces that should be in a museum," Malorie said, and couldn't help glancing at the museum just across the street. To which the Monsards had not been invited to contribute. She looked back at her own space. If she could forge her own way, by herself, in big, harsh, indifferent New York, couldn't she forge a way for the name Monsard again here in much smaller Grasse? Grasse wasn't indifferent to the name Monsard, though. It was hostile. "And multiple two- and three-tiered marquetry tables by Gallé."

"Shit." Tristan whistled. "Holy *shit*. And no one ever sold them or brought them out to show them off?"

Her father had sold a lot of smaller pieces to support his gambling and womanizing, but her grandmother had locked this storage up and not given him a key, once she realized what was happening.

"I guess not," Malorie said.

"I could help you carry some up," Tristan said greedily. "Get a couple of my cousins in here to help with the cases."

Of course he could. No matter what the problem, Tristan always had a group of cousins willing to get together and help. What must that be like, to live a life where male strength surrounded you, could always be counted on for support?

She shook her head. "Once the floors and walls are redone. I don't want the Gallé to get chipped or paint spilled on them."

"*Merde, non,*" Tristan agreed. He eyed Malorie sidelong. "You say that as if it's in the works. Are you planning on restoring this place?"

Was she?

Why would she even think of doing that? It would take months of work. It would take a lot of money—she'd have to sell her apartment in New York. Give up an important, high paying position in the New York perfume industry—a launching pad for becoming CFO somewhere next—to...what? Try to relaunch her own perfume house? A chasing rainbows kind of task in the best of circumstances, much less as a Monsard in a town where family mattered and the family that mattered the most, the Rosiers, still cursed her family name?

And who would benefit? She had no kids. It wasn't like her sisters were going to care. In fact, she'd probably have to get a loan to buy out their shares. She'd be relaunching a family house for a family of one.

She'd have to be an idiot to think of doing that.

She pressed her toe against the carpeted floor. Underneath which lay such gorgeous parquet flooring.

That someone else could lay claim to, put their name on.

"This staircase is absolutely gorgeous." Tristan's heat brushed her clasped hands as he came up behind her to rest his own hand on the slim iron railing. She loosed her hands, startled, and turned.

He smiled at her, his body *much* too close now that she was facing him. But being Tristan, his need for personal space was minute. That guy could see five centimeters free on a bench in high school and cheerfully squeeze down in it beside her. How many times had she found herself in intimate little stances with Tristan at perfume launch parties in New York, when he didn't even *like* her then, he was holding a grudge about Fugace?

Of course, she'd spotted him in very similar intimate stances with famous actresses and gorgeous models more times than she could count. And all those gorgeous women had all looked very happy to be in that position of intimacy, too. The man had a gift.

A gift that made her want to smack him every time she saw him leaning over an actress, teasing her, but Tristan was nothing if not generous in his largesse of himself to the female world.

"I would love to see this place a showcase again," he said, his whole body too close, so that she had to tilt her head back to look up into warm eyes and that inviting curve of his lips.

She was tall, but so was he. The top of her head came just to his lips. It meant his breath always blew over her hair at this distance, tickling her roots and warming the top of her head. It meant she always had to look up at him, when he was in close, unless she wore ten-centimeter heels. And it meant that a kiss was literally only a careless sway of her body away. One lift onto her toes, and that supple, wicked, amused mouth was hers.

"Could I talk you into showing me the Guimard and Gallé?" Tristan said, his eyes holding hers with that warmth and invitation that could talk a woman into doing anything. *Could I talk you into inviting me up for a cup of coffee? Inviting me into your bedroom? Taking off all your clothes?*

Was he imagining owning this place already? Yeah, she bet he was. She could probably sell it to him before the afternoon was over.

Cut loose. Go back to New York.

A bleak void seemed to open right under her heart when she thought of doing that, just one big breath wrong and her heart would teeter into it and be lost forever. But—

"Sure," she said, because Tristan was Tristan. And even in her own defense, there was only so rude a woman could be to a hot, muscled, kitten-cradling guy.

40

Chapter 5

Tristan brushed in front of her as they started down the dark stairs to the underground storage areas.

She frowned at the pushy rudeness—which was really *not* Tristan's style—until she realized that it wasn't rudeness. Tristan, drilled in manners in an extremely patriarchal family, just automatically led the way descending stairs, in case her poor little self couldn't handle them on her own.

Stealing her right to lead her own adventure, into the treasure trove and dangers of her own past.

Her father had done that kind of thing—performed elegant, *I'm-the-man-of-the-family* manners. In his case, though, he hadn't really given a crap about all the *real* ways his wife and daughters could get hurt by him. It had been part of his vision of himself, of the man he thought he was, but he'd never really considered who *they* were, other than as props in his performance. She frowned more deeply at the back of Tristan's head as he lifted his phone, using it as a flashlight to lead their way.

The door into the great room where all the old furniture had been stowed was locked. She slid in front of Tristan to take back her leadership position in her own adventure and pulled out her key.

He reached for it.

She tightened her grip and angled her shoulder to keep him back.

His fingers brushed over her wrist instead of the key and lingered there, as if he had to figure out what he was touching in the dark. The brush of calluses and warmth fell away as Tristan set his hand against the doorjamb and leaned in close behind her, holding his phone up to light the lock with which she fumbled. With her head bent and him leaning in so close, his breath brushed over her nape and sent little shivers of warmth all down her spine, shivers that spread out over her shoulders and down her arms all the way to her elbows. She curled her toes against them.

Tristan didn't say anything at all as she fumbled and fumbled with that stupid lock. He stayed silent in the dark just behind her, except for the soft sound of his breathing, felt more than heard, a cascade of warmth over her nape each time his breath released. He didn't reach for the key again, either. It was funny that he could be so patient. He'd been such a restless boy. The only things that had ever settled him down were things like perfumes, things rich with sensory possibility, as if those were the only things he found compelling enough to go still. To think.

He was still now. Her fingers just could not get that lock open, and Tristan's phone shone quite mercilessly on that fumbling. But he never said a word. While all the warmth of his body soaked into her, while the brush of his breath kept shivering through her, until her body worked the way it was supposed to and everything...just...clicked.

The key turned.

He slid his hand off the frame to push the door open for her, angling his body to give her clear passage in front of him. At least that one patriarchal bit of manners actually required him to step back and quit taking over.

Stepping into the great room was like an escape. Finally her body could stop shimmering. She focused on her surroundings, trying to forget that sensation of him curling her toes without even touching her.

The lights in the ceiling were dim and yellow, shining through dust. Tristan took a quick breath behind her.

A little surge of pride in her middle to show him this. *Her* heritage, her family's old glory. And a sting of pain. Her last foray into the storage room had been with her sisters and her grandmother, a visit that now seemed like a wake, their last Christmas together. Maybe her grandmother had taken them down here that Christmas in one last bid to convince them their past was worth saving. That it wasn't all shame and humiliation. That there was a future in who they were.

Malorie moved into the room. The Guimard chandelier hung from the ceiling, its flirtatious, Belle Époque gloriousness reigning dustily over shapes muffled in cloths like so many burial shrouds. Packed up in boxes. Put away on old cabinet shelves.

"*Merde*," Tristan said reverently. "Look at that." He was gazing at the chandelier, with its curtain of long slender crystal rods, the four green glass teardrops that concealed the light fixture itself. It was a gorgeous specimen of its era. Everything down here was.

No wonder gorgeous Tristan felt right at home, she thought a little wryly. For one second, it even seemed as if the two fit: the glories of her family's pre-war past and Tristan's easy, glorious present.

He could probably annex this place into his Rosier life and barely even notice it hadn't been his to start with.

But still, she pulled a dust cover back, to show off an exquisite two-tiered table with graceful legs, its marquetry so delicately and beautifully done that the shadings of the wood formed a golden-brown layering of light—like the shadings of a sunset, perhaps—behind a tree trunk and leaves.

Dusty memories of coming down here as children, when they had no idea what a collaborator was and no one told them, when this was a treasure trove with a veil of sadness around it that they couldn't understand. It was just something in the way their grandmother...didn't speak, as the little girls hid under cloth draped tables or touched the perfume bottles in wonder. A knot grew in Malorie's chest. *I miss you, Mémère.*

Tristan came to stand on the other side of the tall, slim table from her. "Wow, Malorie." He traced one finger over the glossy surface as if he just had to touch. "This is incredible."

Did he think so? Even with all his own glorious heritage to compare it to? The ache in her throat eased a little. She looked away from that one stroking finger of his that made her wish she was as silky-smooth as that wood.

"There used to be all kinds of perfume bottles, too. Rare Lalique bottles." *How* she had loved those as a kid. "I remember one with a beautiful, opaque, amber-toned glass that cradled the form of two paired black hearts. With that trademark brushed, softened look of Lalique's. And there were all these others—just beautiful." She opened an old binder lying on top of a dust cover to show him the images of that inventory. The insurance records shouldn't be in the same place as the things that could get burned or stolen; she'd have to move the binder.

Tristan came to stand at her shoulder to study the page. She touched a photo of a chatelaine perfume bottle that had belonged to her great-great-grandmother, from back in Monsard's beautiful days. It had been a honeymoon present bought for her in Venice, the little blue bottle crowned with tiny orange blossoms.

"Did they get sold?" Tristan's tone was as sympathetic as a squeeze of her shoulder.

"My father," she said flatly. "He liked to charm, you know? And he had a real need to impress people with his ability to throw money around. Some of the bottles were worth tens of thousands of francs each, and they were the easiest to carry out without anyone noticing."

A little silence. Then Tristan's hand did close on her shoulder, a warm, strong weight. "I didn't realize that about your father."

Really? "Your parents and grandparents didn't talk about it in front of you when we were kids?" She looked back at him.

His eyebrows were flexed, as if something had given him a great deal of food for thought. He shook his head slowly. "I'd picked up that they thought he was a jerk. I didn't realize the details."

Oh. Well, damn. She'd just admitted unnecessarily yet another layer of shameful behavior in her family past. Sometimes she wished to God she had been adopted.

She moved away from him, because it would have been far too tempting to lean back against him as if he could make everything all better, when she knew damn well that making things better was her job.

"You're used to it, aren't you?" She stopped under the chandelier and waved her hand. "A glorious heritage. The Rosiers have so much."

"Not like this. We've never had our own perfume house. Nobody back before the wars was spending money on display this way, in my family. We've always been more of a peasant class."

Yeah, yeah, yeah. The Rosiers and their peasant family myth. They loved emphasizing their salt of the earth nature, but Malorie had had to study Grasse history, too. Glove-makers had been a central part of the Grasse economy back in Laurianne's day—meaning Niccolò Rosario, the mercenary bastard of some Italian prince or whatever legend the Rosiers currently had going about him, had had his eye on the main prize and landed himself quite the wealthy widow. And he'd immediately gone into land with that wealth, obtaining the Rosier valley.

His descendants had built on that beginning. They hadn't exactly been eating black bread and walking around in sabots back during the Revolution. They'd more likely been part of the annoyed, wealthy merchant class who wanted to limit aristocratic abuses in taxation and land confiscation, and who then found themselves scrambling to re-focus their marketing after the initial revolution got out of hand and their wealthiest clients had their heads cut off.

"We did have several very old heirlooms, from our ancestor Niccolò's day, but they disappeared during the war," Tristan said.

Oh, hell, she hoped her great-grandfather hadn't stolen them.

"Or at least that's one story," Tristan said wryly. "My grandfather always said Tante Colette took them, and he does seem to have been right about that. She still claims she doesn't have the one heirloom *I* really would love to see in person, but knowing Tante Colette she's just being cagey. I haven't proved myself worthy of it or something, and she'll share it with me in her own good time. I hope."

"What's the one heirloom you would like to see so much?"

A reverence came into Tristan's face, a kind of hushed longing. "Niccolò and Laurianne's perfume recipe book. Written in their own hands. Can you imagine? Sometimes I have nightmares that it's lying out in the rain, destroyed. That the Nazis took it and burned it or it's in some Nazi descendant's secret vault somewhere." He took a breath. Gave that duck's flick-shrug to his shoulders. His optimism came back. "But I bet Tante Colette is really just hiding it somewhere. Maybe she'll surprise me with it as a wedding present or something."

A little shock to Malorie's stomach. "Are you thinking about getting married, Tristan?" How the hell had he managed to choose, from all his beautiful options?

Tristan laughed. But an odd, puzzled wistfulness slid across his face and knit his eyebrows. He shrugged and it disappeared. "I do want that old perfume book. But I should probably wait until I've found someone I want to spend the rest of my life with before I get married just in the hopes of it as a wedding present."

Yeah. She just bet it was hard for someone with as many options as Tristan had to settle on only one for fifty years.

"Or find someone who wants to spend the rest of her life with me," Tristan said.

Malorie suppressed a snort. If he didn't realize half the women he knew wanted to spend the rest of their lives with him, it was because he was deliberately refusing to admit it. Not ready to settle down.

"Really me," Tristan said and slipped his hands in his pockets, so over-relaxed it was immediately obvious this subject mattered to him. "Not try to change me into someone else."

Change him into someone *else?* "Who the hell else would she want you to be?" she asked incredulously. Sexy, sweet, gorgeous, athletic, creative, brilliant, funny, perceptive, capable of making a woman feel like a million bucks with a smile and a compliment...*merde.*

Tristan blinked at her, energy running through his body again. "She might want me to be good with money," he said a little dryly. Something about his gaze on her was disconcertingly alert. Like he was trying to see right into the center of her brain to what was behind her words. "Capable of prioritizing it. Thinking about the bottom line."

Malorie laughed affectionately. "You need to marry an accountant, Tristan," she said, reaching up to set a perfume bottle back on its shelf. "Just focus on your art and let her take care of that stuff."

For a moment there was absolute silence.

So silent that Malorie could hear the sound of her own heels on the floor as she lowered herself from stretching up to the shelf. She glanced back at him. His hands still in his pockets, he was gazing at her in the oddest wa—

All at once, the implication hit her. Heat raced up her cheeks. "I mean...obviously, I didn't mean..." Oh, *hell.*

Tristan turned away, gazing at a cabinet shelf of 1920s perfume bottles, beautiful but less rare and therefore less valuable, so safe from her father. "You don't think the accountant would drive me crazy?" he said idly after a moment. "Or me her?"

"Oh, definitely." Malorie seized on that. "Definitely you would drive her crazy. I don't know why I wished you on some poor, sane accountant."

He slanted her a glance under his lashes, so discreet she wasn't sure he wanted her to see it. It made her feel ridiculously vulnerable, as if he was trying to see through her clothes to her soul.

"Well, if you ever find an accountant who actually cares about my work and respects it, you let me know," he said finally, the words a little crisp, and turned his back on her, going to stand in front of another cabinet and gaze at the perfume bottles.

Her gaze traced over his back. Tristan had such an easy way of carrying himself, and yet his shoulders were always straight, his head always up. Even in high school, his cousin Damien walked as if he was a knife and the world something he had to cut through. His cousin Matt had seemed to think the world was something he'd have to growl at and wrestle to the ground. But Tristan had always walked into the world as if it was the most beautiful thing ever and he wanted to experience every part of it.

He was an intensely physical being. It was one of the reasons school had been so hard on him. And that physicality showed from those broad shoulders down the definition of back muscles under his T-shirt, to the lean waist and that tight a—she cleared her throat.

"Maybe I should break into Tante Colette's attic again in the middle of the night like we used to do as kids," Tristan said. "Well, we tried to do once, and Lucien broke his arm."

Oh, thank God, they were talking about that family treasure of his again. *Thank you, Tristan, for not hanging me out to dry here.*

Tristan grinned at her over his shoulder, as if the whole faux-pas about accountants had never happened. "Although given that we had the free run of the attic in daylight, I'm not sure what our logic was. Not that we ever found the heirlooms in daylight either. It's amazing how easy it is to hide small treasures amid the masses of things attics accumulate when a family has lived in one place for hundreds of years."

She looked around at all the objects crowded in this storage room. If there were any surprises from *her* family's war history...she winced. They would probably be ones that layered her in shame.

"How is Lucien?"

Tristan said nothing at all for a moment, his face shadowed. And Tristan's face was almost never shadowed.

"He's been hurt?" Her voice dropped. He'd joined the Foreign Legion. What if he'd been *killed?* Her hand flexed and lifted toward Tristan's arm, of its own volition.

"I don't know." Tristan was frowning at the floor. "We never hear from him."

Her heart tightened again, and this time on Tristan's behalf. Even on Lucien's. He'd been five years older than she was, but insofar as she knew him, she, like most of the budding teenage girls, had thought quite well of him. Fit, fine, and, like all his cousins, a protector. No one messed with the girls, or with the smaller kids, when the Rosiers were around.

Her hand closed, tentatively, on Tristan's forearm. A mistake. That touch felt both too dangerous and too inadequate. A need to do more pushed at her—a need to stroke or wrap her arm around his waist or...

But then, Tristan always had pulled all the emotions and energy in a room to him. Or was that just her emotions and energy he pulled?

Tristan's gaze shifted from the floor to her hand. He gazed at it a long moment, his eyebrows faintly flexed, until she pulled back and hooked her thumb in her pocket to make her hand behave.

His gaze lifted to hers.

She turned away, touching a dust cover. "You don't know how to contact him?" she said huskily.

"We don't even know his name in the Legion."

Yeah. That was what the Legion was famous for. Letting men disappear and become someone else entirely.

Malorie grimaced. For a family as tight as the Rosiers, the wound must never close. And Tristan, for all his ability to absorb all attention, returned that attention in spades. He had such a generous damn heart.

She didn't know what to say. She wanted to reach out and squeeze his arm again, and obviously she couldn't allow herself to do that.

"I'm sorry," she said low. Even the Rosier family had its problems, didn't it?

At least the Rosiers had each other to fall back on, in times of hurt. She and her sisters had helped each other at her grandmother's funeral, of course they had. But most of the time, she just had herself.

A hand ghosted over her hair and lightly touched her shoulder. "Thank you, Malorie," Tristan said quietly.

For some reason her throat clogged. As if somewhere in that grazing touch, there was some hint that someone had thought of *her*. How bittersweet it must be for her to be down here, how lonely and lost she must feel.

"How are your sisters?" Tristan asked.

Her throat hurt worse. "Oh, fine. Angèle's in Tierra del Fuego having the time of her life researching penguins." She laughed a little and rolled her eyes, inviting him to share her ruefulness over such an obsession. "And Lise is with SOS Médecins right now in the Central African Republic."

She *hoped* Lise was fine. Penguins didn't seem inherently dangerous, but Lise's job exposed her to far more trauma than Malorie would ever be able to handle.

It would be nice, the thought whispered through her, *for Lise to be able to come home to that garden of bitter orange trees if she ever needed it. Just like we could when Mémère was alive.*

She was the only one in her family since her grandmother with a practical bone in her body. Maybe that practicality could be on behalf of more people than just herself.

"And how's your mother?"

"In French Polynesia." Malorie smiled. "She certainly set out to have a second life once we left home. She runs a little resort on Ruahine, paints, and has a boyfriend ten years younger than she is." The boyfriend reminded Malorie a little of her father, in fact—charming and quick to use that charm to get what he wanted out of people, such as her mother's financial support. But overall they seemed happy. Her mother had well and thoroughly washed her hands of her time hooked into the Monsard family and was not looking back. Even her daughters had to go see her rather than the other way around. But then who could complain about an excuse to vacation on a Polynesian island?

"How are *you*?" Tristan said suddenly.

Malorie met his gaze. For a moment neither said anything at all, his eyes brown and steady, until a weird heat started to gather in her chest.. She raised an eyebrow at him. "Fine. Obviously."

"Well, it is *obvious*," Tristan said slowly, watching her. "But it's obvious a duck is calmly floating on the water without the slightest effort, too. And underneath it's really paddling like mad."

Her breath felt tight. Threatened. Hopeful. As if something was about to break free and it might be dangerous. Or an utter relief.

Tristan lifted a hand until callused fingertips just grazed her cheekbone. "Malorie—"

She twisted away and sneezed. Once, twice. "Sorry." She held up a hand, warding him away. "It must be the dust."

Tristan's hand dropped. He slipped both his hands into his pockets and took a step back, just watching her. "*À tes souhaits*," he said, after too long a delay. *To her wishes, may they come true.* It had been a long time since she had heard *that* phrase, instead of the American *bless you.* And for two sneezes, he was supposed to say— "*À tes amours.*"

To her loves. Yes. In that warm, rich voice that grazed over a woman's skin. She sneezed a third time.

"*Qu'elles durent toujours,*" he added. *May they last forever.*

Their eyes met, just for a moment, and then she turned away, rubbing her arms, trying to capture that sense of warmth grazing over her skin that Tristan's voice always brought.

Tristan thrust a hand through his hair, a gesture that always made her palm prickle with the desire to know what his hair felt like, and looked around him as if searching for help. "Would you be willing to show me more?" He gestured to the covered furniture. "I love this kind of thing."

He seemed to gather his charm and then send it her way in a glance, breaking through the seriousness with it. Inviting, warm, *how can you possibly resist me?*

She sighed. But it had always secretly made her so happy to make Tristan happy. She'd had to read Gloria Steinem every night to keep from ruining her career for him for Fugace. He'd been so passionate and so upset and so, so sure that if he asked the right way, any woman in the world would give him what he wanted. She honestly thought she might be the first woman to tell Tristan no in his entire life. He sure used to wrap their teachers around his finger, all while getting away with the most outrageous behavior.

It was probably just as well she'd known him all her life and knew better than to fall for his bullshit.

At least the thing he wanted this time didn't hurt her. So she showed him all the pieces that had once made a glorious showroom upstairs. Lamps and tables and cases and perfume bottles.

"I never even knew Monsard had all this," Tristan said. "The showroom upstairs could be *amazing.*"

The hunger in his tone sounded disconcertingly possessive. If she wanted to sell this place to him, she could move in and close the deal right now, couldn't she?

Parfums Rosier it could say over the door. Not *MONSARD*.

"It needs a lot of work," she said.

"I told you I don't mind work," he said. And then suddenly, decisively, "I'll take it."

The jolt ran all the way through her. He'd *take it*? Just like that? All that was left of her family, his for the snap of his fingers?

"What do you mean, you'll take it?" she heard herself ask between her teeth.

He looked confused by her tone. "If you want to sell it." He made a big gesture with his hands, as if to indicate all the wonders of the world, right here within his reach. "Promise me you'll see me first. I'll take good care of it for you, Malorie. Don't sell it to someone like LBRH."

LBRH was one of the huge international fragrance companies that had reached out to Malorie's grandmother about buying it so as to have a presence in Grasse, just for the marketing romance of being able to say they were part of the historic perfume capital of the world.

She folded her arms. "Maybe I don't want to sell it." Her voice sounded hard even to her. That moment of intimacy and understanding retreated. Maybe it had only ever been a trick to soften her up. Her father used to do that kind of thing.

Tristan's shoulders slumped a little. "You're just going to shut it up again and let it go to waste?"

Her arms tightened. She wanted to strike out at him, as if he was hurting her, and yet he'd said nothing that should be painful.

Tristan pinched the bridge of his nose. "I suppose in your mind that's the *rational* thing to do." His tone turned *rational* into a dirty word.

No. Selling it was the rational thing to do. Take the money, manage it wisely, retire at fifty. Or do whatever the hell else she wanted to do with her life.

Shutting it up again was the can't-face-a-tough-choice thing to do.

"I think I *will* restore it," she heard herself say, her voice harsh.

Tristan stilled. Really still, like that stupid moment when she'd said he should marry an accountant. Under the hand that still pinched the bridge of his nose, his eyes locked with hers.

"Why not?" she said fiercely. "It's *my* family heritage."

Tristan's hand slowly lowered, but his eyes never left hers. "I never said it wasn't."

"I can keep it if I want to," she said. "It's *mine*."

He said nothing. Just watched her, those supple eyebrows of his ever so slightly drawn together.

She gave him a cool look. "You don't think I can make anything of it?"

Here. In Grasse. Where the world belonged to the Rosiers and her very name was against her.

Tristan's eyebrows went up just a little. "I think you can do whatever you set your mind to, Malorie." He sounded surprised this was even a question.

She blinked, caught off guard. She *could* do whatever she set her mind to, yes, she absolutely could, but...how did Tristan know that?

"You set off on a hike with friends one day to celebrate your *bac*. And when you decided that you liked it better away from here, you just kept going and never came back."

Again that faint thread of darkness in his voice, but mostly it was full of a genuine admiration that felt like having two strong hands curve around her shoulders and grip them in approval. And *no one* had gripped her shoulders in approval. Not...well, ever. She'd tried some relationships in Paris and New York, but...There'd never been a man in her life to be proud of her.

"How did you do it, Malorie?" Tristan said wonderingly. "Go from a girl just out of high school hiking into the Alps with nothing but a backpack to the head of accounting at a major perfume house in New York?"

Her lips were starting to relax into far too vulnerable a smile. Like she *needed* his admiration. Craved it.

Another thing her father had been good at. Giving just enough admiration to get the women around him to depend on it and let him get away with murder so he wouldn't withdraw it.

But Tristan is nothing like your father. You should know that. She did know it. But sometimes it was hard to *trust* it.

Tristan shook his head. "Up to the point when you started destroying my perfumes to advance your career, I don't even *know*."

Oh, thank God. Something she could get exasperated about. Saved by the Tristan-the-artist bell. "I destroyed your—first of all, I did not *destroy* them. I insisted on less expensive formulas to do my job correctly, which, yes, when you do a good job that does tend to advance your career. As I believe you may have noticed yourself, in your own career."

He folded his arms. "Fugace was special."

She sighed. "I take that back about you marrying an accountant. You'd drive her to an early grave."

His eyes narrowed.

"Well, you would."

"Maybe she'd drive *me* to an early grave by insisting on destroying my perfumes all the time."

She gripped her hair. "Excuse me for not jettisoning my own career to advance yours."

He scowled.

She scowled back.

They eyed each other a moment, and then humor glinted in his eyes, and his lips quirked, inviting her to share it.

She sighed at the laugh that ran through her in response. She'd spent her whole life seeing Tristan charm every teacher or any other woman who ever got annoyed with him into laughter instead, and yet the trick *still* always worked on her. "I never had a powerful family to fall back on if I messed up my career, Tristan," she managed to say coolly.

She'd had, in New York, absolutely nobody. In that whole huge city, the only person she'd had was her.

"I've never fallen back on my family," Tristan said, clipped.

Was he kidding her? When he said *I'll take it* about her entire heritage like that, who did he think was giving him that power? He meant Rosier SA was going to buy it, on his behalf, or he meant that he'd get a loan with a single phone call because no bank around here would ever refuse to loan a Rosier scion money. Or even if he meant he'd use his own money, what did he think had given him the entrée into the perfume industry so that he could become the star perfumer that he was?

She gritted her teeth. "You've always had so much power and strength around you that you don't even know what it's *like* to start falling. It wouldn't be possible. None of you would let the other fall."

He started to speak, clearly angry, but as he opened his mouth, he took a long breath in and let it slowly out. Thinking. Which was another Tristan trait. He had a *really* fast, bright brain, and he assessed what other people said and did constantly. It was one of the things that probably made him so good at landing so many hot women. He paid attention to their words and actions. "Did I ever tell you about the time I was seven years old and the first to dive off the cliffs at Bonifacio?"

Twenty-seven meters above the sea. *Merde.* He'd done that at seven? Of course he had. That was Tristan all over.

"I can't even remember whose idea it was. None of us were supposed to be out there at all, but we were always getting in trouble. Because we were always daring each other, egging each other on. And I was the youngest, and I wanted like anything to lead. To win. This impossible thing, right? For a seven-year-old boy to win against a twelve-year-old boy. So I ran ahead of Raoul while he was yelling after me to try to catch me, and I just went straight over without even stopping."

"*Merde*, Tristan. Your parents must have died. Did they kill you?"

Tristan gave her a sweet smile. "Conversely, I very rarely got in much trouble for any of the things we got up to. After all, *I* was only little. The older boys were supposed to keep an eye on me."

Malorie had to laugh a little. Yeah, Tristan probably played his mom like a violin.

"So I understand your point," Tristan said, "about always having support. They probably *wouldn't* let me fall, if there was a way they could help. But (a) I don't think you have *any* idea how strongly my grandfather values independence and self-reliance and how much we all wanted to live up to him, and (b) I don't think you have any idea how much we challenged each other. We might not want to *let each other fall* but we sure as hell come up with ideas like 'let's jump off a twenty-seven-meter cliff face', and then race each other to see who gets there first."

Yeah, she could totally see that, in the way the Rosier cousins related. "But you're missing *my* point. Which is that you can take all the risks you want, because you might kill yourself, but you'll never find yourself out on the street."

"Neither will you, Malorie. Unless you switched nationalities while you were in New York. You'd have government aid."

"Because you think I want to live off handouts from the government?"

"Because you think I want to live off handouts from my cousins?" Tristan held her eyes. "I'm pretty sure there's a greater risk to my pride and self-worth to me failing than you can quite wrap your mind around."

Malorie frowned. A vision of his grandfather rose in her mind. That tough, tough old man with his blue eyes that looked at you as if he could see the swastika printed on your soul from a thousand meters—and hit it at that distance, too, ridding the world of one more element of evil. When he came for talks in school, she sank down as low as possible in her desk and hoped to God he didn't spot any resemblance to her great-grandfather that would make him realize who she was.

Yeah, she wouldn't want to fail in his eyes. She, personally, often didn't even want to *exist* in his eyes. (*Which would be a shame,* she reminded herself fiercely. *You're a strong person. You're living a full life. Don't let that gaze make you quail.*)

She thought of Tristan's grandmother and his aunt, Colette Delatour. Women who had looked Gestapo in the eye and smiled as if no children at all hid only a few feet away.

Of his cousins, who back in high school already walked as if the world was theirs for the making.

"There's a risk to me failing, too," she said. "It's the risk that a failure is all we'll ever be."

And she ran back up the stairs, moving quickly to get out into the light of day.

Chapter 6

Dark hair. Green eyes. Cool quiet. Focus.

Sometimes it seemed as if all his life Tristan had been just outside the edges of Malorie's secret, shadowed pool, trying to escape the noise around him and slip up to her, to have the right to just dip his fingers in the cool water of her. As if she was a shelter he was never allowed to rest in.

Discipline and ambition, determination and courage.

All his life, he had been pushing himself at Malorie, from stealing her pencils to trying to force her to respect his perfumes, always, always, always trying to tell her, *Look at me.*

Play with me, talk to me, notice me, admire me. I admire you.

What the hell was wrong with him? It wasn't as if there weren't other women out there. He loved women and it had been with considerable delight and relief in high school—especially after his crash and burn with Malorie—that he had discovered a lot of them loved him, too. It *wasn't* as if he'd spent the past fifteen years mooning over her, damn it.

But...

He gazed out over the valley and consciously kept himself from folding his arms, tightening his jaw.

"Do you think I'm only who I am because of my family?" he asked his grandfather.

They stood on the slope of the valley, looking across the fields of roses that were leafing out. He and his grandfather used to hike all through these mountains, Tristan as a boy running and shouting and playing with his cousins around him, or hunting, going careful and quiet, or just one on one, especially as Tristan grew into a teenager and more and more needed to walk with his grandfather, a man with standards like a great, majestic cliff to climb. He'd loved that—the challenge his grandfather offered him, to be the best man he could be.

Pépé gave him an incredulous look from faded blue eyes that still seemed capable of spotting a German soldier slipping through pines all the way on the other side of the valley. Those old hands might still be steady enough to pick him off at this distance, too.

"Yes," Pépé said dryly, in that *was your cradle rocked too close to the wall?* tone. "If you need any other obvious information today, I also think the sky is blue."

Tristan sighed.

Pépé's face was as wrinkled and weather-stained as a map that had been crumpled up and carried in the pocket of Time for a century, pulled out and consulted in all conditions, at every emergency. "Of course, I also think your family is only what it is because of you."

Really? That felt oddly...true. Powerful. Tristan found himself taking a deep breath, the rich subtle scents of home filling him. Pine. Earth. That fresh greenness of the land unfurling.

"You think I change my family?" he asked, awkward unexpectedly and almost shy. Not emotions he felt ever. But...he was the youngest. In a family that had a history that lost itself back in the Middle Ages. Had he actually made a mark?

He'd fought like hell to become one of the top perfumers in the world, but even that...there had been plenty of perfumers in his family's past. *Merde*, Niccolò and Laurianne were supposed to have single-handedly introduced new perfume techniques that changed Grasse from a city of glove-makers to the center of perfume for centuries. How did you make your mark in a family where multiple members of it had changed the entire course of history?

That old blue glance clearly questioned Tristan's sense. Such a familiar look that Tristan's lips relaxed into affectionate amusement. Damn, he loved his grandfather.

"I think you hold it together," Pépé said, so astonishingly that Tristan actually moved his feet to catch his balance, as if the ground was shifting under him when in fact it was holding just as rock steady as ground around Pépé was supposed to do.

Blue eyes pinned him. "You didn't realize?" From Pépé's expression, this was a failure in self-assessment on Tristan's part.

"No," Tristan said honestly. For one thing, it wasn't together. Lucien and Raoul had both run off and left him. So had Malorie, for that matter, although at least he'd always known his crush on her was one-sided. Unlike what he had thought about his absolute love for his older cousins, which, as a child, he'd just assumed was returned. Until they walked away from him without ever even glancing back.

If he was the one who held things together, he'd done a shit hell job of it when he was a teenager.

"Mmm," Pépé said.

Tristan watched him expectantly.

Pépé studied the land before them.

"Pépé," Tristan said between his teeth.

"I don't want to make you start overthinking it," Pépé said. "Getting self-conscious."

"*Self-conscious?* Have you even met me?"

"Yes," Pépé said calmly, as if he knew far more about Tristan than Tristan did.

Tristan narrowed his eyes at him. He did, of course, want to prove to his grandfather that if there was one subject in the world on which Tristan was more expert than Pépé was, it was himself. But he also desperately wanted to know what his grandfather was thinking.

Maybe Tristan really was spoiled in some way as the youngest. Some of his older cousins had had their doubts they could ever please Pépé. They'd done crazy things to try to live up to him.

Lucien had joined the Foreign Legion to impress him, Raoul had run off to Africa and gotten shot by a rebel warlord while defending Rosier SA suppliers, Matt devoted his whole being to becoming the patriarch Pépé wanted him to be, Damien drove himself so hard as the ruthless businessman that it was a good thing Jess was saving him from an early grave.

But Tristan, somehow, had always been absolutely sure that Pépé loved him.

It seemed so obvious to him. In the demands Pépé made of them, in the time he spent with them, in the way he had taught them these hills and fed them their first taste of truffle, in the way he never, ever faltered in his expectation—his conviction—that they would be good men.

To Tristan, all his cousins' doubts that they could be good enough for Pépé had come from inside them. From how much they hero-worshipped the old man. The grandchildren of a superhero who worried that they only had ordinary mortal powers. Pépé had clearly never doubted their worth at all. He'd invested in it and believed in it with every stride he'd taken across these lands, with them scampering, or running, or eventually also striding strongly alongside him.

But how did you ever live up to a man like that? A man who was not only great but *good*? How *did* you stand as tall, cast a shadow that was as long?

"You siphon them off," Pépé said absently. He was watching a pair of vultures spin over the cliffs at the head of the valley.

What?

"When they're getting twisted up in their own emotions, you make them laugh. You straighten them out. So they can fit together. You love them for who they are. So that they can be happy in who they are."

Tristan stared at his grandfather, a slow wave of heat climbing up his cheeks. He felt as if he was ten years old again. Awkwardly thrilled to have someone understand him. To have impressed his grandfather.

Without jumping off a cliff. Without shooting something. Without working tirelessly in the fields, no complaining. Without even realizing he was doing it.

"We had a guy like that, back in our cell."

Tristan perked his ears. It was rare that his grandfather referenced his Resistance days, but all the cousins had always scrambled for any knowledge of it they could get.

"When it was raining on us and cold and we'd screwed up an attack and everyone in the group was ready to go home, give up, or possibly kill each other...he'd make us all laugh instead. He was the guy who'd sit down beside you on a rock while you were brooding, tangled up, and say that wry thing that made you take yourself a little less seriously—and know you were accepted even if you were screwed up. He'd ease the tempers and the trouble so that people could put forward the best of themselves. *Be* the best of themselves."

Tristan was silent for a moment, trying to digest this. He'd never even thought about himself this way before. It felt too rich and buttery golden to digest.

"What happened to him?" His grandfather had that expression on his face—the one that meant memories were both good and sad. At ninety-one, he'd outlived most of his peers.

"He was deported three months before the Americans pushed up from Italy," his grandfather said, crisply, that way he always had to talk about the worst things, if he talked about them at all. "When Monsard sold us out. We never saw him again. I used to wonder how long he kept people's spirits up on the train and in the camp." That sheen moved across his grandfather's eyes, that shadow of a grief that could never really heal. "Used to imagine him keeping them up until the bitter end."

The hair on the back of Tristan's neck lifted. He bent his head. Memories of a war that had ended decades before his own birth had formed the bedrock of his existence. They had filled history books in schools. They were the subject of multiple museums around here. But hearing that oral memory, from his grandfather who had lived it, always made it hit...well, home.

"Pierre Monsard?" As if there was any other Monsard family around here. "Your friend was one of the three he betrayed?"

His grandfather nodded once and looked away.

Tristan gazed out over the valley that his family had held for centuries. And saw Malorie's green eyes against the evening pines.

There's a risk to me failing, too. It's the risk that's all we'll ever be.

"It's funny how his descendants have turned out so different from him," he said casually, studying the land.

"They didn't defend their land, did they? All three of those girls left."

"Maybe they went off on a quest," Tristan said. "To grow strong enough to defend it."

"What is this, a fairy tale?" his grandfather said with that faint note of irony he used sometimes when he just wanted to confuse the hell out of everyone. For example, was he being sardonic about anyone believing life was a fairy tale? Or was the irony self-directed, considering they were standing on the edge of a valley of roses and he himself had saved children by hiding them in a wagon of roses?

"If it is, the youngest should have an edge," Tristan teased. His grandfather had also been the youngest, once his father had remarried and given him Colette as a stepsister. Tristan was both an only child and the youngest of the five cousins, so who knew how that worked out.

His grandfather just gave him that look, the one with an extra crumple around the edges of his lips, a compressed smile.

Yes, Pépé loved him.

"Do you blame everyone who leaves?" he asked cautiously. "Who doesn't stay and fight for the land?"

Did Pépé still love Lucien? He never talked about him at all, except that when he mentioned the number of grandsons he had, it was still always five. Tristan thought the fear of not being loved by his grandfather and the *stupid-assed* fear of not having a place among his cousins anymore was what had driven Lucien away. So if he ever, ever managed to see Lucien again, he wanted to be able to tell him: *You're an idiot. Pépé misses you. Come home.*

Pépé was silent for a moment. "Some people have a reason," he said finally, not looking at him.

But he could be thinking about two of his own sons, Lucien's father and Raoul's father, who kept only the most minimal contact anymore with the family. Raoul's father reacting to his wife's death and Lucien's father, well...

"What about Lucien?" Tristan probed cautiously. No one talked to his grandfather about this. Maybe everyone was afraid of what he would say.

Pépé shot him a sharp blue glance. "Since when is fighting for your country not fighting for this land?" *Ton pays, ce pays.* They were the same word, in French.

All the tension in Tristan's face muscles relaxed, only then making him realize it had accumulated. He smiled at his grandfather in relief and approval.

Pépé said nothing for another moment. "He has leaves, though," he added crisply, as if that was his final word on the subject.

Yes, Lucien did. Leaves he never used to come see them. And there were other ways to serve your country than joining the Foreign Legion and abandoning your entire identity, too. *Damn it, Lucien.*

A sigh slipped out of him. "I didn't straighten Raoul and Lucien out. Didn't hold them together."

Tristan had still been to all intents and purposes a kid when Lucien's mother tossed the hand grenade of Lucien's true paternity straight into the heart of their family. He'd been old enough to pretend he understood what everyone was talking about and young enough that he couldn't quite figure out how Lucien could *not* be his father's son. If Lucien's mom was married to Lucien's dad, how could anyone else have fathered him?

But while he might not have understood why it mattered so much, whether Lucien's father had contributed his sperm to the relationship or not—if he'd been his father for all his life, it seemed as if something so tiny you couldn't even see it without a microscope shouldn't matter—he remembered the way Lucien had changed. He remembered that his older cousin had never wanted to see their grandfather anymore and had grown strange and distant with all of them. And he remembered still the brutal shock a year later of learning Lucien was gone.

Just...gone. He'd *chosen* to just wipe his name out of existence, to walk out and leave them all as if Lucien Rosier and all that wonderful, glorious happiness that had been Tristan's vision of their childhood together had never been.

"Lucien and Raoul are when you learned the risks of not being the glue that holds your family together," his grandfather said. Everything about his wrinkled face compressed, his grandfather's hard control of his own emotions etched by time until it had grown visible, like stone under eroded land. "Learned what you could lose if you didn't get it right."

Maybe. Tristan remembered how anxious he'd gotten about Matt and Damien after Raoul and Lucien left. How alert he'd been to any chance that they, too, were going to break down and disappear on him. Maybe that was when he'd started applying those youngest-cousin emotional manipulation skills to something other than just getting his own way.

Hell, maybe that was even part of the reason he liked to capture emotions in bottles so much. So he could bring them out and relive them again, so they couldn't escape him.

"I don't think I'm nearly as selfless as you make me sound," Tristan said.

His grandfather snorted. "Who said it was selfless? You're the most bloody-minded of the lot. Never seen a kid so determined to get his own way. Not since me."

Okay, *now* Tristan recognized himself. It was really *much* better for himself and everyone he knew if he got his way. Nobody else in his family even properly understood what they wanted, most of the time.

Pépé's lips got a little bit more crumpled, from the suppression of his smile. Affection filled his blue eyes and made Tristan feel like a puppy, delighted to have pleased his grandfather. Damn it. He was twenty-nine years old. You'd think he could grow out of that.

"It's just that what you want is to have your people all around you, happy," his grandfather said. His smile softened, a rare sight. He gripped Tristan's shoulder. "I told you that you were a lot like me."

Chapter 7

Brown eyes. Black hair. Callused fingers, on her inner wrist, warm and gentle and sure.

Malorie tossed and turned, caught between a tough decision and the figment of her imagination who was always so good at reassuring her when things were tough.

She needed to be careful of Grasse. Tristan's proximity might make her imagination of him start to seem all too real. Possible. It might have calluses that grazed against her skin, long black lashes that lifted when his eyes suddenly met hers, the faint lines at the corners of his eyes of a young man who spent a lot of time in the sun or on the water and the way they tightened just for her.

It was still dark out when she woke in the twin bed she used to use when she spent the night at her grandmother's house as a child. The scents of orange blossom carried through the open window, with the chill of the spring night. She rose. In New York, she would have been stuck inside four walls with her worry, at this hour before dawn. But here, she could go out among the orange trees, in that hush of scent and darkness, the orchard a patch of shadow amid the lights of the developed coast that sparkled down the slopes to the sea.

She got her grandmother's scythe and went to work, clearing back the growth around the first half dozen trees, then stretched out the old ground cloths and pulled out one of the several ladders. White flowers fell softly from her fingers in the pre-dawn light, pattering against the cloths below.

The gloss of leaves against her skin, the silk of petals in her fingers, the sting of scratches she accumulated on her forearms from the overgrown brush as she worked. The scent everywhere, until she could no longer even really smell it. It became part of her again, like it once had been. Until the rhythm sank back into her fingers, the sun rising, the birds waking.

Tristan would love it here. The thought ghosted across her mind. *If you ever let him in.*

The sun rose gently, flushing the sky above the sea. The flowers twisted and fell, silk between her fingers. The scent of orange blossom surrounded her, rich and sweet.

She hadn't realized that it had been a very, very long time since she had felt at peace.

***

Depth and dust and secret. A treasure gleaming in the dark. Long, gorgeous legs in a crisp pencil skirt striding toward it. It was a scent, that treasure. It was a perfume bottle, almost lost to time and war. It was a story that could still come true.

To an outside observer, Tristan stood perfectly still in the middle of his office, but in his head, everything was happening. Scents came together, multiplied, spun off, a kaleidoscope of possibilities all started from one idea. Many of them he could smell just standing there with his eyes closed. Some he wanted to have the lab blend to see if the components bonded the way he thought they would.

To see if he could capture that glimpse of a past and future story.

It needed a flower. He needed to figure out what was in that perfume bottle at the depths and let its secret scent rise out of the dark and mysterious base.

Flower.

A flower.

Floral.

Floral. Floral. Why did that make him—

Oh, fuck.

That damn beach floral he was doing for LBRH. He still hadn't figured that thing out.

He broke his stillness and went to his desk to write down all his initial ideas for a dust and secret scent before he lost them. He sent two to the lab to mix for him.

Then he gave all his beach floral vials and notes a disgruntled look.

Merde, this stupid beach floral. Who the hell wanted to make *another* beach floral? And not, of course, one where you could do something creative and difficult that people would talk about and think about. No, it was basically just supposed to be mangoes and coconut and sand and sea.

He banged his head down on the sketches he had spread out all over his desk and growled at them.

Then he turned his head enough to unsquoosh his nose and took a deep breath of the paper, the graphite from his drawing pencils. His fingers stroked over the old wood of the desk. Paper and thought and time, all the time up here under the roof of Rosier SA, all the people who had filled this building and thought and worked and created, and the way the noises from the pedestrian street would have reached them, century after century, and the way even the scents that wafted in from the window would have been so much the same—some restaurant had put beef on its grill with tomatoes and thyme, and the wind stirred with a far hint of the sea.

Or paper and time like his grandfather's face, like that impression of a map crumpled up by use but you could still pull it out of your pocket in every emergency. *That.* How did you catch *that*?

He flipped the nearest sheet of paper over and started to sketch a few formula ideas on—oops. That was the nearly naked bikini butt he had sketched earlier, a curvy woman stretched out on a towel with flowers in her hair, as he tried to give himself inspiration.

Yeah.

He shoved the paper-and-time formula away. You couldn't make money for a major fragrance house or land briefs from the top designer houses with a fragrance that was paper and time.

The pressure of that dream of his again. The one where he wasn't a commercial perfumer, he had his own niche house where he made whimsical perfumes, ones that smelled like dust and treasure for those who thought life held the promise of so many secret treasures, or ones that smelled like paper and time for people who loved to smell like paper and time. A book lover's scent. A philosopher's scent.

An alchemist's scent...

Focus on your beach floral.

But the scents were spinning off in his brain already, a whole series, the variations he would make in the base of paper and time so that one scent would be *Libraire* or *Bibliophile* or *Lecteur*. One would be *Philosophe*. One would be *Alchimiste*. Probably he should let the marketing team come up with the names.

Except he couldn't do this dream. His perfumes made too much for Rosier SA. If he landed the brief for a commercially successful perfume—a beach floral, for example—then the perfume house it was for would use Rosier SA to produce it. That was the way the perfume industry worked. Meaning that each successful perfume he landed paid for more Rosier SA salaries than he could count—he let Damien do that kind of calculation—and spread out throughout all their suppliers around the world, to small producers in Indonesia or the Congo or right here around Grasse who depended on Rosier SA's annual purchases to survive.

He couldn't abandon commercial success to do niche perfumes instead.

Although what would be lovely would be to do both. To land commercial briefs and to, maybe, right down the street, have his own niche house where he created all the whimsies a man enthralled by the world could ever want.

A little whiff of fancy, like a hint of scent. Malorie's Maison de Monsard restored to all that Art Nouveau glory, there at the most perfect corner of Grasse, filled with scents that were magical, that caught at all the history and grandeur and centuries of effort around here. And on one of those beautiful display tables, a fragrance that was paper and time. With a bottle made by the local twins, Manon and Nathan Viale, and...

Focus. Always a challenge for him if he wasn't sensually, physically fascinated by what he was doing. *This* perfume house wanted a beach floral. And since it was likely to be the bestseller of the next summer season, it was up to him to get it right so that Rosier SA could get all the profits from it.

He got up and went to his balcony, gazing down the street. He couldn't quite make out La Maison de Monsard from there, and abruptly he caught the edge of the roof and hauled himself up onto it.

There.

Now he could see Monsard's zinc, a contrast with all the red tiles.

Not that Malorie Monsard was why he couldn't focus. Not anymore, damn it. He wasn't in high school.

It was that stupid beach floral.

He sniffed his elbow. Yeah, no. That latest trial was not going to work on skin. He smelled like somebody had laced sunscreen with mango. He checked his other arm. *Non*, rolling that sunscreened body in sand did not make this scent any more original.

Well, just fuck then. He hated beach florals.

He stretched his fingers and stared at them.

Malorie probably hated them, too. He could not even conceive of her wearing a beach floral. It would be something secret, elusive, not there. What he had tried to do with Fugace. An absence of scent almost, luring you closer and closer until you were in this cool green shaded place where you could just feel...safe...from all the barrage of sensations around you and then...

She lifted one booted foot, planted it in the center of your chest, and just kicked you back out of her safe space.

Challenged your freaking production costs.

He flipped his hands over, staring at the calluses. Rock climbing, windsurfing. Movement.

Maybe that was why Malorie had never responded to him. She remembered him from grade school. Restless, wild, distracting everyone, driving the teacher crazy, learning to charm his way out of the constant trouble he was in.

In several classes, one teacher attempt to get him to behave was to put him next to Malorie so she could be the good example and because she was the only one in class the teacher was sure would resist his efforts to rope her into something more active and interesting than math or penmanship.

He'd tried, of course. Rough in his grabs for attention at first, because, since he spent his childhood tumbling and wrestling his way across the hills with his older, all male cousins, he just thought that was the way people who liked each other interacted. He'd teased her and grabbed papers from her and drawn things for her across them. He'd stolen food from her plate at lunch whenever they ate in the *cantine* instead of going home for lunch, and he'd kicked his soccer ball into her games with her friends at recess and made them chase him away.

Anything rather than sit still and focus on things that had no sensation. Even as a little kid, he'd known that *she* had more sensation than everything else teachers wanted him to do.

He'd been surprised to learn as an adult, from his friends in New York, that in some countries they medicated kids like him. He'd found it troubling—his personality was so bad that some societies would intervene to change it to make him fit, rather than make room for him? In France, no one had thought of medication, but they'd most certainly thought he should

73

conform—all on his own, with nothing but his own will and discipline.

He tried. *Merde* but he'd tried, early on. Failing over and over and over, and when he was very little, only four or five, breaking down in tears over it day after day, in the secret of his home, where only his mother knew. And kept going back, day after day because he had no choice, and trying again. For years and years his will and discipline were never enough. He'd felt like he was failing *everybody.*

So he'd stayed in trouble on a daily basis, and charmed his way out of it as often as he could to save his parents more phone calls. It wasn't *mean* trouble, he just couldn't sit still, and it was best if he could get his teachers to treat that with affectionate exasperation rather than anger.

And then he still remembered coming into class the very last second the first day of school back from summer when he was fourteen. And sliding into the empty seat behind Malorie. And her standing back up a moment to bend over and catch a pen that she'd dropped under a neighboring desk.

The curve of her butt.

The length of her legs.

The fall of her black hair.

And all that greedy, confusing, embarrassing sexual desire that had been building in him over the summer just woke up with a zing and *focused.*

It was the same year Raoul and Lucien left, shattering his whole happy vision of a world in which five cousins played and worked together all their lives. So maybe there were more factors besides his own puberty and falling for a girl that got him to start growing up that year.

He never did learn to do more than survive the torture of school as best he could, but he did get better at it that year. Learned techniques to handle himself. He'd sit there, focusing on Malorie, sketching—her, a cliff face, a green river, shadows, things that had sensations in them—and he didn't exactly become a star student, but he started learning control, to be less disruptive. To channel himself as best he could.

He never could get Malorie to reciprocate the interest, though. He'd tried that charm he'd learned as a restless child on plenty of other girls in school, and it turned out nearly *all* of them responded to it when it was combined with his teenage physical form. The discovery of girls—who were pretty much *packed* with sensation a restless, hungry young man could focus on—had transformed his whole experience of school.

But Malorie stayed unreachable. She'd be polite, but she kept a reserve with him that he'd never managed to penetrate. Maybe he was permanently branded in her brain as the annoying brat from grade school.

In fact, it wasn't until he started working in perfumes, when everything he had to memorize had a *sensation* to it, a *meaning*, that he'd flourished. Scents could hold his brain together. If he could sink into them in his head, those scents carried all the activity and richness of life. Playing with them in his head felt like exploring the world, amassing sensations. He could focus on them.

He loved the world around him. He loved its people and its scents and its textures and the way his own body felt, when he was giving it a challenge.

It's just that what you want is to have your people all around you, happy.

Happiness. Your people happy all around you.

That was what a beach memory was about, right? Having one's people happy all around. Not the sunscreen or the sand or the coconut oil—those were just triggers. *His* job was to catch the happiness and bottle it up, so anyone who opened that bottle could live that happiness again in a breath.

Pretty women in bikinis. Toddlers clinging to their parents' hands as they jumped wavelets. Dogs bounding into the water. A giant sandcastle, from a whole family's hours of sandy ambition. The love-battle with the wind, out on a windsurfing board, all exhilaration and laughing challenges and insults with his cousins.

Wistfulness. Wanting to capture that time again.

That was what a beach floral should do.

Not too brash, not a slap of coconut. His beach floral wouldn't be a perfume people wore in the summer so much as the winter, when the skies were too gray. Condensed happiness and longing for the sun to come again.

He went back to his desk to sketch out ideas, sometimes in drawing form because he couldn't think how to capture the image with a scent yet, sometimes with formula components. He pulled out vials, including new molecules labs kept sending him. Sniffed them and tapped his fingers and paced and climbed the walls—literally, gripping door frames and curling himself up until he could touch his feet to the beams in the ceiling, like a monkey.

Finally he sent a half dozen formulae down to the lab to blend for him and went back to the balcony. And looked toward the zinc roof of La Maison de Monsard again.

You're the most bloody-minded of the lot. Never seen a kid so determined to get his own way.

Well, he knew what he wanted.

So why didn't he go get it?

Chapter 8

"Why do you smell of orange blossom?" a gorgeous, rich-timbred voice asked.

Malorie was pacing the corner office above the courtyard, what had once been her grandmother and her great-grandfather's command center for La Maison de Monsard, phone against her ear. She gave up on the hold and hung up, turning.

Tristan, of course. Leaning in her doorway, all that lean form packed with energy, hot and sweet and full of life. Tall, lean, strong, beautiful cheekbones, supple, precise, amused mouth, kissable as hell. That man was walking sex. It was no wonder women threw themselves at him wherever he went.

From the corner office, she'd actually been able to witness that while she waited on hold. Tristan bending to pet a curly-haired dog, while its blond owner talked to him and ended up with her hand on his arm when he straightened, leaning into him. Tristan talking to the owner of the women's clothing shop, come out from her work on her display window to catch him and kiss his cheeks. Tristan giving an appreciative smile to a pack of pretty tourists who looked a sexy twenty or so, the young women walking on just a little way, whispering to each other and glancing back, and then suddenly turning back to him to ask him to take photos of them. He'd clearly enjoyed every minute of it, but Malorie had gotten so annoyed she'd turned and paced away from the window and hadn't seen if any exchange of numbers resulted.

The annoyance crisped her tone when she spoke. "Can I help you?"

"Who knows, Malorie? You've never tried to be helpful."

She sighed and gazed at the ceiling. That was Tristan for you. If a woman wasn't tripping over herself to be the first to sit in his lap, he took it as a personal insult. It wasn't even his fault. He thought eager, flirting willingness was how women normally acted.

"Is that...no, that's not Molini's Neroli," Tristan said. "Who made it?"

He straightened and strolled forward, as unhurried as if she was a pretty girl he was about to flirt with. For someone who almost always seemed so laid-back, it was amazing the intensity he brought to a room. Everything else faded to background around him.

"And you have scratches on your arms." He took her wrist as calmly as if it belonged to him and lifted her arm to study the scratches. "A little early in the year to be tangling with rose bushes, isn't it?"

She tugged at her wrist.

He brought her arm all the way to his face and took a long, deep breath of the back of her wrist before he let it go. "Hmm."

Little shivers ran through her. She quelled them with a firm smoothing of her skirt. "Do you mind, Tristan?"

"Hmm?" he said absently, his mind clearly focused on scent and nothing else.

"Can you even imagine if I grabbed your arm and started sniffing you as if you were my personal scent strip?"

Brown eyes rested vaguely on her a moment. And then slowly focused. His eyes honed in on her and darkened. His lips parted and—he blinked and gave his head a shake. A wry, devastating smile curled his lips. "As a matter of fact, I can, Malorie *chérie*. Are you glad you asked?"

Her head bending over his naked, ripped torso as she gently, deeply...breathed him in. "It was a rhetorical question."

He held out his upturned wrist. "Want to?"

Her toes curled slowly inside her pumps. "Are you just bored, Tristan?"

"Well, I'm not *now*." His eyes gleamed. Her middle heated, the gleam glowing there like honey in the sun.

"You know, most people turn to social media when they can't concentrate."

"Yeah, I never got that," Tristan said absently. "There aren't any sensations. Seriously, what do you think? I've been skin testing some ideas for this damn beach floral I'm working on." He stretched out his arm more fully and pointed to his elbow. "This is my favorite but it's still not right."

Malorie hesitated but curiosity got the better of her. "What's its production cost?" she murmured, just to be on the safe side, as she bent her nose to his elbow.

Tristan didn't make an annoyed noise, though, as he should have at that question. His arm bent as she leaned in, so that his biceps hardened into a strong curve just as her lips got close to them. Heat rushed through her and brought a tingling ache to her lips and hands and even her teeth—all the parts of her that weren't just sinking into enjoyment of those biceps right now. His skin had warmed the scent he had tested, a promise of sand and sun and happiness, full of energy and *joie de vivre*. Once you knew perfumes, you could always pick Tristan's scents out. They always had that base note of happiness. Sensual, playful, intense, wistful, but there, at the base, every time.

"Where's the floral?" she said.

Tristan sighed. "*Et voilà*. Every time I up the floral, it turns into a clichéd mess. I don't know why I ever had to land this brief."

Because a successful beach floral would make millions for Rosier SA, that was why. A responsibility that Tristan, for all his artistic complaining about the role of money in his work, assumed like the pillar of his family that he was.

Must be nice to have a family with so many strong pillars.

"It's fun," she said, a little wistfully. It smelled like their Sunday afternoons at the beach when she was a kid, before things went more and more to pieces or at least, as a kid, before she'd perceived the pieces they were already in. It smelled like that, only a little more secure, like a Mediterranean beach, not like those wide open American beaches where the sand was constantly washing away under your feet. "Sweet and...solid, somehow." Like his family afternoons at the beach must have been, compared to hers. "I like it without the floral."

"Yeah?" Tristan contorted his arm to smell his own elbow. "It might have some possibilities as a masculine. Unfortunately, what I'm supposed to be producing is most definitely a floral. The brief was clear on that. A big floral."

Malorie grimaced sympathetically. It was the unfortunate nature of a perfumer's work that his art was supposed to be commercial. It didn't bother *her*—she liked for things to make enough money you could depend on them—but she could understand how frustrating it was for Tristan to contort himself for marketing departments. Mostly she could understand because he'd been *very very clear about it* when arguing with her over Fugace.

"Why are you doing it, if you hate the idea?"

Tristan raised a supple black eyebrow at her, as if she of all people should know. "It could make millions for us."

Yes. As artistic as Tristan was, he took his responsibility to earn money for his family and, importantly, for every single person whose livelihood depended on Rosier SA's success, as a matter of course.

And he'd probably say something deeply sardonic about accountants if he knew she found that trait so attractive it made a prickle of arousal run through her just thinking about it. Her father had not considered it his responsibility to earn money for his family. He'd milked Monsard's failing resources until they were dry, to feed his own sense of self-worth. So she knew better than to take such an important character trait for granted.

"What about this one?" Tristan held out his other elbow.

Ah, interesting. Darkness and time and somewhere a treasure. It made her want to bite the swell of his biceps to see what that scent tasted like on his skin. "This is a beach floral? What is it, a pirate cove? It makes you smell like Indiana Jones."

"Hmm." Tristan sounded dissatisfied. "Maybe a little less dusty, then, and a little more...something. I'm not sure I meant it to be a masculine."

Malorie shrugged. "You know what I think about masculine and feminine perfumes." She thought that women needed to be able to dream of cracking a whip at their problems and swinging through the air after lost treasure and dealing with everything, even with snakes, just as much as men did. And very few "feminine" perfumes allowed women any kind of adventure other than sexual ones.

"Yeah. I like your thoughts about masculine and feminine perfumes. We should talk more about them, some place less noisy than a perfume launch party."

They'd started to discuss it once on a quiet terrace at a perfume launch party. For a few minutes. Soon after Tristan wandered out and joined her there multiple other people—most of them about ten times as beautiful and a hundred times as rich and famous as Malorie—had followed after him. Tristan, the human magnet.

"Is it just orange blossom water?" Tristan said, back on her scent. "Is that what you use? I'd like to know who makes it, because it's remarkably full. Almost fresh off the flower, with this hint of human honey in it."

"Hint of human honey" might not make sense to anyone outside the perfume industry, but Malorie had spent her entire life surrounded by people who talked like that.

It was just...strange, in a way that tickled in inappropriate places in her body, to know that she herself was the hint of human honey.

"Farelli made me a one-off scent," Malorie murmured, naming one of Tristan's rivals just to see what happened.

Tristan laughed. "Good one. He never made something that full of light in his life. But I could"—he grabbed her wrist and sniffed it again, this time the inside of it, completely forgetting the line she had just drawn in the sand about not doing that—"well, maybe...hmm."

"Tristan." She pulled her wrist back, and the calluses on the tips of his fingers grazed over her skin. "I am *not* a perfume *touche*."

"No, of course not," he said absently. "You're *much* more interesting. Paper is always such a sad substitute for human skin." He reached for her wrist again and frowned at her when she shifted it away. "Would you let me concentrate for two seconds?"

Just because he offered up his bare arm to her didn't mean she had to return the favor. She folded her arms, tucking her hands securely into her elbows. "No. I prefer to remain enigmatic."

Tristan narrowed brown eyes at her.

She gave him a cool, aloof look back.

He looked just a tiny bit pissed off.

She fought to keep her lips from curving in self-congratulations again. To the best of her knowledge, she was the only person alive who could get ever-amused, ever-unruffled Tristan to look pissed off. And she did it just by being herself—sticking to her guns.

Apparently women didn't do that too often around him.

"I'll buy you chocolates," Tristan said.

"What?"

"If you'll let me sniff your skin," he said in a *what-else-could-we-be-talking-about* tone.

She pressed her hands into her elbows, in instinctive self-protection against the stirring in her middle at this negotiation. "Tristan—"

"I have to be up in Paris in a couple of weeks. I'll bring back whoever you want. Who's your favorite? Richard? Marquis? Would you rather have macarons?"

"Tristan! You cannot trade chocolates for the right to—to—" She tightened her arms. She didn't know what was going on here, but one thing was for sure—he was a lot easier to handle when his head was exploding on her ceiling. *Quick. Think of a cheap perfume component you can substitute for an outrageously expensive one.*

"Well, what can I trade?" He eyed the spot where her wrists tucked tight against her arms and flexed his fingers a little, as if it was all he could do to not start prying them free. "What would you like?"

"You can't trade *anything* for the right to touch me, Tristan! That's not for sale."

His eyebrows crinkled. "It's just for research purposes! It wasn't like I was trying to bribe you for sexual favo..." His voice trailed off, like a robot that had run out of battery. He closed his eyes a moment and curled his fingers into his palms.

"Oh, go away," Malorie said, disgusted. With herself. He was making her insides get all frantic and, and...curly.

He gave her a reproving look. "You know, you're not very friendly."

"I smashed your life. Into pieces! On the floor!" She made exaggerated stabbing motions with her hands, mimicking him when they met on the trail.

"But now we're neighbors," he said. "So I'm trying to forgive you and move forward."

She stared at him with her mouth open. *He* was trying to forgive *her*? For what, how badly he behaved when he didn't get his way?

"It's hard," Tristan admitted. His lips turned down in what looked like genuine grief. "Every time I think about Fugace—"

"Oh, for God's sake," Malorie muttered.

He stiffened. "You know what your problem is? You have *no* heart. None!"

"Sure I do. And it's bleeding for you right now."

Tristan glared at her.

Guess I've still got it.

Tristan made a gesture with thumb and forefinger to evoke the sublime, a gesture so very French that it hit her middle. *I'm home.* "Fugace was beautiful. It could have changed the entire perfume industry. Changed the lives of people who wore it, changed the lives of people who *met* the people who wore it. And you sliced its heart out surgically and replaced it with a pig's. To save money."

She sighed very heavily.

He pulled back, offended.

She raised her eyebrows. "Moving forward, are you?"

"Well, I'm *trying*," he said between his teeth. "If you would show one milligram of regret..."

"I have no heart," she reminded him. "And I'm a sociopath. So I can't."

His lips pressed together as he eyed her. "And apparently you like to throw every irrational word a man ever says in the heat of passion back in his face the rest of his life."

She shrugged. "If you don't want to be reminded of irrational words, maybe you should stay rational."

He gazed at her a frustrated moment, and then slowly that wickedness curled his lips and that dangerous gleam came back into his eyes. "But I don't *like* to stay rational, Malorie. I *love*...the heat of passion."

He shifted in closer to her with the last phrase.

Malorie held up a warning hand. "Don't you start."

The gleam grew brighter and wickeder. "Scared?"

Yes. She made a pffing sound of dismissal. "I can handle you with both hands tied behind my back."

Tristan's brown eyes trailed down over her body, and that honey glint in them just glowed like she was a fly and he was about to catch her. "Let's try it," he purred. "I'll tie your hands, and then we'll go from there."

The thought of the reality of what she'd just said—of having her hands tied behind her back while Tristan moved up to her with that gleam in his eyes—stole all her breath. Dissolved cells. Woke heat in the worst possible places.

She wanted to *do it*, suddenly and so badly—tie her hands behind her, see what he did to her body—that not doing it *hurt.*

"Just think," Tristan purred. "How many more irrational words you could get out of me, with your hands tied behind your back. Why, you might end up with things to throw in my face for the whole rest of our lives."

And now she had a vision of Tristan losing coherence in his passion, hungry, muttering, stroking her harder and harder as he...

"Is this all just because you're having trouble with one of your juices?" she said suspiciously. "Is that what's going on? Because I really don't appreciate being used as a distraction, Tristan."

"Why? Your work is insanely boring. I'd think you'd be grateful."

That kicked a laugh out of her. It should have insulted her, but thinking it—and saying it out loud— was so very Tristan.

Their eyes met on her laugh, his alive with his own willingness to share her laughter.

No wonder so many women wanted to wallow in Tristan as if he was their catnip. He just promised sexy happiness with every breath he took.

Every time he met her eyes while his own were laughing she wanted to kiss him.

"Maybe our mutual lives will be short," Tristan suggested. "Maybe the sight of you in those pencil skirts nearly every day will make me explode and that will let you return to your boring accounts again."

She looked down at her perfectly professional skirt. Sleek. Hem just slightly below the knee, where her legs looked good but she didn't show too much of them for a business setting. She liked these skirts. They made her feel brisk, in control, perfectly attired, ready to take on the world. She slanted Tristan a wary glance.

He was looking at her legs.

She crossed her ankles uneasily.

A blissful smile relaxed his lips, and his eyes gleamed.

She stroked her hands down her skirt, as if that could somehow make it longer.

His smile grew.

"There is nothing wrong with my skirts!" she snapped.

"*Merde*, who said there was?" Tristan asked. "Tell me, and I'll kill him."

Maybe she should wear pants. Except that now it tickled at the backs of her knees, the thought of Tristan watching her legs. The thought of his head exploding for reasons other than her effect on his perfumes. *Will you quit letting him get to you? You know he says this kind of thing to all women.*

She'd dressed today to sound out bank officers on the kind of financing she could get if she did decide she wanted to get this place back up and running.

Which she wasn't saying she did. Some days she didn't know which felt lonelier—going back to her life in

New York, where at least she had friends and good colleagues, or staying here and yet again forging a path on her own. Her lips twisted wryly. Once again, and this time in real life, Tristan was proving to be the bright spot in that loneliness, the energy and warmth. *Don't you dare rely on him for that. You know how that would play out.*

"Hungry?" Tristan's warm, low voice.

Damn, was it that obvious? She blinked him into focus.

He'd half-turned and was gazing at the courtyard fountain, hands in his pockets, posture über-casual. "It's lunch time and, in a strange way, you're new in town." He held out a hand. "I thought you might rather put up with me than eat by yourself."

A warmth infused her. It sounded much less lonely, to eat lunch with Tristan rather than by herself either at a restaurant terrace or in the courtyard below—pulling out the little yellow wooden table and chairs still tucked for that purpose in a storage closet near the main doors, just like every other shop on this street.

"But I smashed your life into pieces on the floor," she said slowly. Why in the world would he try to make *her* life easier? Warmer?

"It's part of my nefarious plan. If I make it easier for you to find your footing here, you'll quit Abbaye and my perfumes for them will be safe." He took her wrist and pulled. "Come on, Malorie. If worse comes to worst, you can always stab me with one of those ice stakes I'm pretty sure you carry around in your purse."

Yeah, she wished. The whole damn point of never letting Tristan get too close to her was that she was pretty sure that once he got in close it would be too late.

Chapter 9

"I thought you meant lunch in Grasse," Malorie said warily, one hand resting on the top of Tristan's silver Audi while he held the door for her.

"My nefarious plans have layers. Kidnapping, extortion, and didn't we say something about tying you up with your hands behind your back?"

Malorie gave him her most repressive look.

"Will you get in already?" Tristan put his hand on top of her head and pushed downward. "What do you think I'm going to do to you? Actually hold you for ransom?"

"Who'd pay it?" Malorie murmured, yielding. It was pretty hard to find a reason to refuse to get in a car with someone you'd known since childhood, when the only thing you had to fear from him was that he was so damn sexy you might throw yourself on him and then get really hurt.

She looked back up at Tristan, who stood frozen with one hand on the door, as if he'd just suffered a shock.

What? She smoothed her skirt uncertainly. No, her ass was still covered. Plus, it didn't seem to be that kind of shock.

He slowly closed the door, his face oddly sober as he got behind the wheel. They were out of the underground parking garage before he spoke. "I'd pay it."

"What?" Oh, the ransom. "Weren't you the one doing the kidnapping?"

His eyebrows knit as he took the road winding down out of the upper old town. "If you needed someone to pay a ransom for you—I'd pay it. You could call on me."

For some reason that hit her right in the heart. *You could call on me.* Actually have someone to call on if she was in trouble. And not just any someone but someone who might be capable of rescuing her.

"*Merde*," he muttered suddenly and slipped his hand off the gearshift to close it around hers.

Her eyes prickled. She turned her head to gaze out the window as they left buildings behind for hedge-hidden houses and then the *maquis*. She didn't pull her hand free.

He gave it a little squeeze and had to release it to shift as the roads got steep and twisty. "So how is the decision going?"

Malorie hesitated, but networking was important anywhere and all the more so in Grasse, and no matter how hard it was to trust any aspect of her life to someone else, in her head at least she really did know that Tristan would never mean her harm. He might *cause* harm, but it wouldn't be deliberate.

Of course, even her father's harm to them hadn't been *deliberate*, she thought darkly. It had just been a mismatch in desires. They'd wanted a father's love, and he'd wanted…well, everybody else's love. Their love, too, of course, but their love wasn't nearly enough. Not worth the effort of keeping.

"Well, first I need to see if I even have financing options. And the banks will probably want written confirmation that I have my sisters' proxy before I can go much farther with that."

"What percentage of shares did you each end up with?"

"Twenty percent each. The rest were sold at different times." And usually at rock bottom prices, such as when her grandmother was struggling so desperately back in the fifties, as an eighteen-year-old with a toddler, no husband, and an utterly disgraced father and family name. When the men buying had been either making pity purchases or lurking around like predator hyenas, hoping to end up with the whole business when the pack of them wore her grandmother down.

Yeah. For a whole layering of reasons, the women in Malorie's family loathed letting men into positions of power over their lives. It *never* worked out well.

Tristan whistled softly between his teeth. "So no majority unless you can convince both of them to support you. Or find the rest of those shares."

She sometimes forgot that Tristan had probably been sitting in boardrooms since he had received his first voting shares in Rosier SA, presumably around the same age as she'd been heading off with nothing more than the pack on her back to seek her fortune. He wasn't "just" an *artiste*. He might have spent each meeting sketching like he used to do in school, for all she knew, but in some ways he might be more familiar with the way a company worked than she was.

Her next step, if she continued on her Paris-New York career path, was to aim for CFO of a company, but that was a jungle gym step she hadn't managed to make just yet. Head of accounting for a major perfume house was already pretty damn good for a twenty-nine-year-old who had only ten years before hiked her way to Paris and started out as an au pair putting herself through school.

"I think they'll support me initially," Malorie said. "They're pretty focused on their own careers and don't really care, beyond worrying I've lost my mind to think about throwing away my own career and coming back here."

Tristan's eyebrows drew together again. As if he'd like to say a word or two to her sisters.

"But eventually they might need their share of their heritage, of course," Malorie said. "And they might want it in liquid form."

Tristan's eyebrows knit more deeply. Disturbed, puzzled, close to uncomprehending. Maybe he had paid less attention in Rosier SA's quarterly board meetings than she thought. "Even if it pulled the rug out from under your feet?"

"Well...they do deserve their share of their heritage, Tristan."

"Not if it makes the whole family weaker."

Malorie blinked. It fit with what she knew of Tristan and the Rosiers as soon as he said it, but until he said it, it hadn't occurred to her how fundamentally different his attitude would be. A man was supposed to be strong enough, independent enough, capable enough that he enriched his family, not took from it.

She sighed a little. Sometimes it was so hard not to be jealous of the Rosier family it hurt.

"What banks are you seeing about financing?"

"This afternoon, I'm meeting with Banque Provençale and Banque Alpes-Maritime. But I haven't made up my mind I want to quit my job at Abbaye, Tristan. I'm just looking at possibilities."

He nodded, easing right up to the edge of the cliff they were on to let a car fit by in the other direction. "Who are you meeting with at Provençale? Sophie Girard?"

Of course he would know everyone in a position of power in Grasse. Especially the women. Malorie sighed. "Yes."

"And who is it at Alpes-Maritime? Hélène?"

Malorie narrowed her eyes at him, wondering how pretty Sophie and Hélène were and what had happened to all the old white men who used to hold all the banking positions in Grasse. And every other position of power, pretty much. "Yes."

Tristan nodded absently, a faint smile on his lips. Probably he had good memories of Sophie or Hélène or both. Malorie fought the urge to slouch in her seat and kick the floorboard. Then sat upright as they headed upward on another twisty road. "Sainte-Mère? You're not thinking of your cousins' place, are you?"

He was distant cousins with the Delange brothers, who had the Michelin three-star restaurant Aux Anges in Sainte-Mère. Well, "distant" in Rosier terms, which meant that they all stayed pretty close, even though they were only second or third cousins or something like that. She'd thought they were just going out for a casual lunch. If he went three star on her, she wasn't sure what that meant or how to deal with it.

Tristan's lips quirked as he adroitly navigated the car into the impossibly angled, tiny parking lot below the walls of Sainte-Mère. "Somewhere less formal."

Well, thank God for that.

The medieval walls rose above them as they made the short, steep climb up to the great arch that cut through those walls. All the muscles in Malorie's shoulders relaxed as they passed under the arch, a wash of peace as if she had come home. Sainte-Mère wasn't her home town, and she hadn't been back inside these particular medieval walls in years, but the stone, the age, a village steeped in time...those were her. For all her ability to succeed in Paris and New York, this land was her origin story.

Tristan turned them up a steep, shadowed stair-street that ran along the homes built into the medieval walls. An ancient vine so thick it took both her hands to encircle it ran up the other side of the stair-street like a banister. She stroked her hand over the stone and rested it on the vine, letting it slide under her palm as they climbed the stairs.

The whole place smelled of stone and shadow, and—

"Orange blossom," Tristan murmured. "Even your hair smells of orange blossom. You haven't been getting married this morning, have you?" He pulled a small leather journal out of his back pocket as he spoke, flipping it to a clean page and sketching.

In the old days, a bride would wear a crown of orange blossoms, and the flowers were still hugely popular for spring weddings. Innocently white, sensually sweet. To her, orange blossom was the scent of the safe space of her past, a shelter and peace and happiness in a world where she'd often felt wary. But to most people, orange blossom was the scent of happily ever after.

"No, I'm saving myself for you," Malorie said solemnly. On Tristan's page, an arch of stone was taking rough shape, plus a fall of dark hair from a person not fully drawn, an orange blossom in that hair.

Tristan cut her a dark glance that suggested the urge to strangle her just never really died.

And for some reason, Malorie felt a little flush try to run up her cheeks. She concentrated on the feel of the vine under her hand to keep it at bay. *Stop making stupid jokes about Tristan and happily ever after. You can't pull them off.*

"Well, I'd never expect you to be good with money," she said cheerfully, forging ahead nevertheless. She had to prove she was just joking, after all. Tristan of all people should be able to handle this kind of conversation. He'd promised, hand over heart, to save himself for ninety-year-old grandmothers at least twice in her hearing.

And those old eyes had just sparkled.

Damn him for being such a sweetheart.

"Or capable of concentrating on the bottom line," she added. "So there's that."

"I produce money very well," Tristan said, a little coolly. Which was true, his perfumes often grossed hundreds of millions. He shoved the journal in his pocket and started back up the stairs. "But I do it best by thinking about that money as little as possible."

Yeah, that seemed to be a common trait with artists. Thus the invention of gallery owners or agents or, in Tristan's field, accountants and perfume company executives. "Good thing I was there to think about it for you with Fugace, then," she couldn't resist saying.

He stopped dead on the uneven stairs and pivoted. "Okay, you know what—" He glared at her. "I had already made Fugace's production cost as low as it could be without detriment to the juice. That's part of a perfumer's job. Just because I don't like to think about it in the brainstorming process doesn't mean I'm oblivious. I'm a professional, Malorie."

She'd been twenty-five, the accountant on his perfume but not yet head of accounting, recently arrived in Abbaye's New York office, which had become the once Paris-based company's real center of power in the past decade. She'd been determined to prove how good she was. Tristan had been twenty-five, a rising star perfumer, Fugace the biggest brief he had landed for Rosier SA yet.

"Me, too," she said. "I'm a professional, too."

And way, *way* too smart, after the havoc and insecurity her father had created in their lives, to let a man's emotions override her own financial control.

Tristan sighed sharply and turned toward a door. He ignored its rose-shaped knocker and pushed it open. There was a restaurant here now? All the restaurants used to be up around the main *places* and surrounding streets.

He pulled her inside after him, and a chill ran right up her spine as she saw photos on the walls, a hall, a homey kitchen with orange-red pots hanging on the walls. "Tristan!" she hissed. She yanked on her wrist.

That climber's hand tightened into an unbreakable grip without the slightest effort at all. "Tata?" he called. He poked his head in the empty kitchen, then pulled Malorie along behind him down the hall, checking a laundry room next.

"What are you doing?" Malorie said. "Tristan, please tell me this isn't your—"

"Tante Colette?" Tristan pushed through another door and into a great walled garden.

Malorie felt as if she'd been expecting a friendly dip in a warm pool and he'd plunged her into ice water. *Colette*? Colette Delatour? His Resistance hero great aunt who was one of the people who had born witness against Malorie's own great-grandfather in his trial for collaboration? Colette Delatour, whose closest friend,

Élise Dubois, had been betrayed to her death by Pierre Monsard to advance Maison de Monsard power.

Oh, God.

"Tristan, please—" Malorie dug at his hand with her nails, trying to pry it off her wrist. Before she could switch to open violence like punching him in the kidneys, they were in the garden.

An old, old woman sat in a rocking chair in the sun, her eyes closed, not moving.

Tristan stilled. His grip on her wrist finally relaxed, but his hand slid down and closed around hers, his fingers linking and clinging for a moment, in a weird shift, as if he was clinging to her for safety.

A little shock of fear. Surely Madame Delatour was just sleeping? Although...she was *old*. She'd been an adult during the war. Malorie's own grandmother had only been a child then, and she'd already succumbed to her own old age.

Tristan loosed her hand and strode forward, kneeling by his great aunt's chair, his hand closing around her wrist. His face relaxed as soon as he touched her. "Tata?" He gave her hand a little shake.

The old woman's eyes opened and Malorie went still as a mouse hoping not to be noticed by an owl. But Tristan broke into a smile, and watching him, she thought: *He is so freaking adorable. God, how can anyone that sexy and arrogant and irrationally artistic have that much generous love in him to give to his people?*

It made her so damn jealous of his people.

Colette Delatour frowned down at him. "Sneaking up on me?"

A little brown and white floppy-eared dog that looked as if it might be a cross between a Jack Russell and a King Charles trotted out from somewhere to lick Tristan's hand. Tristan scratched its ears. "I'm going to buy you a mastiff. Patapouf here has lost his ferocious guard dog edge."

From the way Colette Delatour's time-worn face relaxed in amusement, it was possible the little dog had never had a ferocious edge. She let her hand rest on Tristan's head and gently ruffled his hair. Another thing that made Malorie jealous. She'd spent most of her teenage and adult life wanting to ruffle Tristan's hair. Or yank it out.

And she'd still never touched it once.

Colette stood, in that careful way that meant her knees hurt, which Malorie recognized from her own grandmother. Colette Delatour must be, what, sixteen or seventeen years older than Chloé Monsard? But she didn't look older. Meaning either that at a certain point age just stopped showing in the same way or that Colette Delatour had really good genes.

Which would just figure for a Rosie—oh, right. Colette Delatour wasn't genetically a Rosier, was she? Her mother had married Jean-Jacques Rosier's father, right?

Maybe that valley of roses just had particularly good air.

Or maybe having all her grandnephews around, instead of being left all alone, gave her something to live for. Malorie bent her head, on a wave of grief and guilt again.

"I brought a friend for lunch, Tata." Tristan sprang up with the ease of an intensely physical man nearly seventy years Madame Delatour's junior, kissed her cheeks, and offered his arm.

His aunt patted it but didn't take it, standing straight and tall and on her own steam.

As usual when Malorie saw her, she was so impressed that she desperately wished she could hide behind that old garden shed over there and be overlooked. And, as usual, she had too much pride to actually do it. She took a deep breath, standing straight and tall herself.

"How nice," Colette Delatour said, studying Malorie across the garden. Then those old, dark eyes slanted Tristan a very thoughtful look, a faint curve to her lips. "I'm trying to think when you've ever introduced me to a friend."

"And let you scare them off?" Tristan retorted.

"So what does this mean? That you don't care if she gets scared, or that you're finally dating someone with guts?"

Tristan gave his aunt a profoundly disgruntled look. One of those *will you shut up already?* looks common to close families that liked to embarrass each other. Malorie wondered how to correct the impression they were *dating* without having to draw more attention to herself and thus brave the old woman's judgement of her. Tristan might not mind the word *dating*, but she'd like to set herself apart from the thousands of other women he'd taken to lunch, dinner, or bed.

"Malorie." Tristan beckoned. Malorie braced herself and kept her chin steady, not low but not defiantly high either, as she crossed the garden. "Tata, may I introduce Malorie Monsard?"

A subtle shock around the old woman's eyes at the name. Malorie tightened all her muscles.

"She and I went to school together," Tristan said blithely. "Malorie, this is my aunt, Colette Delatour."

"It's an honor," Malorie said very low. She was afraid to hold out her hand and have it rejected, and it would be far too much presumption for someone her age to kiss such a venerable old lady's cheeks on first introduction. So her hand flexed uneasily at her side, and she kept straight and still.

Colette Delatour gave her a steady, searching look from head to toe. Her expression was thoughtful and, now that she had schooled away that first flicker at Malorie's last name, unreadable. "I knew your great-grandparents," she finally said neutrally.

Malorie flushed in a painful, inexorable wave of shame and shot Tristan a look she wished could stab him. Oblivious, secure *bastard*.

"And your grandmother," the old woman said, and Malorie folded her arms over her middle. Someone of Colette Delatour's age had probably severely judged a sixteen-year-old who had found herself pregnant back in the fifties.

"And your father," Colette Delatour said.

Malorie's jaw tightened. Tristan's eyes narrowed on his aunt, his face gone grave and his lips parting as if he was about to speak.

"Your grandmother was a strong woman," Colette Delatour said. Simply and flatly, as if no one could ask for a better compliment so there was no sense putting flowers around it.

"I know." Malorie held the old hero's eyes with a sudden flash of anger. *How dare you test me? I test myself.*

Her whole life, she'd been testing herself. Trying to make sure that on the exam of life, her own results were different.

"What about you?" Colette said.

Malorie said nothing, her arms folded, her eyes holding the older woman's stubbornly.

"When she was nineteen, she hiked all the way from here nearly to Paris, and made friends with a family on the trail, and worked as their au pair so she could have a place to stay in Paris, and put herself through school there, and now she's head of accounting at Abbaye," Tristan said suddenly.

Malorie took a little breath. He'd just defended her. No one did that. It felt so good to have someone fighting at her side it hurt.

Colette's gray-white eyebrows went up a little. "Is that so?"

Malorie gave a jerky shrug of one shoulder, not unfolding her arms.

"I always wondered if I should have had more adventures," said the woman who had faced down Gestapo, been a central point of a spy network of perfumers throughout France, and helped thirty-six children escape through the Alps. Her tone was a little wistful.

Malorie felt her arms relaxing on the urge to give an incredulous laugh. She didn't dare go that far, but still.

"Oh, because you haven't traveled enough, Tata." Tristan rolled his eyes, clearly opting to pursue a possible lightening of this moment. He looked at Malorie. "Do you know she went to Nepal, Kenya, and New Zealand before she was fifty? This was traveling back in the fifties and sixties, you understand. She's been more places than I have!"

Colette relaxed her gaze on Malorie and raised her eyebrows at Tristan. "I've had close to seventy more years of opportunities, last I checked."

"There you go, rubbing your age in to one-up the rest of us again." Tristan shook his head.

Colette laughed. Laughed. For his next feat, Tristan was probably going to get a stone statue to unbend and become human.

Tristan leaned forward and kissed his aunt's cheek again, spontaneously. "Shall I go make lunch, Tata?"

"I've got a soup on already. You could cut some herbs and greens for a salad and slice the bread and bring everything out. If your friend has the courage to stick around."

***

Tristan had always found happiness easy. Unhappiness was hard and painful, and he avoided it if he could. But happiness was everywhere.

In the slide of his fingers over stone. In the scent of mint released as he clipped the greens for the salad. In the scent of the almond tree, its blooms pale and their fragrance irresistible, filling the garden with a gentle sweetness. In the walls rising around him, this safe, quiet, sheltered space where he had hunted treasure as a child with his cousins, sat and talked to his aunt as a teenager and adult.

He worried about Malorie, who didn't seem to have access to as much happiness and who never seemed to trust it when it was offered. Who'd cut his heart down to the size of a business deal, when he'd held it out to her in Fugace. Who'd kept her quiet concentration when they'd worked together on that Occupation project in high school, as if the Occupation was more important than the present was. Or just safer.

His aunt had challenged her courage, but Malorie was always going to win that challenge. It wasn't her courage at question, quite the reverse. It was how she never let her guard down at all. She was worse than Damien, and almost as bad as Tante Colette and his grandfather.

He offered her a sprig of mint, one of the most compact sources of happiness he could lay his hands on, its crisp, vivid fragrance like a miracle. He knew it wasn't in fashion to really *believe* in miracles and go to church and all that, not beyond weddings and baptisms, not since his grandmother had died. But it was hard for a perfumer to harden his heart to all possibility. All the scents in the world that were all around him, that *anyone* could have, always seemed to be a way that someone had said, *Here. My gift. Be happy.*

So he just tried to pass it on.

Malorie was clipping the butter lettuce, but she crushed a couple of the mint leaves between her fingers and brought the sprig to her face, breathing slowly, her eyes closing. Her face grew wistful and a little sad. Ah. Scents could do that, too—remind someone of something lost. Her grandmother?

He crushed some thyme and brought it close to her nose while her eyes were closed, to see if she caught the change of scent. Her nose crinkled, and her eyes opened, meeting his with a little leap of warmth in them. "A garden is your idea of heaven, isn't it?"

Heaven was a concept he'd never attached to. It seemed so pale and bland. No one ever talked about the scents in heaven, or the dirt, or the little earthworm curling back into the soil there. There didn't seem to be any granite cliffs to offer a man a challenge, or harvests to bring in with his cousins, or roofs to repair for his aunt on a Saturday morning. No sweat and work and he was pretty sure that meant no laughter, because where did the bonding come from if it wasn't through the efforts you made together? He bet no kid ever broke his arm sneaking over his aunt's wall in the night, in heaven, or burnt the sole off his shoe leaping over a bonfire when his parents thought he was in bed, or jumped off a twenty-seven-meter cliff that could have killed him.

"I like life right here," he said. He didn't know what he'd do when everyone he loved started leaving him by *dying*, and then he'd have to choose between the world he loved and following after them. As the youngest, there was a real possibility that one day he'd be the last one of his cousins here.

His heart twisted hard. He slid away from the thought, back into happiness, taking the basket they'd filled and heading into the house. Malorie followed while Tata smoothed a tablecloth over the teak table outside.

"Do you worry about her?" Malorie asked quietly behind him.

He set the basket by the sink and looked around.

"Earlier, when you first saw her," she said, a little awkwardly, "I thought you acted a little...scared, just for a second."

"She's ninety-seven," Tristan said, and his throat tightened suddenly, and his eyes stung. He turned on the water, angling his shoulder so she couldn't see his face. He hated having so much emotion sometimes. It had been the bane of his existence when he was a child, before he'd learned to hide it from his older cousins. "So sometimes I...I mean sometimes..." He saw Tante Colette sleeping in the sunlight, and fear jolted through him that this time she wasn't sleeping. He washed herbs in this kitchen and imagined that moment when all the life in it would die, and the kitchen and the garden would become new holes in his life, like the hole Lucien had left. Like the hole Raoul had left for so long. Like the hole *Malorie* had left, damn her for being so oblivious to it.

And some day his grandfather wouldn't be there to walk the hills with him, and some day...

Malorie's hand touched his back lightly. As if he might be contagious. "I wish you weren't such a nice guy," she said softly.

His nose crinkled, because it was still stinging, and he had to get that down before he turned. "Why the hell would you wish that?"

"Oh, you'd *never* understand." A thread of darkness in her tone. She turned to pull the big country loaf out of its linen bag and set it on the heavy wood cutting board.

"I might be smarter than I look," Tristan said dryly. At least she'd helped that stinging go away. "Why don't you give explaining it to me a try?"

Malorie just angled him an ironic look and took the bread knife to the big country loaf. The scent of fresh bread released into the kitchen, along with the mint and thyme and freshness of the salad and the cozy comfort of a soup full of roots—potatoes, carrots, parsnips, puréed together and simmering to wait for them. A spring meal—the rests of the winter and the promise of the summer. Anything could grow in the spring. Even things that had been frozen by winter again and again and again.

"It makes it hard to resist you," Malorie said suddenly.

A jolt ran through Tristan's body. Malorie had never, in their entire lives, given any sign that she found him hard to resist. She had always kept herself like a secret garden, behind the only damn wall in the world that he couldn't manage to climb. "That must be what I don't quite get, Malorie." He cut off the faucet and turned to face her. "Why would you want to do that?"

She rolled her eyes. "I don't trust you as far as I could throw you, Tristan."

She might as well have hauled off and punched him. "Why *not?*"

He'd trust anyone in his family. They'd been, for generations now, the absolute bedrock of this region. It was his own generation's most fundamental responsibility, never to fail in that trust. To be honest and honorable and strong and ready to fight for what was right. He couldn't imagine failing in that duty; who would he *be* if he wasn't those things?

And beyond that, he was the *emotional* bedrock of his family. Even his grandfather realized it. *Merde*, when his grandfather and great aunt died, he might be the only one left to keep his family sane. To keep them together. He was the youngest, and yet all that responsibility to be wise, to give the right advice, to redirect someone with a wry word down the right path, would fall on him. What the hell had he ever done to *anyone* that was untrustworthy?

"You could have any woman you wanted, Tristan," Malorie said dryly. "And you do."

He pressed mint-scented thumb and forefinger to the crease between his brows. "No, I obviously don't, Malorie. Or we wouldn't be having this conversation."

She gazed at him blankly.

Seriously?

"Really want," Malorie said. "Not like some game. Although that might be the problem. It's all just a big fun game to you. And for most of us, it's a little more serious."

What was wrong with games? What was wooing a woman supposed to be, a war exercise?

"I know you're more serious, Malorie," Tristan said between his teeth. "Trust me, that has been repeated to me, ad nauseum, since we were four years old."

"I didn't mean like our teachers would say in school," Malorie said uneasily. *Sérieux.* Willing to focus, hardworking. Or in Tristan's case, *pas sérieux.* Not willing, not a good student, not disciplined. "I know you work hard."

His jaw had set harder than he wanted it to. He searched her eyes. "Do you?"

"Of course I know that!" Malorie said, exasperated. "Tristan, come on. You're one of the top perfumers in the world, and you're only twenty-nine. You just can't focus well when you're sitting still. Any idiot can see that."

"Yeah, but you're not an idiot," Tristan said dryly. Which *he'd* been called, by teachers. *Arrête de faire ton imbécile, Tristan. Stop acting like an idiot.* "So maybe you can't."

"What are you trying to say, that I've got my head up my ass?" Malorie folded her arms. "Of course I can see that. Hell, the perfumes you've made. I mean Fugace was beauti—" She broke off, wincing.

He felt as if he'd taken a blow to his middle. It stopped all breath and it hurt and he couldn't figure out what to make of it. "*You* realized Fugace was beautiful? And you still ruined it?"

Malorie's teeth snapped together. "*No one* can tell the difference between the original formula and the profitable one, Tristan. No one."

"*I* can."

She waved her hands. "Well, no one that *matters.*"

Tristan glared at her, beyond outrage.

"You know what I mean!" She waved her hands more. "*I* can't. Normal people can't. No one who was going to buy it could! *Merde,* probably *you* couldn't even tell yourself if it was a blind scent test."

"Oh, trust me," Tristan said grimly. "I could."

She snorted. "Seriously, I should blindfold you and try it sometime."

Tristan paused. An image rose up in his mind inexorably, and temper just kind of spread out in a lazier, hungrier heat through his body. His lips curled. "You thinking about bondage *again*, Malorie?"

A tide of red climbed up her cheeks and she made a sound between her teeth like a frustrated tiger. "Grrr, you are so annoying sometimes!"

She had no idea how much heat flamed inside him when he made her blush. Eager, wall-climbing heat, the kind that made him want to just *do* something. "I like the way you flip it," he said agreeably. "Sometimes I get to tie you up and sometimes you get to tie me up. Although I'd prefer you drive me mad with something besides Fugace if you do it."

"Oh, seriously, do not tempt me," Malorie muttered, picking the bread knife up again.

He devoutly hoped she wasn't imagining using that on him instead of what he wanted her to be imagining. He'd always had trouble getting Malorie to take the non-ice-water path in her fantasies. "So in this blindfolded image, do I have any clothes on, or am I completely vulnerable?"

The bread slice fell ragged and uneven to the cutting board.

Tristan allowed himself a slow, slow grin. "In mine you start with your clothes on," he said helpfully. "I like to take my time."

Malorie turned and glared at him.

It was so hard not to kiss Malorie sometimes it just about killed him. "What, weren't you saving yourself for me?" he asked innocently.

Malorie set her knife down with a thump. "What am I doing here?"

"Slicing bread. But I think you forgot how to do it in America, so maybe I should take over."

"Here," Malorie hissed. "In your aunt's house. That was a *bastard* trick to pull, Tristan."

Had it been? He could be pretty damn bloody-minded about getting his way, as his grandfather had pointed out. "I thought it was best to get it over with. Then you wouldn't worry about it anymore."

Malorie stared at him. "And that wasn't up to me to decide?"

Possibly. But then she might not have decided the thing he thought was best. People had a really bad habit of doing that.

Malorie's record in that particular regard was abysmal.

"I should have been more subtle," he admitted. "I didn't expect you to start yanking on your wrist like that. I think you have trust issues."

Malorie gaped at him. "You're blaming me for not trusting you while you tricked me into doing something I didn't want to do? And the only problem you see in the trick is that you weren't more *subtle* about it?"

"You didn't want to meet my aunt?" Tristan lifted his chin a little to convey that she had not only wounded him but was insulting his whole family. When you were wrong, always best to redirect.

"Merde, Tristan." Abruptly Malorie bent over the cutting board and put her head in her hands. "My great-grandfather reported her best friend to the Gestapo. He got her *killed.*"

Élise Dubois, a schoolteacher with her own young son to protect, who had never wanted to have to be brave, but who had had a little Jewish girl hiding among the kids in her classroom and who hadn't been able to let that little girl be taken. That had been how Élise started, working with his great aunt and his grandfather's Resistance cell.

Tristan put his arm around Malorie and pulled her into his chest. Just concentrating on being her warmth. There was nothing else he could possibly do. "It's in the past, Malorie," he whispered finally. "It's nothing to do with *you*."

Malorie made a weary noise against his chest. "Everything's so much easier in New York. You don't have all this *crap* dragging you down like a ball and chain on your ankle."

His arms tightened. Kind of the way his hand had tightened on her wrist when she tried to get away. "Those are roots, Malorie. Not a chain. They're where you get your nutrients."

"That's easy for *you* to say! Your roots are beautiful!"

He dropped his hand to her wrist and pulled her after him to the door to his aunt's house. He opened it and stood her on the steps in front of him, facing the great banister vine while he gripped her shoulders. "Look at it."

She stood stiff under his hands.

"Look." He gestured to the bottom of the stair. Where the vine grew out of a small space of earth in the cobblestoned street. He gestured to the top of the stair. Where, after being trained to climb under shadow, for the whole length of the stair street, trimmed back from every attempt to reach earlier for the sun, it had finally been allowed to strain upward again. And there, at the top of that thick vine that was as old as his aunt, a young growth had headed upward, and the fresh spring leaves of the grape vine were shifting gently in sunlight and breeze across a latticework of support.

Malorie still said nothing. But under his hands, her body shifted in a long, slow sigh.

"I like to climb," he said. "So I've seen plenty of trees that started in a pocket of earth under a boulder, split that rock, and grew to be centuries old. I've seen trees that got crushed by another tree or split by lightning and still grew, in their new shape."

"I'm not a tree," she said. "I'm human. I have feet, to hike away."

Tristan was silent for a moment. Then his hands caressed her shoulders. "You're ruining my metaphor, Malorie," he said gently.

And it was the gentleness that unstiffened her. That let that braced tension in her shoulders ease away. He savored it a moment, the loosened muscles under his hands, and then turned her back to him. "I didn't bring you here to hurt you, Malorie." Which she should damn well know, if she knew him at all. But Malorie's distrust of his intentions didn't really have anything to do with him, did it? It was about time he figured that out. "I just thought...it's like a bandage, you know? Sometimes you just have to rip it off and let the wound get a little air."

Malorie stood a step down from him, making her have to look much farther up than she usually did. Maybe that was why she looked so vulnerable and her eyes searched his as if she might actually be listening to him. She nodded slowly, still a little tired and sad.

He slid his hand down her arm to link his fingers snug and warm with hers and pull her back into the kitchen.

***

The lunch was...kind of nice, actually. Sitting in the walled garden, surrounded by the scents of herbs and the almond tree and stone and earth, reminded Malorie of her grandmother. Madame Delatour did keep testing her, but maybe because Malorie had been testing herself her whole life, she found she was almost pleased with the test. *Finally, a chance to show I pass.*

But after lunch, when Madame Delatour sent Tristan upstairs to change a lightbulb in a high ceiling, Malorie filled the sink with hot water and braced for whatever the grand old woman wanted to say to her in private.

"So what do you see in my nephew?" Madame Delatour asked, a little amused, stuffing mint into a tea pot.

108

So the old war hero was going to soften her up, chat about inconsequentials before she got to the real test. Fine. Malorie could deal with this. Although she'd almost find it safer to talk about Pierre Monsard.

"We're not actually dating," Malorie corrected. "We're just"—what had Tristan called it?—"friends since school."

"See too many of his flaws to take a chance on him, do you?"

"What flaws?" Malorie said, confused.

Old dark eyes lifted from the teapot and held hers, Colette's eyebrows lifting.

Seriously? Malorie had guessed Tristan's great aunt and grandfather had impossible standards, but did Colette Delatour actually look at Tristan and see *flaws*? "He's a sweet-tempered, disciplined, creative genius who loves his family so much he takes time for them every day. He's athletic and funny and perceptive and the only grudge I've ever known him to hold is when someone 'hurts' one of his perfumes. *What* flaws?"

She tried not to openly glare at her elder, but she knew her gaze was far too challenging, maybe to the point of disrespect. It made her mad, the thought that anyone Tristan loved and looked up to could be so demanding that they thought *he* had flaws.

Colette Delatour turned away from her to pick up the kettle, and possibly there was a very faint curve around those old lips as she poured the boiling water over the mint. "Disciplined?" she asked after a moment.

Malorie controlled the need to roll her eyes like a teenager. "Just because he needs to move, you all act like that! To even get through perfume school, you have to memorize thousands of scents, and all their chemical formulae. He's produced multiple top ten perfumes and he's only twenty-nine. He's disciplined as he—he—heck."

She plunged her hands into the hot dishwater. It would normally be very offensive for her to try to wash the dishes in a near-stranger's house, but Colette

Delatour was ninety-seven and leaving them for her didn't sit right. Besides, Malorie could claim America had worn off on her. Everybody knew Americans had no *savoir-vivre*.

"All those qualities, and I'm sure he would prefer you thought he was sexy," Madame Delatour said mildly, setting the pot back on the burner and double-checking that she had turned that off.

"Oh, he's far too sexy for his own good," Malorie muttered to a dirty plate. Or at least for her own good.

There was the small sound of a shoe against wood in the doorway. She winced and glanced back.

Yes, sure enough. Tristan. *Merde*, how long had he been standing there?

He was staring at her, but when he saw she'd noticed, he came forward and pulled her hands out of the water. "I'll do this. You can't wash the dishes here." And, *sotto voce* in English, "You'll embarrass her."

Colette Delatour didn't look the least bit embarrassed to Malorie. If anything, she looked very faintly pleased with herself.

Well, at least Malorie had run out the clock and escaped whatever last test the merciless old hero had had planned for her. "I'll go wash up," she said, escaping to the bathroom.

***

Tristan watched Malorie go thoughtfully—always glad of a chance to watch that ass in motion in one of those skirts of hers—then glanced at his aunt with a raised eyebrow. "*Merci, Tata.*"

Tante Colette was smiling very faintly. "She'll do."

Yes, he had thought Tante Colette would like Malorie. The lunch had gone perfectly. Malorie had been respectful of his aunt's age while still gathering her own pride around her like a shield, and Tante Colette had accepted that pride with considerable approval. He'd known something was up when he got sent upstairs for

110

a lightbulb, but he'd figured by then that Malorie could handle it. Malorie had a wariness and vulnerability around warmth and praise from others that he was only just beginning to perceive, but when it came to fighting her corner, she could do just fine.

"What qualities?" he said.

His aunt raised her eyebrows at him. "Was she talking to you when she said it?"

He should have pressed a damn glass to the ceiling instead of actually changing that lightbulb. "Tata, have I ever mentioned you have a mean streak?"

Colette poured the tea into cups, the scent of mint surrounding him until he was wallowing in the comfort and challenge of home. "I believe that perfume recipe book was lost in the war, Tristan."

"I wasn't even talking about that this time!" he said, aggravated. Lost in the war, his ass. Although Tante Colette had honed her ability to lie calmly and convincingly in a time when not convincing would have meant torture and death for herself and others, so sometimes he had a doubt. He hoped she was just being mean, though, and making him wait for it until he'd— whatever the hell Raoul and Matt and Damien had done to deserve one of those precious heirlooms. "Come on, tell me what she said. I'll wash the dishes."

That faint smile. "You'll wash the dishes anyway, Tristan."

Well, yes. In fact, he was halfway done already, enjoying the way the lemon of the soap mixed with the mint of the tea. "Taking advantage of a man's good nature," he grumbled to a soup bowl, very audibly.

Tante Colette brought the tea cups to the kitchen table. "I guess if you want to know what qualities she thinks you have, you'll have to get her to tell you herself."

As if that was ever going to happen.

A flashing memory of Malorie's incredulous face in the dimness of the Monsard store of treasures, that *who the hell else would she want you to be?*

111

"If you'll take my advice, though, Tristan—"

"Always," Tristan said promptly. Well, he at least thought about it most times. And usually learned to regret it when he didn't take it.

"—you'll tell her about those Monsard shares you bought from me."

"*Shh.*" Tristan darted a glance toward the doorway. He wouldn't put it past his aunt to—but no, Malorie wasn't back yet. "Not yet."

Tante Colette shook her head and took a sip of her mint tea. "Just don't let her sell soaps to tourists in that place, whatever else you do. Or sell it to one of those giant New York fragrance houses looking to use Grasse to pretend it has a history."

Tristan held up soapy hands. "Trust me, Tata, I am on it. Malorie may not know it yet, but that place is going to be beautiful again."

Chapter 10

In the late afternoon, the great old doors of Monsard stood wide open, as did the windows, and dust particles stirred in the slanting sun across the courtyard. The boring old seventies-era display cases had been hauled out and pushed against a wall of the courtyard.

Malorie, her hands full of bank folders, strode forward and stopped dead. Shirtless, Tristan Rosier was on his knees in the main showroom, ripping up carpet.

Oh, wow. How the hell was she supposed to recover from *that* view?

Lean-hipped and strong-shouldered, his back had excellent definition from all that climbing and windsurfing and who knew what else he did—hauling things on the family farm, probably. The Rosiers sure were attached to their belief that they were peasants. Maybe back in the Revolution, they'd seen the value of keeping their feet firmly planted in the earth and their heads well away from a guillotine, and they'd been clinging to that strategy ever since.

Or maybe they just liked the land that much. Having their fingers in dirt or clinging to stone, their hands buried in roses and jasmine.

Her shoulders still felt so...eased, from that moment on the steps of his aunt's home, when his tone had softened from insistent to gentle, accepting, and those long, strong fingers had stopped forcing her to look where he wanted and changed to a caress, letting her turn back around. She could have stepped right into him then and pressed her face against his chest, but of course she still knew the difference between fantasy and reality. But she'd faced his aunt far more easily after, her shoulder muscles warm all through lunch from that touch.

So maybe she had forgotten how to be properly braced against him, and that was why seeing him half-naked now zinged through to the end of every nerve she had.

His back muscles shifted as he sliced a roll of carpet and taped it closed, then tossed it sideways onto a pile of similar rolls. It was only April, but his back was already tanned from his insatiable need for outdoor living, and the glimpse of abs when he twisted for the throw made her mouth go dry.

"*What* do you think you're doing?" she demanded, outraged at herself. This was getting out of hand.

Tristan always had been someone who, given an inch, would take a mile. All with a bewitchingly charming grin just to make sure no one stopped him sooner.

He sat back on his heels, gloved hands resting on his jeans, a black lock flopping over his forehead, started to grin at her—and held up a hand, his face scrunching. Abruptly he twisted away and sneezed.

"*À tes souhaits*," Malorie found herself saying automatically.

He sneezed again.

"*À tes amours*," she said, a little more warily.

He peeked at her over his elbow and sneezed one more time, this one clearly forced.

She narrowed her eyes. "*Qu'elles durent toujours*. If you *want* your loves to last forever, which, with so many fish in the sea, you probably don't."

"It's a good thing you told me about your father so I don't have to take your cynicism personally anymore," Tristan said cheerfully. "How was Hélène?"

"Suspiciously helpful."

He nodded. "That CV of yours must have knocked her socks off. Who wouldn't want to loan money to someone who could become head of accounting for Abbaye before she was twenty-nine?"

"She seemed particularly impressed with the fact that I could curb *you*."

Tristan looked indignant. "You actually mention ruining Fugace on your CV?"

"I'm guessing you mentioned it to her. Would that have been in pillow talk or in a little call just after we had lunch?"

"If my past love life ever turns out to be your business, I'll let you know, Malorie."

Ouch.

He pulled off a glove and waggled his bare left hand. "If you like it, you gotta put a ring on it."

She folded her arms and glared at him.

His gaze drifted down her body in a way that made her pencil skirt feel too short, all the way down to her ankles, then drifted back up. He gave a dreamy little sigh.

The problem with that dreamy sigh was the way it made her nipples ache. "Are you going to explain any time soon what you're doing in my building ripping things up without my permission?"

"'My building.' Nice ring to that, isn't it?" Tristan said. "You like saying it?"

Yes. She gave him her most repressive look.

"What, you're trying to pretend you wanted this carpet to stay?"

"I know you Rosiers think everything in Grasse belongs to you, but where do you get off waltzing in here and doing whatever you choose to my family property?"

"Well, it provokes you. That's always fun."

She fisted her hands in the crooks of her elbows.

"*Allez*, Malorie. I'm helping you. You know you want to see that floor again."

Malorie flung out her arms. "*Why* are you helping me?"

115

"I want to make sure you do things right. I've got a vision for this place."

She stared at him. "Oh, you do, do you?"

"Yes," he said firmly. "It's restored to glory. All those Gallé display tables below are back up here and on them are the most beautiful perfumes. There's only one flaw in the vision, actually—you."

That would hurt more if it wasn't perfectly obvious that Tristan was just trying to get a rise out of her. Odd thought—did he get as much of a zing out of provoking her as she did out of provoking him? "Do I spoil your perfect little world, Tristan?"

He wrinkled his nose. "You'd want to focus on the bottom line. When this place could be a show house. Everything that's best about perfumery. Can you imagine? A company where the *perfume* took priority. Where it was about making the best, not making the most money."

"Okay. I imagined it. It already failed spectacularly in my vision, and it only took six months."

He cast her a dark glance. There she went, shattering his illusions again. Waking him out of his blissful, sun-kissed dreams to make sure he didn't get skin cancer. Talk about a lousy role in his life.

On the other hand, it would be perfectly crappy to get skin cancer, wouldn't it?

"What happens in *your* dream world?" she said. "You buy up Monsard and run it like a tax write-off?"

"Maybe you're underestimating the public and the power of a great perfume," Tristan said haughtily.

Right. Malorie pinched the bridge of her nose. "You do remember this is the same public that has kept Spoiled Brat in the top ten for the past four years?"

"*Niche* perfumes," Tristan said. "To people with *taste.*"

A glimpse of that passionate artist heart of his showed through his eyes. It was always hard to say no to Tristan when that happened. Well, it was always hard to say no to Tristan period, but that was the worst—when she knew it truly mattered to him.

"I really don't think it's smart to limit your market to such a tiny group."

He shook his head. "It's the perfect place to make it work, Malorie. Here, maybe eventually another shop in some expensive part of Paris. It's what Monsard was so good at it in the old days, before the war, right? Appealing to the clientele who wanted something unique to them, something with taste."

The old glory days. Of glamor and happiness and hope.

Could *this* place nourish hope? This place that was all past, so much failure. Was it roots or a ball and chain?

"Is that why you're helping?" Malorie tried to keep her tone cynical. Tough. Not about to be taken in. Not even by Tristan. "Softening me up so you can take it over?"

Tristan looked puzzled. "Malorie. We've known each other most of our lives. We've been friends at the very least since high school."

"You never even spoke to me in high school," Malorie said, confused.

Tristan looked as if she'd slapped him. "You don't even remember, do you." His voice had flattened. It wasn't a question.

"I mean, just the kind of automatic exchanges when we crossed paths. *'Pardon'*, when you brushed too close to me in the hall. 'Excuse me, do you mind if I reach past you to get that book?'"

Tristan closed his utility knife and rested it on his knee. "And how often did that happen, Malorie?"

She stared at him. He held her eyes, his gaze straight and a little stern, reminding her oddly of his great aunt's gaze. That gaze that wasn't going to let someone wiggle away from the truth.

"You were always friendly to everybody," she said, slowly. "That was just the way you were. Even to me."

"'Even'?" Tristan said blankly.

She made a little wave of her hand. "You know, the...nerdy girl. With the cheap clothes. A Monsard."

Oh, here we go again, Tristan thought. "You know I never even thought about what your last name was? Not ever."

Or maybe, well...once in a while had he thought about it, on those museum field trips, when he'd noticed the blankness of her expression and the way she stood far to the back and so he'd gone to stand a little too close to her, so that she'd have a shoulder pressing against hers. If he'd had the right, he would have put his arm around her, but he didn't, so...he'd done what he could.

He tried to wrap his mind around it, but he couldn't imagine what it would have been like to grow up as the great-granddaughter of a collaborator. His entire existence had been dominated by the pride and glory of his grandparents and great aunt, Resistance heroes. He had always had a lot to live up to. He couldn't imagine what it was like to have a lot to rise above.

One corner of Malorie's lips twisted so wryly he felt vaguely as if he'd been guilty of white male privilege or something. Privileged oblivion to someone else's point of view.

"You wore cheap clothes?" he said blankly. Hadn't they all just worn jeans and T-shirts?

"Compared to most of the girls who hung around you, yes," she said, back to that dryness of hers.

He frowned a little. He had no idea what the clothes cost, but yeah, now that she mentioned it, he did remember short skirts and nice quality boots and some absolutely vile perfumes in the circle of girls around him. Some people thought every woman should have a signature scent, but like many aspects of adolescence, the search for that identity had sometimes manifested itself in glaringly over-sexualized, awkward ways.

Malorie had left no sillage behind her at all, in the high school halls. Or rather her sillage had been a space, a wake of quiet where a man could take a deep breath and almost hope to clear his head. But usually she was gone far too fast for him to reach that hope.

"Did I ever do anything that suggested I gave a crap about any of those things?" Tristan said, profoundly irritated. He'd spent all those years in high school unable to touch Malorie not because she was busy dismissing him as an immature trouble-maker but because she was too proud to risk him looking down at her?

Didn't that just figure, about Malorie.

"You know, you are very annoying," he said.

Her lips quirked in that dry way that made him want to just kiss the hell out of her. "You've mentioned."

"One of these days you're going to quit screwing my life up for ridiculous reasons." Tristan attacked the carpet with a vengeance. "'Oh, this ingredient costs too much.' 'Oh, my clothes don't cost *enough*.' Whatever, Malorie."

"You do a terrible falsetto."

"Thank you. That's the first nice thing you've said about me in our whole freaking lives."

Chapter 11

He'd managed to get another swathe of carpet sliced, rolled, taped and tossed over with the others, just getting back into the rhythm, when Malorie's shoes appeared to his left, on still untouched threadbare carpet.

It had been a long time since he'd knelt at Malorie's feet, and a wave of erotic nostalgia washed through him. Hell, too bad he didn't have a pencil or a textbook to drop at them.

Malorie must mean to help him, because she slipped out of her elegant heels, standing on the carpet in bare feet. Her toes flexed into their freedom, and hot blood pounded in his head, taking him right back to when he was fourteen, fifteen, sixteen.

Only he knew a lot more about women now. He knew those heels made her feet sore. So if a man caught her foot in one strong grip right now and squeezed, how long would it take him to have her moaning and twisting in that pencil skirt and begging him to push it higher up her thighs?

In fact, if he rolled her back on the rest of this dusty carpet and took one of her feet in his hand and—

Heat flushed up under his skin. *Damn* Malorie got to him.

"That's not true," Malorie said, and the sexual fantasy was so vivid in his head that he almost argued with her about it. *Oh, yes, you do get to me, Malorie. Just because I never get to you doesn't mean we're all as immune to maddening sexual desire.*

"That it's the first nice thing. On that report on our group that our teacher made each of us do on our Occupation project, I said you were an excellent partner, easy to work with, contributing lots of ideas, doing your part."

It was ridiculous how much that warmed his insides. "Really?" He felt all fuzzy with pleasure. *Get a grip, Tristan.*

But he'd liked working on the group project. It had been the kind of academic work he could actually do well—not pinned to a desk, able to sprawl out in an empty classroom after school, move, minimize distractions, work on a subject that interested him. Watch the way Malorie's neck curved over their poster as she was carefully etching letters. Plus, he'd been dying to prove to the smart girl in school that *he* was smart, too, even if he couldn't fit his brains the right way into the school box. So he'd really put his all into the project.

Malorie shrugged.

Hey. Was Malorie blushing a little?

Now *that* was interesting.

"What did you say about me?" she challenged.

He'd actually had to rewrite the whole group evaluation several times, because every time he got to the part where he had to reflect on his partner's work, he blinked after a while to find he'd sketched Malorie's face and beside it notes for how to capture her in a scent. How to grasp that sense of *space* in her sillage, of cleanness and refuge.

He still hadn't quite figured out how to do that with a scent. A perfume seemed inherently that space's antithesis.

He'd come the closest with Fugace, but...well, anyway.

"Pretty much the same," he said. *Merde* but her legs went up forever. And his mouth went dry and his brain short-circuited just like it had every single damn time he'd dropped his pencil at her feet in high school. "That was before you went into financial management so it was still true."

Just crouching to tape the next carpet roll for him, she stiffened upright. "Tristan. You know, sometimes it is very hard to not just"—her hands flexed in the air in a frustrated motion—"*do* something to you."

"Yeah." He retracted the blade of the utility knife. "Tell me about it." He took his time pulling off his work gloves, savoring the anticipation. "Although it's hardly my fault you sold your soul to the devil."

If she was one of his cousins, he'd make some joke about "it must run in the family"—just put his finger *right* on that old wound and make it into something they could laugh about. But she'd probably take him seriously and shut down like a light. Worse, she'd probably be *hurt*. So he sat on that bit of humor.

"You know, one of these days I may strangle you," Malorie said.

He shrugged. "My neck's right here." *Bring it, baby.* Tristan had been picking up girls since he was five years old, when three or four of them at once, none of them Malorie, had insisted he "marry them" on the playground in a mass ceremony that had involved some kind of dancing and them chasing him and throwing flowering weeds at him. A lifetime of experience had taught him one thing for certain: if annoyance got her to grab him and break that physical barrier, then he had won half the battle.

Her eyes flickered over the hollow of his throat, over his shoulders, down his chest. She turned her head away and focused intensely on the carpet.

Yes.

"Look," he said. "I'll even help." He took her free hand, a jolt of intimacy right up his arm, and curved her fingers around his throat. "Go ahead." He lifted his chin bravely. "I'm ready to die."

Malorie laughed involuntarily at that, but her laugh broke on an indrawn breath. Her eyes flickered to her hand on his throat. .

She jerked her hand away and looked back at the carpet. But not before he had seen her dilated pupils.

Yes.

"Your legs kill me," he said. "Remember back in high school when I was always bumping into you in the hall so I could pick up your textbooks?"

"What?" She looked so blankly astonished that it set his teeth on edge. Maybe if he bit her thigh *that* would get through to her.

"You don't remember." Had he penetrated her sexual consciousness *at all* back then? "You know, it's a good thing there were other girls back in high school, Malorie, or your brush offs would have given me a complex."

She gave a faint snort. "Yeah, I noticed you and the other girls."

Well, good. He hoped she'd wanted to scratch his eyes out over them. *That* would have been an emotion. "You had the first option." He dropped his gloves on the exposed plywood. "You just turned it down."

"I don't even know what you're talking about. Why do you keep harping on about high school? We happened to sit next to each other in a few classes, but come on, Tristan. We didn't hang out or anything."

This still had the power to annoy him so damn much. "We did not just happen to sit next to each other, Malorie. It took some strategizing on my part." Usually he'd aimed for the desk behind her. It probably sounded creepy now, but it was about the only way he had gotten through high school. Watching girls, and most particularly her. He'd branched out more than a little when it became obvious that his crush on her was a lost cause and that plenty of other girls were more than happy to give him all those sensual experiences he craved. But somehow or other, even when he was surrounded by pretty girls, she'd always pull him back to her.

She stared at him as if he'd just turned her whole world upside down.

"You don't remember all the times my pencil rolled under your desk?"

"Not really." She was watching him as if he was transforming into a werewolf right before her eyes. "I mean, people were always dropping things."

They were, because it gave them an excuse to shift in their seats. Tristan wasn't the only restless captive.

But still—pretty nearly the only thing he'd retained to this day from high school math class were those little zinging memories of stretching a hand past Malorie's legs for his pencil, and she didn't even remember at all? "What the hell were you focused on, the Pythagorean theorem?"

"Well...probably whatever the subject was."

Bon sang.

That was probably why she could go into financial management and accounting. She had the ability to stay focused on maddeningly boring things as if they mattered.

More than him brushing her legs?

Damn.

"It would roll right here. If I aimed it right." He stretched his hand forward until his thumb and then his forearm brushed her ankle, pretending to pick up a pencil. Malorie went very still. Not shifting away from that brush of his hand. "I guess I was harassing you, but I was a stupid teenager and didn't realize."

Malorie stared at him. "I thought you were just being you. When we were four, you used to spill crayons all over the place on purpose just so you could get up and pick them up."

"And you'd always have to help me," he remembered. His hand curved around her calf. Not tentative. He made it warm and sure, as if it had the right to be there. As if it had always had the right to be there. "And even though you should have appreciated the opportunity I made for you to get out of those little desks and crawl around on the floor chasing colorful things, you still considered it highly unfair. I don't know why. You didn't even have to get in trouble for it—I was the one who shouldered all the blame."

Her lips twitched a little. That warmth came into her eyes, the warmth that always got to him, as if fundamentally, deep down under her need to protect herself, Malorie really liked him. "I should have known that was your perspective."

His thumb ran down over the front of her ankle, tracing that tendon, his fingers massaging subtly into her lower calf. Her calves had been pale in New York, but here they had already flushed warm gold again from her hike through the hills. "I should have known it wasn't yours."

Her head was bent so she could watch his hand on her calf, dark climber gold against spring hiking gold, both of them with sun-loving Mediterranean skin. She gave a little shrug of one shoulder. "Charming guys are always getting away with murder while the women have to do all the work."

Ouch. "That's not who I am, Malorie." His palm rubbed, slow and firm, up her calf. He looked up at her parted lips, at that confused, hungry expression she was trying to control. She still hadn't pulled her leg away. "You know that now, don't you? That I like to work. And I don't like, ever, to let people down."

A sudden rush of emotion trembled across her face, almost like the brink of tears. "You're such a nice guy, Tristan," she said, muffled, her hand covering her face. "Do you have a mean bone in your body?"

Merde, if he ended up in the friend zone after all this, he was going to lose his mind. Malorie right down the street from him treating him like a sexless friend might actually be a more misery-inducing prospect than Malorie in New York, dating other men as if both she and her dates were cool, independent skyscrapers.

He scraped his calluses very gently behind her knee, and she shivered from her toes to her head. "Some of my sexual fantasies about you are kind of mean. You beg in them for a long time."

Malorie lowered her hand enough to cover her mouth and stare at him, green eyes a little dazed, as if those dilated pupils of hers were letting in too much light.

"And they almost all start out like this." He rubbed his hand up to her lower thigh, pushing her skirt up, watching her face. "Your legs are the first spot on your body I touch, in almost every single one."

"I had—I had no idea you had such a fertile imagination," Malorie said, struggling visibly to pull together her ironic, repressive tone.

That made him laugh softly, low in his throat. He scraped the calluses of his fingertips very, very lightly against her inner thigh. "No? And yet you're the one who always likes to call me an *artiste*." He let his fingers drift in little circles up her inner thigh, wielding the calluses deliberately. *Sensation.* Oh, yeah, that was something he knew all about. "I think it's safe to say that I like to get...creative." He smiled, a wicked, rich heat rising in him. "If you think touching your legs is imaginative, just wait."

How long was she going to let him keep letting his fingers climb in slow, teasing circles up her thigh? He was so *pissed* at himself for respecting her boundaries all this time, if all he had ever had to do was transgress them like this.

But shit...her boundaries were her boundaries. That was what he was supposed to do—respect and protect them.

She took a quick, deep breath. "Tristan—"

He fisted his other hand around her skirt before she could martial her forces to shut him down and pulled. "That's how you say my name in my fantasies, too. The first time you say it. The fun is getting that tone to change."

He must have weakened her at the knees, he thought triumphantly. Because her knees started to buckle at the pressure of his pull, and he was just adjusting his position to catch her when every single muscle in her body stiffened right back up.

Damn it.

She jerked back from him, tripping over her own shoes, flushing dark as she stared over his head.

Tristan turned, coming to his feet.

Oh, shit. Damien. With a lilt of gleeful amusement around the corners of the usually so controlled line of his lips. He was already turning away, Tristan would give him that, trying to retreat before he interrupted, but it was too late.

Tristan glared at him. That was the problem with having so many cousins. Ubiquity. *Fifteen years of fantasizing about those legs and you show up just as soon as I get to touch them.*

"*Pardon*," Damien said urbanely, recovering control over his expression with the skill he always had. Only those gray-green eyes promised Tristan that this was going to be a hilarious subject of teasing for his cousins for some time to come.

Realizing his mistake, Tristan immediately dropped the glare for a casual raised eyebrow, as if he got caught half-naked kneeling at a woman's feet seducing her all the time and what was wrong with his cousins that they didn't? He didn't reach for his shirt either, just tightened all his muscles subtly, in a way that he hoped made Damien want to hit a gym competitively.

"I didn't mean to interrupt anything," Damien said, with the urbane confidence of a man who knew *he* hadn't been caught kneeling at a woman's feet trying to get his hand up her skirt. "I saw the doors open and thought I'd check in."

Meaning Damien hadn't been able to stand glimpsing work being done on such an essential element in Grasse as La Maison de Monsard without finding out what was going on. You'd think having a wedding in less than three weeks would give him enough things to keep track of, but no.

"*Bonjour*, Malorie." Damien crossed the great room to kiss her cheeks.

Malorie was trying to slip her feet into her shoes without making it too obvious they weren't already on, her face flushed, and she stumbled when she had to look up for the kisses. Damien caught her arm smoothly and braced her while she got her shoes on.

From Damien's manner, helping women get dressed again after they'd been around his youngest cousin was so familiar it didn't even merit a reaction. Only that little glint of glee when he met Tristan's eyes over her head proved how much he was enjoying the anticipation of teasing Tristan to death.

Malorie gave Tristan a fulminating glance.

Oh, great. Now she was going to blame him for his own behavior. He offered her his quirkiest, most charming *how-can-you-be-mad-at-me-really* smile, which he had been perfecting ever since his crayon spilling days.

Malorie, who had seen that smile progress through all its stages of mastery, looked the polar opposite of impressed.

Damn it, Damien. You have lousy timing.

Although Tristan supposed Malorie would have been even more pissed if Damien had shown up one minute later, when he'd just gotten her rolled under him on the carpet.

He might have been more pissed at Damien at that point, too.

"So you're ripping up the carpet," Damien said, politely redirecting his focus away from Malorie's flushed face. "Starting restoration work?"

"A few touch-ups," Malorie said noncommittally. She was getting control of herself, her manner returning to that cool, proud, ironic style of hers that had always gotten under Tristan's skin when he was arguing with her about perfumes. She wasn't going to give Damien one iota more information than she felt he needed to have.

Watching the two face off against each other, Tristan wondered if Malorie, too, would have been the right-hand man—woman—of an international company by now if she'd been born a few rungs higher on the ladder the way he and Damien had.

"To make it more sellable or thinking of re-launching the company in some version?" Damien probed.

Malorie glanced at Tristan. "I'm considering options. Did you text him about the banks as soon as you dropped me off, Tristan?"

"No," Tristan said, although that was a reasonable question. Where had his loyalties lain there? Usually he would have told Damien immediately of any shift in the Grasse socioeconomic system that he thought would affect Rosier decisions.

"Banks?" Damien said.

"Just looking at my financing options," Malorie said dismissively, as if it was no consequence. Nice to know Tristan wasn't the only Rosier she distrusted. Meanwhile, that distrust made her about the lousiest networker in history.

"It's not a bad idea. Re-opening this place. It's got a perfect location and beautiful bones." Damien didn't glance at his cousin when he said it, not that Tristan had ever had any fears that he might. Tristan was the only person who could read straight through Damien's poker face. Like Malorie, Damien walked through a business world where people were constantly trying to stab him in the back.

Although, unlike Malorie, he had a whole family to watch his back. It was amazing the kind of rumors Tristan, for example, picked up just hanging out and being friendly at perfume launch parties. And because people sometimes confused his dislike of business with an incomprehension of it, they often had no inkling he understood some subtle reference. As did the models whom top executives treated like deaf and brainless arm candy, but whom Tristan took the time to treat like real people.

"And all that history," Damien said.

Malorie stiffened.

Tristan gave Damien a quick, warning glance.

Damien's black eyebrows went up a little in confusion and then he realized. "I mean the glamorous history. There are plenty of great houses that have something to be ashamed of from the war."

True enough. Some of the greatest Paris fashion houses had been accused of being far too friendly with their Nazi occupiers. The fact that none of their heads had suffered *une dégradation nationale* spoke more to their power and contacts than to innocence.

"Not yours," Malorie said.

Damien chose his words carefully. "For two people who risked their lives to save children, they could have perhaps shown more mercy," said the man who had such a reputation for being merciless, "to the young child left with nothing to believe in, after her father fell from his heights."

Malorie's grandmother. Tristan looked at Damien with deep approval.

"I'm not saying they were deliberately hard on your grandmother, too. I just think that when they pursued vengeance against your great-grandfather they forgot that his daughter would suffer so much as a consequence. And you always have to think about the consequences of your actions," said the Rosier shark, who took over businesses for them, who weakened rivals.

Tristan gazed at him thoughtfully. It was surprising the insights you could gain into the hearts even of the people you were closest to, at the oddest moments.

People were utterly fascinating.

"So." Damien looked at the corner of plywood revealed and at the great expanse of floor, and his fingers went to his cufflinks. "Need some help?"

Chapter 12

If anyone six months ago had tried to tell Malorie that she would soon be back in Grasse and the Rosiers would be down on their hands and knees helping her restore La Maison de Monsard, she would have recommended that person for rehab.

But there they were. And *merde* but it was a hot view. She undid a couple of buttons on her shirt and went to work so she'd have an excuse to keep stopping to fan herself.

"Have you guys ever thought of doing your own charity calendar?" she said dryly, to get control of those emotions. Damien raised an eyebrow, but Tristan immediately grinned and flexed. Yeah, he knew what he was doing, all right. "The sales would probably fund half the charities in Grasse."

"Yeah, but Damien's *pudique*," Tristan said with a wave of his hand. Modest.

Malorie choked on a laugh and tried to focus on the carpet again.

"Everyone's *pudique* compared to you," Damien told him.

"Well, if you've got it," Tristan said humbly. Damien threw a carpet roll at him.

Tristan caught it and tossed it over to the growing pile, showing off the power of his shoulders. Malorie bit hard on the inside of her cheek and tried not to think about those shoulders bunching as he started to pull her down to him, of what they would have felt like under her fingers when he rolled over her on the carpet.

"And Matt would blush," Tristan said regretfully. "He'd probably be one constant blush for the rest of his *life* if we ever got him drunk enough to get him to pose nude for a calendar."

Malorie was pretty sure a picture of big, growling Matt Rosier mostly naked and blushing would only increase sales, but she dropped the subject before it could get out of hand. Tristan was so good at twisting her attempts at ironic self-protection around on her and making her laugh and let down her guard instead.

Damien's fiancée, perfumer Jess Bianchi, stopped by, enjoyed the view herself for a few minutes, then left and came back a little later with several cold bottles of water. That was good. Malorie could press her bottle against her cheeks, which flushed hot every single time she thought about getting caught with Tristan's hand up her skirt. And every single time she sat back on her heels and accidentally watched him work too long and thought about what those strong hands and his thrill in everything physical would have felt like if Damien hadn't come by and...

She took a long swallow. Damn Tristan anyway.

Tristan got a late call from Paris about his beach floral and stepped out into the courtyard to take it. Malorie stood to haul a few rolls of carpet to the main pile, and Damien scooped them up from her and took them with his.

"You really aren't dressed for this." He nodded at her reddened knees. "I know Tristan has already suggested this five times, but why don't you just let us do it?"

"I'm fine." It felt surreal to have him and Tristan helping her at all, let alone to just leave them to it while she took care of something else. Also, being this close to Damien half-naked was making her blush again. Damien was far too cool and controlled for her tastes— none of the easygoing warmth that made Tristan so irresistible—but there was no denying that standing this close to him while he had his shirt off provided for a very enjoyable perspective.

In high school, girls used to argue cheerfully with their friends about which of the Rosier cousins was the hottest, and the more Tristan matured, the more Malorie had found herself secretly in his camp. He strolled through the high school halls like a human-size sun, spreading warmth and gorgeousness wherever he went. Still, Damien definitely had a sexy dangerous thing going on.

Damien tossed the rolls of carpet down on the larger pile. "So," he said thoughtfully, "you and my cousin?"

Malorie flushed hot all over. "No! *Not* me and your cousin." Only three days back in Grasse and already all the Rosiers were assuming she was yet another one of Tristan's many female friends. Tristan was a...a...*plaie. Une vraie plaie.* A plague on her existence. "That was just, just—"

"Ah, just sexual attraction, then?" Damien said, as unreadable as if they were talking about financial reports. He nodded understandingly. "That happens with him a lot."

"Yeah, tell me about it," Malorie growled, foot-shoving a carpet roll back onto the pile.

"He suffers," Damien said very blandly. "Only used for his body—"

"Oh, give me a freaking break, Damien."

That quick grin of Damien's flashed and was brought back into line. "If only some woman could see past the sex to all his other qualities."

How a single one of the Rosier cousins had survived this old without being strangled was beyond her. And here she had always thought Damien was the one with sense. "*All* women can see all his other qualities, Damien. We're not idiots."

Unfortunately. It would be really helpful if at least ninety-nine percent of the rest of the female population were idiots.

"You can?" Damien glanced, confused, toward the courtyard. "*What* qualities?"

"Not you, too." Malorie said, outraged. "What the hell is wrong with you Rosiers? Are you so freaking *spoiled* that you can't see what a treasure you've got?" She gestured dramatically toward the courtyard. Her hands were feeling more Gallic with every hour back in this country.

Damien made a dubious moue. "It's just Tristan."

"*Just?*" Her fingers itched for Rosier throats. What was it, because he was the youngest? "He makes you guys millions, which you of all people should appreciate, Damien. He makes you laugh instead of walk around with a stick up your ass all the time. He's the damn *joy* in the family. And you don't even *appreciate* him?"

She broke off. Why did Damien have a very faint curve to his lips, like he did when he'd just lured a rival CEO into revealing a very important weakness about his company?

"Treasure is an interesting term," he said thoughtfully.

Malorie flushed to the roots of her hair. "*Whatever,*" she snarled. "I was just trying to, trying to—oh, forget it." She folded her arms and turned to stare at the revealed plywood. "You know what? I appreciate your help, but I need to close up now and, and, and...meet someone for dinner."

***

In the courtyard, Tristan finished his call and looked around, startled, as the doors closed behind Damien. "Wait, what?"

Damien shrugged into his shirt without buttoning it, coming forward. Above them, the colors of the soft ochre and dusky orange buildings had gone softer in the evening light, drying clothes strung between balconies. "I think I got us kicked out."

"How the hell did you do that? You didn't start giving her any more crap about her family history, did you?"

Damien shook his head. Instead of fastening his cufflinks again, he was rolling up his sleeves. Down the street, Jess waved at him, heading back up from her little perfume shop—which used to be Laurianne's and which Tristan rather strongly felt should have been kept in the family, but apparently Damien was going to take care of keeping it in the family his way, so that worked out.

For Damien and his heirs, at least. If Tristan, the only perfumer of his generation, had ever nurtured any secret hope that that invaluable piece of family history should be passed on to him and *his* heirs, then Tante Colette's gift of it to someone else entirely had been a slap-in-the-face reminder. He was the youngest and the youngest was supposed to make his own fortune.

He wondered again how Malorie had just walked away to make her fortune somewhere else, without feeling that she was cutting her own self off at the ground, slicing the flower off to put in a vase, leaving all roots and life behind.

"Are you holding something else against her?" Tristan asked warily.

Damien's lips held a very faint curve. "Oh, no, I think she'll do."

"Do for what?" Tristan said, a little confused.

Damien shrugged. His eyes held a little light of...laughter? Supreme satisfaction? "I'll leave that up to you."

"Thanks," Tristan said sardonically. "I appreciate that." The last people he wanted to have interfering in anything about his relationships were his cousins.

Jess reached Damien, the waft of smoked ambergris when Tristan bent to kiss her cheeks making his nose prickle with curiosity to find out what she was testing today. Then she stepped into her place at Damien's side, and Damien slid his arm around her waist like he was sliding that arm into its home. The place it was always meant to be.

"Although if you'll take my advice—"

Yeah, right. Damien had made a complete cock-up of his relationship with Jess initially, and it had taken considerable discreet intervention on Tristan's part to get those two to act sane again.

"Always," he said dryly.

"—you'll let her know how many shares in Monsard you've accumulated."

Damien might understand strategy in business but apparently in relationships it went right over his head.

"I'm saving them for a surprise," Tristan said. Until Malorie realized how much she really wanted them.

Damien and Jess exchanged one of those couple glances, the ones that said, *we know worlds beyond this poor single fool if only we could open his eyes.* Which was rich, given how completely nuts the start of their relationship had been. Damien had gone *completely* off the deep end. How could any man fall so hard for a woman after just a one-night stand? Tristan liked most everybody, and had had plenty of fantastic one-night stands, but the people he *loved* were all people he had known for most of his life, as if his soul had grown around them and enclosed them inside it.

"Tristan, I know you think you're the only one of us to understand women," Damien said.

Ha. Tristan was the only one of them to understand any people period. His cousins just bumbled along like blindfolded wolves.

"But allow me to let you know one thing about business people. We really don't like that kind of surprise."

Chapter 13

Malorie was so pissed off by the time she had gotten home that she could hardly stand it. Once she escaped the thrall of Tristan's hot body, annoyance was a conscious choice. She could be pissed off or she could be desperate, and she had not gone through hell, fire, and New York to come back to this town desperate.

Her annoyance with Tristan was even more exacerbated by the sneaking suspicion that Damien had played her somehow. Why the hell had she said *treasure*?

Well, she knew whose fault it was.

Tristan Charm-Your-Pants-Off Rosier had gone *really* over the line this time. Wrapping his hand around her calf, sending heat climbing straight up to her head and flushing every part of her body on its way there, then following after that heat with that slow, slow rub of calluses. How dare he?

That man would do *anything* to disturb her focus, to demand her attention. He treated her body just as he'd treated his damn boxes of crayons back when they were kids. And it worked, too. She felt spilled out, a fascinating sprawl of colors.

She had *had* it with him. What did he think she was, an actress? A model? *Used* to his bullshit?

You'd better hope I don't stay at Abbaye. I'd strip your next perfume down to something sensible.

And then he'd die, and then she'd dance on his grave.

Kicking up clods into the faces of all those other women prostrate with grief, sobbing their eyes out, their perfect bosoms heaving in their beautiful, sexy party dresses.

So there.

Tristan's specter rose up out of the imagined grave like some movie version of a perfume escaping a bottle, thumbed its nose at her with a grin, and proceeded to curl around her shoulders and whisper flirting, sexy promises to haunt her for the rest of her life.

Grrrr. She growled at him and strode out under the bitter orange trees. And a deep slow breath moved through her body.

The sun was setting. The light was soft and rosy to the west, flushing southward over the Mediterranean. The scent from the orange blossoms was warmer than the night, sensuous and fresh and sweet all at once.

Romantic. Hopeful.

She slipped off her shoes and stood barefoot on one of the drop cloths. She'd found a little distillery that could handle her small quantities of orange blossom from the few trees she could harvest a morning. It had been the same one her grandmother had used, and the older man who ran it had been surprised and pleased to see her, reminiscing about her grandmother, while from time to time one of the handful of other people in the region who had small bitter orange groves showed up with their burlap sacks of orange blossom, too.

Some white flowers scattered on the cloth, fallen during the day. She stirred them with her toes. *Tristan would love it here.*

Yeah. He would.

But a vision flashed through her mind of Damien's amusement, of Tristan's blasé attitude. *Oh, you caught me with my hand up a woman's skirt again? Nothing new to see here.*

Sexual attraction? Yeah, that happens to him a lot.

Tristan's fatal flaw, at least where women who fantasized about him were concerned. Every other woman fantasized about him, too, and he was never going to settle for only a few sensations when he could have all of them.

He'd still love it here, though. She sat down on the cloth, picking up one of the fallen flowers and wrapping her arms around her knees. On a night like this, surrounded by scents and flowers, with his own body and hers to enjoy, Tristan would turn the night into a one-couple orgy.

She could imagine it in far too vivid detail. Tristan's eyes black in the night, his hair falling over his forehead, the way that lean, muscled body would move, the way he would react to every touch, every sensation, craving all of them.

The way she would react to *him*. To his hands on her skin, to her hands on his, to the texture of his hair and shoulders under her fingers, to the scent of his skin.

Tristan's scent was fun. You never knew what he might have been skin-testing on his arms that day, which made his natural scent elusive, like a game of tricks and mirrors. Only a woman who had the right to bury her nose regularly against his bare skin would ever learn his naked scent. On a lazy Sunday morning, late enough for the scents of the shower and his toothpaste to have calmed down, only Tristan left, warm, inviting all the exploration a woman could ever want.

She curled her fingers into her palms. And finally stretched out on the drop cloth, staring at the stars. He'd really had a crush on her?

Of course, he'd probably had a crush on half the girls in school. Discovering sex and eager to have as much of it as he could.

Whereas she'd been walled off. Like her grandmother. Creating a barrier all around herself, a safe space. When she'd set off on that hike, maybe it had felt so incredibly freeing not only because she was escaping Grasse but because she was escaping the confines she had created for herself.

Stepping out.

She pulled the drop cloth over herself, wrapping herself in flowers and the thought of Tristan—the imagined Tristan, who was hers—and fell asleep.

***

The parquet flooring gleamed in the afternoon light. It made her throat tighten and her chest hurt, how beautiful it was. A few dust motes lingering from all they had stirred up still danced in the rays of light, luring her back into another time, when her family was strong and glorious.

"Got any old flapper dresses in an attic somewhere?" Tristan murmured, as if he saw the vision, too. He'd had to haul all the plywood that had been under the carpet outside to reveal the floor, and his chest and shoulders gleamed faintly with a hint of perspiration.

It was probably why he had left an arm's stretch of personal space between them instead of standing with his shoulder brushing hers like he usually did, but it made her want to touch one finger to his biceps to see what that hint of moisture felt like on his skin.

Hell, she just wanted to sink her fingers into those biceps completely and test what his muscles felt like. Pumped from the labor right now, his eyes glowing with his own satisfaction.

"I guess we should paint next before we move the furniture up here," he said, a little regretfully, a man who had a vision of this room he wanted realize faster than paint dried.

"Why are you doing this, Tristan?" Seeing that beautiful parquet flooring revealed made everything seem so *possible*.

Or was it having Tristan here to help with the work, to share his energy and enthusiasm, that made things seem so possible?

So desirable.

He shrugged one powerful shoulder. "I want to see this place restored. It's beautiful." He slanted her a somehow indulgent glance. As if he had come to terms

140

with some aspect of who she was and was giving it understanding and acceptance. "Plus, as I've mentioned, Malorie, we've been friends since grade school."

Yeah, he did keep mentioning that. She'd had friends in high school, and in Paris and New York, too, but sometimes, the way he talked about it, she wondered if she understood what friendship was. Like maybe she'd been missing something, all this time.

A narcissistic father could really do a number on a girl. Her therapist in New York had taught her all the ways she compensated for that in her relationships with others—distrust being her primary one, an unwillingness to let down her guard and let people in— but knowing what caused that wariness didn't mean Malorie found it easy to let those survival instincts go. They were a part of her, older even than her relationship with Tristan.

"Well, I just want you to know I really appreciate it. If there's ever anything I can do for you in return..." Besides sell this place to him at a discount, which he'd better not be maneuvering for.

Tristan sighed dramatically. "You could grab me and kiss me in gratitude any time. Break that twenty-five year streak of shutting me out."

She rolled her eyes. And tried not to remember his fingers, stroking up her thigh, while he kneeled at her feet.

Instead, she focused on remembering both his and Damien's easy amusement when he was discovered in the act.

"Twenty-five years and never even kissed," Tristan said sadly. "The dearth of physical affection in this relationship is stunning."

The man made flirting with him so damn enticing. She bit the inside of her lip. "You don't remember, do you?" she said, taking his sadness and upping it a quotient of woefully wounded.

"Kissing you? Unless you drugged me first, I can promise I'd remember that."

"In a tunnel on the playground. We were five."

Tristan gave her a blank look.

"My first kiss." She clasped her hands to her chest and gazed heavenward romantically.

"Probably mine, too, if we were five. Seriously? This really happened?"

"You said you wanted to marry me."

To her astonishment, a light flush climbed up Tristan's cheeks. He thrust his hand through his hair. "Are you making this up?"

To be honest, her vague memories mostly involved fragmented images of the bright yellow of the inside of the tunnel and coming face to face with a blurred-by-time Tristan as they were each crawling through it from opposite ends. But she was pretty sure that was how it had played out. "You forgot." She turned her head away tragically. "I knew it."

"I can't figure out if you're shitting me," Tristan said warily.

"Then later that recess, you married four or five other girls in this big ceremony over by the playhouse set, and I wasn't even invited to the wedding."

"Okay, I remember *that*. They caught me! And threw weeds at me. My cousins made fun of me for weeks."

"I think the weeds were supposed to be flowers. Your cousins were probably just jealous."

"That's what *I* said, but they kept laughing."

Malorie was starting to laugh herself. She knew she was supposed to be stomping on his charm so that he couldn't get his hand up her skirt again, but Tristan was so damn irresistible it was *ridiculous*.

Tristan gazed down at her. As an adult, she was used to facing off against Tristan while wearing heels, but today, having planned ahead to help with the work on the floor, she was in minimalist tennis shoes, and the fifteen centimeters or so he had on her when she wasn't wearing heels made her feel unfamiliarly small. His gaze was caught on her laughter.

"So this would actually be our second kiss." His voice deepened, sensual and hungry, as he lifted his hand.

She stepped back before his hand could curl around her nape or cup her cheek or...*just don't think about all the ways he could touch you. Don't think about a "second" kiss.* "We've kissed cheeks more times than I can count," she said dismissively. Twice on hello, twice on good-bye, every single encounter. Even in New York. Even when he was so mad at her that his lips pressed against each cheek like the cold points of an exclamation mark at the end of an insult. "What's so different about lips?"

Tristan laughed deep and soft. "Malorie." He took a step forward, following her retreat. "Let me show you."

She took another step back, bumping into the wall.

Tristan stopped. Standing close, but not putting his arms to either side of her on the wall, not using his greater size and strength to close her in. Sometimes it hurt her heart how much she really, really *liked* Tristan.

"Do you know how pretty you are?" Tristan said softly. "I mean, really, really beautiful. I don't even know what it is, exactly. It's just when I'm up close to you, I feel like I can breathe." He paused. His lips quirked. "Sometimes much too hard. Like I'm getting ready for something...very physical."

Oh. The urge to turn physical ran through her. Tried to turn all her defenses into pliable, yielding things.

He lifted a hand to pull on a strand of her hair, drawing it gently through his fingers. "I bribed Antoine to blow off our project that time," he murmured. "So that it would only be me and you. I kept wanting to kiss you, all the time we were working on it. But I knew I was too over the line in how much I hit on you already. That you had to show *something*, some sign you wanted it, too, before I could try for a kiss."

"And I never did?" Malorie said, surprised. And then she flushed and turned her head away, embarrassed by what she'd revealed. "You know damn well you were one of the hottest guys in school," she muttered.

A flash of pleasure in Tristan's eyes at that admission.

"Well, that's what I wonder now." He ran his thumb over her cheekbone. Pleasure shivered through her. "If maybe I missed a chance because I just didn't know how to read your interest. You weren't giggly, like some of the girls. You've always been so...strong in yourself, is the best way I can put it. Maybe quiet didn't mean untouchable, and I just didn't realize back then. I was pretty insecure."

Malorie made an incredulous noise. "You don't have an insecure bone in your body."

"Maybe not now," Tristan allowed. "But back then I was still going through my growing pains. And you've got to admit, Malorie, that during our entire school years, you were the girl who had everything together, and I was the boy teachers kept telling to act more like you."

She'd seemed like she had everything together? What? Surely not in *high school*. Right after her father died with another woman in his car, when everything had been falling apart at home and her social support at high school had been, at best, unreliable, and she'd mostly just tried to keep her head down, focus on getting through each day, and definitely not look at the mirror too much and obsess over all the changes happening to her body that would mean she could never feel like a safe child in her grandmother's garden again.

"Your grandfather would have killed you if you'd gotten involved with me."

"I don't think my grandfather operates quite the way you think he does. He's always told *me* that you judge a man on his own mettle, and that's the only thing you can judge him on. Family's just a preliminary indicator that may be entirely off."

Malorie searched his face, wondering how true that was. His aunt, Madame Delatour, had tested Malorie's mettle, but not in a mean way, not—surprisingly—as if she was visiting the sins of her great-grandfather upon her. More as if she tested everyone's mettle, particularly that of women her nephews brought to meet her.

Tristan ran his fingers over her head, as if the texture of her hair fascinated him. "I bet he will like you. He loves strength and pride and independence and trying to do the right thing."

Malorie fought the sudden sting in her eyes.

"You didn't realize?" Tristan's voice gentled. "That anyone else saw that in you?"

"Tristan, *stop it*," Malorie said frantically, her face twisted away.

He stepped back. But his gaze stayed on her face. It was unnerving how steadily he studied her.

Tristan was freaking smart. People forgot that sometimes, because he maintained such a laid-back, humorous persona. But Malorie had spent her life in the perfume industry. She knew he had memorized several thousand molecules that he could identify from the smell, and when he did, their chemical formulae appeared in his brain, and all the ways he could connect that molecule to any of the thousands of others, and whether they would bind well, how long they'd last in the bottle before they broke down.

She knew that that was just the *basics* of his career. Tristan was arguably the most brilliant perfumer of his generation. Meaning he was inarguably brilliant.

Genius-level brilliant. Amused, lounging, windsurfing, rock-climbing, hating to sit still...and a genius.

And one of the areas on which he had chosen to focus his intelligence was people. He enjoyed them, and he liked to understand them.

And right now, he was focused on her.

"What do you *want* from me?" she asked, furious with him for how desperate and confused and wanting he made her feel. How much he made her long not to step away from her guarded keep and head out on a quest for better prospects but to claim the keep and open it wide and let him in. No matter how much opportunity that gave him to hurt her, once he was inside.

Tristan caught up his T-shirt and toolkit. "I already told you that, Malorie." He went to the doors, paused, and looked back over his shoulder to capture her eyes one last time. "You."

Chapter 14

You.

You.

Seriously, Tristan was indefatigable where women were concerned. He had to experience every damn one of them.

She wrapped her arms around herself under the bitter orange trees. Of course, what if that woman wanted to experience Tristan?

That's how he lured so many of them in. Women knew he would be an incredible, sensual, once in a lifetime experience.

And she never had experienced him, not once in her life. She'd always kept focused on her goals. Protecting herself from anyone who might require her to abandon those goals in the service of his wants and ego.

What if your goals and his are the same?

The flush of enthusiasm and happiness at seeing those parquet floors gleaming, for example. Standing shoulder to shoulder imagining what the showroom would be like painted, the display tables restored to their positions, perfume bottles on display.

What if they made a team? Him with his perfumes and creative vision and passion and her with the financial sense and drive to make sure those visions could come true.

Her lips quirked. How they would fight. How many times Tristan would grow impassioned and persuasive and convincing.

She wouldn't even be sabotaging her career if she gave in to that passionate persuasion. If she ran Monsard, then as long as profits were good, those profits wouldn't have to be maximized to the last cent every single time. She could decide where priorities lay, not a higher up executive watching to see if she proved herself worthy of the next promotion.

Or they could decide where priorities lay.

Funny how exasperatingly delightful that sounded. As if the exasperation was part of the delight. The zing and the arguing and the convincing.

She laughed a little. If their work arguments happened in a situation where Tristan getting his hands on her wouldn't be sexual harassment, she bet he would win every single time. A woman would have to be *very* stubborn, to resist Tristan when he could bring his full sensual arsenal into play.

As stubborn and hardheaded as they came.

She considered herself. Well, hell, she was pretty darn hardheaded, wasn't she?

She rapped her knuckles against her skull. As usual, she could only count on herself to be reliable enough for that job.

***

Dust particles caught in light. That stirring awake of old time. Hope born anew.

Tristan climbed, stretching out his entire being with every reach for the next possible hold, until it felt as if he could stretch his soul from earth to sky. Everything made sense to him, when he was alone on a rock face. Sense, back deep into the oldest roots of the term, when wisdom and feelings were inextricably entwined.

He climbed too much alone, probably—his mother definitely worried about it—but he needed this time by himself as much as he needed his time with everyone else, time with his family, time with fascinating strangers. It was his balance. His time with only him.

Today was an old, familiar climb, one he had been doing since boyhood, on the limestone cliffs at the head of the valley of roses. Every reach of it was imbued with laughter and challenge and solace and escape, pride and accomplishment, solidarity and fun, all those things the cousins had enjoyed together and alone, from the moment they had first set out to climb these cliffs like their fathers and grandfather and great-grandfather had done, all the way back, probably, to Niccolò Rosario himself.

He could climb it more by memory than by concentration now. He knew where each hand and foot should go.

He let the scents and thoughts of scents drift in and out of his mind as he climbed, forming hazy combinations. Dust. Light. Hope. A slim green pride in the middle, standing, turning, wondering. Maybe that green would spread her arms in delight. Maybe she would start dancing.

Atop the cliff gazing out at the valley of roses, he drew all over the pages in his leather bound notebook, in the usual frustrating sense of inadequacy and ever-hovering failure that it was to try to get an olfactory dream down into chemical formulae. He knew that if he listened to that promise of failure—that he could never capture life as beautifully as he imagined it—that he would be paralyzed and never produce anything. So he made a practice of forcing himself to write everything down, even if he had to doodle all around it or write it slanted to prove it was just brainstorming, no commitment to the wrong formulae implied.

Eventually he logged into the Rosier SA system to send the most promising brainstorming ideas to the lab to mix for him. That was one of the good things about being the perfumer and thus being able to send his formulae to the lab to mix—he couldn't get paralyzed there, too, wondering if the next drop in a trial blend was actually one drop too many and would ruin it.

When he came into his physical office space mid-morning, the trials were sitting in brown vials on his desk, the only labeled, orderly thing there. But they weren't what drew his eye.

His desk held its usual black bowl of perfumes *touches* or white test strips, a mill with more strips sprouting out of it like white sunflower petals, papers full of sketches, notes, and formulae spread all over it, multiple small brown vials, some of them toppled over, and, since he was working on a beach floral, some tactile inspiration—a big, polished green-tinted shell and a tray of sand that he had formed most recently into a lopsided sandcastle.

And sitting on the curving butt of a bikini-clad beauty he had sketched while he was brainstorming was a giant box of crayons. Next to it, a black bowl full of orange blossoms.

Staring at them, he felt like one of those children's tricks, where you touched a few drops of water to a small bit of foam and everything about it started to soften and grow.

Saw these and thought of you, a message said, on a sheet of his own sketch paper. *Thanks for all the help with the floor. Malorie.*

"One of your women friends stopped by," his assistant Gaëlle said cheerfully from the doorway.

"Gaëlle, come on," he said uncomfortably. *One of his women friends?* That didn't seem right at all. He ran his finger over the edge of the box of crayons. Then dipped his hand into the bowl of blossoms and brought them, dripping water, to his nose for a long, deep breath of romance and dreaming.

"I have to say, she understands you better than most," Gaëlle said.

Tristan gave her an irritable glance. At twenty-two and with perfume ambitions, Gaëlle was supposed to be gaining her first grasp of the perfume industry under his wing, but like most twenty-two-year-olds, she already thought she knew everything. Especially about her boss. Gaëlle, brown hair twisted up on the back of her head, raised her eyebrows over the cat glasses she was currently favoring and looked thoughtful, disappearing back into the outer office.

Tristan opened the box of crayons, a smile breaking out at all the colors, lined up, as yet unblunted by use. The wax scent brought with it a flashing vision of spilling them all over the floor. Of the happiness of crawling around under the desks chasing colors with Malorie instead of being stuck in a seat trying to do math worksheets.

It wasn't that he had found the math hard, exactly—when his father took him outside and asked him to do the same problem with real world examples, he could do it without even a pause, just as he could later in life when calculating parts of a perfume—but it had been really hard to *focus* on. Colors, now...colors were different. Colors and scents had a lot in common.

He stroked the orange blossoms over his face, turning his head back and forth to feel more texture.

Aww, hell. This was so damn like Malorie. The note, brisk and kind of distant, *thanks for the help.* And the actual gift it accompanied, that intimate and warm understanding of who he was.

It made his heart all freaking mushy.

He had actually sat down and drawn a heart on the sketch paper, and around it another heart, and then another, going through six colors of crayons, before he blinked to realize what he was doing. He flipped the paper over, but on the back of it, again before he could stop his restless hands, he sketched an orange blossom and a fall of black hair. With maybe just a—he pulled out another crayon—a hint of brown in the dark of it, like his.

And now he wanted to make a scent that was wax and colors and childhood happiness, not nostalgic but all grown up, as if it had never been lost.

That would be an awesome perfume. He wondered if Malorie would want to sell it on the display shelves of La Maison de Monsard. If it would mean to her the same thing it did to him.

That was the fascinating thing about perfumes. They never told the same story to two different people. And yet every time someone smelled your perfume in a store and bought it to wear against their skin, you knew that something about it—something that you felt, something that mattered to you—was universal.

***

"Hey, Malorie."

Malorie, going through still more of the generations-accumulated papers and small items, barely recognized the voice. It still had that warm, rich, sexy timbre but there was something quiet about it, maybe even kind of shy.

She tucked the little brass key quickly back into its crackling yellow envelope, marked *Rosier*, and shut the letter box on it. Shut away its cold chill. *Please, dear God, don't tell me we have something else to be ashamed about where the Rosiers are concerned.*

Maybe it was something innocuous. Before the war, the families had been frequent business allies, even friends.

"*Bonjour*, Tristan." Her fingers curled into her palms surreptitiously. She felt stupid and over-exposed. Leaving him a bowl of orange blossoms and a box of crayons was the dumbest, most vulnerable idea ever. Sure, she needed to find a way to thank him for his help, but that particular way...showed she wanted to make him happy.

But he seemed kind of shy, too, leaning in the doorway of the office. The brightness of his supreme self-confidence was softened around the edges, as if some film maker had been playing with misty, romantic lighting.

It made him seem infinitely approachable somehow. As if she could walk right up to him, tuck her sense of over-exposure against him, have his arms circle around her, and be home.

The hairs on her neck prickled with a wistful rush of sensation at how good that might feel, to rest her head on his shoulder, and she looked back down at the worn box.

"I, ah, brought you something." It was so rare for Tristan to show shyness, that she could pick the hint of it out, despite his sexy, gorgeous physicality that made it hard to think about anything but how hot he looked. That blithe charm and confidence made it hard to remember he might be human and vulnerable, too.

Unless a woman had known him most of her life. In which case maybe, if she relaxed her need to to defend herself, she might be able to understand something about him.

"Yeah?" she said. Shyly. People didn't really bring her presents much. She felt heat trying to climb her cheeks, and she fought it hard.

He crossed the room to her, still that long, easy stride, a man who knew that every single cell of his body would handle exactly what he wanted it to, kissed her cheeks, and stepped back enough to offer her a small glass object on his palm.

An exquisite chatelaine perfume bottle, with a vivid swirl of blue colors in the glass, around its neck a delicate gold and white crystal crown of orange blossoms, like a bridal crown. It looked exactly like the one her great-great-grandmother had had, stolen and sold by her father when she was twelve. And its image had been on one of the pages of missing items she had casually shown Tristan that day in the storage room.

Her eyes started to sting. She bit the inside of her lip, fighting her sense of vulnerability with everything she had.

"I know a guy in Nice who collects that period," Tristan said. "He, ah, was finally persuaded to part with it."

Tristan could persuade a rock to sprout flowers for him. Sweetly scented ones, too, to make him happy.

Malorie stroked her finger over the glass, tentatively.

"It's the same one," Tristan said. "He had the records, right back to Monsard."

Malorie curved her fingers under the bottle and lifted it. "My great-great-grandparents went to Venice just after they married. My great-great-grandfather bought it for my great-great-grandmother there as a present to remember the trip."

"Really?" Tristan sounded pleased.

Malorie didn't dare look up at him. "That's the story." Her voice sounded husky. "*Thank* you, Tristan."

"Yeah." His voice was deep and warm. His hand lifted to curve against her cheek. "Of course."

"How much was it? Can I pay you back?"

The hand dropped from her face. "No." The word was flat and hard.

When she looked up at him, so were his eyes.

She covered her face with one hand. "I'm sorry. I'm sorry. I just—"

"Okay." He still sounded a little angry, but resigned to it. Patient. Two big, warm hands closed gently over her shoulders. "It's okay, Malorie. Just...don't ruin things because you don't trust them, okay?"

Her eyes filled. "I'm sorry," she said again.

"Hey." Tristan's hand curved warm against her cheek again. His thumb rubbed just under her lower eyelashes, and she was very afraid he might have felt a brimming tear. "I said it was okay." He smiled at her. "New Yorker," he teased gently.

She shook her head. "It's not that, it's just—" She didn't know how to explain to him that with her father, gifts were always a Trojan horse—a way to get in past your defenses, then tear down your walls for his own gain. She'd been on the fringes of that kind of attention, fortunately, although she'd suffered from it. Her mother, of course, had suffered the worst—love bombed every time she started to gather up the determination for divorce, dragged back into that craving for her husband's attention and approval. *Malorie* had been mostly love bombed by her father when he wanted to use her adoration for him as a weapon against her mother.

So yeah...Malorie didn't trust people to do things just to be generous to her, to have her back. She assumed she should pay Tristan back, because, well...

"You've spent way too much time climbing the rock face on your own," Tristan said. "It's like that's the only way you know how to do it. You need some cousins."

Malorie laughed with a kind of despairing irony. Trust Tristan to instinctively think of family as a positive. "I'm pretty sure my family is at the origin of my desire to stand on my own. That's what my therapist in New York said."

Tristan made a face. "You know what's sad? I mean, I think it's probably good you talked about it with someone, but you probably did it with a therapist instead of a friend because you felt safer if you were paying."

Malorie wanted to fold her arms as a barrier, but the chain of the chatelaine perfume bottle tangled in her fingers, and she couldn't brace against the man who had given it to her. It was so damn...sweet. This piece of her lost history, from back when that history held honeymoons and happiness. "Also, a therapist has training," she pointed out coolly, nevertheless.

"So a person has to have professional training for you to let your guard down with them? Hell, you're worse than Damien. At least he has his family."

Malorie took a breath to argue...and then let it out, stymied. She didn't like to show weakness to other people, that was true enough. And other than her grandmother, family had not really been a safe space for her.

When her dad played the good, charming *I adore my family* man and got his wife and daughters to confide their doubts and fears to him, he was very good at exploiting those doubts and fears to his advantage later.

Sometimes Malorie wondered how much of a mess she might be if he hadn't drunkenly raced himself and one of his wannabe-glamorous girlfriends right off a twisty cliff road between here and Monaco when she was thirteen. Talk about a guilty thought. Thank God for therapists.

Thank God she'd known Tristan long enough to realize, deep down past her instinctive emotional wariness, that he really was different. If he gave a gift, he meant it to bring happiness. Not as a crowbar to crack open someone else's soul for his advantage. "Thank you," she said again. "That was a really, really sweet thing to do, Tristan."

He shrugged one shoulder, but he looked pleased again. "I didn't realize it was a part of the collection with such personal meaning. I hope you don't mind, then— there's a...something I was fooling around with in it."

Her eyes prickled again. She darted a glance at him. "Really?"

Even after Fugace?

He shrugged, his eyes on the bottle. And then, just as she looked down again, lifting to focus on her face.

She untwisted the tiny orange blossom stopper.

The scent of dust a sparkle in the light. Dancing like it could float up into the sun. A deep rich floral base, gleaming under it like a fresh-finished parquet floor, an orange blossom with an age to it, as if it had been lying in wait, layered in and packed away, until someone opened a chest full of some great-great-grandmother's wedding dress and the scent could release again.

"Oh, wow." The impact was like a punch to the chest. "Tristan." She looked at him, her eyes full again. She, who didn't believe in crying before others, who knew much too much better than to show weakness—he kept reaching that strong hand deep into her chest and *grabbing* her.

Maybe he wasn't cracking her open for his advantage, but he was cracking her open nevertheless.

"It's raw," he said quickly. "It needs a few months to mature. And I need to play with it some more. But for a first draft..." He let his voice trail off.

Tristan might not be a narcissist the way her father and quite possibly her grandfather and great-grandfather had been, but he was most definitely an artist, vulnerable when he held his art out, craving praise in return.

"I'm really sorry about Fugace," she said suddenly. It just tumbled out of...who knew where. Her cracked-open chest, perhaps.

His lashes flickered, and his gaze locked on hers.

"I don't—you shouldn't have asked me to sacrifice my career for you. You really shouldn't have, Tristan. But I'm sorry I couldn't protect it the way you wanted me to, just the same."

Brown eyes held hers for the longest time. A deep breath expanded his chest and slowly released. He leaned forward suddenly and kissed her cheek. "I didn't realize I was asking you to hurt your career chances for me," he said quietly. "I didn't see it that way."

Yes. He might not be her father, but, caught up in his passions, he could absolutely, adamantly be focused on getting his own way. Passionate stubbornness and a complete lack of empathy weren't the same though.

"And this is beautiful," Malorie said of the perfume. She was still caught in the wonder of it. It was as if he had captured that moment of brightness and hope the day before, when they stood side by side gazing at those parquet floors, and put it in a bottle for them to keep. To wear on her wrists, to surround herself with on darker days, more subtle and more powerful than a photograph of it could ever have been.

Tristan pulled a folded scrap of sketch paper from his back jeans pocket and handed it to her.

She opened it. It was a list of the ingredients with their cost written in black pen, the total production cost per gram at the bottom. Entirely surrounded by curlicues and doodles in multiple bright crayon colors.

"Don't say I never did anything for you, Malorie," Tristan said, and she started to laugh and cry a little, too. Her hands lifted to her face before she remembered the open chatelaine bottle, and a little of its perfume spilled onto her wrist.

"Oops. That's going to be a bit strong," Tristan said, catching it and capping it, even as the scent surrounded them.

The hope of old time.

His hands framed her face, her laughter and her crying, and he studied her, looking entirely pleased with himself.

Malorie managed to point to one of the ingredients on his list, right by a doodle in yellow. "I'm sure the synthetic version would do just as well here, and be a lot cheaper."

Tristan's eyes narrowed. "If it would have done just as well, I would have used that."

Malorie sighed a little in relief at his exasperation, so much easier to handle than his sweetness.

His eyes narrowed just a tad further. And then he laughed suddenly. "Living in Paris and New York certainly taught you how to fight your corner, didn't it? In high school, you were mostly quiet, like this walking refuge you wouldn't let me into. But by the time I ran into you again as an adult, you had sparring skills to defend it."

"I certainly hope so," she said, with a lift of an eyebrow. New York and Paris would eat you alive, if you didn't know how to spar. "Wait...I was what?" A *refuge*?

"You helped me focus," he said. "You didn't realize that?"

Tristan had focused? She stared at him.

"*Allez*, Malorie." He looked a little frustrated. "Since we were four years old, teachers would sit me next to you because you were supposed to help keep me focused. Teachers would actually openly *say* that was what they were doing. When we were old enough that teachers stopped assigning seats, *I* would sit myself near you. And you never figured that out?"

"I didn't realize it was true," Malorie said, stunned. "I just thought—you know how teachers are. Always making it the girls' responsibility to behave well, while the boys—you—get away with murder."

"You had this space around you." Tristan shaped his hands, something supremely tactile about the way his fingers cupped around empty air, as if he wanted what he imagined to come alive, to be touchable. "That was so...quiet. Clean. I felt like a dog distracted by every single noise and scent around me and you carried with you a purity of air. I never could understand why, the older we got, the more you locked me out of it, when I needed it so much."

She couldn't even figure out what to make of that. School had been a place where she felt good, where the expectations tended to be consistent. The teachers had liked her, a quiet, disciplined, smart little girl who never caused trouble no matter how much a certain classmate tried to drag her into it, and that liking had felt safe. No teacher had ever used her reciprocal liking and respect against her, except insofar as always putting their most distractible student in the seat beside her might have been a bit of a use.

And it was true that she'd always tried to keep herself kind of...clean, yes, of the noise of other people, because she'd seen too clearly what her father's clamor of *me, me, me* did to her mother, and, well...to his daughters. She'd felt the multigenerational societal consequences for choices made by people before she was even born.

Don't let anyone else get to you, she'd always told herself. *Keep your center. Keep your focus.*

But...a purity of air? A quiet?

Tristan's tone, his words, the way he shaped that empty air with longing hands, made her sound kind of...wonderful.

"I was just trying to keep that space safe," she said, muffled. Herself safe. Free to become herself.

Tristan turned his palms up and held them out to her. Callused and strong. "It's not safe with me?"

Malorie thought she was going to strangle on her own emotion. It swelled up in her, so clogged and thick and wanting, like some sluggish, old liquid just before the clean fresh water welling behind it broke through and washed it all free. "Tristan—"

His hands did look safe. As if she could put herself right in them, and he would hold her. And never use that trust against her ever.

Even though she *knew*, right down to the bottom of toes that even now tried to grip harder to the floor in her defense, that she was better off standing on her own two feet.

The longing grew painful, so dammed up by her need for self-protection.

Tristan took her hand, set it in one of his hard palms, and cupped his other palm over it, closing it and the bottle she held in, snug and sure and warm. "What about this much?" he said gently. "Maybe this much would be safe?"

Her eyes stung *again*. He was killing her.

"As a trial," Tristan said. "If it turns out your hand is safe, maybe we can go a little further after a while. Maybe I could keep your elbow safe, too."

Her lips twisted in a smile that didn't offset the prickle in her eyes.

"Or just...this much." Tristan turned her hand over, exposing the paler skin of her inner wrist. Then stroked his top hand over it, fingers curling loosely around most of her forearm. The hardness of his palm combined with the gentleness of his touch sent shivers up her arm, curling over her shoulder, sliding down her nape, and melting all through her.

"I keep myself safe, Tristan," she said with difficulty.

"Yes, I got that, Malorie. You're queen of your own castle. But if you ever open up and let someone inside your walls, I think that person then has a responsibility to help defend those walls, too. You can't really open up walls to someone who's just coming inside them to use you or is planning on letting the enemy in while you're asleep."

Yes. Exactly. Just as you couldn't venture out in the world to seek your fortune if you couldn't manage to successfully defend yourself when fortunes went wrong.

It was perilously reassuring that Tristan understood that. The man who didn't really seem to have walls against anybody.

Oh. Oh, right. That was why he'd said he'd always wanted inside hers.

She laid her free hand on top of his suddenly, closing his in warmth, too.

His lashes lifted. Their eyes held for a long, sweet moment of clarity that seemed to grow clearer and sweeter the longer it went on.

And then his hand ran up her arm and around her nape, pulling her toward him as he leaned in. Her breath caught just before his lips touched warm and firm to hers.

The sensation that jolted through her was nothing like that vague peck in the tunnel at five. But all around her, color seemed to fragment in great glowing yellow panes, the sun shining through them, and the scent of orange blossom and dust-gleaming sunlight rose around them.

He lifted his head just enough to take a breath, his eyes searching hers once from centimeters away before his lashes fell to his cheeks and he angled his mouth over hers, his lips parting this time, exploring. A breath moved hard through his body, and his fingers flexed on her nape. It was as if he squeezed sweetness through her from that point, sweetness and arousal that had no outlet but her lips. Her hands caught his shoulders as her lips parted under that wave of sweetness, as she kissed him back.

Tristan half sat on the desk and pulled her onto it from her side, their bodies twisting into each other across its awkward barrier, his hands rubbing hard down her back to pull her in tighter and then gentling, one hand rising to cup around her head. He kissed her with wonder, and passion, and a strange and heady *comfort*. He kissed her as if they had known each other all their lives...and he'd been wanting to kiss her all that time.

God, he was good at it.

She'd known he would be. Not known in high school, when she hadn't really understood what good kissing was. But when they'd run into each other again in New York four years ago, it had been clear that he'd spent that gap from nineteen to twenty-five learning everything his body enjoyed and everything women enjoyed, too.

Tristan *liked* kissing. He liked kissing her. He took his time, shaping, exploring. Textures first. Lips brushing. Firming. Sliding and changing angles. Parting. And then tastes. Him. Taking more and more of her mouth as she gave it to him, his fingers kneading into her body, rubbing, stroking her closer.

The heat of his body. The muscles of his shoulders and chest...and arms...and abs, under her hands as those hands strayed farther and farther. That sound he made deep in his throat, that vibrated in her breasts and deep between her legs and made her ache.

Orange blossom might not mean safety to her any more. It might mean sex.

She twisted into him, fighting the awkward position to try to get closer, and knocked the letter box onto the floor.

It fell with a thump and a scatter, and she broke away from him, breathing in deep expansions of her lungs. Her lungs, her whole torso felt as if she had just been released from a corset—as if she was expanding everywhere, seeking, stretching, wanting all this new range of motion.

Her hair spilled around her shoulders. Tristan's fingers tangled in it, flexing still against her head. He stared at her, eyes dilated, those sensual, supple lips of his flushed and full.

They stared at each other, Tristan's eyes wide and almost wary, as if the world had turned upside down and neither one of them knew how to approach it from this angle.

Malorie broke free abruptly, crouching to gather the spilled papers, pausing long enough to rub her hands once hard over her face and through her hair. She felt so shaky. She felt so wide open.

Oh, crap, the old yellow envelope with the word *Rosier* written on it was visible. She flipped it over and dropped it back in the box, glancing up at Tristan.

Maybe he hadn't seen it. His eyebrows had drawn ever so slightly together, but he, too, ran a hand over his face and through his hair, looking dazed. Looking *much* more overwhelmed than she had ever imagined Tristan could be from a kiss.

Of course, he did always live on all his senses. Could easily be subjugated by them.

The idea drew her in, fascinating. So if she touched him...was it possible he might actually be even more vulnerable than she was? At least for as long as that touching lasted?

She stood slowly, setting the letter box back on the desk. Her thoughts were a disorganized tangle, as if she was a ball of yarn and Tristan had just batted her all over the room.

It was pretty, though, that yarn. All rainbow colored.

"I wasn't planning—" She took a breath and tried again. "When I came back here, I didn't mean—" Restarted. "Tristan, you're *really* complicating my homecoming."

He shrugged one shoulder, but the intensity of his eyes didn't match the carelessness of the gesture. "So why don't you stay long enough to figure all those complicated things out?"

She gave a half-laugh, frustrated and despairing. "That would probably take a *lifetime*."

If it was possible, his gaze pinned her even more intensely. "Last I checked, you had a lifetime. Why not spend it on something that matters to you?"

Arrested, she stared at him. What mattered to her. She had done what she set out to do in Paris and New York. Made it. Succeeded. Become herself.

But now that she was all *become*, was succeeding for other companies in a world full of skyscrapers and people she barely knew really what mattered to her? Mattered enough for a lifetime of it?

"You're not complicating my life, Malorie." His hand closed around her chin and pulled her toward him as he leaned in. "You're making everything feel simple." He hesitated, and his voice went absent, as if he was trying to understand it even as he said it. "As if you cleared all the other half-assed ideas off the page and left the only formula that was true."

She took a long, sweet breath, staring at him. What a beautiful thing to say. To *be*.

Tristan took a deep breath, too. Then he kissed her again, a kiss that started out firm as if it was meant to be short and then melted into something longer, deeper. He pulled her in suddenly to his body, his hands running up her back and down to her butt, driving her closer until she was pressed all against that lithe hard muscle.

He kissed her greedy. Like a thirsty man gulping water before he got dragged away from it.

A long, hot, intense kiss, while his arousal pressed harder against her, and his fingers dug more fiercely into her butt, until finally he broke apart and fell back a step, breathing hard. His hands flexed by his sides like they were still craving more texture.

Malorie pressed the back of her hand to her mouth and stared at him over it.

He closed his hands into tight fists and took a hard breath. "Still not bringing back any memories of that tunnel," he managed.

Malorie had to laugh, a tiny, choked laugh that struggled to get past all the other, bigger emotions. But it was nice, to have that little spurt of laughter in among them. It made the size of them seem less overwhelming and scary, like a ray of sunlight breaking through huge trees you were lost among.

"What did you tell me?" Tristan said abruptly.

Just now? Malorie looked at him, confused.

"When I asked you to marry me in that tunnel. What did you say?"

Malorie pressed her hand through her hair. "I don't remember."

Tristan reached behind him and gripped the doorframe. He had incredibly strong hands. Her gaze traced the tendons and muscles of his forearm and the tendons of his hand, all delineated by the tension in his arm. "I think I need to go now," he said. "I mean...unless..." His gaze went to the big desk behind her. His eyes went darker still.

Malorie folded her arms across herself and nodded rapidly. "Um-hmm. Yeah...okay."

"Right." From the looks of his grip he literally pulled himself backward through the door. Took one stop out of sight. Silence in the hall. Then he leaned back in. "Doing anything tonight?"

Malorie stared at him while a huge sense of being a snowball about to start rolling downhill grew in her. Dating? Was he going to ask her out?

"Want to come to a party?" Tristan said.

A—oh. Malorie's snowball flattened out. "A perfume party?"

"More like an important local social event."

Malorie took a breath, held it a moment, and then let it despondently out, staring at the painted toenails that peeked from her pumps. Maybe they could go back to kissing instead.

"Be a good chance to network," Tristan tempted.

Trust Tristan to think that was tempting.

"*Youpi.*" She sighed.

"*Allez*, Malorie, you've been out of the social loop around here for ten years. If you want to make a go of this place, it's a good idea to start making contacts with people."

"I never was in the social loop, Tristan."

He hesitated. "Well, you were a teenager when you left. Of course you weren't."

"*Monsards* weren't." She had been to a few of the larger perfume-related events around here—the ones so big *everybody* got invited to them. Even them. And when that happened, her grandmother made them go, determined they not lose that little bit of *entrée* into Grasse society, as if she still dreamed her granddaughters...would be able to stand on her stubbornly unbending shoulders and one day make something of this place again.

Malorie frowned a little, looking around at the high-ceilinged office, the arches that no fifties and sixties remodeling could conceal.

"Anyway, I know *you*," she said after a moment. "You're like a one-stop essence of human contact all by yourself."

At those parties where she stood awkwardly with her sisters off to the side, Tristan, even at sixteen and seventeen, had moved through talking to *everybody*. Even powerful people fifty, sixty years older than he was, he could talk to with a kind of respectful, friendly confidence. Which just went to show the social advantages of being born a prince. Meanwhile she and her sisters didn't talk to anybody at all, beyond the awkward introductions her stubborn, proud grandmother insisted on making no matter how much it cost her to do it.

And well, of course, to Tristan. Who was so sociable, he even made sure to chat with *them.*

With her. She'd always thought he was just taking pity on her, when he came to chat with her off in a corner by herself. Nice guy Tristan. Or in her more cynical moments that he needed the adoration of every single last one of the people at that party, even hers. It had never occurred to her that he just needed her ability to stand separate sometimes. Needed her.

"Well, then." Tristan extended a hand. "Don't say I never gave you anything important."

Chapter 15

"Interesting choice of a woman to bring to my birthday party," Tristan's grandfather said, with a level of dryness only he and Tante Colette could manage. Malorie and Damien both had a nice way with a dry voice, but Pépé's dryness had been *aged*. Laid out under the sun and just desiccated for nine decades.

"*I* certainly thought so," Tristan said cheerfully, grinning at his grandfather.

Pépé gave him one of his looks. Tristan just smiled. Pépé's looks weren't for the faint of heart, but somehow or other they always just made Tristan feel...loved. Like Pépé thought he could stand up to them.

"Pierre Monsard's great-granddaughter." Pépé shook his head. "Have you lost your mind? Her father was a piece of work, too. Not to mention her grandfather."

"You knew her grandfather?" Tristan searched Pépé's face quickly. *Malorie* didn't know her own grandfather. Of course, Malorie wouldn't have been born.

"Maybe." Pépé's face went its most unreadable, the man even Gestapo couldn't get an indiscreet slip out of. And he had the scars to prove they'd tried. He glanced across the outdoor crowd to Tante Colette.

The two nonagenarians practiced so much acerbic stubbornness that they could never really manage to speak to each other, kind of like the same pole of two magnets couldn't be forced together. The closer they got to each other, the stronger the repel force, but add family to the mix to keep them slightly apart, and it kept that repel force down to manageable levels.

Plus, it wasn't as if they actually had to talk to each other anymore. They both had smart phones these days.

They could text each other to coordinate strategical victories over their wayward descendants.

"Is he still alive?"

"No." Pépé's voice was clipped.

"Then why don't you tell her who it was? It's not like anyone could be hurt by it."

Pépé said nothing.

Granite. You could climb it, but you couldn't really tear it down.

Tristan frowned at him.

"I said maybe," his grandfather said. "I've never found any good to come of spreading rumors."

Yeah, when Pépé was a teenager, rumors got people killed. Rumors that some child recently moved here from Paris was really Jewish. Rumors that so-and-so had been out all night the night a German supply depot was blown up. And in the first year after the war, rumors that so-and-so had maybe managed to survive the Occupation by letting a German soldier in by the back door.

Pépé might absorb rumors, but if he released one back into the world, it was a verified fact, and you were in the need-to-know.

Tristan looked across the gathering at Malorie. She had about climbed out the passenger window of his car and thrown herself off the cliff they were edging when she realized where they were going. Then she'd muttered bitter comments the rest of the way about, *Fool me twice, shame on me,* as she slouched against the door. But once they'd arrived, she'd pulled herself together, of course—tall and cool and proud. So he'd put her with Layla and Allegra, who could make friends with cliff faces. Layla, in fact, would go down in history as the only threat to this valley his grandfather had ever smiled at. Jess had joined the three of them, possibly not realizing that Malorie was a perfumer's most-feared creature—an accountant.

Malorie laughed as he watched, and Tristan felt smug. He'd known he could count on Layla and Allegra. Plus, Layla had busked and small-gig performed her way through Europe when she was about the same age as Malorie had been when she hiked off on her own to make her fortune, so Tristan figured the two would find they had more in common than one might at first assume between a musician and an accountant.

He smiled at his wine and took a sip of it in a very counter-productive effort to cool his head. There was one way that letting Malorie assume this social event was just a perfume industry party had come back to bite him. She'd worn a silky, nearly nude sheath that would have been glamorously simple and appropriate in New York or Paris and was a bit much for a local extended family birthday party, and also for his entire body. *Merde* but that dress looked strokable.

Just all over slipping and sliding and stroking and—

A big arm draped around his shoulders. "Tristan," Matt said affectionately.

"No," Tristan said immediately, stiffening. Damien and Raoul were strolling up to join them, herding him in and blocking his view of the rest of the party, grinning as if they lived in one great, glorious world.

"Isn't life beautiful?" Matt sighed and toasted the sky.

Tristan slipped his arm around Matt's waist, leaned his head against his shoulder even though that was an awkward bend, and sighed romantically. "The sun setting. The stars coming out. *La vie est belle.*"

"Will you get off me?" Matt pushed him away, and Tristan stood free, grinning and smoothing his clothes.

When you grew up with four older cousins who loved to pin the youngest and tickle him and engage in various other demonstrations of how much bigger they were— back then at least—then you learned more methods than tests of strength to break free and control a situation.

"You boys behave," their grandfather said with no particular firmness to it. Tristan had often suspected that their grandfather would have found good behavior on their part much less interesting to observe and ultimately bad for them.

"What, you don't think it's beautiful, Pépé?" Matt asked, gesturing expansively. Get one glass of wine in him and growly Matt turned into the guy who wanted to hug everybody. Tristan gauged him to be at about half a glass now.

Pretty soon, he'd be all cuddle bunny with Layla. On cue, Layla looked across the gathering at Matt with a kind of affectionate warmth that made Tristan wish someone was looking at *him* with affectionate warmth, but Malorie just gave him a cool, you-have-messed-with-me-one-last-time look. Which, to be honest, was hot in a whole other way. Made him want to mess with her more.

"I mean, twenty-five years," Matt said. "And finally, finally Tristan gets the girl."

"That's devotion for you," Damien said mildly, twisting his glass so the wine could release its scent.

"Oh, is devotion what we're calling it?" Raoul said. "Not desperation?"

Tristan slanted him a dirty look, but he still got kind of a kick out of it when Raoul teased him. As if the oldest cousin and prodigal grandson was solidly back in the fold and no longer distrusting of his welcome.

"I was thinking it was more like incompetence," Matt said cheerfully. "I mean, how long does it take you to get a girl to pay attention to you, Tristan?"

See, this was why he never brought anyone to meet his family. Well, that and...his family was forever. You didn't want to introduce someone into your forever space too easily.

"She needed to grow up first," he said coolly.

"Or one of you did," Damien told his glass.

Talk about the injustice of *that* blow. Of course, Tristan was the youngest. If he hadn't also been an only child within the confines of his own household, he never would have gotten a respite from unjust blows.

"I seem to remember," Matt said. "I don't know— Damien, let me know if I'm confusing Tristan with someone else—but I seem to remember someone acting as if *I* was a total idiot about women. Yeah. Either of you two remember anything like that?"

"Well, in Tristan's defense, you are a total idiot about women," Raoul said. Rule of thumb among the cousins, never let the fact that you were living in a glass house prevent you from throwing stones. All that glass was going to get shattered one way or another anyway.

Matt looked indignant. "*I* grabbed my fiancée as soon as I saw her."

Yeah, and he meant that literally. "Some of us prefer not to behave like apes," Tristan said.

Mistake. All three of his cousins looked at him with a glint in their eyes.

"Okay, one of us prefers not to act like an ape." Tristan gestured to himself with his glass. "I can't speak for the rest of you."

Lethal, urbane Damien raised one eyebrow, gray-green eyes glinting. Generally speaking, people didn't associate Damien with apes. Damien had grabbed his fiancée the first time he saw her, too, pretty much, although he'd been a little more refined in the grabbing at least. Hell, so had Raoul grabbed Allegra, come to think of it.

And those women had *let* them. More or less.

They hadn't coolly sat on the male ego, every single damn time.

Tristan frowned in the direction of Malorie, currently hidden from his view by Raoul's big head. "You know, this story about my twenty-five year crush has been greatly exaggerated. I've hardly been mooning over her my whole life."

"Bravely pretending to live his life without her. Making do," Matt said sadly to his other cousins.

"Okay, that's just insulting to any other woman I've been out with. *Making do.* Come on," Tristan said. Their grandfather stood just a tiny bit removed from their group now, listening without looking at them, his lips compressed into that aged hint of a smile as he watched the extended family chatting and laughing before him.

"Hiding his fragile heart," Raoul said solemnly as if Tristan hadn't spoken. Tristan glanced at him suddenly, feeling as if Raoul had touched far too close to something that was almost...true. Raoul's amber wolf eyes met his in surprise, and then a flicker of thoughtfulness passed across his face.

"Probably desperately hoping his cousins would watch his back," Matt said.

"Fight for him," Damien agreed.

"Help him out," Raoul said.

All the hairs on the back of Tristan's neck rose. "Oh, no," he said. "No, no, no, no, no. I definitely wasn't hoping that."

"He's the youngest," Damien said, looking to Raoul. "I mean, we're supposed to watch out for him, right? That's what the moms always said."

"I like that," Tristan said indignantly. "I'm the one who always looks after all of *you.*" Made sure they functioned together, that none of their fights ever got so serious they couldn't come back from them, that none of his cousins ever got so drowned in a well of their own emotions he couldn't reach down a hand and haul them back up and make them laugh at themselves and see more clearly.

And no one even noticed.

"*Ingrats,*" he said darkly.

"Yes, that's why I feel so obligated," Damien said. "I owe you."

Merde. Tristan scrambled through his memories, trying to think what he might have done.

"A lot," Damien said.

You know, sometimes it would be helpful to have a grandfather who actually *did* make the older cousins behave, instead of standing over there to the side looking as if he'd be laughing if that wouldn't betray his dignity.

"Forget it," Tristan said. "I did it out of the goodness of my heart. You don't owe me anything."

"He doesn't think we have hearts," Matt said sadly, deeply wounded.

"We don't," Raoul pointed out.

What was Damien holding against him anyway? Tristan was probably the reason he and Jess were together. Using humor to plant sense on one side and the other, getting his aunt to bring out old photos to show Jess Damien's soft sid—oh, yeah.

His cousins parted, revealing Malorie and the gathering of women again. Tristan's mom was just reaching them with a big photo album in hand.

Ha.

Was that all they had?

"You damn jerks," Tristan said agreeably, just to give them the impression they had succeeded. Had he put enough heat into that? He didn't want them so disappointed that they tried to come up with some *other* way to drive him crazy.

Matt, Damien, and Raoul exchanged faint, smug smiles.

Tristan raised an eyebrow. "Glad to see you three are accepting your colorful past so well these days."

If anything, the three of them looked smugger.

Seriously? They really thought this would get to him? Tristan sighed. "You do know Malorie and I were in school together when we were four, right? One time the teacher even let me play with finger paint." And play he had—he'd covered his face and arms and clothes with all the colors of the rainbow, then cupped his hands to Malorie's cheeks to give her rainbow splotches, too.

He was pretty sure she'd liked it back then. In the picture his teacher had given his mom, they were both laughing.

His cousins exchanged slightly discomfited glances. As if they'd forgotten that part.

Tristan took a smug sip of his wine.

Across the way, over there under the blooming almond trees, his mother gave a shriek.

Tristan's eyebrows shot up. His brisk, competent, *I've-got-everything-but-my-son-under-control* mother did not shriek.

She used to, once in a while. Like that time he'd covered a whole wall in their home with more "finger paints" he'd found in a shed and that, it turned out, were regular adult paint and not washable, or that time he'd left a snake on her pillow as a present to surprise her when she woke up. She'd screamed pretty loud for that one.

But after twenty-nine years of that kind of thing, plus her share of handling whatever trouble the five of them got into together, she was pretty hard to get a shriek out of.

Now Damien's mother, Tata Véro, was looking over his own mother's shoulder at the album, and uproar was ensuing.

"Okay, what did you do?" Tristan set his glass on the nearest table and jogged across.

Malorie was laughing by the time he got there. That was probably a good sign. But all the other women were glaring at Matt, Damien, and Raoul as if they'd just massacred a herd of kittens. He got the photo album away from them.

It *was* the alien photo, exactly as he'd suspected.

Edited.

So that Tristan stood naked all by himself, entirely covered in paint, while his cousins had been digitally cut from a formal wedding line-up of the five of them and pasted behind him, all in their little tuxes looking long-suffering while Tristan grinned in purple paint, arms raised up with a wooden spear in his hand. (Alien technology having apparently been focused more on developing space travel than a weapons system.)

"Hey!" He turned on his cousins, outraged. He loved that alien photo. It spoke to everything happy about their childhood, before things started to break apart and he developed that sense that he had to learn a strong and supple grip to keep them all together. "What did you do with it?"

A flood of indignant female exclamations overwhelmed his, Tata Véro, Layla, Allegra, and Jess all landing on Matt, Damien, and Raoul until pretty soon those three were swearing on their lives they hadn't destroyed the original and humbly apologizing for having ever tampered with the sacred albums.

Tristan relaxed and glanced at Malorie, a little space of quiet now cleared around them.

She raised one eyebrow at him, but there was laughter in her eyes. "Do you *ever* get in trouble?"

"Hey, I didn't do this one! Why should I be getting in trouble?"

She grinned at him, her eyes alive with humor. Oh, wow, that was a *great* look on her. It got right down into his middle and warmed him from the inside out. She tapped the photo. "You haven't changed a bit, have you?"

Tristan considered the image of him naked and covered in purple a moment. "My dick's bigger."

Malorie burst out laughing. She laughed so hard she nearly choked and Tristan had to put his arm around her to help support her, while she buried her head in his shoulder and laughed and laughed.

The women re-converged on Malorie with phones out to show her the *real* photo, so that Matt, Damien, and Raoul had to suffer through her seeing them naked and covered in colors, too. The three of them squirmed. Some people were *so* insecure about their masculinity.

His arm around Malorie, his cousins writhing in embarrassment, Tristan grinned in triumph, all right with his world.

Chapter 16

"Plotting your takeover?" an old, dry voice said from a little behind and to Malorie's left, and her hand tightened around her wrist behind her back. She'd stepped away from the gathering to stand at the edge of the fields, gazing out across them and up at the hills. And she knew without looking exactly who had come up beside her.

"Of this valley?" she said dismissively. "I'm not sure the money in this industry is in agriculture." She refused to indulge Monsieur Rosier in a belief that she was jealous of what the Rosiers had.

Even if she was.

Oh, not of the land, per se, although there was a sense of peace and security in this valley that filled her with wistfulness. But of that *happiness* in Tristan's family. That solidarity. Hell, the worst his cousins could think to do to him was edit a photo of him standing in his full Tristan glory—naked to the world around him and thrilled to be in contact with it with every bit of his skin, and colored in purple paint to celebrate. They weren't hurting him with that, they were showing him off.

She'd never seen so much love in one place anywhere as in this family, and they didn't even *know*. They took it for granted. They probably doubted it sometimes and wondered if their family really loved them, like idiot teenagers.

Well, except...maybe Tristan didn't take it for granted. She had a sense that Tristan nurtured it and grew it, tending to his family happiness as if he was its gardener and he liked the sweet scent when it bloomed its fullest.

Oh. And Damien went out and fought the corporate world for it, and Matt growled and tried to hold together the heart of it, this valley, and the old man beside her paced the family territory and still to this day fought all comers. Maybe they didn't take it for granted. That just made what her own family had become hurt worse.

"You sound like your great-grandfather," Jean-Jacques Rosier said, and her nails flinched into her wrist. "He never cared about the land either." Except in French, the word he used for land, *le pays*, also meant the country.

Malorie tightened her jaw. Kept her shoulders straight. Said nothing, because what could she say?

"And I'm not sure there was anything your father cared about. Besides himself."

True enough. Malorie's eyes burned. *"Bon anniversaire, monsieur,"* she said flatly, as respectful a slap back as she could possibly make. She'd told him happy birthday twice already—when Tristan introduced her and over the dinner table when they sang it. But it still made her point—*I'm just trying to honor your day. Leave me alone.*

"I suppose it makes sense you would go for someone like Tristan," Jean-Jacques Rosier said. "A charmer just like your father."

Malorie's head whipped around in pure shock. "Tristan is *nothing* like my father!"

Oh, Tristan would be so *hurt* if he knew about this conversation. He adored his grandfather.

Malorie, on the other hand, thought he was a ninety-one-year-old bastard. She glared at him.

Monsieur Rosier just raised white eyebrows faintly, studying her. "You don't think so?"

"They're as different as two people can be!" Malorie snapped, fed up with trying to be respectful to Tristan's arrogant elders. Okay, fine, they'd saved the world. Maybe resting on those laurels for the last seventy years had stagnated their brains.

"How do you figure that?" Monsieur Rosier said, as if the matter was of academic interest only.

"How do I *figure*?" Malorie threw up her hands. "He *cares* about people, that's the big difference. He tries to charm them into doing what's best for them, not what's best for *him*."

"Trust me." Jean-Jacques looked ever so faintly amused. "Tristan is very effective at getting his own way."

Malorie gestured even harder. "*This* is his way. Happy family, everyone together and laughing. Oh, why do I even bother with you people. You're utter idiots." She dropped her hands back to her sides, found no pockets to shove them into in this silky dress, and gripped them again behind her, glaring out at the fields.

"I'm an idiot?" the old war hero said mildly.

Malorie slanted him a glance and very, very carefully made sure she didn't let herself answer that one.

"You think you're more perceptive about my own grandson than I am, do you?"

Malorie flung up a hand again. "He's got *all this*." She gestured to the valley, to the happy family gathering. "And what does he do? He tries to bottle it, to share it with the whole world, so they can have it, too. And when he likes someone specially he...he...he tries to capture some beautiful thing that person loves, some moment, something important, and hold it for them in a bottle so they can always have it." That warm dust-in-light perfume, that wish that time could wake up and all its old promise come true. He'd made that for her. She snuck a glance at the difficult war hero. "Has he ever done that for you?"

Jean-Jacques Rosier looked out across the fields. "Yes," he said, so quietly that Malorie's irritation grew quiet, too. She wondered how many scents had filled that man's life and how many, by now, carried loss in their fragrance.

He'd lost his wife. He'd lost a son. He'd had two other sons go to far countries after their own losses and rarely come back. Most of his lifelong friends were gone by now, and one of his grandsons still fought in the Foreign Legion.

"Excuse me, sir," she said, and bent her head. "I didn't mean to be rude."

Monsieur Rosier studied her thoughtfully. She made herself lift her head and meet his eyes.

"You've got your grandmother's bones," he said after a moment. Since she didn't look that much like her grandmother, she thought he meant something other than literal bone structure.

"Good," she said firmly, making sure he knew she would *not* stand for any aspersions on her grandmother. "She had strong bones."

The old man smiled very faintly, as if all those wrinkles on his face were time-scars that didn't let his face stretch into a full laugh anymore. "That's what I just said."

***

Tristan eyed his grandfather sidelong as the old man came to stand beside him while he opened three fresh bottles of wine out of the *cave*. People liked to plan to live long in his family. They laid choice harvests down and set them by for birthdays ten years in advance. In the belief that if worse came to worst and they weren't there to drink them, the rest of the family would drink them in their honor.

So far, they had not yet had to drink his grandfather's bottles in his honor without being able to hand him a glass of his own.

Tristan handed his grandfather a glass. "It's the 2006."

His grandfather cupped the glass and turned it to let the wine stir, took a breath of it just the way he'd taught his grandons to do, his eyes closing a moment, and then tasted it. "It aged well," he said, satisfied.

Tristan glanced across at Malorie, who was now talking to Léa and Daniel. Having helped run a restaurant and served as its hostess since she was a teenager, Léa was very good at putting almost anyone at ease and making them feel welcome. Tristan was, too, but he liked letting his family do it here—letting Malorie's welcome expand more and more, so that she realized she could be welcomed here in Grasse by more people than just him.

Malorie valued independence. Had a deep-rooted need to prove to herself that she didn't need anyone but herself. So he figured it was a long-term game. Instead of helping her deal with his family, which would make her feel as if she needed that help and therefore trigger her profound rejection of any possibility of *needing* someone, he would let her handle this party mostly on her own. Once she proved to herself she could do it, she wouldn't brace against the fear that she needed him anymore, and the next party, he'd get to hang out with her more and wrap his arm around that silky, maddening dress that kept sliding over her hips every time she moved. Once she'd proven she could stand on her own and didn't need him, she'd relax more and just enjoy his company.

He hoped.

"Did you try to scare her off?" he said.

"Yes," his grandfather answered imperturbably.

Tristan smiled just a little and tried the wine himself. His grandfather was right—it had aged well. Some vintages were like that. They needed time to grow. They were fuller and richer if you waited and came back to them later. "And how'd that work out for you?"

His grandfather smiled very faintly, that little compression of his lips that was like being brushed by the sun. "She'll do."

Chapter 17

"The purple paint doesn't faze you?" a woman's voice asked wryly, and Malorie looked around to see a chic, competent, dark-haired woman stop beside her. Tristan's mom. Malorie might once have stood off to the side awkwardly at Grasse parties, but at *this* party, any moment by herself seemed to be an open invitation to every single one of Tristan's family members to isolate her and interrogate her. She couldn't even make a trip to the bathroom without someone seizing the opportunity.

You'd think the man had never brought a woman home before.

"At least he didn't pour the paint all over me, too, that time," she said, amused. "You forget, we went to school together."

Annick Rosier shot her a quick, searching glance. "Oh, *you're* the girl who—" She broke off. "*Malorie*," she repeated. "That Malorie. Of course you are. No wonder he never told me your last name back then."

Malorie looked away across the fields.

Annick winced. "I mean—" She brushed the faux pas away briskly, her wedding ring glinting on her hand in the lights strung through the trees, and fell silent for a moment. Her expression softened, reminiscent. "He had *such* a crush on you back then," she said fondly, turning to spot her son's head, where he was filling his grandfather's wine glass.

Malorie folded her arms, not so much to defend herself but to keep the fuddled, happy feeling in her middle nice and warm. Like it was a newborn kitten.

"And now he's finally got you to go out with him." Annick gave a low laugh of pure maternal wonder. "There's persistent, and then there's Tristan. He smiles at you like he's the most laid-back person in the world, and underneath he doesn't let go of what he wants *ever*. If he mentions he'd like to hike all the way to Grasse, you'd better *not* blink just because he looks as if he's happily distracted onto other toys."

As far as Malorie could tell, Tristan had been distracted onto *plenty* of other toys. Not that he treated other women like toys exactly, or not any more so than they did him, but still. Malorie gave his mother a dry look. "No offense, but Tristan has hardly been brooding over me all his adult life."

"Well, he's very…physical," his mother said, flushing slightly and looking up at the stars as if asking them why she was having to discuss her son's sexuality with anyone.

Hey, you started it, Malorie thought. *What, I wasn't supposed to fight my corner?*

Annick hesitated, searching for words. "You know how his cousins are all like emotional bears tumbling blindfolded over a cliff?"

Malorie didn't know that, but she snorted at the image. Particularly in regards to elegant, lethal, controlled Damien, it was one to be cherished.

"Tristan's not like that. He…roots. He likes everybody, but the people he *loves*…he's grown that love for them for a really long time. It's very…stubborn." Annick flexed her fingers in the air, as if that stubbornness was so strong it had a texture. Then she spread her arms up high above her head like the arms of a spreading tree, making Malorie savor how much more vibrant conversations were on this side of the Atlantic, where people spoke like their bodies were part of the conversation. "And it's very big." Annick's fingers spread at the uppermost limits of their stretch, a star shining just at the edge of her wedding ring like a diamond.

Malorie turned to look at Tristan, who was grinning at his cousin, dramatic, expansive chef Gabe Delange.

Now she couldn't identify the emotion surging in her middle. Inside it, at its heart, there was still that fuddly golden warmth, like a dream curled up tiny and purring. But that gold nestled in the heart of something as rushing and enormous and scary as that hurricane that had hit New York.

"I think you probably shouldn't give yourself ideas," she said carefully to Tristan's mother.

Annick gave her an odd look. "You do remember he's my son, right? I know him pretty well."

Malorie held a fair degree of skepticism about parents, but she inclined her head politely.

"I wasn't giving myself ideas," Annick said. "I was giving you a few."

Malorie met her eyes. The older woman's were searching and, underneath, wary. As if she thought Malorie could hurt her son.

Malorie frowned a little, automatically seeking Tristan's dark head. She had at various times in her life wanted to strangle him, break a perfume bottle over his head, or throw him out a skyscraper. But she'd never wanted to *hurt* him.

It had never occurred to her that she could.

Annick was overprotective that was all. Maternal instinct. Malorie tried a reassuring smile. "Tristan's not as vulnerable as you think."

Annick looked worried.

"Trust me," Malorie said dryly, "where Tristan and women are concerned, there are always plenty more fish in the sea."

Now Annick looked exasperated. "No, there aren't. There are plenty of women Tristan can have *sex* with." His mom was annoyed enough she even said it without wincing. "But there *aren't* plenty of women he can fall in love with. He doesn't know how to do that—change, let go. I know he seems very distractible on the surface. But emotionally he's very constant. I just told you."

Malorie was silent, not sure what to respond. Not even sure what to think. She felt as if Tristan's mother had just given her one universe-size idea to chew on.

"He's not really distractible," she said after a moment. "You're thinking of what his teachers said. He can't sit *still*, I agree about that. But it's more because his focus is too big. He focuses on *everything*. Now that he can work in the way that suits him, it's almost like he is himself a distillery. He pulls everything about the world into him and then gives the essence of it back out."

Annick's face softened into a smile. Her gaze lingered on Malorie, thoughtful. Assessing.

Malorie looked back across the party, not sure what to do about that gaze except to let Annick assess. It seemed a reasonable thing to want to do before you let someone closer to what mattered to you.

Across the way, under the great plane tree, Tristan joked with his cousins and fragrance chemist father, an interestingly geeky older version of Tristan with gray wings in his hair and glasses. A little kid was trying to climb up Tristan's pants, and without missing a beat in his conversation, he picked the girl up automatically and set her feet on his shoulders, bracing her so that she could stand on them and proudly wave.

"Did he drive you crazy in school?" his mother asked quietly. "When he was little I mean. I know he got in a lot of...trouble."

Malorie heard the faint note of anxiety, even all these years later, of a mother who had not known how to help her son. He'd had to figure out how to help himself. But that one was an easy one to reassure her about.

"He was fun," Malorie said. All those spilled crayons and finger paints. As she watched, he flipped the little girl forward over his head and down in front of his chest, holding her with strong, sure hands and grinning at her before he set her down on her feet and ruffled her hair. "He was the life of the place," she said softly.

***

"Don't tell me," Tristan said a little while later, putting his arm around his mother's waist as she came up to him and hugging her to his side. "She'll do."

"Maybe," his mother said. "She might."

Tristan gave his mother a rueful look.

His mother held up her hands. "I'm still judging."

He laughed and kissed her head. "Right, Maman."

Little Lexie Delange had stopped in front of Malorie under the almond trees and was gazing at her solemnly. Malorie squatted down in front of her, her knees tight together in her little sheath as it pulled up her thighs and made Tristan's head go blurry hot. He took a slow breath, focusing on Malorie's face like women were always trying to get men to do. Her manner was a little over-careful, as if she hadn't been around many kids but was respectful enough of a little girl to give her attention just the same. Lexie handed Malorie a broken twig with a few white almond blooms still clinging to it. Malorie's face softened into pleasure.

Four-year-olds had such an unfair advantage, when it came to charming women.

"I wonder who vets for Malorie," Tristan said suddenly. "Makes sure the man who's interested in her is worthy of *her.*"

His mother raised a maternal eyebrow—clearly Malorie would be damn lucky to get him, in her mind.

"I guess that's why she has to do such a careful job of it," he realized. The same reason she fought her own corner. If she let her guard down to the wrong person, then she thought no one in this world would help defend her when that wrong person tried to strike her down.

He would defend her, but...it was really hard for her to understand that. It had taken him a long time to start to guess how hard, and now it wrenched at his heart.

"Her father was a piece of work," his mother said suddenly.

Tristan slid a glance at her. "You knew him?"

"We went to school together, too. All charm and no heart. The kind of guy who'd talk a girl into making out with him and then ruin her reputation with the rest of the school just so he could brag about it."

Tristan grimaced. And wondered what it was like to grow up with a man like that for a father, a man whose ego was infinitely more precious to him than another person's well-being.

"She seems very different from both her parents," his mom said. "Tougher than her mother. I guess that makes sense, that she'd want to be tougher."

Tristan was pretty sure that Malorie wanted to be tougher than at least three generations of her family, even perhaps tougher than her grandmother, the woman who had also had to be tough enough to stand alone.

"I'd like to see her in finger paints," his mom said musingly. "See if the tough woman looks like that little girl in that old photo when you make her laugh."

"She gave me crayons," Tristan said, and flushed, even though of all people he should be able to talk about something intimate with his mom.

"*Did* she?" His mother smiled, watching Malorie tuck the almond blossoms into her hair and pull the orange blossom out to give Lexie instead. "You know, *mon chéri*...I think she likes you." And after a moment, "*You*, I mean. Not that idiot sexy hot shot thing you like to do."

Oh, hell, not that lecture again. Some people's moms still asked their adult sons if they'd washed their ears. Tristan's liked to double-check on a regular basis that he was using condoms. With a slight disapproving moue as if he shouldn't be needing to use them so often in the first place. It was freaking embarrassing. "*Maman.*"

His mom shrugged. "But if you'll take my advice, *ma puce*—"

"Always," Tristan said immediately. "Maman, do *not* start about the cond—"

"—you'll let her know about those shares."

Okay, talk about a non sequitur. "It's a surprise,"
Tristan said. Remind him never to organize a surprise
birthday party for anyone in his family. They *clearly* did
not get the concept. "I'm waiting for the right moment."

Chapter 18

In her dreams, a thumb stroked Malorie's hair back from where it had caught in her eyelashes and tucked it with the rest of her hair. *Sweet.* She smiled as the thumb drifted back along her cheek and turned her head just enough to kiss it. It stilled at the kiss, then stroked the shape of her lips. So sweet. She kissed it again, blinking slowly awake, her cheek pressed against the leather passenger seat.

Tristan's face close to hers, long, black eyelashes shielding his eyes as he gazed at his thumb on her lips.

Tristan. Of course. She smiled at him and kissed his thumb one more time.

His eyelashes lifted and his eyes caught hers. Close and brown and magic.

"Malorie." His voice was husky. His hand sank into her hair, cradling her head. He lowered his head.

His lips were firm and warm and gentle, too, parting hers, and—

"Wait, you're real?" She jerked back, startled.

"Now that's an interesting comment," Tristan said softly, lifting his head just enough to look at her. "What does that mean, exactly? Do I kiss you sometimes in your dreams?"

Malorie flushed.

Warm brown eyes widened. "*Do* I?" His fingers kneaded into her nape. "Now how long have I been doing that?"

Ten years at least. She could remember tucking herself into fantasies of Tristan those early, terribly lonely days in Paris and then again after the move to New York. He'd be there the most when loneliness was toughest or she'd had a bad day, and even after a happy, busy day that had finished with a late night dancing with friends, she still sometimes liked to cuddle up into the thought of him as she dozed off. She'd gotten into the habit.

She tried to give him a dirty look, but their faces were so close the look couldn't get up much power. "The man in my dreams knows far better than to trick me into going to a Rosier family party. Your *grandfather's birthday.*"

Tristan smiled just a little. "Oh, yeah, I bet in your dreams I do exactly what you want me to. In real life I'm a lot more fun."

He kissed her again right on her mouth as she started to argue, sinking in, luxurious and hungry. Far more demanding than any cozy dream.

Malorie's whole body clenched and then released in one long wave of pleasure, her fingers kneading into his shoulders. "Jerk," she managed.

Tristan laughed and nipped her lip. His lips slid to her ear. "Pépé liked you," he whispered. "I told you he would."

That made Malorie's throat tighten. "He said I had my grandmother's bones."

"He must have had a lot of respect for your grandmother, then."

Her throat ached more. Tristan just *gave* her things, so easily—these words that strengthened her, that made her feel as if she was someone good. Still on some level it scared her, because her father had done that, too— made a person feel wonderful about herself, all because of him, and then, once she lived for that admiration, used it against her as a weapon.

But that's not Tristan. That's never been Tristan.

"It's too bad your grandfather never told her that," Malorie said low. "Rosier respect could have made a big difference to her life."

"Your great-grandfather hurt him and Tante Colette pretty badly," Tristan said gently. "And Pépé was only about ten years older than your grandmother. You have

191

to remember that right after the war, he was barely out of his teens. He was a hero of the Resistance not because he always made the right decisions but because he made decisions at all. He acted. He tried."

Yeah. She didn't want to blame Jean-Jacques Rosier or anyone else for all the old wounds in this country. *Let's let that blame go. Let's bring out the good again, let its dust sparkle in the light, the old Art Nouveau gleam from before the war ever was.*

"Malorie." Tristan loosed her clasped hair and twirled the almond twig that fell free between his fingers. "What is this place? There's this hint of orange blossom coming over the walls, and...you know damn well if you don't show me, I'm going to climb the walls on my own to see what's inside."

She'd given him her grandmother's address to pick her up, but she'd met him outside the gate then. He'd gazed at the walls a moment with his eyes narrowed, his head slightly tilted, but then he'd looked at her in her dress and seemed to forget pretty much everything else.

"You wouldn't call the police on me if I did, would you?" Tristan said.

No. Which he knew damn well. Malorie rolled her eyes. "There you go again, getting away with murder just because people like you too much to punish you for it."

He smiled, running his thumb over her cheek to tug at her lips. "So you like me a little bit, Malorie?"

"Well." She managed a shrug. "We've been friends since grade school."

His smile split into something wider, rich and warm. "Or we've been something." His thumb ran over her upper lip and then traced down, down her seatbelt, following its path over breast and hip, to release it.

He kissed her once again, quickly, and got out of the car. She barely remembered to pull her act together enough to get out herself before he made it around to open her door for her. He still managed to be there in time to hold a hand out to her as she straightened from the low seat.

"You know I can get out of a car by myself," she told him. Even though that callused strength felt wonderful around her own strength.

"I suspected," Tristan said, amused. "But if you thought I was going to miss an opportunity to watch that skirt ride up your thighs while you got out of the seat, you don't know me nearly as well as you think."

She had to laugh a little, shaking her head. And a little heat ran up her thighs and clenched between them. "Just so you know I can take care of myself. I hiked through the Alps on my own. I made my way to Paris from them on my own. I found a place to live, and went to school, and got a job, and made my way to New York...all on my own. I opened every single door I needed open...for myself."

I don't need anyone. I do not depend on you.

Tristan just looked at her for a long moment. His face had gone stern, such an unusual expression for him that it had a visceral impact. "Do you know I went by your house, a few days after the bac? And your mom said you were hiking with friends through the Alps. I stopped by a couple weeks later, but she said, 'Oh, she's still hiking.' *I thought you were with a group of friends still.* Later it was, 'Oh, she's going to school in Paris now.' I thought she and your older sisters had helped you get there, get set up, find a place to stay. I didn't realize you'd done all that on your own until it was far too late to, to...make sure you were okay."

"Why did you stop by?" she said, confused.

A very dangerous look. "Why the hell do you think, Malorie? I couldn't see you in school anymore, so even though you never gave me the slightest sign of encouragement, I was going to go ahead and take the risk of asking you out. I kind of had...visions for that summer, actually." His tone was dark, and he opened a hand as if letting something drop and then pushed that dropped thing away. "That was all a long time ago, and it's gone now, but to be honest, if I'd known you were hiking and hitchhiking by yourself through France, I would probably have tried to find you. To make sure you were okay. So I could sleep at night."

"But your cousin could go off and join the Foreign Legion after *his* bac. And that was okay," Malorie said dryly.

Dark look. "No, it wasn't okay, actually. But he was a ma—" Tristan broke off, too late. *A man.*

"Sexist much, Tristan?" She pushed vines aside from the lock again and slid the key in.

Tristan's mouth set stubbornly. He said nothing.

Let five men grow up together under Jean-Jacques Rosier's tutelage and you could *never* cure them of their patriarchal worldview. Hell, the family still had an *actual patriarch.* Tristan could act as laid-back and amused about life as he liked, but his core showed, over and over.

And she was not jealous at all of that solid male strength at the center of their family when her own family's patriarch had crumbled in a storm like a rotten tree.

She sighed and rested her head on the ivy covering the door into the orchard. And fantasized that he stroked his hand over her bent neck and sent shivers of reassurance and pleasure down her spine. Damn. Even *imagining* it sent shivers of pleasure down her spine.

It was exceptionally dangerous to her emotional health and well-being to let him into her grandmother's orchard.

But he would love it so much. She could see his face now, as he walked through the orchard in the moonlight and all those scents rushed to kiss him.

Like the eager women at every party he went to, she thought wryly.

He put himself in danger, too, didn't he? Every single time he made a perfume. All the life he could absorb distilled into a gift for everyone else. That they might honor, or that they might spit on.

She sighed again, very softly, and turned her head, the ivy tickling her face. "Do you want to come in, Tristan?"

His stubborn expression flickered. "Isn't that what I just said?" He blinked at her, his eyes growing searching in the dimness, and then took a step toward her. "You mean—is that an invitation?"

"I think I have something that will make you very happy," she said quietly.

Those supple black eyebrows of his drew together. He searched her face again, his expression incomprehensible. "Wow." His voice was barely audible, but he looked kind of stunned. "And you're only just now realizing that?"

She didn't understand what he meant, so she didn't try. She opened the door. Tristan clicked his keys, and the car lights died.

She let him in.

Chapter 19

The scent that had been teasing at Tristan, as elusive as Malorie, ever since he stepped out of the car, just rushed right at him and wrapped him in its silk. He took a step forward, surrounded by weddings and innocence and sensuality, dresses and flowers in a bride's hair and sweet hope in her eyes, and promise. It fell on him, like a village dance in simpler times, petals tossing through the air.

He breathed it in, blinking, focusing on what was actually there.

Trees whose white flowers tempted in the moonlight, against the dark gloss of their leaves.

His heart stopped.

His lungs expanded. He stretched out his arms as far as they could go, spreading his hands, as if the scent caressed the web between each finger. Tickled in under his fingernails. Stirred the follicles of hair all over his body. Reached everything about him.

"You have a bitter orange orchard," he breathed. "*That's* where you picked up that scent."

He walked forward, reaching up to the first tree, his fingers trailing over bark and glossy leaves. He grabbed two branches and pulled himself up into them. Into that scent, into the moonlight.

The orchard stretched around him, quiet night. Lights glittered in the distance, and a few bobbed gently on the sea, but here, this space of terraces was a refuge from that world.

He cupped a blossom and buried his face in it, a scent swirling with textures—the silk of a bed, a woman's skin, a hope of a future. The bark of the tree, the softness of the petals, the gloss of the leaves. Even the moonlight seemed to have a texture now, tingling over his skin.

He was pulling in too much. He was growing giddy with it.

He looked down for Malorie, like looking for an anchor.

She stood with her hand resting on another tree, smiling just a little as she watched him. She blinked when he met her gaze and turned away immediately, walking a little way through the grove of trees, trailing the fingers of her free hand through the low-hanging leaves and flowers. Cloths had been stretched under the cleared trees, a scattering of flowers fallen on them. He wanted to help with the harvest. He found all harvests of flowers irresistible, but this one, in Malorie's secret garden with the far view of the sea...it would be his idea of heaven.

He picked a flower from his tree and dropped back down to her, very conscious, with all the sensations pouring in, of the sensations *inside* him—the athleticism of his own body, how lithe and strong and full of life it was. It was good to have his body. It was good to have his senses, gorging on the pleasures all around him. It was good to be alive.

"Malorie."

White flowers against night-dark leaves formed her backdrop and, farther away, seen between the slope of trees, the sea.

"This is wonderful. Thank you." He stroked her dark hair back from her temple, just as he had in the car, and tucked the flower in her hair to replace the one she had given little Lexie and the almond blossoms that had long ago fallen free.

Perfect.

Well. One thing would make it more perfect. He bent and breathed in the scent of them together, the orange blossoms and her hair.

Mmmm. Now that was perfect.

"My grandmother willed it to the three of us," she murmured and gave a little shiver of a grief too recent.

197

"It was where we came after school. She would pick us up and..." Her voice fell away as she swallowed.

He pulled her in against him, wrapping his arms around her. "I'm sorry, Malorie." What else was there to say? He stroked her hair, in lieu of words.

"You'll make me cry, Tristan," she said, very muffled.

"You can if you want. I'll just stay right here until you've done as much as you need, okay?"

He didn't know if that was the right thing to say, because all the tears in her just welled up out of her eyes that fast, and she pressed her face into his chest and started to shake with them.

Her family was so damn...shattered. Everyone gone off to their end of the world, as if family had no holding power left for them anymore. Had she had no one to grieve with at the time? Or was this moment just one of those waves of grief that came back, like the wistfulness that still hit him sometimes for his own grandmother at the almond scent of Christmas? Like the way he sometimes still missed Lucien, when the wild herb scent of the hills hit him too hard, and cursed him for joining the Foreign Legion.

"I loved it here," she said. "With her somewhere around and me and my sisters playing in the orchard or coming inside to help slice up strawberries for our dessert or whatever she asked us to help with."

Of course. Who wouldn't love it here? What a perfect secret place in the midst of the eager, glittery world that sloped to the coast.

"And now there's no one left."

Tristan had had nightmares about that, when his older cousins first ran off on him. He'd imagined all of them leaving what mattered most to him in the world—family—one by one, until out of all that beautiful, wild pack of joy they'd been as kids, he was the only one left. The shock of Lucien and Raoul's departures had layered itself over his own complexes, as the youngest who had often had to fight not to be left behind by the older boys when they were little. But Matt and Damien, maybe partly in reaction to Raoul and Lucien's departures, had held firm. And he had held firm. They were family. The country here was their country. *J'y suis, j'y reste.*

I am here and here I'll stay.

Poor Malorie. He hugged her closer.

"I think I broke us," she whispered. "Angèle and Lise were still at university here. But when I started that hike...I just felt so clean, away from Grasse. I felt like I could be me. I didn't have to be part of an old, decaying pattern. I could be something new and strong. But it was like I was the first hole in the dam or something. Then Angèle finished her degrees and left, and Lise finished hers and left. And Maman had only been holding on until we were grown—talk about someone who wanted to get away from everything Monsard meant and be her own person again. We all left. And then there was only my grandmother. Can you imagine how sad that must have been for her?"

It made his chest tight to think about it, the small, quiet, and stubbornly proud old woman keeping her store, selling those soaps, while all her grandchildren left her. How many tourists who stopped him on the street to ask him to take pictures of them had he sent into that store, just so the old woman would have company?

"She tried so hard to keep us together. Do you think it was easy for her, to hold her head up with her father's shame on it and the way people must have treated her, after she got pregnant? But she did it. She stayed. She stuck with it. And all for what?"

"For this, I think," he said quietly, gesturing to the secret grove of orange blossom around them. "To give you this as children."

Because wasn't that vital? The safe, magic spaces you had as a child, even if you grew up and left them behind. It must have been the only thing her grandmother knew to do—fight to preserve their heritage, no matter what. She wouldn't have thought to cross seas and start over, the way Malorie and her sisters had.

Malorie was silent for a moment. "Well, I want to give *my* children something," she said fiercely into his chest. "I want to give *my* family something. I don't want it to be only about me. I've done that too long already."

He tightened his arms around her, on a surge of emotion he didn't know how to name. He just lov— admired her so much.

She pressed her face into his chest, crying again.

He ran his fingers through her hair, caught the orange blossom as he knocked it loose, restored it to its place, and just waited it out.

***

Hot, strong, muscled chest.

Cradled.

Warm.

You're not a kitten, Malorie.

But that was Tristan, rescuing her just the same.

Grief twisted her like two hands on a wet rag, wringing all the water out of her, and then relaxed slowly, into that comfort he offered.

If Tristan's family was all patriarchal, her grandmother had been her family's matriarch. Quieter, more subdued, more withdrawn from a world where the shame from her father had had such a direct and devastating impact on her own life possibilities, but there for them, just the same. Malorie had never even realized how much she took her grandmother for granted. And now the hole she had left could never be filled.

Tristan's hand on her back was strong and easy, rubbing through her hair. His scent was subtle, probably something he had designed himself. Warmth and wickedness and something indefinable, impossible to catch.

Of course. That was Tristan all over. She was surprised he didn't smell amused, too.

The scent of orange blossom and night wrapped around both of them, a great, caressing promise. A cool, crisp spring midnight and a warm hold. Tristan's heart beating under her hand.

She hadn't known that grief and consolation could be sensual, and as soon as she noticed that sensuality, it uncurled. Flourishing where grief had made room for other emotions. Her fingers kneaded once into his chest, to savor his heartbeat. His strength. His heat.

That heartbeat picked up, just a little. A hint of heat came into his scent. His fingertips flexed into her back, adding a gentle new texture to his rubbing that rippled pleasure down her spine.

Her breasts pressed against a hard chest. Her hips nestled against his. Their bodies fit together in all the right places. Even the sensitive, smooth skin of his throat was only a nuzzle away.

He drew a quick breath, his fingers dropping to her lower back, kneading her closer, and she realized that she *had* nuzzled his throat, on the thought. He smelled so good. Now she wanted to lick him.

She actually had to bite on the tip of her tongue as it started to sneak out.

Tristan, damn it. Why do you have to be so damn enticing? It's not fair.

She was pretty sure he wasn't even trying. Right at that moment, he was just focused on being a nice guy.

She'd never been attracted to bad boys. Maybe because she'd known Tristan all her life. She'd always known, up close and personal, that the sexiest creature on Earth was a really good guy.

An exasperating *artiste*, but a good person. It was just too bad for her that, belying a world-wide impression that women were idiots, every other female alive realized it, too.

"Malorie." His voice had deepened and roughened and held a hint of question. But no amusement whatsoever, for once.

Hey, at least she knew he remembered her name.

There didn't seem anything wrong with anonymity, though, not here in this secret grove of scent with the sea that hush of a promise in the distance, past all the glittering lights. She wished they *were* anonymous, strangers, and she could just yield to this beautiful night without having to deal with the awkwardness of having been one of Tristan Rosier's enjoyable encounters for the rest of her life.

She gathered strength at the thought and almost started to pull away—but just then his fingers stroked lightly right up the curve of her spine, through her silky dress, and that shivered through her, weakening all her muscles again.

Her fingers spread on his chest and then stroked up it to curve over his shoulder. She didn't mean to. She swore she didn't. She'd just always wanted to know what those shoulders felt like. Shoulders that could pull his entire body weight up a cliff face with as much ease as if it was just an enjoyable way to work the kinks out from a morning in the lab.

They felt *good.* The kneadable hardness of muscle over strong bone. Why did a man's strength offered to a woman have to be so damn *erotic?* For two hundred thousand years, she bet women had been falling for that.

Who's going to look after you, Malorie? If you go through with this.

Nobody, she told herself fiercely. *Nobody needs to. I'm tough.*

"Tristan," she said, lifting her head.

"Malorie," he said again, rough and low, as if she had answered his question.

And he bent his head and kissed her. Slow, leisurely, nibbling, melting her, and determined to eat her all up.

His hand slid up, up, up her back with the kiss, pressing her into all that lean hardness of his body—growing harder—until his palm curved over the nape of her neck and his fingers sank into her hair. His other hand shaped over her hip, then curved over her butt as his kiss didn't nibble and didn't test, didn't invade, didn't take. It met her own kiss, a perfect fit of energy and hunger, as if their mouths had been made for each other.

It wasn't like what they said, about yielding to temptation—the first bite is the best, and then it loses its savor.

No. His kisses just got better and better. Until her hands were shaping his face, fingers threading through his hair, palms stroking down over his shoulders and back up. Until he was breathing very hard, and when he finally lifted his head, she thought he looked dazed, but it was dark enough that she couldn't quite tell.

"Malorie." The question was back in his voice, and it held a note of wonder. As if he'd spotted a falling star and wanted to know if she'd seen it, too.

She touched his lips. They were soft and parted and moistened from her kisses, and when she touched them, he drew another sharp breath and caught her hand and sucked two of her fingertips into his mouth, nipping and tasting.

Oh.

He reached up suddenly with his other hand, loosing her body, and fisted it around a branch, crushing a flower that released more scent. "Malorie." His voice was low and tight, that gorgeous timbre it had vibrating against her, on a note of incredulity. *"Bon sang."*

He locked both hands above them in the branches as he kissed her again, not holding her at all. She found herself pressing into him, gripping his head to hold him deep in the kiss, missing the pressure of his hands on her body pulling her in still tighter. His hair was just as silky as she had always imagined it. Leaves rustled overhead as his hair slid under her fingers, and a white bud fell in his black hair, another cascading off her shoulder.

What a lovely, lovely offer of his body. She ran her hands down his chest and back up his ribs, unable to resist such a present, and all the way up his arms to his wrists, tugging his hands back down.

He released the branches and pulled her into him again. This time, as he kissed her, his hands stroked all the way down to her thighs, the silk sliding cool against her skin and then warming instantly at the heat of his hands. He pushed it up as he kissed her, until her thighs were bare almost to her panties...and then he caught himself and stroked it down, smoothing it out.

Then, sinking into the kiss, pushed it up again—caught himself and stroked it down. Up, down, a sensuous slide of heat and restraint and desire.

His hands gripped her harder with each passage, lingered longer on the up stroke, kneaded into her butt through the silk. Malorie got lost in the heat of him, in the great, giddy rush of kissing him, of pressing herself into that hot body.

This was a terrible place for staying rational. She should never have let him in here. So what if she knew it would give him pleasure? That was a *really* stupid path to start down. Once a woman started giving Tristan pleasure, it was a short road to addiction. She'd overdose on being his pleasure.

"And I had all these plans," Tristan muttered, a faint thread of self-mockery in his voice.

"Plans?" Malorie couldn't even form the word properly. *Don't stop kissing to talk.*

"Fantasies."

Wait, this didn't match his fantasies?

"Never mind." Tristan pushed those fantasies away. "This is beautiful." He cupped her face in both hands. "You're beautiful."

She hesitated, but she felt beautiful, held by him like that, his eyes on her like that. Never in her life had she felt as beautiful as she did right then.

Don't let a man make you feel beautiful. Don't need *him,* some little voice begged in her head.

I know, she lied to herself. *I'll be all right.*

Tristan slid down her body. Lips brushing over her chin, under it, down her throat—more intimate and more maddening than the kissing, because she could not kiss him in return. She could only tilt her head back, helpless to that vulnerable pleasure.

His hands slid over her shoulders, down her arms, as he kept dropping, his head rubbing over her silk-clad breasts, down to her belly, until he was kneeling on the cloth stretched under the tree, a scattering of blossoms around him.

"Malorie." He looked up at her, so gorgeous like that it should be illegal, and his fingers circled her wrists and tugged.

She stared down at him. On the brink of a need for someone else greater than any she'd let herself feel since before her father died.

And yet...she'd let Tristan in here because he should be here. She'd known he would love this place, the most precious memory of her childhood. She'd *trusted* him with it.

They fit here. Her wrists turned in his hold until their palms met, open. Her hands smaller than his. And yet as their eyes held, as their palms pressed together, their hands seemed perfectly matched.

A bloom loosed from the tree above and drifted down between them.

Malorie's fingers linked with Tristan's, and she followed that bloom to the cloth.

Chapter 20

Tristan had fantasized about Malorie in a pencil skirt. He'd imagined her on her desk with her legs apart, moaning and frantic for more. He'd imagined her in his car, parked somewhere private. He'd imagined her in a closet at a party, so overwhelmed by lust for more of what he was doing to her that she didn't even care where they were and by God wasn't giving him cool looks anymore.

But this...this was like the dream he should have had. This was the dream a very young man could have had, driving to Malorie's house determined to ask her out no matter what, just before he found out she'd left and wasn't coming back.

He stroked her dark hair out on the pale, faintly rough cloth. This dream was almost too beautiful. It betrayed him into intimate hope and belief, the kind he'd had about her as a teenager.

As if he'd found that quiet place with her that had always been so erotically alluring. She understood how beautiful this night was. He couldn't think of anyone, ever, who had offered him a more perfect gift than this— a moonlit night in this quiet, secret space full of the scent of sensuality, with now and then a white flower drifting down around them. And her body, for his delight.

Her hair was so silky under his climber's fingertips, and the faint roughness of the cloth under her hair made him wish he had more silk for her. Silk sheets instead of calluses and ground cloth. He took an orange flower and touched it to her cheek, twirling it between his fingers gently against her skin. *There. There's silk.*

Her eyes clung to his, wide and confused and vulnerable.

Yeah, me, too.

"Shh," he murmured, because he knew it was his job to reassure her. He was bigger and stronger and otherwise she might run away. "It's okay." He brushed the flower over her nose, and somehow that one gesture clenched in his gut and squeezed longing right through to the blunt end of his cock. He'd always wanted to touch her nose caressingly. Always wanted to have that teasing, possessive privilege.

That vulnerable set to her mouth trembled into a smile. Her lashes fell against her cheeks.

He teased them with the flower, trailing it over her eyelids, then tracing it over her eyebrows until her eyes had to flutter open again. Propped on one elbow, he smiled down at her and blew her a kiss.

That, too, he'd always wished he had the teasing, possessive right to do. In class. Across the school cafeteria. Across a party full of people. Across that table at the meetings over Fugace, before he'd realized she was the one behind Abbaye's determination to destroy it.

Fugace brushed across his mind, a wisp of an old ghost now, its power fading away. Weakened by her apology and his, and by this pale cloth, in this sweet-scented night, with her hair spread by his fingers.

"Malorie," he whispered again, just to make sure it was really her. She'd fooled him that way before. Been other women, who'd never been quite right.

How many mornings had he woken from a night of mutually enjoyable sensuality wondering why he felt so empty inside, why he so desperately needed to go climb a cliff?

Malorie touched his lip. Traced over it, just as he was tracing her with flowers.

And that had never even crossed his dreams at all—that Malorie might treasure *him*. She'd moaned and responded in his dreams, and, fine, okay, sometimes, especially after she'd given him that librarian's look while in one of her pencil skirts, she had done some things that in real life she might have slapped him for suggesting. But she'd never treated him as if he was precious, too.

It was wonderful.

He kissed her fingertips, trying to encourage more of it. And it seemed to work, because her fingers spread over his cheek, delicately, shaping his cheekbone as if it was a work of art.

He drew his orange blossom over her temple, twirling it there until her eyes fluttered closed again, then drawing it over her cheek to her lips. He brushed her lips, gently back and forth, while her thumbs traced circles and figure eights over his cheeks and her fingers spread further until she could pet the edges of his hair.

It was so incredible it hurt, to be treated so preciously. She was going to break him like an eggshell and find him all raw and messy inside and wishing he had managed to boil hard before she got to him.

She had all this scented, moonlit night on her side. She'd known when she opened the door to this secret garden—she must have known—how vulnerable he was to a night like this.

Malorie could have seduced him at any time, anywhere—it wasn't as if he would have said no. She didn't need all this. She didn't need to break him wide open.

"You're so beautiful," he whispered, because he couldn't help it. It was true.

She opened her eyes just long enough for this look that was so damn...*vulnerable* that...

Was she breaking open, too?

Shit, that...

He shifted his body more over her, his thigh pinning her now, possessing her. *You can break open. I've got you.*

His flower trailed over that proud chin of hers. It would never soften, but her lips could—that trembling half-smile.

He caressed the corners of that smile again with his flower. *Shh. See? Everything is all right.*

Her thumbs tugged gently at the corners of his lips. Caressed and teased those corners. Stroked just the edge of his lower lip, following the line of it to the center, then shaping the bow of his upper lip.

That made him feel so...fuddled. Confused. Happy. Hopeful. Arousal was this leaping, eager thing, trying to surge forward and take all even while it tried to linger in this moment.

He traced the flower up her jaw to her ear, played it over her tiny emerald studs, and then caressed it down her throat.

"Tris—" she started to whisper, but her voice broke off before she even finished his name. Her fingers traced down his throat, shaped the muscles at the back of his neck that were holding his head up at this angle as if those were special, fascinating muscles, then down over the shoulder muscles that were activated by the same position.

He drew his flower to the hollow of her throat and twirled it slowly there, watching. Her pulse was beating visibly near the tip of the petals.

She petted her fingers down to the unbuttoned collar of his shirt, teasing under the edges as if to reach more of his skin. If she started to unbutton it, then that would mean...

Damn, he wanted to unbutton it for her. Just rip the thing off and hunt buttons with her in the grass tomorrow. His heart was thundering too hard. Were they making out, like teenagers on a picnic? Or was she all in?

It would be helpful, right now, to know if she didn't want to go all the way. So he could rein himself in early, before he over-engaged.

But he knew better than to ask her. She might make up her mind too soon, before he'd had a chance to use all his persuasive tools.

He guessed that was why men had invented pants with buttons. So they'd stay on through all the making out she wanted until she made the choice to take them off.

And he was getting a little ahead of himself. Right now, her fingers were still hesitating above the top button of his shirt.

All the focus of his body seemed to rush up to her fingertips brushing under his collar, as he willed her and willed her and—her fingers stroked back up his throat.

Damn it.

He snuck his hand up and undid another button. Okay, two.

Fine, three.

Then he pulled her hand back down to stroke his chest more fully.

And snuck open button four.

Oh, fine, fuck. He ripped the whole rest of his shirt open, buttons popping. There. Now *that* was better.

If only he didn't have this damn T-shirt on under it.

Malorie hesitated just a moment, as if maybe he was rushing her far past the point she wanted to go. But then her fingers spread over his chest through the T-shirt. And then, again as if she was touching something very, very special, she started to spread her stroking over the rest of that revealed T-shirt.

Her hands followed his ribs, slid around to stroke the muscles of his back, exploring all the ways he was shaped. His nose stung at the way she touched him. As if he was...*incredible* or something.

He kissed her again, trying to take his time, trying to be as tender and sensual as this night.

And she forgot he was so precious, as her body arched into his, as her hands started to drag on him and pull.

Yeah. That worked for him, too.

His hands slid up her silk dress, which was headily addictive against her body, it was impossible to touch her enough. But he tried. He got lost in it all, so much sensation. Silk and lips and the muscles of her thighs— *merde,* he could not believe that he was finally touching those fantastic legs of hers. And they were even *better* to touch than in his fantasies.

All of this was better.

Infinitely more dangerous to his happy life, but much more real.

He lost himself completely to it. Stopped thinking, stopped hoping, stopped planning. Just lost himself to the sensation of her body, to the scent in the air, to the glorious delight of something beautiful finally coming true.

***

Tristan broke Malorie's heart open. As if all the sensations he drank in so greedily from the world, he condensed and poured into her until her carefully tightened heart couldn't keep itself whole anymore and had to split to hold it. Flowers crushed around them, the scent of orange blossoms mixing with the scent of their greed.

She got his shirt off—oh, wow, the silk smooth skin of his back over those hard muscles. He finally pushed her dress up past her panties. His thumbs hooked under the elastic of the string bikini, and then followed that elastic all, all, all the way down to where his thumbs met.

She shivered and jerked, already melted from all the kissing. Tristan was so damn good at this. His clever, clever fingers didn't hurry. They petted gently through curls, as if venturing into uncharted territory held under the sway of a powerful sorceress. They treated her mound like a chancy hill to be slowly, slowly crept up. They found the lush part and delicately, delicately tested it, as if making sure they had the right to go there. Every centimeter he progressed into her vulnerability, he made her feel so damn powerful.

211

As if pleasure *was* the power. The ability to make him want to give it to her was all the power a sorceress could ever need.

Wasn't she supposed to be giving *Tristan* pleasure? Wasn't that the addictive path she'd started down?

Was she good at it? Would she stand out in his mind later, from all the other encounters he'd had?

Did it matter? She could guarantee that *he* wasn't thinking about later. He was entirely focused on the now.

The heat of passion.

But she drew her hands down his back as she wondered. Curved over that tight ass of his and pulled him to her, arching up into him. He helped with that—pressed his hips right back down into hers, took part in that grind together. But he didn't unbutton his pants.

Instead, when her hips dropped back to the ground, he ventured more deeply into that uncharted territory. Explored up the lush folds, watching her face, until she jerked and shivered again and maybe even moaned.

He stroked there, never looking away from her face. He looked so utterly disheveled now—hair a tousled mess, lips damp and bruised, eyes black in the dark as he fought to see her as well as he could in the moonlight. Shirts abandoned, all that lean, rippled, muscled torso bare. Black curls there. Her fingers curled into them and then drew down, down, down, grazing over his taut belly, until she hit the waist of his pants.

She tucked her fingertips under the waistband, pulling on him.

He stroked his thumb over her and very, very gently, very, very delicately, pulled a little, too.

Oh, God.

She bucked up to his hand. He soothed her, rubbing gently again, watching her face.

She yanked at the button of his pants, fumbling, the stupid thing wouldn't fit through the buttonhole—

He pressed his thumb more firmly down, in a little circular motion.

She started to pant, her fingers slowing on his button, caressing it, caressing farther down, to his erection through his pants.

He pressed into her hand. He was breathing very hard. But he kept his focus.

Rubbing, rubbing, rubbing, watching her as if she was the most fascinating thing he had ever seen.

God, Tristan knew how to live in the moment. Who knew how many women he'd seen orgasm? And yet he kept his entire focus on her, as if this moment was unique in all his life.

It was unique in hers, too, but of course it would be. She'd never made love with Tristan before.

Gorgeous, sexy, exasperating, overprivileged, beautiful-hearted Tristan Rosier.

She managed to make his button obey her this time, slower with it, more determined. His breath grew rougher. His thumb a little more insistent.

She pushed his pants down, scooped him free of his briefs.

Tristan jerked so hard he might have been stabbed.

So she soothed him. Soothed his cock. *Shh, shh, shh, it's okay.*

He swore. Softly, eagerly, dirty, dirty words. Pressing into her hands. His thumb slid down the length of her, delving between her folds as he drew it back to press right where she wanted it.

She pulled at him. *Tristan, come on. I'm not doing this alone.*

No. At least she'd know for this one moment, that she'd had as much power over him as he'd had over her.

Besides, it really was addictive, giving him pleasure.

"Malorie. Damn it." He scrabbled for his pants pocket, finding a packet.

He opened the packet with one hand and his teeth, so that he could keep his other thumb on her. His hair had fallen over his forehead. As she ran her thumb up his length, he looked utterly wild. "Hold *on*, Malorie." He grabbed both her hands and locked her wrists above her head.

That left them both deprived. She bumped her pelvis up against him, rubbing herself against him to get that texture she was now missing, lifting her thighs to close around his hips.

"Fuck." Tristan rolled away from her for a second.

She didn't like the texture of the condom nearly as much as the silk-hard feel of him bare. But then, Tristan almost certainly didn't like it as much either, and *he* wasn't complaining. She closed her hand around him again, tracing her thumb over his base, that half-centimeter that was still bare. Tightening her hold.

Tristan looped one hand under her and kissed her again, pulling her into him, deep, deep, as his fingers kept playing with her. She even liked, in a way, that his fingers were growing a little clumsy, that he was losing his rhythm as his focus pulled down and down into his own body.

She sank her fingers into his butt and arched her pelvis up into his, pulling him inside her.

Oh.

Oh, wow. She arched into him as Tristan made a rough sound, and his hips thrust him deep, deep.

Mmm.

She found his fingers and brought them back to where she wanted them.

He laughed a little, an incredulous, joyous sound, as his gaze drifted down her body. He braced his weight on one hand, arm hard against her side, and stroked her as he sank deep into her.

Too much. Feelings grew bigger and bigger in her, pressing at her as if she was a balloon too full of helium, about to pop. And yet the pressure kept building,

building, until she was frantic to release it, to burst so that she could come back down to earth...even in pieces.

And then she did burst, her nails seizing his shoulders, her body jerking hard just as Tristan gave a rough sound and thrust hard into her. She threw her arm over her face. That was better. All in the dark. Now she couldn't see him when they came. She could pretend he couldn't see her.

As she didn't fall to earth like limp pieces of a balloon at all. As a stroking, coaxing hand eased her down as gently as if she was an orange blossom, drifting, floating, gently rocked by the breeze, to the ground in the night.

She grabbed a fold of the cloth and pulled it over her face, not looking at Tristan. The man she had known all her life and never really known at all.

He slid his face up just to the edge of the fold that protected her and kissed her temple. His hand rested on her belly, rubbing in a small, possessive motion. After a while, he moved away and then came back, laying his shirt over her upper body and then curving his to hers, pulling her back against him as he drew the scented cloth on which they lay up around them.

Something tickled her shoulder.

Tristan, twirling one white flower against it, idly, sometimes stroking it up and down her arm, his breath warming the top of her head. The flower traced over her knuckles, came back up her arm. Neither spoke. She was still being caressed by a flower when she fell fast asleep.

Chapter 21

The white flower snapped from the tree at the twist of her fingers and floated gently down to rest on Tristan's body. Malorie smiled a little as she harvested, almost humming under her breath. The early light of a spring morning, the sun starting to warm away the chill of the night. The scents of orange blossom freshened again by the way the oils were starting to get absorbed by her arms and hands. The familiar, old gestures of harvesting with her grandmother and sisters, here in this place safe from all the world.

And below her, one gorgeous specimen of manhood getting slowly covered in white flowers.

Stay in the moment. There was really no more beautiful moment to be in.

It wasn't so bad, waking up to face the fact that she had finally slept with Tristan Rosier. Yes, she'd let the man who had everything have her body, too. But she'd also had his. If they were going to have to meet up in the streets for the rest of her life with a memory of this night in Tristan's head, well...she'd *also* have the memory. And it was a pretty damn good one.

It was when she saw him with other women that it was going to hurt.

A vicious pang, just thinking about it.

She hoped that the smell of orange blossom didn't make her hurt like that, ever after. This was her safe space. What had she been thinking to let him in it?

Stay in the moment.

In this moment, if she could stay in it, the scent of orange blossom didn't hurt yet. It carried with it more sensuality than she had ever experienced in her entire life. She'd woken a little bit ago to find Tristan still curled snug around her, heavily asleep but warming her against the spring night with his body, his shirt having slid mostly off her but the drop cloth still pulled around them, flowers caught in her hair. Even the aftermath of their love-making was incredibly sensual.

A bud only partially open twisted in her fingers and fell onto Tristan's forehead, a little harder without open petals to provide air resistance. He blinked awake sleepily, then stayed still, taking a moment to orient himself.

A slow smile started to grow on his face. He pushed up onto one elbow, the blanket of white blossoms sliding over his body, a crown of flowers caught in his black hair, like some sybaritic god of spring. He looked down at the flowers sliding down his chest, bemused, then ran his hand over his stomach to come up with a handful of flowers that he let drift down again.

He smiled up at her, two rungs up the ladder. "This is definitely better than ice water. But didn't that guy in the stories have to marry Sleeping Beauty when he kept waking her up like that?"

Her hand tightened around a branch as that one jabbed straight through her. No joke was taboo to him, was it? "I'm hardly Prince Charming, Tristan."

His smile faded. He sat all the way up and looked at all the flowers piling in his lap, lifting another handful of them. "I'm charmed."

Could they *not* go in this direction? Pretend there was some happily ever after in here somewhere? "I thought I made your head blow off."

He shrugged. "I'm the youngest of five cousins. I'm used to people trying to drive me crazy as an expression of affection."

Her lips twitched. She was the youngest of three sisters. Their family might not have been as solid as Tristan's, but, yes, she recognized the symptoms.

Tristan lifted double handfuls and let the flowers slide off his hands again, clearly in love with the sensation.

217

Her instinct for self-protection faded, and she
reached out and snapped a flower free just over his head,
watching it drift down as he turned his face up to it and
let it kiss his lips. *You're so gorgeous. It's really not fair.*

That generous, hungry sensuality of his, as if every
sensation in life was one he wanted to savor. Yes, those
good fairies had given him a lot of gifts. But Tristan had
appreciated every one. He could have been truly spoiled.
But he chose to see the world as one great present, and
to appreciate every detail. And to try to offer it in turn to
others.

Tristan stretched out again, folding his hands
behind his head. During the night, he had pulled his
pants back on against the chill, but that ripped torso
remained bare of anything but flowers. "Do you know I
had my first sexual fantasy about you when I was
fourteen years old?" he said meditatively. "And now,
finally..." He twirled a flower in his fingers and smelled
it, a little smile curving his lips.

"All your dreams have come true," she said
ironically, back to self-protectiveness.

"Hard to imagine a better dream than this," Tristan
said softly. He stroked his chest with a flower, absently.
Then raised an eyebrow at her. "What about yours?"

Malorie's fingers stroked over a petal, as if she was
trying to feel the same sensation he was giving himself
as he brushed his chest. "Mine were more comfort
fantasies," she said, a little shy to talk about them. "Not
so explicit."

He laughed. "Teenage boys and teenage girls are like
two different species."

She found herself laughing back down at him.

He reached a hand full of flowers up to her. "I can do
comfort, too. Come here."

A vision of just sinking down with him again in
broad daylight, cuddling up with him.

It made her take a step higher up the ladder.

Tristan watched her thoughtfully a moment. Then rolled to his feet in a flex of ab muscles that sent a wave of possessive heat through her—*mine*—and came to the ladder. Wrapping his hands around the rung to either side of her hips, he just leaned his head forward until it rested against her back.

Malorie twisted around, and he let his face stay against her as she moved, until she was facing him, and his head rested against her belly. His eyes closed, and he nestled his head against the silk of her dress and let his weight sink against her.

Malorie didn't know what to make of it, the sweetness and warmth that ran up her middle from where his face rested and stole its way into her heart. It was so like all her fantasies of him when she was lonely or upset, except the reverse—he was the one seeking tactile comfort from her. She touched his hair, tentatively. Such silky, thick black hair. Her fingers sank into its waves, knocking a white flower loose from the careless crown of them still caught there.

He ran his hands up her sides under her arms and lifted her off the ladder, lowering them both back down on the cloth. "You're right," he said, when he had her settled on his chest. "This is very nice."

His fingers ran through her hair, stroking it as if the sensation of every strand was fascinating to him. His heart thumped, steady and reliable, under her ear. His breaths eased slow and deep through his body, as if he was profoundly at peace. "Perfect," he murmured, his tone oddly wondering, as if the man who had everything had never had anything as perfect as this.

And it was perfect, that was the problem. Solid and warm and tender. So tempting she wanted to fall right into it, even though she knew that once she let go, she would fall forever. *I'm in love with him.* It wasn't even a surprise to think it. More like an "about time you accepted that". *I think I've been in love with him a long time.*

It should have felt like falling.

219

It didn't.

It felt like cuddling up against a strong, warm body that held her in perfect happiness.

"It was you," Tristan said suddenly.

What?

His fingers moved in her hair, the stem of a flower brushing the crown of her head. "Fugace. I'd been trying to capture you most of my damn life, and I finally did, I almost had you, it was almost perfect, I was *that close,* and I gave it to you, and you just pushed it away and broke it. Because you wanted to focus on your work. You always did that shit to me, Malorie. But I couldn't believe you'd do it even with Fugace. It was beautiful."

Malorie's fingers curled into the dark hair on Tristan's chest. She stared at them, at that precarious grip on such a beautiful person, inside and out. Maybe she should have spent more time climbing, like Tristan did, to have a grip that could hang on to anything. "Me?"

Fugace was *her*?

"You had to recognize it, Malorie. The green and the shadow, the quiet and the toughness, the elusiveness, that fairy-tale courage of the youngest daughter who went off to seek her fortune and slipped through the prince's hands."

She lifted her head to stare at him. That beautiful perfume? No. She had not seen herself in it. And it had never even occurred to her that Tristan Rosier, the industry's most gorgeous and most popular scion, had made a perfume for her.

Just as it had never occurred to her that he had a crush on her. Never occurred to her that when he came and talked to her at parties, or sat down on a bench too small for them both, he was doing anything but treating her with the same charming friendliness he treated everyone else.

Maybe she didn't only have trust issues. Maybe she had some freaking self-esteem issues. Which were probably textbook for a narcissist's daughter, but damn it. She'd been positive she was too strong to fall into that trap.

"Me?" she said again, her voice very small. Tristan Rosier had made a perfume for her?

That shadowy, elusive promise of a perfume, like a whisper of white flowers on a spring night. Like a cool green swimming hole in the shadow of trees in a hot summer. With its core of courage.

That perfume that all the critics had described as *wistful. Full of longing.*

"Yes, you," Tristan said, impatient and annoyed as only a wounded, unappreciated *artiste* could be.

She'd thought that courage was *Tristan's* courage, because he always took creative risks with his perfumes.

That elusiveness was Tristan's elusiveness. The quintessential fantasy of a man who could never come true in her real life.

The way he'd described it had made her seem so...special. Heroic and poetic and romantic, all together.

You didn't realize? His voice had been so gentle. *That anyone else saw that in you?*

She sat up and curled her arms around her knees, and so he sat up, too, wrapping his arm around her.

Should I tell him? That she was in love with him, that she'd never climbed up this high before and she was afraid of the fall. The last man she'd believed in had enjoyed giving women brutal falls. And she knew that was a long time and a lot of therapy ago, but when things hurt you as a child, they hurt you forever. Those scars never went away.

Tristan shifted and found his phone on the drop cloth, stretching his arm out in front of them to take a photo.

In it, they looked like two wood gods that the Romans or their predecessors here might have come upon. Tristan's fingers shifting in her hair had woven in a crown of flowers to match his own. White blossoms against their dark hair, golden skin, her green eyes and his brown, her pale silk dress crumpled and him shirtless. She'd smiled for the camera, but in her eyes or her posture there was a little wariness still, as if this wood goddess wasn't sure what it might mean for her, to be caught. And in his, a profound and possessive contentment, as if everything was right with his world.

I think he knows.

Chapter 22

Happiness opened for Malorie like a scent bottled and brought to maturation. Sprayed on a white strip, waved under her nose to test it out.

She liked it. So now she had to try it on skin. See how it developed over hours, from that first quick, volatile top note to the longer notes that came out as her skin warmed. It changed her identity, this new perfume. Could it become her signature?

Who was she?

Because she had not made the scent. She wasn't a perfumer. Tristan had made it, and her skin had married to it and made it glow.

This happiness depended on someone else.

A flash of a brown vial through the air, her hands just barely managing to clap together around it. Tristan had just climbed through her office window. He really did treat her like some people treated social media—popping over whenever he couldn't focus anymore.

She found she liked it. She was her own boss now, not a kid who had to please her teachers in school or her superiors at her new job, and her priorities were finally, finally aligning themselves with what, deep inside, she really wanted.

Tristan swung his legs over the sill and came across to kiss her. "What do you think?" He nodded at the vial, his body relaxed, his tone casual, as if he couldn't care less if she liked it or not.

Yeah, right.

She vaporized the trial on her elbow for lack of a test strip—if she was going to run a perfume company, she'd better fix *that* little lack in her office supplies—and brought her elbow to her nose.

Mmm. Neroli, like the warm, rich shadow and amber tones of wealth and glamor. Risk and a hint of mischief, like a woman's calves exposed under flirty flounces for the first time in two thousand years. Depth and curling grace, like history becoming new.

"Lovely," she said quietly. "It's like..." She looked around her office, the control center of La Maison de Monsard.

"We'll have to run a range," Tristan said. "Between that and the dustier one I gave you the other day and a few more ideas I want to try. Plus, I have to see how they mature, of course. When do you want to start thinking about bottles and packaging and lining up production? Do you want to use Rosier for production until you bring Monsard's facilities back on line again? Or do you want to focus more on just being the showplace for the perfumes and maybe think of a long-term agreement with Rosier to make them?"

Malorie knew perfectly well what he was doing. Assuming her decision was made, that she was going to re-launch Monsard, and that he was going to be involved in it, as a way of directing her down that path. It should have been annoying. Instead, it was profoundly warming. She *loved* the idea of having Tristan by her side and even often butting heads with her, but either way, tangled up in the bringing back to life of this place. What better person was there, to fill a place with life?

"I still need to hear back from my sisters," she said. "Without their cooperation, there's not much I can do. I can't afford to buy them out at this point." And secretly, she'd kind of prefer it if they didn't want to sell. If she fought for this place for the sake of a family, like the Rosiers did, no matter how much more shattered the family was. The healing had to start somewhere.

Maybe it could start with her.

"If you had the majority of shares, would you be ready to commit to it?" Tristan asked, watching her as if he'd like to pierce right through to the center of her brain and figure out what she was thinking.

Good luck with that. Malorie didn't even entirely know what she was thinking. And that was his fault. If he hadn't been around, it would be simple—take back this place and relaunch it or sell it, fish or cut bait. But his existence layered that decision with so many more emotions, delicate silky ones, like orange blossoms she was afraid to crush.

Or maybe they were powerful dragon emotions she was afraid to get eaten by.

"I don't know," she said. She had made so many life-changing decisions briskly, without ever glancing back. But this one would so clearly dominate the whole rest of her life. The rest of her descendants' lives. Hell, it would even, to a certain degree, reshape Grasse. The thought of being someone who had consequences again, whose role in her family and in a region's history might be powerful and pivotal, was terrifying. Her great-grandfather had had that role, and look what he had done with it.

"Mmm." Tristan looked as if he'd decided not to say something he really wanted to say.

"Look, you had the training to be a patriarch," she said. Training in honor and courage and standing up for what was right. No one ever messed with the girls or the smaller kids in their high school, not with five Rosiers there. That was the kind of influence they wielded. The power they had for good. "If I'm going to become the Monsard matriarch one day, I'll be making everything up as I go along and trying to get it right."

"Like Niccolò and Laurianne," Tristan said.

Malorie rubbed the vial he had tossed her, bemused. Had he just compared her to the legendary founders of the Rosier clan? Casually, not as if he was flattering her but as if that was quite simply who she reminded him of. "What, Niccolò the hardened mercenary?" she said dryly, to defend herself.

"The romantic," Tristan said reprovingly. "He was the bastard son of a prince and he married a glove-maker. Honestly, Malorie, it's not all about money."

She'd bet it was if you had lost everything and didn't even have a pair of gloves to your name, as their stories claimed about Niccolò. "I thought he was a mercenary on the losing end of a war in Italy who came here dead broke. Laurianne was a smart, wealthy businesswoman. If he was a romantic, he certainly had a gift for landing on his feet."

Tristan frowned at her.

Seriously? He really didn't think financial security had been a factor in Niccolò's choice of wife? "Sometimes it's more obvious than others that you never breathed a financially insecure breath in your life," she said.

There was a little silence. And then quietly, "Maybe he was as capable of forging his own way as you always have been. And so falling in love was extra."

Maybe. It was a nice thought. The open compliment of her in it was the kind that worked inside her and made her bones feel stronger.

Tristan smiled a little. "So then Laurianne, the glove-maker perfumer businesswoman, is the romantic? Willing to risk all her life and fortune on a hardened mercenary?"

Malorie shuddered. That had been really true back in Niccolò and Laurianne's day—that if Laurianne married, she yielded control of her entire life and finances to Niccolò. How the *hell* had she brought herself to do that, instead of staying a widow? "He must have been quite the charmer," she said very darkly.

Tristan frowned at her. "*He* was the one who brought so many perfume techniques here out of Italy. Maybe she was getting quite a lot out of the relationship, too."

Frankly, if she lived to be a hundred, she would never understand the risk that Laurianne had taken on Niccolò. Hard to deny it had paid off, though, at least for their descendants. "The sex must have been good," she said. "That's all I can figure."

Tristan laughed. "Good to know that might be a factor in a tough businesswoman's decisions."

This conversation was brushing close to...something that made her roll her eyes quickly and grow more ironic.

Tristan tweaked a strand of her hair. "So does that mean you get to be like Niccolò and I get to be like Laurianne? Damn it. And I always wanted to be the tough, cynical mercenary starting over out of the ruins in the story."

Yeah, right. "Tristan, I'm afraid you completely failed to get the hardened mercenary part down."

"Luckily I've got you," Tristan said cheerfully, and she had to laugh.

Again, she couldn't think about the assumption that seemed to underlie their conversation. But she *could* think that...well, maybe he was a little lucky to have her. He wasn't very good at setting up his own walls, was he? Or of thinking about things like the bottom line, which were fundamental to a family's security.

A reassuring thought. That there really were things about her that the man who had everything needed.

That too-handsome-for-his-own-good face tilted down toward her. Not too far. She was in heels. Brown eyes turned warm and wicked. "Have I ever told you about all the fantasies I had, when we were arguing about Fugace, that started right here and ended up with you pushed back on your desk with your legs spread while you moaned for more?"

A jolt of heat and indignation right through her. "No. That's terrible."

"I know," Tristan said, savoringly, as if the very terribleness tasted delicious. "Well...show is better than tell any day." He put his hand on her shoulder and pushed.

***

Happiness unfolded for Tristan like the scent of a limestone cliff. A scent he had known all his life and yet never once managed to capture in a perfume in a way that conveyed its beauty.

Limestone and a man's sweat, and no sound but the scrape of his own body against rock and the breeze, or in summer perhaps fading below him the sound of cicadas. Familiar and beautiful and it seemed like a good perfumer should be able to do something with it, but he had never before managed to capture it in this form.

Happiness was like the blank page when he went to put down his first formula ideas for the scent that would capture that limestone hope. That anguish of doubt that he could never let anyone know he had, that sometimes drove him right back away from that page and up the limestone cliff again until he could force himself through the barrier.

But he had to write the ideas down. Had to start the trials. Would this work? What about this? This idea was promising, but how would it smell two weeks later? How would it smell on skin?

Happiness closed around him in a vast embrace like the great walls of a scented orchard where he could roam both safe and free. The happiness was bigger than he'd ever realized it could be—or maybe when he'd first started dreaming of it, it had been smaller and he hadn't known how much it had grown. She was bigger. He was bigger. Together, they both were.

He thought Fugace didn't suit her anymore. If he made it again, he would have to bring a warmer note into the cool green and shadow, would have to capture that heart of orange blossom, rich with sensuality and hope and promise. It would have to be a stronger scent, a scent that had gone on great, long adventures. But a spring scent. Like two people with flowers in their hair, smiling tentatively at a camera, two wood gods who had known each other for all time and still, with the spring, found a new beginning.

He scythed the great overgrown orchard down so they could move among the bitter orange trees, and he fixed the motor on her grandmother's old mower so they could more easily maintain it. He helped paint walls in the building in Grasse and scrub clean the old fountain and set it to flowing again. Malorie set orange blossoms floating in it. He dreamed the scents he would make to flow in its waters.

He discovered that Malorie liked to get up when the stars were still out just like he did. The two of them harvested orange blossoms in the quiet dawn before they went in to Grasse. He dreamed things that he still felt too shy to tell her, like what it might be like to have his perfume lab here in the orange blossom orchard instead of at Rosier SA, or maybe—would he prefer it?—in the Monsard building not far from her office, or maybe in both places, depending on whether he needed quiet or needed people that day.

And as night fell, he could never resist pulling her down onto one of those drop cloths sprinkled with orange blossoms fallen during the day and catching her body under his. Then the beauty of everything overwhelmed him, and he fell into it, and then later he fell asleep into the arms of this absolutely perfect life and his dreams of it lasting forever after.

Chapter 23

"You and Malorie," Antoine Vallier said, an eyebrow lifting at Tristan over their beer. Around them was the usual happy conversation of the post-work hour at all the restaurants around the *place*, the fountain rippling softly in the center of it all. "So all this time we thought you couldn't settle on one woman, but in fact you're just slow to close."

Unruffled, as a life policy, Tristan took a swallow of beer and enjoyed the people strolling by. He didn't ask how Antoine knew about Malorie. He was used to Grasse knowing more about his life than he did. "Well, it turns out I *did* ask her to marry me when I was five, but she doesn't even remember what she said." He gave a heavy, sad sigh. "Life is tough with Malorie." But he was grinning. He loved her toughness. Her bones were so strong that he knew exactly what she was made of.

"So you've told her about the shares," Antoine said. "And she's okay with it."

Tristan looked at his friend blankly. His old classmate and he had lost contact when Antoine went off to university, but Tristan had looked him up as soon as he learned Antoine was now Tante Colette's lawyer and standing up to Damien and Matt and Raoul as if he was born to challenge arrogance. Tristan *deeply* approved of younger men who managed to get the better of the more established, more arrogant, older men. Plus, while Damien and Matt and Raoul responded with hostility to any perceived threat and made things worse, Tristan figured he'd rather respond with friendliness and see if he could make things better.

Antoine had a lean, mean, touchy thing going on, but Tristan was used to that kind of stuff, too, with all the *I-am-a-badass-and-emotional-teddy-bear* shit he had to put up with from his cousins. In fact, it was amazing how much, when he grabbed Antoine for a drink or coffee these days, he felt as if he was talking to one of his own cousins.

In a sardonic, blond version.

"Why wouldn't she be okay with it?" Tristan said. "I've got enough that I can give her the majority. It's perfect. If she decides she wants that."

Antoine gave him that long, ironic green look of his. Tristan grinned at him. When you grew up with Damien, ironic looks lost a lot of their impact. "Tristan," Antoine said, drawing on the word as if he really needed a cigarette and was only restraining himself for the sake of Tristan's sensitive nose. "Pretty much no one close to you ever meant you harm, did they?"

Tristan gazed skyward and asked heaven to grant him patience. "You know, people have *no* idea what it was like to grow up the youngest of those gorillas."

"Real harm." Antoine's words sounded crisp, like he was cutting them out of a great block of forbearance with some difficulty. "Not mud-wrestling."

"Well, no," Tristan said, patiently. "If they did, they wouldn't be close to me." Sometimes people misunderstood his easy ability to get along with most of the world; they thought it meant he trusted most of the world. "But even though they didn't mean it, that doesn't mean they never caused it."

Raoul and Lucien.

"Yeah." For some reason, Antoine's voice was so dry it was almost bitter. He reached for his cigarettes, then curled his fingers into his palm just as they brushed the package and brought his loose fist down to the café table. "But let's just say your assumptions about what people close to you are capable of doing to you are very different than those of people who grew up in a less...happy family."

The expression on his face made Tristan worry about Antoine's family. The two of them had been friendly back in high school, or at least as friendly as Antoine let anyone be to him. But they hadn't exactly been blood brothers—Tristan had four of those already, in the form of his cousins. He knew nothing about Antoine's family at all.

"*Have* you told her about the shares?" Antoine said.

Would people quit nagging Tristan about that? "I'm waiting for the right moment. Speaking of surprises, Jess says you're coming to their wedding?"

What Jess had actually said, apologetically to Damien who reacted to Antoine somewhat like a cobra reacted to a mongoose, was that Antoine had put her on the spot, congratulating her on the wedding and saying he was looking forward to attending. So she'd felt as if she had to send him an invitation. But Tristan didn't bring that up, just watched Antoine. "You're not going to show up like the bad fairy and curse their children, are you?"

Because Antoine had some kind of thing about Damien. Tristan couldn't put his finger on what it was, but even back in school, Antoine had closed off if Damien even wandered their way in the school courtyard.

"I think I'll stick with a traditional gift," Antoine drawled, bored. But there was something in his eyes as he looked out over the esplanade toward the sea in the distance. "I must be able to find diamond-studded platinum spoons somewhere."

Tristan just laughed. "They're asking guests to contribute to a scholarship fund for Grasse kids wanting to study perfume in Paris."

Antoine said nothing. This time, he drew the cigarette halfway out of the pack before he remembered Tristan's nose and tapped it back in, putting the pack away. Emotions seemed to crowd under that carefully neutral surface of his, but Tristan couldn't decipher a single one of them.

He'd better keep an eye on Antoine at Damien's wedding.

"But how did we get on me?" Antoine said, tapping his fingers restlessly against the table as if a cigarette should be sliding through them. "If you'll take my advice—"

"Always," Tristan said, resigned. Take advice from the guy who'd been idiotic enough to skip their group project with Malorie just because Tristan talked him into it? Some days he wondered if he should be a little more upfront with people about how hardheaded he was. He *liked* for them to incorrectly assume his compliancy, but this was getting ridiculous.

"—you'll tell Malorie about those shares before she finds out on her own."

***

Happiness expanded outward for Malorie through the streets of Grasse. It warmed the colors of the buildings, made the clothes hanging to dry between balconies wave a familiar welcome to her in the breeze. *Welcome home.*

She knew, by the way people reacted to her—curious and bemused and, in the case of quite a few women, jealous—that Tristan was acting differently with her than he did with other women. That the knowledge that she and he were together was rippling out through Grasse society and bringing all kinds of people peeking through the doors of La Maison de Monsard, intrigued to meet her and to see if they could find out more gossip than the person who had passed their current supply of gossip on to them.

It was the first time in generations that anyone in her family had been at the center of Grasse gossip that wasn't negative. It was hard to get used to. Sometimes she dreamed of hiking up into the hills again so she could just be herself and not have to think about any of it. When she told Tristan, he said, "That's why I like to climb so much," and took her out to build on her rudimentary gym skills so she could climb, too.

In her grandmother's and great-grandfather's old office the next day, she stared at the envelope with the little key, the envelope marked Rosier, and hesitated, and while she was hesitating, Tristan wandered in with a present for her.

The Lalique bottle of frosted glass amber twin hearts with their frosted, dusky dark centers. "I found it," he said proudly, and she had to bend her head as her eyes teared up.

Sometimes she thought she should tell him that her father used to give presents only as manipulation—to get you so addicted to his admiration and present-giving that he could use that need on your part for his own ends. But then she thought she never should, because she didn't want to put a single dark note into Tristan's warmth and generosity. It wasn't his problem, that the men in her family had been such assholes. It was hers, and she'd traveled a long road—literally—to become her own person and not let her father and grandfather and great-grandfather control her future.

There was an unleashed tenderness now in the way Tristan touched her face or stroked back her hair or played with her hand that was overwhelming her. She'd never experienced anything like it, and when their eyes met, she thought, *I don't think he's ever felt anything like it either.*

And she'd always thought Tristan had felt everything there was to feel.

"What's in it?" she managed huskily.

"Something that needs to mature still, I think," he said, watching her.

She opened the bottle and dabbed the stopper against her wrist. Tenderness, here again. A delicate, hopeful, starlit scent, orange blossom like a thread of a path you could follow through the night. Or like two people sitting in the early dawn together, sensual and vulnerable and with flowers in their hair.

She reached out and linked her fingers with his. He tightened his grip and pulled her in snug against his hard body. Her head against his shoulder, she closed her eyes. Taking slow breaths, letting herself just sink into the sensuality of being with Tristan. What did he smell like today? A little bit of this tender scent. He'd tested it on his own skin first, sometime earlier, hadn't he?

"I have something I wanted to ask you about." She showed him the envelope. "Do you recognize this key?"

His eyes lit with interest, but he shook his head. "It looks old. Do you want me to ask my aunt and my grandfather?"

Malorie winced. She'd kind of wanted to absorb whatever this key revealed before she had to tell his aunt or grandfather about it. You never knew, in her family.

Tristan turned the key in his hands. "Maybe it's to one of those cabinets downstairs. Or to some little box in one. I don't know what it might have to do with the Rosiers. Can we go on a treasure hunt?"

Malorie had faced the envelope and key with dread, but Tristan looked like a kid who'd just been handed a real pirate's map. Her own wariness softened. Tristan made everything seem as if it would be all right.

Mostly, she realized, because from his perspective it would be. Whatever the key revealed, he wouldn't think less of *her*.

"I always loved treasure hunting," he confessed, doing that *thing* that just aroused the hell out of her, that combination of sexy, hard-bodied man and boyish enthusiasm. "Did I ever tell you about the time we climbed over Tata Colette's wall in the middle of the night and Lucien broke his arm?"

"You mentioned it, yes," Malorie said, amused. She had a flashing vision of Tristan, old and white-haired, repeating the same story yet again to tolerant great-grandchildren. It was an oddly enticing little glimpse into a possible future—he was still full of life and enthusiasm, even wrinkled with age. His grandchildren, she was pretty sure, adored him.

"Oh," Tristan said. And then, unabashed, "Well, it's a great story." He grinned at her.

"So you want to go on a treasure hunt through my family's treasures?" Malorie took the key from his palm and held it up.

"Hell, yes." He grabbed it from her. "Let's go. Anything in here it might fit, do you think?"

***

Tristan was still going strong, but Malorie was getting rather sick of trying keyholes in the storage room an hour later and was delighted to have a FaceTime ping from Angèle to give her an excuse to take a break. Plus, she'd been trying to get in touch with Angèle ever since she got back to Grasse.

"I'll be back," she told Tristan as she put her phone away and went up to take it on her laptop in the office.

Pixelated face, a warm jacket with the hood pulled over her head, Angèle's brown hair escaping in wisps in the wind. Behind her a beautiful old building in warm golden tones. The building blurred in the background as Angèle shifted to, presumably, a less out-in-the-open place to talk.

"Well, look at that," Malorie said. "You're finally speaking to me."

"Really poor reception at the penguin colonies, Malorie."

"How are they doing? The penguins?" She'd been down there a couple of years ago. Angèle did retreat to Rio Grande from time to time, where she must be now, but as for the colonies themselves...talk about remote.

Angèle's face relaxed. "Pretty well. Although if people would let the King Penguins get established before they showed up en masse to take pictures, it probably wouldn't hurt." She rolled her eyes.

"By *en masse*, you mean ten to twenty people a day? Who sit respectfully at a distance with cameras, crossing their fingers that a penguin will wander up closer out of curiosity?"

Angèle gave her a disgruntled look. "That's how it *starts*."

Malorie grinned. Angèle had come to visit her in New York a few times, too—mostly because so many major conferences in wildlife biology were in North America. She always loved the restaurants, but she always asked Malorie how she stood the noise for more than a few days at a time.

"So what the hell are you doing?" Angèle asked. "Have you lost your mind?"

Malorie lifted her eyes to heaven a moment, hoping the pixelated connection showed the gesture properly. You could put Angèle all the way down in Tierra del Fuego, but you could never take that older sister *I-know-better-than-you-do* tone out of her. She probably bossed every single other biologist out there. "I'm trying to restore La Maison de Monsard," she said. "Somebody has to do it."

"Why? Let the thing die."

Malorie tensed. All the hairs on her arms lifted when Angèle said that. As if she'd been cut loose from the world, to float without roots for eternity. "It's our heritage, Angèle."

Angèle either just looked at her for a moment or the connection was freezing up.

Malorie made a gesture. "It doesn't have to matter to you, too." It *didn't*. Even if it hurt. "I just need your shares. Or your proxy for them, if you want to keep official ownership of them."

"I think you're crazy," Angèle said. "Why don't you just sell your shares to the Rosiers? Tristan's begging for them."

Malorie blinked. "...Tristan?" Wait, what?

"Surely he's asked you for yours, too."

"I—no. He hasn't done that." Her thoughts were starting to slow, as if they were stuck in honey.

"Really?" Angèle sounded surprised. "That's weird. He even told me he'd create a grant for young women from Grasse who wanted to study biology if I signed them over to him."

Oh, smart. Tristan was always so smart about people. He knew that would tempt Angèle far more than money.

While Malorie always thought of practical things— money—Tristan always knew that there were far more buttons to push on people to get what you wanted.

He knew about honey.

It smelled so sweet, it tasted so good...and it trapped way more flies than vinegar.

Those poor, stupid flies probably even thought it was a good way to go.

"Lise, too?" she said slowly. "Has he asked her about them, too?"

Angèle's eyebrows drew together in a little frown. "Maybe. It's really hard to get in touch with Lise anymore." Said the person who spent half her time observing isolated penguin colonies in the southern tip of Argentina and Chile and in Antarctica. "I wish she'd give up on saving the world and go somewhere safer."

Yes. Even at the far end of the world, even though they'd all chosen to make their own road, Angèle still had some latent instinct to keep an eye on her younger sisters. Hell, she probably kept an eye on penguins because of that instinct—penguins were something she actually *could* take care of.

"You're not going to do it, are you?" Malorie had to speak carefully. Her tongue felt clumsy. Tristan had been trying to accumulate shares in La Maison de Monsard. Tristan had been asking her about *her* shares in Monsard. Tristan had shown an eager, possessive interest in restoring Monsard, had talked about it like he would be part of it.

"Well, not if you want them, of course not," Angèle said. "But I still think you're crazy. Chasing after some windmill from our past. *Merde*, Malorie, who do you think you are, Don Quixote?"

Okay, Angèle was trying to save penguins from global warming. And she claimed *Malorie* was tilting at windmills?

Wasn't that just like her oldest sister's convictions she knew best. And could take control, keep her charges safe, fight the world for them. Maybe she'd chosen penguins because she'd known she'd never, ever manage to keep human charges safe.

"It matters," Malorie said. "I want this. It matters to me. It matters to us." She had to believe that. One day, surely, it would matter to Angèle and Lise. Or to their kids. Or to her own kids. If she ever found anyone to have kids with.

A vision of Tristan Rosier, gorgeous and half naked and strewn with flowers.

Tristan. Who could charm anyone out of anything. Her pants. Her shares. Her dreams.

Who had switched from fighting with her to flirting with her right about the time he had learned she had Monsard shares.

"Did he say why he wanted them?" she asked.

"He didn't have to," Angèle said blankly. "I mean...it's Tristan. Obviously the Rosiers are thinking of going into direct perfume sales, and Tristan's name is the one they can do that with."

And so, just like that, because he wanted it and he couldn't conceive of a world that didn't do everything he wanted, Tristan had decided to take over her family company? *I'll take it*, he'd said, what seemed like years ago. But was really only a few days.

Had he only needed a few days? To wrap her around his finger and take it from her?

"Look, don't worry," Angèle said. "If you want the shares, they're yours. You can have my proxy. I'll send the signatures you need so the banks will work with you. But you'd better get in touch with Lise somehow, because you don't know how many other shares he already has. He might only need one of us to sell to him to get the majority."

Malorie sat for a long time after they cut the connection, staring at the amber hearts bottle. When she was a little girl, she at first used to love it when her father brought her mother romantic gifts. They meant he loved them, that he was going to convince her mother to stop being mad at him. When she was very little, she hadn't understood the real causes of her mother's anger—his cheating and his draining of all their income for his show-off purposes. She'd only been happy that their father was doing all that work to keep them together, and she'd often been taken into his confidence behind her mother's back, as he explained how difficult her mother was being over nothing, how much more the family mattered to *him* than it did to anyone else. Didn't *she* care about the family? he would say. If she did, she should tell her mother.

As she got older, she'd learned to hate the gifts. She learned to see through her father's lies, learned what was going on behind the fights. She learned that staying together would only keep them stuck in the same situation, that the presents would just weaken her mother's conviction yet again. Weaken even her grandmother's, because how could her grandmother stay stern against her son acting so sweetly? Even if he was stealing away their financial security to feed his own addiction to showing off in Monaco.

She'd never liked gifts, as an adult. In fact, she'd never liked relationships, because how could you, if everything nice the guy ever did made you worry you were about to be caught in the clutches of a narcissistic spider? Someone who just wanted to suck the blood out of you for his own ends and, if you were really unlucky, keep you alive enough to give him more blood the next time he needed it?

She buried her head in her hands and took deep breaths. While her entire past rose up in her like the girders of a great building and twisted in a scream of rusted metal.

Tristan bounded in with a carved wooden box in his hands. "I think I found it!"

Chapter 24

Tristan stopped short just inside the door as he took in her expression.. He cocked his head, concerned. "Is everything okay? Angèle's okay, isn't she?"

Malorie stared at him. It would help so much if her father hadn't been capable of exactly the same expression of concern, when inside he didn't give a damn about anything but what he wanted.

It's Tristan. Not anybody else. Him. Think.

It was so hard to think when everything *hurt*.

She spoke slowly, having to sort through each word and choose the next one with care. "Tristan. Have you been trying to buy up Monsard shares?"

"Oh." The smile just slid off his face. "She told you."

Oh, God. It was true.

"She's still my sister, Tristan. I know we're only Monsards, but that still means *something*."

"She could have kept her mouth shut about this at least," Tristan said, irritated. "It was supposed to be a surprise."

That side-swiped her. She couldn't figure out what it even meant. "A *surprise*?"

"Don't tell me you don't get the concept either."

"You were buying up shares in my family company as a *surprise*?" From the screaming rust-girders of her past, she felt as if she'd just found herself instead strolling through the candy cane structures of la-la land.

"*You're* the one who's always focused on business, Malorie. I thought you'd appreciate it."

"*Appreciate* it?" Her fingers pressed so hard into the desk she hurt her knuckles. "And when were you going to share this surprise with me?"

"I don't know! I couldn't figure out the right moment." He frowned. "It's just so...dry. I mean, when would *you* have said it?"

Malorie shoved to her feet. "As soon as I got them?"

"But you were barely speaking to me back then. I bought the first ones two years ago when your grandmother was going through a tight spot and didn't want to tell you girls."

That one was like a punch in the gut. Malorie had trained her whole life to be *good* at finances, so she'd never be helpless before someone else's misuse of them again. But when her grandmother had needed financial help...she hadn't even known.

"Of course you three are women, now, and should have been told, but she was your grandmother. I guess you were always girls to her."

And Tristan had known. And she had two ways she could think about that—he had either exploited an old woman's weakness, like every man in her grandmother's life had ever done, or he had seen someone who needed help and offered it.

Like Tristan would have done.

That emotion he kept rousing in her swelled up to press in her chest. This wondering, panicked *love* of him that was so freaking painful.

Terrifying. She'd seen it over and over as a child. It was so, so easy to love someone who could never love you back. Someone who would always be out for himself.

But that's not Tristan. You know it's not Tristan.

Although...although...he did really like to get his way. His mother had said it herself, had said to never make the mistake of thinking he'd been distracted onto other toys.

Toys. Her heritage. Her life. Her? He had so much, how could he *ever* value *her* as much as she did? He had everything. She was all she had.

"And anyway, I didn't think you were interested in anything here then," Tristan was saying casually. That casualness made it worse. This struck at the heart of her world, and to him it was nothing. His pocket change. Her whole fortune. "Once you came back and told me you were thinking about restoring the place, I figured I'd tell you once you were sure you wanted them. If you were going to decide to sell the place, I wanted to keep them so we could buy the rest of the shares from you more easily."

"How many shares do you *have*?"

"Twenty percent."

A cold shock. Twenty percent. That was how much *she* had. Her entire inheritance. Tristan had acquired the equivalent of her entire inheritance so casually he hadn't even thought it was important to mention it. All those treasures of which he had been so possessive in the storage room really *were* just as much his as hers.

"I got Damien to sell me Rosier SA's, and I got Tata Colette to sell me the ones she had from a long time ago, when your grandmother was struggling as a young single mother, I guess."

Oh. Malorie had never known that Colette Delatour had tried to help her grandmother. Her teenage grandmother had needed all the help she could get, having had her life swept out from under her by her father's fecklessness, and then given another life to take care of on top of it, by the fecklessness of some man who had left her pregnant. Charming men, who got what they wanted, and left the women to pick up the pieces.

"I got the ones your father signed away in Monaco to cover gambling debts."

A sick vulnerability knotted in her stomach. Tristan had managed to exploit every single weakness the men in her family had created. Malorie could feel herself tightening and tightening, like a guitar string about to snap. She hadn't been able to control the damage her father did to their family, because she was a child.

And now she still couldn't control it. Because of Tristan.

"And I was trying to get Angèle or Lise's twenty percent, which would between us have brought us up to a safe majority so the banks would deal with you, but your sisters are a lot harder to negotiate with than perfume bottle collectors."

Between us.

Right. Right. Malorie struggled to breathe past that knot that seemed to grip her whole torso. *It's Tristan. Tristan. Not your father. Tristan.*

Between us.

Tristan doesn't think of it as him against me. He thinks of it as "us".

And that was vital.

Still her voice felt harsh, parched, words peeling off one by one. "You have a fifth of Monsard shares. And you thought it was more important to give me perfumes?"

Tristan's expression flickered. "Wasn't it?"

Tristan. It's Tristan.

Of course he would think perfumes were more important.

Malorie fought that knot in her, fought to make herself breathe. Long breaths. *Think. Think past the past. Stay in the moment. It's Tristan.*

And what mattered to *him*? The pretty crayons he spilled on the floor. The drawings he slid across her desk. The perfumes he made, to offer her.

Tristan stiffened at her silence, and for the first time, it looked as if *he* had been wounded in this conversation. As if something had shaken his confidence. And she almost felt glad—because maybe, if he was wounded, too, he could halfway understand how much this hurt.

"It wasn't," he said. His face emptied.

Oh, God, she hated to see that empty look on his face. She squeezed thumb and forefinger below her eyes. "Of course it was," she said low. His perfumes were the most beautiful thing he could imagine. And he gave them to her.

Sometimes she wanted to shove him off a tall building for being so blithe and oblivious. And yet...she never wanted him to have to hit the ground. She liked it, that he was so damn happy in who he was.

"No," Tristan said. "It wasn't." He was searching her face, his expression growing...tired? As if he was never, ever going to find what he wanted, when he searched her face.

Malorie's jaw worked. She didn't want him to pull this out of her. She didn't want to. He didn't deserve it. She *knew* he was just clueless sometimes. She *knew* it. She knew he loved the crayons more than the math sheets.

And that was all this was.

It was just—"Twenty percent, Tristan. Twenty percent."

"I haven't been able to convince the old Monsard board members or their heirs to sell. For now, we still need your sisters."

"And I still need *you!*" she snapped suddenly. "If you have twenty percent."

His expression flickered. "Well...yeah," he said, staring at her.

She didn't want to hurt him. She really didn't. He wasn't her father. He was such a *good* guy. But her arms hugged her middle, where all of this hurt *her* so damn bad. "*Twenty percent.* Tristan. That's how much I have. My entire legacy. Everything I have from my family. And all you needed was to use your Rosier money and connections to scoop up the same amount on the open market, which is only *out there in the first place* because my father and his father and grandfather were such *bastards.*"

The box he'd held so excitedly when he sprang into the office dropped to bump against his thigh. His other hand flexed as if it wanted to find a tricky cliff face to grip. Far away from here. "Malorie," he said persuasively. "You're making too big a deal out of this. It—"

The exact words her father had used over and over, about and to her mother, who was always *making too big a deal out of things*, and only when Malorie got older had she realized her father's modus operandi. To do something horribly damaging to the family, cheat on her mother, steal their financial security to show off in Monaco—and then diminish her mother's right to be mad about it. Shift the blame onto her, for overreacting.

"No," she said very quietly. "No, I'm not."

Something about her tone stopped Tristan cold. He stared at her.

She straightened her shoulders. Lifted her chin. "I'm not making too big a deal out of this," she said. "To me, this matters."

"It shouldn't," Tristan said quickly, brushing her claim aside. "I didn't think about it at all. It was just someth—"

Malorie's jaw tightened until it felt as if it would snap. "I know you didn't think about it at all, Tristan," she said, locking eyes with his. "Trust me, I figured that out."

His eyebrows knit slowly as he stared back at her, as if they were speaking two different languages and he could only make out one word in ten of hers. "I thought about the perfumes I gave you. I thought about those a lot."

Oh, God. Were they right back to Fugace? She pinched her brow.

"But then, you still don't think those are important," Tristan said, his voice so...flat. As if that uncrushable little boy in him had been crushed. By her.

Her insides tightened even more in a kind of panic. She didn't want to hurt him. She really didn't. But if he didn't hurt, too, then he didn't *understand*. And over and over her father had shifted the blame for the hurt in a situation from him to his wife or daughters. It wasn't that *he* had done anything wrong. It was that *they* hadn't considered *him*.

Of course Tristan wasn't her father. Of course he wasn't. But all of this, the past and the present, snarled inside her and made such a huge, painful mess.

Malorie didn't know how to handle this and keep her center. It was as if Tristan had stolen not only shares but that most important thing of all to her—her sense of who she was and who she wanted to try to be. She'd worked so *freaking hard* to establish that.

"I don't know why you never think the perfumes are important." Tristan sounded numb. "I mean, *merde,* Malorie, did it *ever once* occur to you that those perfumes are worth more than your shares?"

She recoiled, feeling as if Tristan, of all people, had just found the one point where she was most vulnerable and shoved the knife in.

Tristan. The one person in the world she'd been learning to trust.

"They are," he repeated, stubborn and hard. "I picked those shares up at bargain basement prices, and if you properly marketed those perfumes they'd make you millions. But by all means, dismiss them as the *art* of someone who never *works.*"

What?

"That's not what I'm doing!" she blazed. She *never* said that kind of thing about him—well, maybe she used to. But only when she was trying to fight him back. To his family, she'd made it crystal clear how highly she thought of him. He had to know it, *merde.* Tristan had more self-confidence than anyone she knew. "And I don't need you to tell me how much more every single damn thing you have is worth than anything I have. I think you've clearly established that." She slashed her hand through the air to indicate those shares.

Or maybe to indicate him. The prince. Who always seemed to be worth so much more than she was, every time. Even right down to emotionally, the one with all the heart, while she was the mercenary one. Heartless.

Tristan made a hard gesture, as if he wanted to shove every emotion in this room out the window, and rolled his shoulders, that old gesture of shaking water off a duck's back. "Malorie." He tried to make his voice calm. "This is ridiculous. I think it's all just a misu—"

Hurt and fury surged up, obliterating her last grasp of sense. *Ridiculous?* "Damn you. You steal twenty percent of my entire family legacy, and you think that doesn't even matter."

"I didn't *steal* it. I *bought* it, with the money I earned from making those perfumes you think are so worthless. And I was going to g—"

"I don't care what you were going to do!" she yelled, all control abruptly breaking. "I don't want you to have that much power in my life in the first place, to be the one who decides. I don't want to depend on you, can't you get that through your fucking patriarchal head? *I don't want to need you!*"

The words dropped into the room as if a church bell had been rung right there, reverberating too loudly, all other sound stopping. Tristan stood very still.

Malorie stared back at him, trapped by the truth of what she had just said. She'd gone too far. She'd gone way too far. She was going to break them. Oh, God. She didn't want to break them.

And yet to apologize, she would have had to pretend that she didn't mean it.

And she did.

Tristan's eyes crinkled up as if she'd hurt him hard enough to make them sting. He took a long breath. "Malorie." His voice sounded rough. "Do you really think I'd ever use those shares in any way but to help you? That's all I wanted to do. Help."

He didn't wait for her answer. Didn't wait for her to absorb or recover. He turned around and walked out.

He still had the box from the storage room under his arm, but of course he didn't notice. Like he didn't notice that he walked out with her heart and her happiness. A man who assumed the world was his by birthright would never notice that he was taking something so minor that didn't belong to him.

Chapter 25

"You were right," Tristan said. "I should have told her about those shares."

Matt slammed the sledgehammer down on his head. Okay, not quite on his head, but on a wrought iron post about a meter above his head, the impact ringing all the way through the iron, through Tristan's bones, and almost certainly contributing to premature deafness. Jess had decided that she wanted to line the drive to the old *mas* where the post-wedding party would be with hanging pots of jasmine for the wedding celebration, which sounded very pretty and all that, but somebody had to drive all those thin, graceful wrought iron poles into the ground. When it was your turn to be at the top of the ladder swinging the sledgehammer it wasn't so bad, but being the man holding the post steady was crappy.

"What was that?" Damien called, pulling two more posts out of the back of the truck. "I couldn't hear you."

Tristan gritted his teeth. "I said you were *right*."

"Sorry, one more time?"

Bang went the sledgehammer. Tristan clenched his jaw, but it still shook from the vibration. "You were RIGHT. Happy now?"

Above him, Matt let his hand slide up the sledgehammer handle to loosely grip it near the head, promising a moment of reprieve. He gazed at Tristan in open astonishment.

"I'm generally right," Damien said. "But could you be more specific?"

"About Malorie," Tristan said between his still-vibrating teeth. "And the shares."

"Hell, I could have told you that," Matt said. "No one likes to find out someone else has something that's valuable to him. Or her."

Just after Matt met Layla he had discovered Tante Colette had gifted her a part of this valley, Matt's heritage, which he was supposed to guard for the family. He had not handled it well.

"Layla was a stranger," Tristan said. "It's not the same thing at all. And you got over it. You didn't even make her give it back."

"That's because by then I knew I could trust her," Matt said.

Tristan scowled.

"Face it, Tristan, no one likes to feel as if she trusted you and then you stole from her," Raoul said. And frowned, brooding. "Even if you *weren't* stealing from her. I mean...not really. Well...it was complicated."

That's right, Raoul had tried to steal that perfume box from Allegra when he first met her. For God's sake, his cousins were crazy. And *Tristan* was the one who couldn't get the woman he wanted to trust him. He squeezed his furrowed brow, but it refused to relax.

"Or feel betrayed," Damien said. "No one likes to feel he—*she*—made herself vulnerable and then was betrayed."

Damien's idea of betrayal seemed to have been having a woman walk out on him after a one-night stand. Tristan, who couldn't really think of a single one-night stand on which he would want to build a relationship but who had known Malorie his whole fucking life, did *not* see the similarity.

"I did not betray her!" he snapped. "I was trying to help."

"Where have I heard that before?" Raoul said.

"Remember when he knocked down our fort when he was five?" Matt said. "He was trying to help then, too."

"Or that time he nearly started a forest fire and our grandfather discovered we'd been building bonfires in the middle of the night?" Raoul said. "Oh, yeah, I remember *that* help."

Seriously, it was such a damn pain to be the youngest sometimes. "You could try remembering all the times I saved you three from acting like total idiots and ruining your lives," Tristan said. "Instead."

Matt grinned at him. "You know, *you* could try listening to your wiser older cousins once in a while. Instead of assuming we're total idiots."

Tristan gave him an incredulous look. "This from a man who can't even put a T-shirt on correctly when he's got a crush on a girl?"

Matt started to blush.

"And don't even get me started about you," Tristan told Damien.

"Hey, I did all right," Raoul claimed. "With Allegra."

Tristan gaped at him. "You tried to *steal* from her—" He broke off. Frowned. "Well, she *thought* you tried to steal from her—" He broke off again. Damn it. "You're just lucky she was so generous and trusting."

And Tristan was not lucky. Malorie was not trusting. She didn't believe anyone in this world had her back, not even him.

Shit, she was nursing her wounds somewhere thinking he'd stabbed her in the back. And even though that hurt like hell, that she would think that of him, he knew he was going to have to go fix it. Because...how did you nurse a wound in your back? You needed someone else to help you recover from that.

"But just to make sure we're clear on the basics," Damien said. "You are hereby acknowledging that you do, in fact, screw up with women at least as much as we do when your heart's involved?"

Tristan gave him a disgruntled look. "*As much* might be exaggerating."

"Fine." Damien dropped his poles on the gravel with a clatter. "Then I won't help you out."

"I do not need help," Tristan snapped, although he slid a glance at Damien. Damien had a good idea? "I know exactly what I need to do."

All three of his cousins looked at him expectantly. Like hyenas waiting for him to toss them a juicy tidbit.

Tristan ground his teeth. "Apologize, okay? It's not that complicated. I'm not one of you idiots."

Damien gave him a faint, cousin-cruel smile. "Then why are you here miserable? If it's that simple."

Okay, you know what—? Tristan stepped back from his pole, shaking his numb hands and wrists. "One of you guys can hold this thing for a while. *I* want to hit things with sledgehammers."

Matt yielded his sledgehammer and his place on the ladder, while Raoul dragged the second ladder into position to start another pole on the other side of the drive. "Apologizing always works," Matt said. "I mean, if it doesn't, you need to rethink whether she's the person you'd want to spend your life with."

Spend your life with. Tristan felt heat climb all the way from his shoulder blades up to his hairline. Oh, hell.

All three of his cousins stilled, staring at him in greedy delight. Yes, the hyenas had just gotten a very tasty morsel.

"Did you just blush?" Matt elbowed Damien. "Did you see that? He just blushed."

"It's the exertion." Tristan hefted the hammer. "Are you sure you want to provoke me while I'm holding a sledgehammer above your head?"

Matt grinned up at him and gripped the pole. Then stopped grinning in favor of clenching his jaw as the first *bong* went through him.

"I didn't do anything wrong," Tristan said abruptly, with another hard slam. "So why the hell should I apologize?"

From his own ladder above Damien's head, Raoul stared at him from across the drive. "Apologizing isn't about whether you did something wrong or not," he said incredulously. "It's about whether something you did got her hurt. You didn't know that?"

Yes, of course he knew that. Damn it. He was the one who was *good* at emotions. His cousins were the ones who were bumbling, blindfolded bears. But...Tristan tried hard to unclench his jaw, but the effects of holding that iron post while it was battered with a sledgehammer seemed to have permanently tightened it. "She doesn't care if *I'm* hurt. She thinks I'm just...I don't know. That I'm just the same kid I was in school, and that my perfumes are worth nothing."

He hated it, he *hated* it, when Malorie dismissed what he did as silly and inconsequential. It made him think of all those times in school, when teachers had told him, *Arrête de faire ton imbécile*, while Malorie had bent studiously over her work and tried to ignore him. She'd always been in the right, and he'd always been in the wrong. The kid who goofed things up.

"Well, if she thinks you're still the same kid you were in school, she sure as hell liked the kid you were in school," Damien said.

Tristan tightened his grip on the sledgehammer, trying to search Damien's face from across the drive. "What do you mean?"

"Please." Damien touched his flat belly. "I've got a weak stomach. I can't repeat that kind of thing."

Tristan controlled a very strong urge to drop the sledgehammer and go for Damien's throat so he could strangle it out of him.

Damien looked amused. "She thinks you're some kind of wonderful."

Tristan blinked a moment.

Matt made a noise like an indignant bear. "If someone could explain to me why Tristan manages to fool all of the women all of the time, I would really appreciate it."

Tristan knew he was supposed to make some gloating *I'm so hot I sizzle* kind of gesture right about then, but his heart wasn't in it. He took a step down the ladder, closer to Damien. "Could you be more specific?"

"*Merde, non,*" Matt said. "I just ate."

Damien laughed. "Tristan, why don't you focus on getting these posts done, and who knows? By the end of it, maybe some sense will have been pounded into your head."

Tristan hesitated. But there was something very satisfying about pounding things with a sledgehammer right about then. He couldn't stop thinking about Malorie. No cousins around her to help her process things, just keeping her shoulders as straight as she could and trying her best to handle everything life threw at her—even the emotional curveballs—all by herself.

Chapter 26

Malorie slapped mortar onto the wall of the old orange orchard, mending cracks. You had to keep up with these things. If you didn't pay attention, walls fell down on you. It was almost as if something in nature didn't love a wall.

But she did. You could get along with people better if you had a good wall between you. You didn't have to trust them.

The wet dust and stone smell of mortar rose around her, making her eyes wet, too. She was *not* crying. She was too mad to cry. It was just that mixing the mortar had made her want to sneeze, and she couldn't quite shake the sneeze out.

Damn Tristan. He was never going to understand her ever, was he? His life had been too different. Too warm, too happy.

She wanted to make up, and yet she wanted Tristan to *realize* what he'd done, too. To understand how much she couldn't bear to let him have that big a piece of her control over her life, and that her need for independence didn't make her a bad person.

Did it make her a bad person? She'd always tried really, really hard to do the right thing. But she'd never been good at self-sacrifice. Growing up, it had been too much expected that the women and little girls in her father's life sacrifice everything about themselves to him.

Sleep on it. It will feel better in the morning.

Plus, you can't break you and Tristan. Surely you've figured that out by now?

Figured out that she and Tristan had known each other all their lives, a relationship that had grown far too big for them to just yank it out casually by the roots over a fight.

Her breathing calmed as she thought about it. She stopped slapping mortar quite as recklessly, slowing to smooth it out. Mending. A wall that would protect this space for a long time, for anyone in her family who needed refuge here.

It was true. She really could trust Tristan. He was probably right this second drawing up a transfer of those shares to her, because he'd seen how she reacted.

Signing away his hope of a role in the company to her. All that bright enthusiasm and energy withdrawing.

How eager he'd been to reveal those floors and make them shine. How his imagination had engaged with the whole story of the place, trying to capture it in a perfume bottle for her.

Her spade slowed in its thrust into the wheelbarrow and she looked at the mortar she brought up. He was so fragile where his perfumes were concerned—the only area in which he was easily hurt. And for Tristan to walk out on her, she was pretty sure she had really hurt him.

A scraping sound came from the top of the wall. She looked up as a long, lean figure swung over it easily and dropped down beside her, the sight of him so unsurprising that she didn't even startle back.

Tristan. His hair gorgeously mussed as always, his cheekbones so perfect, his eyes such a rich brown. He shrugged a small backpack to the ground and took in her spade and her wheelbarrow of mortar.

"Oh, you would," he said, with a mix of resignation and exasperation.

"So would you," she said, unexpectedly wry, looking up at the top of the wall he had just cleared so easily.

She barely had time to drop her spade as he closed his hands around her hips, pulled her in to him, and kissed her.

It obliterated all her defenses in a warm wave of human touch. And she probably shouldn't remember all the times her father had done that kind of thing to her mother, treated her mother's anger as something easily dismissed as soon as he himself was over it. But a part of her did.

"I'm sorry," Tristan said, and she drew a rough breath. His apology struck another crumbling blow to her defenses.

But she tried to keep them strong. "You don't even know what you did."

"I know it hurt you," he said simply.

Tears filled her eyes that fast. *Oh.* That did make all the difference. That he cared.

He pulled an envelope out of the backpack he'd dropped to the ground and handed it to her. "I had to go pound things with a sledgehammer for a while with my cousins, and then I had to get this drawn up. That's why it took me so long. It signs the shares over to you."

Her face crumpled. All her emotions tangled, the morass of them swelling out of control. This should have been the perfect thing for him to do. And yet it felt so wrong. "Tristan. You can't just sign these over to me. Don't you even care about them?"

Tristan stared at her incredulously. "Oh, *bon sang.*" He rested his forehead against hers. "Now you're just messing with me."

"I'm not, I just—" He tangled her emotions up so much she couldn't even pull a single one clear from the mass and figure out what it was. "I thought Monsard *mattered* to you."

His fingers flexed into her hips. "I'm starting to understand why Matt growls so much."

"Is it this easy for you to give them up?" As easy as it had been for him to acquire them. This huge part of her.

That she'd thought he cared about.

Hell. How had what she wanted out of him become the quintessence of a Catch-22?

"No." Tristan lifted his head to gaze into her eyes. "It's not easy. It makes me sad, Malorie. I loved feeling part of this with you. Being there at the new beginning, the idea we were starting something beautiful together."

Yeah. She had loved that, too. Her fingers crumpled the edge of the envelope. Tristan had made relaunching Monsard sound not lonely but *happy*.

"But are *you* ever going to understand that when I gave you those perfumes, when I moved on after Fugace and *still gave you more of me*, doing that was a much bigger gesture than giving you these shares ever could be. *No*, the shares don't matter to me that much. I got the shares because I knew they mattered *to you*."

Oh. Those tears threatened to spill through her lashes. She dropped her forehead to his shoulder, seeking steadiness. His steadiness.

That shoulder obliged by staying steady, even as his chest moved in a big sigh. He pulled a strand of her hair free and twined it around his finger.

Her breath released against his shirt, slow and soft. "The perfumes do matter to me, Tristan," she said. It stuffed up her throat with emotion how much they mattered. "They really do. They're beautiful. I just...you're *never* going to understand."

His arms wrapped around her. "Yes, I am," he said quietly to the top of her head. "You're explaining it to me right now."

"You think I'm just a *mercenary*." She was starting to cry. It was his damn warmth that did it, loosening everything. "You *always* think that. You never, never understand that when somebody else has control of your company or your money, it's, it's...like standing on one of those damn beaches they have in America, where all the sand gets pulled out from under your feet every time you try to brace."

Tristan's arm snuggled her more closely into him. His lips touched the top of her head. "I'm more like Mediterranean sand. I tend to stay somewhat in place."

He was like a damn granite cliff face was what he was like. Or, as his mother had said, like a giant tree, that just grew and grew. *He doesn't know how to do that—change, let go. I know he seems very distractible on the surface. But emotionally he's very constant. I just told you.*

She closed her eyes, focusing on the feel of his arms around her, on his shoulder under her cheek.

The emotional constancy of his. Sturdy. Solid. Forever.

"I just wanted to be part of it," he said quietly. "I guess I did get the shares as a lever, to try to make sure you had to let me in. But I wasn't trying to make you feel vulnerable at all. I guess I overestimated how much you understood you could count on me."

Sometimes, she could know something intellectually and yet still, emotionally, never quite lose the scars.

He kissed the top of her head. "I've always wanted to be part of you, Malorie."

Tears flushed to her eyes again. "You have not," she said roughly, even though she at least partly knew she was wrong to pretend not to believe him.

"I'm pretty sure I have, Malorie. I asked you to marry me when we were just five years old. And you've still never told me yes or no."

She flushed all through her, too many emotions all at once, as she pulled back to look at him. "We were just kids."

He nodded. "But we're not kids anymore."

Her throat clogged so much. His emotions always seemed so simple and honest, and hers were always so dammed-up and afraid.

Honest. Funny how she could think that about Tristan when he'd been buying up shares behind her back to give himself leverage in her family company. And yet...

He stroked her damp hair back from its tangle in her lashes, his hand cupping her cheek. "I don't think you're just a mercenary, Malorie. I think you're the hottest, most capable, most amazing mercenary out there."

She blinked rapidly, lashes smearing dampness, at the completely unexpected nature of that compliment. "Uh—"

"Do you think I'm *just* an artist?" he said.

She slowly shook her head. "I think you're the hottest, most annoying, most amazing artist out there," she said huskily.

He smiled a little, his thumb stroking her cheekbone. "So maybe you can hire me sometimes to make a perfume for you? Because I'd really like that."

To be part of it. Him and her, together against the world.

Oh, hell, this guy made her cry so damn much. She scrubbed her face. "Do you know I *never* cry where anyone can see me?"

"I figured. But then I never thought I was 'anyone'."

No. No, he wasn't just anyone.

She managed some kind of smile. "So I guess crying all over you is a way of letting you in?"

"I guess it is," he said quietly and squeezed her body into him a little more snugly. For a little while, they were quiet. She listened to the thud of his heart. A little faster than usual, showing his emotion. But still steady. Still strong.

"What about nineteen percent?" she said abruptly, pulling back to look at him. "Could you sell me one percent? So I can have twenty-one percent and you can have nineteen?"

One of those supple eyebrows went up a little. He smiled. "You'll feel better if you have them all, Malorie."

She hesitated a long moment. Then met his eyes. "No," she said very slowly. It was amazing how unscary this felt to say. Not like jumping off a cliff. But like finding her grip and climbing up it, toward the sun. "I wouldn't feel better."

That alert stillness ran through him. His eyes held hers.

"I want you in this with me," she said helplessly. It went against her whole life policy. And yet... "You're the life of the place," she said softly. "You know all the sunlight in that perfume you made me yesterday? That's you."

An astonishing wave of color ran up Tristan's cheeks, a startling flush of vulnerability. His smile grew awkward, his expression reminding her of nothing so much as the gangling fourteen-year-old he had been just before he started to fill out. Or of the little boy who had spilled crayons at her feet, over and over again.

She ran her palm down his forearm until she reached his hand and could pull it from her hip, linking her fingers with his and lifting it between them, gazing at the two hands together.

It was kind of the most beautiful sight she had ever seen. Their two hands together.

Her breathing calmed. Slowing, settled.

His fingers flexed gently on hers. "You don't have to bribe me with shares. I'll still be here."

She shook her head slowly. "But those are what matter to me, Tristan. Those shares. So I want you to have them. The way you wanted me to have your perfumes."

"Aww, hell," he said helplessly, and lowered his forehead to hers again, gazing down at their entwined hands. "Malorie. Don't you *dare* make me cry."

"Keep them," she said. "They're yours. We're"—she gave him a quick, searching look, hoping he agreed—"we're in this together."

His fingers flexed gently on hers. "Ours," he said, his voice deep and warm. "That's a nice word. Why don't we say they're ours."

Ours.

Oh. *That* sounded right.

263

Ours.

Yes. It might be the very nicest word ever invented. Warm. Solid. Together. She tried it, carefully: "Ours."

Chapter 27

For a long time after that, they lay under one of the orange trees, not speaking. Tristan played with her hair, freeing it from the clasp at the back of her head, drawing his fingers through the strands of it. A white flower drifted slowly down with the setting sun, and he caught it and tucked it in her hair.

In that hush of space, you could let things out. Open up secret spaces inside you into the safety of that evening. Propped on one elbow, watching the edge of color over the sea, he spoke thoughtfully, words slow. "I guess I wanted them as a lever because I never could trust you would just let me in for what I am."

"What?" Malorie jerked into a sitting position.

He sat up, too, opening his hand. "I never could trust you'd...admire me, too. See any good qualities in me. So I wanted to have something I knew you cared about."

"*What?*" Malorie stared at him for a full ten seconds before she smacked both her hands to her face. "Oh, my God, you people are so *dumb.*"

"Hey."

"You're all so freaking entitled and so spoiled that even *you* can't see what a good thing you've got in you."

Tristan parted his lips as if to say something, then clearly thought better of it and came up with something else. "I don't even know what you're talking about. For half our lives, you've barely been able to stand me."

Malorie ground her teeth. "Tristan. You're sexy, sweet, gorgeous, you can just *smile* and it warms entire rooms, you're hardworking and creative and a freaking genius, everyone says so, and you have this *gift* for reaching into the heart of things and making that heart feel okay. And you don't even realize how *rare* that is? What a freaking *miracle* of a person you are?"

Tristan looked as if he'd been strolling with Tristan-like confidence along the edge of a cliff and she'd just shoved him off it. Well, she always had wanted to shove him off a cliff, but who knew a compliment was the way? He opened his mouth and closed it, and a delicate hint of color came into his cheeks. "...*That's* what you think my qualities are?"

"Some of them," Malorie said sulkily. Sometimes the Rosiers just pissed her off so bad.

"*Some* of them?"

"Well, I didn't want to go overboard." She folded her arms.

Tristan gaped at her. The flush deepened, dramatically. He shoved his hand through his hair. "Wow." And then, "I am going to fucking kill them."

"What?"

"Well, not Tante Colette, I can't kill her, but Damien, I am definitely going to kill."

"Why are you talking about murder all the sudden?"

"I just think certain people could have passed on certain essential information. Instead of leaving me to fumble around in the dark." He suddenly pulled her back into his arms again and just hugged her, very hard. "Wow," he murmured again, low.

She leaned her head against his chest, listening to the thump of his heart. It was such a reassuring sound. She'd gotten scarily close to panicking and breaking everything, and...well, maybe he wasn't that easy to break. Trees weren't, after all.

His chest moved in a slow breath against her cheek. He spoke softly. "The perfumes are the best thing I can be. So when you can dismiss one of those..."

She lifted her head. "You're the best thing you can be, Tristan. Your juices are a lovely expression of that, but if I make them more profitable, I am *not* dismissing you."

A funny little smile on his face. He kissed her. "I love you so damn much."

A shock of joy straight through her. She stared at him.

He was playing with her hair. She wasn't sure he'd even considered the impact of what he'd just said. "You know I've always been insecure about you," he said.

"Tristan. You have *not*."

He shrugged a little, but met her eyes. That way he did sometimes, that insisted that she really look at him. "Sometimes the scars you acquire as a child never really go away."

"I scarred you?" she whispered, horrified. She'd never meant to.

He shook his head. "It wasn't you. You were hard to attain, but you were never mean about it. It was that sense that I was never good enough. That I could never live up to you. Or live up to what anyone wanted of me, really."

What? Oh, because...if he'd learned to charm his way out of so much trouble, it was because he was always getting things wrong. She'd kind of forgotten that. Everything about him seemed so right now.

Because he'd polished himself. Done what he needed, to make his society accept him. They both had had their battles, just different ones.

Her hand tightened around his. "You might have been a pain sometimes, Tristan, but...I always thought you were amazing."

His smile warmed until it was this great ray of sunshine in her life. He kissed her. "Likewise, Malorie."

He made her feel so good. Whole and held, both at once.

He linked their fingers, gazing at their hands. "We're going to butt heads over production costs and perfumes so damn much." The way he said it, it didn't sound like a bad thing.

Did Tristan have as enticing a vision of that as she did? "I bet it will be fun," she said, wistful for a future that seemed as if it might really happen.

That brilliant smile of his. He kissed her hand. "I'll make you some commercial perfumes if you'll let me play around with a niche line, too."

"All right." She was starting to smile, too. Tristan had that gift, of helping, when emotion got too utterly overwhelming, to give that emotion a little outlet of humor and warmth, before it burst a person. "Don't go crazy with the *oud*." One of the most expensive perfume components in the world.

He held up a finger. "Local jasmine. From Matt."

"Hmm." She liked the idea of local, but Matt was freaking expensive. "Maybe he could give you a family discount."

"Maybe Rosier SA could give us a family deal on all of production, since they're family. It will be a while before you could get your own production facility set up again, if you want to do that."

Rosiers would be family?

Okay, wait...what were they assuming here?

"Could we call it Rosier-Monsard?" Tristan said.

Her eyebrows shot up to the top of her head. "No. We could not. You'll only have nineteen percent of the shares, Tristan." To her twenty-one percent. But she had her sister's proxy. Forty-one plus nineteen—even without Lise, they could go forward, if she and Tristan could agree. Sixty percent would be enough to convince the banks.

"How about Monsard-Rosier?"

"Tristan. It's La Maison de Monsard."

"I am not changing my name to Monsard," Tristan said, and Malorie gave one great, big blink, as that sentence went *bam* right through her.

"Well, I'm not changing my name to Rosier," she said. What the hell were they discussing?

Tristan folded his arms and frowned at her. "Why do you always have to be so difficult?"

"Why do you always have to be so patriarchal?"

He frowned at her another moment and then made a flick-the-water-away-from-the-duck's-back motion with one hand. "Fine, we'll work that out later." He turned his palm up so that her hand rested in it and ran this thumb over her ring finger, a little smile on his face. "But that's a yes otherwise?"

She had the sudden impression that she'd been lured down a funnel path until he'd landed her right where he wanted her. And she hadn't even realized that was the direction in which he'd been luring her.

"What was the question?" Malorie meant to sound her usual tough self, but her voice came out husky and wispy, as if she'd lost all her air.

"If you hadn't waited twenty-four years to answer it, maybe you'd still remember it." Tristan turned their palms up, pressed together, and linked his fingers strongly between hers. "This was the question," he said, and kissed her ring finger, right at the base.

Malorie ran her free hand through her hair and actually pulled locks of it across her face, to half hide herself as she gazed at him. It was so disorienting how wonderful he made her feel. She could *not* get used to it. Dizzy and wandering in a fairy world and not sure where her cardinal points were anymore. "Can you actually marry someone you've known your whole life?"

"Who else would you marry? I've never understood my cousins, falling for people they barely know."

Yeah. She couldn't get that either. It seemed as if love took a long time, to establish its roots, to grow so big and take up so much space in your life that you couldn't imagine that life without it.

She couldn't imagine life without Tristan. Even when she'd been living her life on the opposite side of the ocean from him, she'd made him up at night to pretend he was in it anyway.

269

She had to clear her throat, and even so, her voice came out barely more than a whisper. "So you've...fallen for me?" She peeked at him.

Tristan flexed his fingers into hers and was silent for a little moment. "It doesn't feel like falling." His free arm stretched up and expanded, like a tree spreading its branches. "It feels like growing up into the sun."

He did it again. Brought this sudden sting of emotion to her eyes, made her chest swell.

"It feels like finding this quiet place to walk in, where the white flowers are falling, and the sun speckles through the shade of the branches. Or the stars come out."

Malorie covered her eyes with her free hand.

He hesitated. Then shrugged. "It feels like happiness. To me."

She looked at him over her hand, her lashes damp. "To me, too."

His smile broke out. "Oh, that's all right, then." His voice was deep and rich and warm as he pulled her into his body, hugging her tight.

Malorie squeezed her eyes shut and pressed her face into his throat. "Sometimes I think you've been driving me crazy and I've been in love with you my whole entire life."

"Like a seed." Tristan drew a small circle on her lower back. "In a rock. That just kept growing." His fingers spread and stroked up her back. A growing tree, perhaps.

They were both silent for a long time, just holding on.

Until Tristan finally made a nudging motion into her back with his knuckles. "You going to answer this time?"

"What?" She felt almost sleepy with happiness, secure in a way she had never felt in her entire life.

"The question."

She considered a moment. She felt so dreamily happy that she wanted to just say yes to anything, but it might be about using some outrageous component in one of his perfumes, so she finally had to sit back a little and admit, "I don't remember what the question was."

A little hint of color started to show in his cheeks. "The *tunnel*. That question."

"Oh!" A happy sound that startled out of her, a burst of joy in her middle. All that glowing yellow light. But she hesitated, and then bit the inside of her lip, smiling a little. "I don't remember it exactly. Can you spell it out?"

Tristan's eyes narrowed. "You know, for someone who complains so much about patriarchy, you sure do leave a lot on the guy's shoulders."

Well, that was a fair point. Malorie considered it.

And then she actually tried. She definitely could be the cool, confident person who took charge of this situation and asked him. She told herself that, and then she tried it, and the words strangled in an embarrassed, frantic knot in her throat. A tiny bit of them actually came out as a tangled, suppressed sound. She brought one pair of their linked hands to her forehead and pressed it there, her face flaming.

Tristan smiled a little, as if her emotional tangle fed his own confidence and certainty. He kissed one of her fingers where it linked between his, the gesture bringing his face in close to hers.

"How about this question?" His voice had gone deep and easy, that warm, rich timbre that always made her want to either press herself against him or just take off all her clothes. He turned their linked hands until the back of his hand was facing her and touched his ring finger. "Do you like it?"

Malorie had to smile. He had the sexiest hands. Long fingers, tanned, small scars from rocks and probably agricultural work, so damn strong, a relentless grip. She nodded.

"Do you want to put a ring on it?"

271

Her flush deepened again. She looked up into his eyes—brown and sure and inviting. "Yes," she said quietly and definitely. She'd *love* to have Tristan for the rest of her life. If she could get him.

He broke out into that beautiful smile of his. "And I want to put a ring right here," he said, rubbing her ring finger, his hand tightening hard on hers. "So we're okay, then. We've got that figured out."

His hand was so firm on hers, like he was *never* going to let it go. Like she might have to dress one-handed for the rest of her life. "Yes," she said again.

It didn't even feel that brave to say. It felt like putting the last piece into a puzzle the two of them had been building for a long, long time.

He swept her into his arms again. "Oh, good. I never know with you," he said into her hair. His arms tightened on her once spasmodically, as if it was slowly sinking in, and then neither said anything for the longest time, just held on.

Chapter 28

"I found it," Tristan said. "No fair. I want to turn the key."

Malorie knew he was halfway teasing her and halfway just that enthusiastic. "Are you sure you didn't already peek? I can't believe you resisted this."

"I *waited* for you, because it's *yours*," Tristan said virtuously. He had brought the box he'd found in the storage room in his backpack, still locked. The stars were starting to come out over the sea, a scattering of evening-fallen blossoms around them. "But *merde*, you are slow."

She slid the little key into the small box. The wood was cedar, the box simple but nicely carved, with elegant curves at the corners and a curving marquetry design on the top that made her think of Art Nouveau again. "It belongs to my family," she pointed out.

"Maybe," Tristan said. "The envelope had my family name on it." He closed his hand over hers to make her turn the key faster.

Because Malorie was still afraid of what might be inside, and Tristan was just eager.

The key turned. Tristan pushed the lid up.

Linen cloth wrapped a rectangular shape. It parted to reveal cracked, scarred reddish leather. One part of the cover folded over the other, still dangling one leather tie, its mate long since broken off.

Beside her, Tristan took a rough breath. His hand pushed past hers to touch the leather, and he peeled it back.

Niccolò Rosario. A strong, authoritative pen stroke, in bold black ink that time had only partially faded.

Under it: *Laurianne Manosque Rosario.*

Tristan made a sound, as if he'd been punched in the stomach. Malorie looked at him. He was staring. "*Quivi s'incomincia,*" he whispered and she looked back at the motto under the date. Old Italian. *It all starts here.* "It's their perfume book."

It thrust right through her. The Monsards had one of the most precious heirlooms of the Rosier clan.

That sick, sick sinking in her stomach. Oh, hell. How had her great-grandfather gotten his hands on that? During the Occupation. While he was helping the Nazis.

Tristan was muttering. Soft, reverent swear words. He scooped the book out of the cedar box, holding it through the linen, his hands so careful.

"Malorie." He turned the page and stilled. Then looked up at her, his face as suffused as if he'd had a visit from God. "It's their *perfume book.* Niccolò and Laurianne. Tata said it was lost in the war."

It had been.

Tristan didn't notice her reaction, absorbed as he turned another page. "And all this time I thought she was lying to me. That she had it hidden somewhere. I worried like hell she had it up in her attic, I wanted it somewhere more climate controlled."

"You should allow the museum the loan of it, to exhibit," Malorie said. Her throat felt strained. The museum had no exhibits from the Monsards. None. They'd been erased down to meager mentions of the nineteenth and early twentieth centuries, cut from the circle of donors who had made the museum possible. And having this book in their possession wasn't exactly going to win the Monsards any historical points. "They'll know how to preserve it."

"I know." Tristan still focused on the pages he was turning. "Just on loan, though. We'll always keep this in the family."

Malorie looked at her fingers, wondering what in the world that could possibly mean. Hadn't they just been talking about making their family be the same one? She was pretty sure no one would want to pass that book on to Tristan if that meant he would pass it on to Monsard kids.

And he had dreamed of that book most of his life.

She stared at his dark, wavy hair. "Tristan—"

"We have to tell my aunt and my grandfather," he said. "They've been fighting over this thing forever. I wonder if they'll be thrilled or annoyed that they can't blame each other for its disappearance anymore?"

Oh, hell, yes, she would have to face them. "Tristan—"

"What's this?" He picked up a letter from the box that must have lain under the linen.

Malorie grabbed it from him. If it said something horrible about her people, she wanted to see it first and not have to watch his expression and wonder.

It was her grandmother's hand. A short letter, only a paragraph.

"Oh," she said very low. "L...Léo Dubois gave it to her." Élise Dubois's son. The son of the woman Pierre Monsard had gotten killed.

Tristan blinked, visibly taken aback, and then looked over her shoulder to read the letter, too.

"I guess...it was in lieu of child support," Malorie said, dark and rough, full of visions of her grandmother alone at sixteen and pregnant, with a book and no idea what to do, troubles piling up on her. "Oh, God."

In the letter, her grandmother didn't use the expression *child support*, she just explained that...well, a week after she told Léo Dubois about her pregnancy, he brought the book to her. And then he ran away. Malorie wrapped her arms around herself, in lieu of hugging her sixteen-year-old grandmother.

Tristan put his arm around her. Warmth and support. He looked incredibly puzzled by the letter, which he would be. Tristan didn't run away. "Did he

275

think she could use it to leverage support out of the Rosiers?"

"Maybe." Malorie shook her head. Her grandmother would never have done that, unless her child was actually starving. "Can you imagine the shame?"

"Yeah." Tristan's voice was rough, too. "I kind of can." His hand flexed into her back.

Of course the empath could. She bent her head, overwhelmed by all of this. It was all just too much. The shares, the marriage proposal, now this, all in one day. God, life in New York had been simpler. For a second, almost with craving, she thought of that hike up toward Paris when she was nineteen, the clean, pure wind and only herself to deal with.

But she hadn't had Tristan. *Merde*, Tristan must have to deal with family complications *constantly*. As a given.

"So the book is yours," Tristan said oddly. "Niccolò and Laurianne's perfume book."

Malorie was taken aback. "How do you figure that? It was stolen from you!" Even if, thank God, her own family hadn't done it.

Still, her own family had been responsible for how messed up Léo Dubois was.

Tristan spoke slowly and carefully, as if he was picking out the right words—the right choice—with great reluctance from the much more compelling wrong ones. "Tante Colette adopted him. I guess he had as much right to this book as I do."

From his tone, Malorie wasn't sure he truly felt that deep down. But he was trying to feel it. Trying to do the right thing.

"And if this was all her child support for all those years," he said and let his voice trail off. He looked at the book one long moment—and then handed it to her.

Malorie crossed her hands and refused to take it. "It's your heritage, Tristan."

"Those shares I obtained in Monaco were yours. I gather your father didn't have much right to sell them either."

"Fine," she said. "If it's mine, I give it to you. There. That solves that problem. It's yours."

Tristan gazed at her a long moment. Then a little smile crept onto his face. "How about ours? You can be Niccolò and I can be Laurianne."

Niccolò the romantic or Niccolò the hardened mercenary? It wasn't clear anymore.

She stared down at the book. Then looked at Tristan.

Did he realize what he was offering? Shares could be sold and traded. People who got married got divorced and their rings pawned.

But this book was the priceless, irreplaceable heart of his family patrimony. He couldn't inherit the valley, he was the youngest. *This* was his heritage.

You couldn't share something like that with someone else, unless you were absolutely sure her children and yours would be the same. That the two of you would last, that together you would pass this on for generations.

If she cried one more time today, she might have to turn in her credentials as a tough woman and resign herself to being a watering pot. "Madame Delatour and Monsieur Rosier might not agree," she managed huskily.

He kissed her quickly. "Let's go tell them."

***

They took it to his Tante Colette first, since Sainte-Mère was on the road from Vallauris to the valley of roses.

Plus, as Tristan said…they had to talk to her about the contents of the letter.

"Mémère wanted you to know she didn't steal it," Malorie said carefully, watching the old woman. Afraid to hurt her. She knew very well how much a tough exterior might protect a vulnerable heart. "She—Léo

277

Dubois gave it to her when he left. Maybe some part of her thought for a long time that he would come back for it. Or for her."

Colette Delatour covered her eyes with her hand. Tristan immediately put his arm around her.

"I'm sorry," Malorie said, distressed. She didn't know what this made her to the old woman. The granddaughter of a boy Colette had adopted after the war and who had caused a lot of trouble and run away only a few years later. But she knew it must hurt the older woman. "I thought you should know."

She checked with Tristan. He, too, had thought his aunt should know. That she was strong enough to handle anything but being kept in the dark. Tristan gave her a little nod and reached out his free hand to squeeze hers.

"I suppose this explains a lot of things," Colette said quietly, lowering her hand. Her face was sad. "I wonder if he loved all of them, or just wanted to be loved by all of them."

Malorie looked at Tristan. He'd already told her about Layla and Jess. Which made the two women cousins of hers, a surreal thought.

"I think," he said slowly, "that he hit puberty and found girls, girls, girls. And that it's probably a good thing Maman was always after me about condoms," he added ruefully.

That was so like Tristan—comprehension, no judgement, and a little thread of humor, to try to make this more manageable.

"You were just supposed to not *do it*, back in my day," Tante Colette said. "We thought about sex differently then. We thought if you weren't married, only bad people did it. And the fathers were supposed to keep an eye on their daughters, protect them from the boys. But of course, there weren't as many fathers, for a while."

All those destroyed, disrupted families. People killed. Léo Dubois's own father had died on the front in the initial invasion and his mother had been killed before his eyes, and then he'd been, until the end of the war, turned into a kind of pet by the SS troop that had killed her. Tristan had explained everything to Malorie in the car.

"So he ran wild with the girls." Malorie swallowed the *vulnerable* before *girls*. But she was pretty sure that was what it had been. Maybe everyone in the situation had been vulnerable. They'd needed his masculine attention, and he'd needed to fill a hole inside him. "And when he woke up to a mess of three pregnant fifteen- and sixteen-year-olds, he didn't know what to do. He couldn't be that bad in your eyes, maybe, or what he imagined you would see as bad." This was a boy who had been initially "adopted" and turned into a kind of pet by the men who had killed his mother when he was eight, after all. He must have been all kinds of messed up inside already, about whether he was a good or bad person. "So he ran away."

"I can't say I would have been anything but shocked and furious if he told me he had gotten three different girls pregnant," Colette said quietly. "No wonder Jacky didn't want to tell me why he kept riding Léo so hard." She frowned, an old disgruntlement helping her handle the regret. "That was so like him. I was six years older than he was, and had been through the war just like he had, and yet he still thought he should protect me from the fact that a sixteen-year-old might be having sex."

Malorie knelt quietly in the grass in front of the rocking chair, waiting. She had no idea what to do about things that had happened generations before she was born, and yet people were still alive to have been hurt by them.

After a moment, Colette Delatour turned the pages of the old book between careful hands. "I thought he stole it," she said low. "I didn't want Jacky to blame him, so I just thought it was easier to let him blame me."

Behind her head, Tristan squeezed his eyes tight shut a second, in what could only be the profound frustration of a man who thought everything was easier if you just communicated and offered tolerance.

"In a way, it really was lost in the war," Colette added. "So I was telling the truth."

Léo had been lost in the war, she meant. Malorie held Tristan's hand a little more tightly, to handle all the sadness here. Her own great-grandfather was responsible for Léo's mother's death. Probably making it doubly certain that Léo wouldn't admit to Colette that Pierre Monsard's daughter was pregnant with his baby. Hell, what horrible scars that Occupation had left.

"I'm sorry," she said again, because she didn't know what to say. She felt like crying. Again.

Colette reached out a hand and laid it on her head. The old woman held her eyes for a long, firm moment. "Child. You bear the weight of your own life the best you can. You'll help carry the weight of those who come after you, as best you can. Don't bear the weight of those who came before you. You can't do anything about that."

Malorie's lips trembled, and she bit down hard on the inside of her lower one.

Colette withdrew her hand. "And I know you're not a child," she said a little more briskly. "But sometimes all of you are, to me."

Malorie dragged her hand under her eyes. "I'm sorry. I don't mean to—I just really miss my grandmother."

Colette petted the leather cover. If she didn't know for a fact it was impossible, Malorie would have thought the old war hero felt almost shy. "I know it's not the same, but maybe in the circumstances you can make do with me."

Tristan slid his arm around Malorie's shoulders and pulled her in snug against him, so that they were kneeling or in Colette's case sitting in what was very close to a group hug, with Tristan as its anchor.

Malorie rested her head against Tristan's shoulder, very grateful he was there.

"Hey, did I tell you we're getting married?" Tristan said brightly.

Colette sat up a little straighter, distracted from old sadness. Dark eyes went from Tristan to Malorie. "Well," she said thoughtfully. "Isn't that about time?"

"What do you mean, about time? I'm only twenty-nine!"

Tristan was doing it again, using pretend indignation to redirect this conversation into lighter-hearted territory.

"Yes, but you were made to be a family patriarch," Colette said.

Tristan looked dumbfounded by this, sitting back on his heels and blinking several times.

"And for that you need a strong matriarch." Colette smiled a little at Malorie.

Who felt rather dumbfounded herself.

Colette wrapped the red leather carefully back in its linen and handed it to them both. Malorie didn't reach for it, though, unnerved, and Tristan closed his hands around it reverently.

"I would have given it to you a long time ago if I could," Colette said gently. "But this is better. It belonged to two strong people together. So it's best to give it to both of you. I hope it will bring you the same thing they had."

Malorie gave her an inquiring look. She knew Niccolò and Laurianne were a legendary couple, but she still wanted to hear Colette say exactly what she wished for them. Somehow, in this garden, from this old woman, it felt as if any wishes she made for them would come true.

Colette smiled just a little. "*Et ils vécurent heureux et eurent beaucoup d'enfants.*"

And they lived happily ever after and...

"Why does the French version always have to mention having lots of children in it?" Malorie whispered later in the car to Tristan, touching her belly. It was all very well for fairy tale tellers to say, but somebody had to carry those children in her body.

Tristan just grinned, as if all was right with his world.

Epilogue

The wedding started off beautifully. In late April the very first jasmine was starting to bloom, and Jess wove it into a crown for her hair, eschewing a veil in favor of tendrils of jasmine hanging down through her soft brown curls. Damien looked so handsome he was almost lethal with it, in his perfectly tailored black tux, straight and tall and eyes glowing with raw emotion—the kind he never exposed to anyone, now exposed to every single person who knew him, so that they could all squeeze themselves and go *awww*.

They'd chosen to have a traditional church ceremony after the *mairie*, and they'd chosen to do both in the little village of Pont-le-Loup at the end of the valley of roses where Damien and his cousins had so often been dragged to Mass by their grandmother. By French law, the ceremony at the *mairie* was the legal ceremony and came first, and in Pont-le-Loup it was directly across the town *place* from the church anyway.

Hundreds of guests had arrived from as far away as Québec for the first Rosier marriage in a generation, and now filled the *place* between the city hall and the church, waiting for Damien and Jess to finish signing documents in the former and come out. Tristan, Matt, Raoul, and Gabriel and Raphaël Delange lined the steps outside the city hall, and various members of the extended Rosier clan, including (and this still felt a tad surreal) Malorie herself, moved through the crowd, distributing confetti cannons.

She stopped beside Antoine Vallier, who stood with a gorgeous redhead, and handed him her last confetti cannon. He took it with a very odd expression on his face.

"So how'd you end up at the wedding?" she asked him, amused. "If they can't kill you, invite you to join them?"

283

"You could say that." Antoine had grown up tall and lean and dangerously good-looking and in a weird way reminded her a little of Tristan, or maybe more of Damien. Probably just that general French look she was still getting used to being back around—the way the lips were so much firmer and at the same time so much more supple here than American lips, the tight, confident way he held his body as opposed to that loose broadness of the American stance. Americans slumped a lot. Like most French, neither Antoine nor Tristan nor Damien ever did. Even when Tristan acted so relaxed, he did it in a lean, alert way.

Antoine was alert now, too, even tense. His green eyes were still as vivid as they'd been in high school, and right now they were focused on Damien's father Louis, a tough, unemotional businessman who had just come out of the city hall, beaming in acharacteristic open pride. Antoine made a sudden restless movement toward the pack of cigarettes inside his tux jacket. "I don't know why I came," he muttered, darkly.

Malorie's brow knit faintly. But she couldn't figure out Antoine's reaction, and she looked to the other side of Antoine where a gorgeous auburn-haired young woman stood. "And I don't think we've met?"

"We have, actually," the woman said, shaking her hand. "I was a year behind you in school. Elena."

It took Malorie a long moment, and then her eyes widened. "Wow." Maybe that was blunt, but she had *not* expected such gorgeousness from the braces, glasses, spots, and thirteen-year-old pudginess she remembered. She didn't want to say anything hurtful about ugly ducklings, but she was definitely looking at a swan transformation. "You look *fantastic*. What are you doing now?"

"I find people," Elena said. "For example, for Madame Delatour, I found Layla and Jess, and also—well, but—" She broke off, pushing something she had almost said away. Her expression turned frustrated or sad or...wounded?...and she shook her head.

Véro, Damien's mother, ran out of the city hall, waving to everyone dramatically to alert them to ready their confetti cannons, and the sound of a powerful motor cut through the air.

A motorcycle, the motor quickly softening as the driver slowed and opened his hands, coasting to the far edge of the crowd where he could park, trying to keep the motor quiet. He sat there a moment, as Malorie glanced toward him. Straight shoulders in a leather jacket that he shrugged off as soon as he stopped, as if he was too hot in it. A tall man.

He swung off the motorcycle, stood still for a long moment—and then reached up and pulled off his helmet.

The redhead grabbed Antoine's arm.

Antoine stiffened.

Tristan turned his head, but just then Damien and Jess appeared at the top of the steps, and the crowd erupted in cheers. Confetti burst into the air all over the place.

The rider made a sharp movement at the explosions, caught himself, and stood still, staring at the steps where Damien and Jess and all the Rosier cousins stood, his shoulders straight, his hands at his sides loosely fisted, as if he was ready for anything, even a fight. Had been ready for anything as a habit, for a very long time. He wasn't dressed for a wedding. An olive-green T-shirt pulled tight across his chest and clung to hard abs and the swell of his biceps, revealing the bottom edge of a tattoo. A curl of blue confetti drifted toward him on the breeze.

Malorie drew a sharp breath as recognition finally penetrated.

Tall. Lean. Broad-shouldered. Hair cropped short. Sun-worn, his skin and hair almost the same shade of golden-brown. Blue eyes that looked over the crowd as if scanning for attack.

Hard.
Wary.
Weary.
Lucien was back.

***

FIN

AUTHOR'S NOTE

Whenever inserting a fictional store or building or families into a real town, an author is obliged to appropriate the space and history a bit. In this particular book's case, that appropriation is perhaps more noticeable because the location of La Maison de Monsard is so noticeable—right off the esplanade and across from the museum.

There is no exact real world equivalent, but its location is fairly close to that of the real world Fragonard. (There is no resemblance, however, between Monsard and Fragonard in any other way. Monsard is a completely fictional family and house, including its war history.)

There is also a real world perfume museum in roughly the spot it holds in my fictionalized Grasse. However, because the Rosiers are a fictional family and their influence on the museum in my books is large, I've gone ahead and fictionalized the museum as well, giving it another name and different characteristics. However, if you are in Grasse, you should check out the real museum, which is quite fascinating.

Sainte-Mère, similarly, and the Rosiers' valley of roses are created out of "real cloth", if you will, the types of places you see in that region, but they are themselves made up and you won't find them on any real map. (But if you want to see towns rather similar to Sainte-Mère, you should check out the old upper towns of Mougins and Haut-des-Cagnes.)

It can be very tricky inserting influential families into a real place, so just bear in mind that these stories are fictional. They are not *romans à clef* for real families. I like to think they are *realistic*—the situations of the perfume industry, the way it grew in Grasse, the region around the characters, the events they had to live through, the places that formed them.

Real events and real places on a broader scale do form their backdrop (Grasse, the south of France, the Italian and German Occupations, for example).

But that doesn't make these books real. Consider it your alternate history version, perhaps—if the world was a little different, if Niccolò Rosario had actually come out of Italy back in his day and the Rosiers and Monsards actually existed.

THANK YOU

Sign up to my newsletter to be the first to know when Lucien's story is released and for a free copy of the novelette *Night Wish*, the reader-requested story of Damien and Jess's first meeting! And as always, thank you so much for leaving a review, if you can. In the current publishing world, reader reviews have really become the lifeblood of authors.

Keep reading for an excerpt from my next book, *Trust Me*, Book 3 in the Paris Nights series.

Laura Florand

Website: www.lauraflorand.com
Twitter: @LauraFlorand
Facebook: www.facebook.com/LauraFlorandAuthor
Newsletter: http://lauraflorand.com/newsletter

LAURA FLORAND

OTHER BOOKS BY LAURA FLORAND

Paris Nights Series
All For You

Chase Me

Trust Me

La Vie en Roses Series
Turning Up the Heat (a novella prequel)

The Chocolate Rose (also part of the Amour et Chocolat series)

A Rose in Winter, a novella in *No Place Like Home*

Once Upon a Rose

A Wish Upon Jasmine

Amour et Chocolat Series
All's Fair in Love and Chocolate, a novella in *Kiss the Bride*

The Chocolate Thief

The Chocolate Kiss

The Chocolate Rose (also a prequel to La Vie en Roses series)

The Chocolate Touch

The Chocolate Heart

The Chocolate Temptation

Sun-Kissed (also a sequel to *Snow-Kissed*)

Shadowed Heart (a sequel to *The Chocolate Heart*)

A CROWN OF BITTER ORANGE

Snow Queen Duology

Snow-Kissed (a novella)

Sun-Kissed (also part of the Amour et Chocolat series)

Memoir

Blame It on Paris

TRUST ME

Excerpt

Lina was fighting a dragon.

You'd think a dragon would know better than to mess with an international heroine who could take terrorists out with a bucket of liquid nitrogen, but no.

The damn thing was smirking at her.

She revved her chainsaw. *You sure you want to take that tone with me, lizard?* Ice shards flew as she took her saw to the curve of its neck, the cold in the room trying to overwhelm her body heat even through her gloves and hoodie.

Why the hell she had wanted to learn to ice sculpt, she did not know. It had seemed like a fun new challenge when she first took her motorbike out to Brittany to talk a famous sculptor there into teaching her his tricks— after all, she got to wield a chainsaw—but then hell had exploded in the Au-dessus kitchens, and now she was still on the hook for next month's contest and likely to humiliate herself by coming in last place, at the rate she was going.

Of course she'd probably be excused for giving up, in the circumstances. Backing down.

Letting the bad guys win.

She narrowed her eyes at the smirking dragon and revved her chainsaw menacingly—

And a big figure moved in the doorway of the freezer.

She swung violently, the chainsaw slicing straight through the dragon's neck. Ice shattered on the floor around her boots.

Size, danger, violence, freckles, and all her adrenaline shooting into her bloodstream ready to fight him—

Freckles?

Oh.

It was him. The mountain lion.

Jake. Friend of Chase "Smith", Vi's ridiculously over-confident new boyfriend. (Vi had the *worst* taste in men, honestly.) Favored leaning in the doorway of Chase's hospital room, watching Lina as she left the elevator with her police security and went into Vi's hospital room. Watching her when she came down the hallway to check on Chase.

Watching her now.

Long, lean, powerful. Hazel eyes, red-gold hair clipped short. Hard jaw. Controlled movements. And as far as she could tell, covered all over in freckles. This thick, golden-brown layering of them, as if every mote of sun that had ever had the chance to touch his skin had clung to him, unwilling to let go.

Greedy sun, just wanting to get its hot little rays all over that life of him. Would he have the same freckles on those broad shoulders? That hard, flat belly? That tight butt? His...did freckles go to...that is, she'd never seen a freckled man without any clothes before, was it possible that he'd have freckles on his...that the sun would have gotten all hot and greedy with his...

Are you turning into a nymphomaniac in some kind of post-traumatic stress reaction?

Probably worse things she could become. Scared. Weak. Paranoid. *Yeah, all the other options made nympho sound pretty enticing.*

She cut off the saw and set it on the steel table by the destroyed dragon, then bent to pick up the biggest two chunks of the decapitated head in her gloved hands. Totally ruined. After all that work. Her fingers cramped around them suddenly, in a spasmodic urge to throw them across the room, to scream, to grab the block left and just batter it to the floor.

She took a deep breath and let it out, setting the chunks down, pulling off her thick gloves, pushing back the hoodie of her sweatshirt, pulling out her earplugs.

"Little life tip. Never sneak up on a woman fighting a dragon with a chainsaw."

From the subtle amusement in Jake's face, he probably took out six crazed chainsaw-wielders with a toothpick before breakfast every morning. "You know, it does seem as if my training should have included more practical tips like that. I'll have to tell my old instructors they missed a situation."

"They probably counted on you to have common sense."

He cocked his head and considered that a moment. "A group of wild teenage males who thought they could become the biggest bad-asses on the planet? I doubt it."

True. In her eleven years in top-notch kitchens, she'd dealt with more than her fair share of teenage males wielding lethal objects. Common sense didn't come into it.

"The real question is how *do* you approach a woman with a chainsaw?" Jake asked. "Any tips?"

Trust Me, coming April 2017!

Sign up to my newsletter to be notified as soon as it's released.

A CROWN OF BITTER ORANGE

ONCE UPON A ROSE

Book 1 in La Vie en Roses series: Excerpt

Burlap slid against Matt's shoulder, rough and clinging to the dampness of his skin as he dumped the sack onto the truck bed. The rose scent puffed up thickly, like a silk sheet thrown over his face. He took a step back from the truck, flexing, trying to clear his pounding head and sick stomach.

The sounds of the workers and of his cousins and grandfather rode against his skin, easing him. Raoul was back. That meant they were all here but Lucien, and Pépé was still stubborn and strong enough to insist on overseeing part of the harvest himself before he went to sit under a tree. Meaning Matt still had a few more years before he had to be the family patriarch all by himself, thank God. He'd copied every technique in his grandfather's book, then layered on his own when those failed him, but that whole job of taking charge of his cousins and getting them to listen to him was *still* not working out for him.

But his grandfather was still here for now. His cousins were here, held by Pépé and this valley at their heart, and not scattered to the four winds as they might be one day soon, when Matt became the heart and that heart just couldn't hold them.

All that loss was for later. Today was a good day. It could be. Matt had a hangover, and he had made an utter fool of himself the night before, but this could still be a good day. The rose harvest. The valley spreading around him.

J'y suis. J'y reste.

I am here and here I'll stay.

He stretched, easing his body into the good of this day, and even though it wasn't that hot yet, went ahead and reached for the hem of his shirt, so he could feel the scent of roses all over his skin.

"Show-off," Allegra's voice said, teasingly, and he grinned into the shirt as it passed his head, flexing his muscles a little more, because it would be pretty damn fun if Allegra was ogling him enough to piss Raoul off.

He turned so he could see the expression on Raoul's face as he bundled the T-shirt, half-tempted to toss it to Allegra and see what Raoul did—

And looked straight into the leaf-green eyes of Bouclettes.

Oh, shit. He jerked the T-shirt back over his head, tangling himself in the bundle of it as the holes proved impossible to find, and then he stuck his arm through the neck hole and his head didn't fit and he wrenched it around and tried to get himself straight and dressed somehow and—oh, *fuck.*

He stared at her, all the blood cells in his body rushing to his cheeks.

Damn you, stop, stop, stop, he tried to tell the blood cells, but as usual they ignored him. Thank God for dark Mediterranean skin. It had to help hide some of the color, right? Right? As he remembered carrying her around the party the night before, heat beat in his cheeks until he felt sunburned from the inside out.

Bouclettes was staring at him, mouth open as if he had punched her. Or as if he needed to kiss her again and—*behave!* She was probably thinking what a total jerk he was, first slobbering all over her drunk and now so full of himself he was stripping for her. And getting stuck in his own damn T-shirt.

Somewhere beyond her, between the rows of pink, Raoul had a fist stuffed into his mouth and was trying so hard not to laugh out loud that his body was bending into it, going into convulsions. Tristan was grinning, all right with his world. And Damien had his eyebrows up, making him look all controlled and princely, like someone who would *never* make a fool of himself in front of a woman.

Damn T-shirt. Matt yanked it off his head and threw it. But, of course, the air friction stopped it, so that instead of sailing gloriously across the field, it fell across the rose bush not too far from Bouclettes, a humiliated flag of surrender.

Could his introduction to this woman conceivably get any worse?

He glared at her, about ready to hit one of his damn cousins.

She stared back, her eyes enormous.

"Well, *what?*" he growled. "What do you want now? Why are you still here?" *I was drunk. I'm sorry. Just shoot me now, all right?*

She blinked and took a step back, frowning.

"Matt," Allegra said reproachfully, but with a ripple disturbing his name, as if she was trying not to laugh. "She was curious about the rose harvest. And she needs directions."

Directions. Hey, really? He was *good* with directions. He could get an ant across this valley and tell it the best route, too. He could crouch down with bunnies and have conversations about the best way to get their *petits* through the hills for a little day at the beach.

Of course, all his cousins could, too. He got ready to leap in first before his cousins grabbed the moment from him, like they were always trying to do. "Where do you need to go?" His voice came out rougher than the damn burlap. He struggled to smooth it without audibly clearing his throat. God, he felt naked. Would it look too stupid if he sidled up to that T-shirt and tried getting it over his head again?

"It's this house I inherited here," Bouclettes said. She had the cutest little accent. It made him want to squoosh all her curls in his big fists again and kiss that accent straight on her mouth, as if it was his, when he had so ruined that chance. "113, rue des Rosiers."

The valley did one great beat, a giant heart that had just faltered in its rhythm, and every Rosier in earshot focused on her. His grandfather barely moved, but then he'd probably barely moved back in the war when he'd spotted a swastika up in the *maquis* either. Just gently squeezed the trigger.

That finger-on-the-trigger alertness ran through every one of his cousins now.

Matt was the one who felt clumsy.

"Rue des Rosiers?" he said dumbly. Another beat, harder this time, adrenaline surging. "113, *rue des Rosiers?*" He looked up at a stone house, on the fourth terrace rising into the hills, where it got too steep to be practical to grow roses for harvest at their current market value. "Wait, *inherited?*"

Bouclettes looked at him warily.

"How could you *inherit* it?"

"I don't know exactly," she said slowly. "I had a letter from Antoine Vallier."

Tante Colette's lawyer. Oh, hell. An ominous feeling grew in the pit of Matt's stomach.

"On behalf of a Colette Delatour. He said he was tracking down the descendants of Élise Dubois."

What? Matt twisted toward his grandfather. Pépé stood very still, with this strange, tense blazing look of a fighter who'd just been struck on the face and couldn't strike back without drawing retaliation down on his entire village.

Matt turned back to the curly-haired enemy invader who had sprung up out of the blue. Looking so damn cute and innocent like that, too. He'd *kissed* her. "You can't—Tante Colette gave that house to *you?*"

Bouclettes took a step back.

Had he roared that last word? His voice echoed back at him, as if the valley held it, would squeeze it in a tight fist and never let it free. The air constricted, merciless bands around his sick head and stomach.

"After all that?" He'd just spent the last five months working on that house. Five months. *Oh, could you fix the plumbing, Matthieu? Matthieu, that garden wall needs mending. Matthieu, I think the septic tank might need to be replaced.* Because she was ninety-six and putting her life in order, and she was planning to pass it on to him, right? Because she understood that it was part of his valley and meant to leave this valley whole. Wasn't that the tacit promise there, when she asked him to take care of it? "*You?* Colette gave it to *you?*"

Bouclettes stared at him, a flash of hurt across her face, and then her arms tightened, and her chin went up. "Look, I don't know much more than you. My grandfather didn't stick around for my father's childhood, apparently. All we knew was that he came from France. We never knew we had any heritage here."

Could Tante Colette have had a child they didn't even know about? He twisted to look at his grandfather again, the one man still alive today who would surely have noticed a burgeoning belly on his stepsister. Pépé was frowning, not saying a word.

So—"To *you?*" Tante Colette knew it was his valley. You didn't just rip a chunk out of a man's heart and give it to, to...to whom exactly?

"To *you?*" Definitely he had roared that, he could hear his own voice booming back at him, see the way she braced herself. But—who the hell was she? And what the *hell* was he supposed to do about this? Fight a girl half his size? Strangle his ninety-six-year-old aunt? How did he crush his enemies and defend this valley? His enemy was...she was so *cute*. He didn't want her for an enemy, he wanted to figure out how to overcome last night's handicap and get her to think he was cute, too. Damn it, he hadn't even found out yet what those curls felt like against his palms.

And it was *his valley.*

Bouclettes' chin angled high, her arms tight. "You seemed to like me last night."

Oh, God. Embarrassment, a hangover, and being knifed in the back by his own aunt made for a perfectly horrible combination. "I was *drunk.*"

Her mouth set, this stubborn, defiant rosebud. "I never thought I'd say this to a man, but I think I actually liked you better drunk." Turning on her heel, she stalked back to her car.

Matt stared after her, trying desperately not to be sick in the nearest rose bush. Family patriarchs didn't get to do that in front of the members of their family.

"I told my father he should never let my stepsister have some of this valley," his grandfather said tightly. "I told him she couldn't be trusted with it. It takes proper family to understand how important it is to keep it intact. Colette *never* respected that."

His cousins glanced at his grandfather and away, out over the valley, their faces gone neutral. They all knew this about the valley: It couldn't be broken up. It was their *patrimoine*, a world heritage really, in their hearts they knew it even if the world didn't, and so, no matter how much they, too, loved it, they could never really have any of it. It had to be kept intact. It had to go to Matt.

The others could have the company. They could have one hell of a lot more money, when it came down to liquid assets, they could have the right to run off to Africa and have adventures. But the valley was his.

He knew the way their jaws set. He knew the way his cousins looked without comment over the valley, full of roses they had come to help harvest because all their lives they had harvested these roses, grown up playing among them and working for them, in the service of them. He knew the way they didn't look at him again.

So he didn't look at them again, either. It *was* his valley, damn it. He'd tried last year to spend some time at their Paris office, to change who he was, to test out just one of all those many other dreams he had had as a kid, dreams his role as heir had never allowed him to pursue. His glamorous Paris girlfriend hadn't been able to stand the way the valley still held him, even in Paris. How fast he would catch a train back if something happened that he had to take care of. And in the end, he hadn't been able to stand how appalled she would get at the state of his hands when he came back, dramatically calling her manicurist and shoving him in that direction. Because he'd always liked his hands before then—they were strong and they were capable, and wasn't that a good thing for hands to be? A little dirt ground in sometimes—didn't that just prove their worth?

In the end, that one effort to be someone else had made his identity the clearest: The valley was who he was.

He stared after Bouclettes, as she slammed her car door and then pressed her forehead into her steering wheel.

"Who the hell is Élise Dubois?" Damien asked finally, a slice of a question. Damien did not like to be taken by surprise. "Why should Tante Colette be seeking out her heirs *over her own?*"

Matt looked again at Pépé, but Pépé's mouth was a thin line, and he wasn't talking.

Matt's head throbbed in great hard pulses. How could Tante Colette do this?

Without even warning him. Without giving him one single chance to argue her out of it or at least go strangle Antoine Vallier before that idiot even thought about sending that letter. Matt should have known something was up when she'd hired such an inexperienced, fresh-out-of-school lawyer. She wanted someone stupid enough to piss off the Rosiers.

Except—unlike his grandfather—he'd always trusted Tante Colette. She was the one who stitched up his wounds, fed him tea and soups, let him come take refuge in her gardens when all the pressures of his family got to be too much.

She'd loved him, he thought. Enough not to give a chunk of his valley to a stranger.

"It's that house," Raoul told Allegra, pointing to it, there a little up the hillside, only a couple of hundred yards from Matt's own house. If Matt knew Raoul, his cousin was probably already seeing a window—a way he could end up owning a part of this valley. If Raoul could negotiate with rebel warlords with a bullet hole in him, he could probably negotiate a curly-haired stranger into selling an unexpected inheritance.

Especially with Allegra on his side to make friends with her. While Matt alienated her irreparably.

Allegra ran after Bouclettes and knocked on her window, then bent down to speak to her when Bouclettes rolled it down. They were too far away for Matt to hear what they said. "Pépé." Matt struggled to speak. The valley thumped in his chest in one giant, echoing beat. It hurt his head, it was so big. It banged against the inside of his skull.

Possibly the presence of the valley inside him was being exacerbated by a hangover. Damn it. He pressed the heels of his palms into his pounding skull. What the hell had just happened?

Pépé just stood there, lips still pressed tight, a bleak, intense look on his face.

Allegra straightened from the car, and Bouclettes pulled away, heading up the dirt road that cut through the field of roses toward the house that Tante Colette had just torn out of Matt's valley and handed to a stranger.

Allegra came back and planted herself in front of him, fists on her hips. "Way to charm the girls, Matt," she said very dryly.

"F—" He caught himself, horrified. He could not possibly tell a woman to fuck off, no matter how bad his hangover and the shock of the moment. Plus, the last thing his skull needed right now was a jolt from Raoul's fist. So he just made a low, growling sound.

"She thinks you're hot, you know," Allegra said, in that friendly conversational tone torturers used in movies as they did something horrible to the hero.

"I...she...what?" The valley packed inside him fled in confusion before the *man* who wanted to take its place, surging up. Matt flushed dark again, even as his entire will scrambled after that flush, trying to get the color to die down.

"She said so." Allegra's sweet torturer's tone. "One of the first things she asked me after she got up this morning: 'Who's the hot one?'"

Damn blood cells, stay away from my cheeks. The boss did not flush. Pépé never flushed. You held your own in this crowd by being the roughest and the toughest. A man who blushed might as well paint a target on his chest and hand his cousins bows and arrows to practice their aim. "No, she did not."

"Probably talking about me." Amusement curled under Tristan's voice as he made himself the conversation's red herring. Was his youngest cousin taking pity on him? How had Tristan turned out so nice like that? After they made him use the purple paint when they used to pretend to be aliens, too.

"*And* she said you had a great body." Allegra drove another needle in, watching Matt squirm. He couldn't even stand himself now. His body felt too big for him. As if all his muscles were trying to get his attention, figure out if they were actually *great*.

"And she was definitely talking about Matt, Tristan," Allegra added. "You guys are impossible."

"I'm sorry, but I can hardly assume the phrase 'the hot one' means Matt," Tristan said cheerfully. "Be my last choice, really. I mean, there's me. Then there's— well, me, again, I really don't see how she would look at any of the other choices." He widened his teasing to Damien and Raoul, spreading the joking and provocation around to dissipate the focus on Matt.

"I was there, Tristan. She was talking about Matt," said Allegra, who either didn't get it, about letting the focus shift off Matt, or wasn't nearly as sweet as Raoul thought she was. "She thinks you're hot," she repeated to Matt, while his flush climbed back up into his cheeks and *beat* there.

Not in front of my cousins, Allegra! Oh, wow, really? Does she really?

Because his valley invader had hair like a wild bramble brush, and an absurdly princess-like face, all piquant chin and rosebud mouth and wary green eyes, and it made him want to surge through all those brambles and wake up the princess. And he so could not admit that he had thoughts like those in front of his cousins and his grandfather.

He was thirty years old, for God's sake. He worked in dirt and rose petals, in burlap and machinery and rough men he had to control. He wasn't supposed to fantasize about being a prince, as if he were still twelve.

Hadn't he made the determination, when he came back from Paris, to stay *grounded* from now on, real? Not to get lost in some ridiculous fantasy about a woman, a fantasy that had no relationship to reality?

"Or she *did*," Allegra said, ripping the last fingernail off. "Before you yelled at her because of something that is hardly her fault."

See, that was why a man needed to keep his feet on the ground. You'd think, as close a relationship as he had with the earth, he would know by now how much it hurt when he crashed into it. Yeah, did. Past tense.

But she'd stolen his land from him. How was he supposed to have taken that calmly? He stared up at the house, at the small figure in the distance climbing out of her car.

Pépé came to stand beside him, eyeing the little house up on the terraces as if it was a German supply depot he was about to take out. "I want that land back in the family," he said, in that crisp, firm way that meant, *explosives it is and tough luck for anyone who might be caught in them.* "This land is yours to defend for this family, Matthieu. What are you going to do about this threat?"

Available now!

ACKNOWLEDGEMENTS

First of all, I want to offer a huge thank you to Mercy and Dale Anderson, a wonderful editing team whose support and encouragement and insight into story has meant so much to me. And many, many thanks to author Virginia Kantra for all her feedback and wonderful insight into story.

And a huge thank you, of course, to all my readers, as always, for all your support which has kept me motivated to write more books! Thank you all so much.

A CROWN OF BITTER ORANGE

ABOUT LAURA FLORAND

Laura Florand burst on the contemporary romance scene in 2012 with her award-winning Amour et Chocolat series. Since then, her international bestselling books have appeared in ten languages, been named among the Best Books of the Year by *Library Journal, Romantic Times,* and Barnes & Noble; received the RT Seal of Excellence and numerous starred reviews from *Publishers Weekly, Library Journal,* and *Booklist;* and been recommended by NPR, *USA Today,* and *The Wall Street Journal,* among others.

After a Fulbright year in Tahiti and backpacking everywhere from New Zealand to Greece, and several years living in Madrid and Paris, Laura now teaches Romance Studies at Duke University. Contrary to what the "Romance Studies" may imply, this means she primarily teaches French language and culture and does a great deal of research on French gastronomy, particularly chocolate.

LAURA FLORAND

COPYRIGHT

Copyright 2017, Laura Florand
Cover by Sébastien Florand
ISBN-13: 978-1-943168-13-2

CPSIA information can be obtained
at www.ICGtesting.com
Printed in the USA
LVOW03s1620040417
529578LV00004B/949/P